Para Tim, quien me dio la idea   D.B.

EDICIONES
ekaré

Traducción: Carmen Diana Dearden
Primera edición, 2006

Texto © 2004 David Bedford
Ilustraciones © 2004 Emily Bolam
© 2006 Ediciones Ekaré

Edif. Banco del Libro, Av. Luis Roche,
Altamira Sur, Caracas 1062, Venezuela.
www.ekare.com

ISBN 980-257-321-3
HECHO EL DEPÓSITO DE LEY
Depósito Legal lf15120058004089
Impreso en Singapur por Imago Service

Los Cocodrilos Copiones

David Bedford

Ilustrado por Emily Bolam

Ediciones Ekaré

Cocodrilo siempre había vivido
en la misma laguna, y le gustaba.
Pero no le gustaba compartirla con los demás cocodrilos.
Cada vez que se movía, se tropezaba con uno.
Y cuando alguno se movía lo tropezaban a él.

–¡**Estos cocodrilos siempre me empujan**! –gritaba Cocodrilo.
–¡Y tú nos empujas a nosotros!
–contestaban los demás cocodrilos.
La laguna estaba tan abarrotada, que Cocodrilo
salió a buscar otro lugar donde vivir.

La nueva laguna de Cocodrilo era barrosa y resbalosa.

Cocodrilo disfrutaba resbalándose y revolcándose.

Pero cuando los otros cocodrilos vieron lo que Cocodrilo estaba haciendo...

...también empezaron a resbalarse y revolcarse.
–**¿Por qué estos cocodrilos no dejan de copiarme**?
-gritó Cocodrilo.

–¿Y por qué no podemos resbalarnos y revolcarnos si queremos?
-dijeron los otros cocodrilos-. No es tu laguna.
Cocodrilo se puso tan furioso
que salió de la laguna barrosa y se fue.

Encontró un lugar a la orilla del río

y se echó a tomar el sol.

Pero cuando se durmió...

...¡los otros cocodrilos también vinieron a tomar el sol! Cocodrilo apenas podía moverse. Estaba muy disgustado.

–**¡Que me dejen tranquilo ya estos cocodrilos**! –gritó.

Se metió en el río helado y se fue nadando.

En medio del río, Cocodrilo encontró un tronco flotando.
Se montó en él, pataleó suavemente y flotó río abajo.
Le gustaba ver a los sapos en la orilla y a los pájaros en los árboles.

Y, sobre todo, le gustaba estar solo.

Pero entonces, oyó un chapoteo y...

... ¡los otros cocodrilos también venían flotando río abajo!

Cocodrilo pataleó más rápido.
Al pasar una curva del río, se escondió detrás de unos matorrales.
Los cocodrilos copiones estaban gozando tanto que no lo vieron.

Cocodrilo se deslizó por la jungla hasta que divisó
una montaña solitaria.
–¡Esa montaña sí que me gusta! –dijo.

Y empezó a subirla.

En la cima de la montaña, había lugar para un solo cocodrilo.

Cocodrilo estaba feliz.

Pero cuando bajó el sol y empezó a oscurecer...

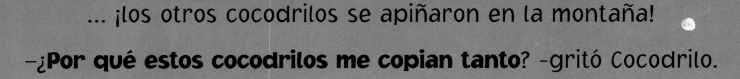

... ¡los otros cocodrilos se apiñaron en la montaña!

–¿Por qué estos cocodrilos me copian tanto? –gritó Cocodrilo.

–Porque siempre estás haciendo cosas nuevas y divertidas
–dijeron los demás cocodrilos.
–Además nosotros podemos sentarnos aquí si queremos.
No es TU montaña.

Cocodrilo
esperó hasta
que los demás se
durmieran. Entonces,
se escabulló en silencio...

...de regreso a su laguna.

Nadó por todas partes y no se tropezó con nadie.
No se había dado cuenta de que su laguna era tan grande.

Cocodrilo sintió frío.
Se acordó de cuando la laguna estaba llena
de un tibio montón de cocodrilos roncando.
Ahora estaba solo en la laguna desierta.

"Ojalá estuvieran aquí mis amigos",
pensó Cocodrilo con tristeza .

-¡Sorpresa!

Los otros cocodrilos se reían, se tropezaban y se revolcaban.
Cocodrilo se sintió DICHOSO.

Decidió que no estaba mal compartir su laguna
con los demás cocodrilos,
aunque estuvieran un poco apretujados.

Pero algunas veces le gustaba escaparse...

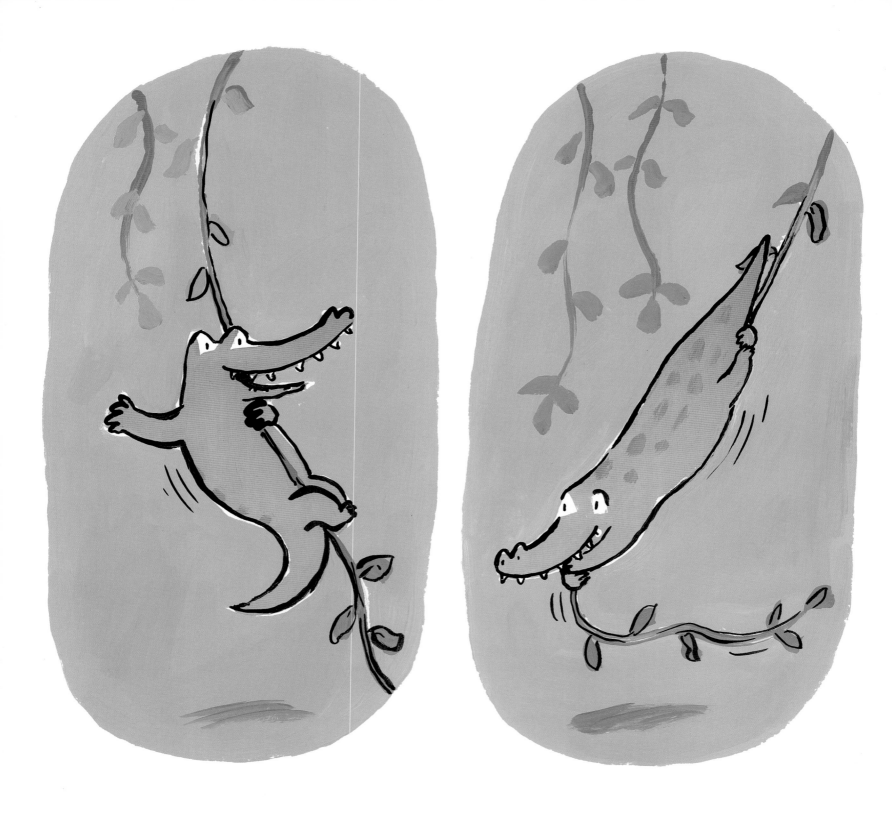

... y hacer cosas solo,

antes de que los demás lo encontraran.

Gotcha!

Nonfiction Booktalks to Get Kids Excited About Reading

Kathleen A. Baxter
Marcia Agness Kochel

1999
Libraries Unlimited, Inc.
Englewood, Colorado

For Riley and Mike.

Libraries Unlimited, Inc.
P.O. Box 6633
Englewood, CO 80155-6633
1-800-237-6124
www.lu.com

Library of Congress Cataloging-in-Publication Data
Baxter, Kathleen A.
    Gotcha! : nonfiction booktalks to get kids excited about reading / by Kathleen A. Baxter [and] Marcia Agness Kochel.
      xviii, 183 p. 22x28 cm.
    Includes bibliographical references and indexes.
    ISBN 1-56308-683-2 (pbk.)
    1. Children's literature, American Book reviews. 2. Book talks-- United States. I. Kochel, Marcia Agness. II. Title.
Z1037.A1B34 1999
028.1'62--dc21   99-34279
                                                                    CIP

Contents

Figures

Acknowledgments

Chapter 1

Cover, from *Summer of Fire: Yellowstone 1988* by Patricia Lauber. Jacket illustration photograph © Erwin and Peggy Bauer. Jacket design by Kathleen Westray. Reprinted by permission of Orchard Books, New York.

Cover, from *Wildfire* by Patrick Cone. Copyright 1997 by Carolrhoda Books, Inc. Used by permission of the publisher. All rights reserved.

Chapter 2

Cover, from Robert Burleigh. *Hoops.* © 1997 Harcourt Brace.

Cover, from *Never Take a Pig to Lunch and Other Poems About the Fun of Eating* by Nadine Bernard Westcott. Jacket illustration © 1994 by Nadine Bernard Westcott. Reprinted by permission of Orchard Books, New York.

Cover, from *Oh, Grow up! Poems to Help You Survive Parents, Chores, School, and Other Afflictions* by Florence Parry Heide and Roxanne Heide Pierce, illustrated by Nadine Bernard Westcott. Jacket illustration © 1996 by Nadine Bernard Westcott. Reprinted by permission of Orchard Books, New York.

Cover, from *Yuck! A Big Book of Little Horrors* published by Simon & Schuster Books for Young Readers (1996).

Cover, from *Snapshot* by Kenneth P. Czech. Copyright 1996 by Lerner Publications. Used by permission of the publisher. All rights reserved.

Chapter 3

Cover, from *The Secrets of Animal Flight* by Nic Bishop. Jacket photograph © 1997 by Nic Bishop. Reprinted by permission of Houghton Mifflin Company. All rights reserved.

Photograph (figure 3.2), from *Nights of the Pufflings* by Bruce McMillan. Copyright © 1995 by Bruce McMillan. Reprinted by permission of Houghton Mifflin Company. All rights reserved.

Cover, from *Watching Water Birds* jacket copyright © 1997 National Geographic Society.

Cover, from Caroline Arnold. *Hawk Highway in the Sky: Watching Raptor Migration.* © 1997 Harcourt Brace.

Cover, from Lynne Cherry. *Flute's Journey: The Life of a Wood Thrush.* © 1997 Harcourt Brace.

Cover, from *Harp Seal Pups* published by Simon & Schuster Books for Young Readers (1997).

Cover, from *Orcas Around Me: My Alaskan Summer* by Debra Page. Illustrated by Leslie Bowman © 1997. Published by Albert Whitman & Company.

Chapter 4

Chapter 5

Chapter 6

Introduction

This book is written for people who want to encourage children to read. Librarians, teachers, parents, and everyone who loves books and kids will find hundreds of fascinating, thought-provoking, and fun books to share with the children in their lives. I (Kathleen Baxter) am a librarian, and I speak frequently to groups of kids about books. In library jargon, we call this *booktalking.* No matter what your profession or background is, this book can help you match up children with just the right books. It is divided thematically into seven high-interest chapters and is written in a conversational style, as if we were talking to a group of children. Choose a chapter and dig right in! It doesn't take special skill to get kids excited about reading, just high-quality books and lots of enthusiasm on your part. Marcia and I will present ideas for more than 350 booktalks, some so short that they simply entail showing illustrations, others somewhat longer—but none so long that you will have to spend hours memorizing them. We have indicated which illustrations are good to show a crowd, and books are placed together so you don't have to come up with your own groupings. I have always insisted that books in my library collections be well reviewed, and you may rest assured that the books mentioned here have received favorable reviews in major library reviewing publications.

THE JOYS OF NONFICTION BOOKTALKING

I discovered the joys of nonfiction booktalking almost by accident. For a visit to a classroom of second graders, I had with me some newer books of all sorts to attract their attention and interest. The title that clinched it was a book about the *Titanic* (this was years before the movie came out). One of the little boys was agog with questions. Soon everyone was asking question after question. Did sharks eat the passengers on the *Titanic*? How come there weren't enough lifeboats? How come nobody came to help? How come men were not supposed to get on the lifeboats? I could make stabs at, and even answer, some of the questions, but the answers to others were beyond my ken.

I vowed that this would never happen to me again. I checked out three adult books about the *Titanic*, read them all, and went into my next classroom armed with a wealth of information and prepared for any question. I learned that the *Titanic* is about as good a booktalk topic as any I can think of. Everybody loves the story, and books on this subject are available for all ages. One thing I really like about booktalking nonfiction is the wide range of reading levels of books available on an interesting subject. Find a subject that fascinates, and a lot of your work is done for you. Pull together a group of books and make them available to your audience. Many times, I have learned, young children will be motivated to read harder books because they contain more and better pictures. At the very least they will try to make out the captions. I have left many a group of fourth graders wailing because I would not leave Robert Ballard's *Exploring the Titanic* in their classroom.

As time went by, teachers spread the word that I was really good at finding books children want to read. They seemed to think I had some mystical power for ascertaining such things. In truth, I did not think that at all. I am a fairly ordinary person with a healthy streak of curiosity and an active interest in a lot of things. I believe that if I find something particularly interesting, it is likely others will too. The main thing I do is look at new books as they arrive at my library and pick out ones that have something intriguing in them. This is hardly a daunting task. In some cases, it is simply a matter of finding a great photograph. Sometimes all I need to do to sell a book to an audience is hold up that photograph. In this book, we will mention some of the pictures that are guaranteed crowd pleasers. For example, show the audience the picture of the puppy eating out of a bowl in Joanna Cole's *My Puppy Is Born*, and listen for the chorus of "oohs" and "aahs." Another approach is to tie the pictures in two books together (e.g., Mavis Smith's *A Snake Mistake* and Alexandra Parsons's *Amazing Snakes*) and enjoy the audience reaction. Alice in Wonderland asked what was the use of a book without pictures. Sure, you can booktalk a book without pictures, but a good picture can make your booktalk.

My goal is to get children to read, to help them see what fun it is, to show them how many doors it can unlock. I tell them this truth about myself: I carry a book with me almost everywhere I go. I carry one in the car and in to see the doctor, the dentist, or the beautician. I even took one into surgery once! When I go on a trip, I always take too many books because one of my greatest fears in life is not having anything on hand to read. I read in bed, in the bathtub, on lunch breaks, and anyplace else you can think of. I *always* have overdue fines, because I am a heavy library user. I usually take good care of my books, but I have been known to drop them in the bathtub accidentally—and I have to pay for them as does every other person who destroys a library book. I warn kids about this as a person who understands the problem, not as a threatening librarian; in fact, I deemphasize taking good care of books. I do warn them about taking good care of their library cards—not letting their mom wash it or their dog eat it. This usually gets a laugh, and I love getting a laugh. I believe that people who are laughing are listening.

When I do a booktalk, I seldom limit it to a single theme. I like to mix and match a hodgepodge of materials. It is very important to stay in touch with your audience. Kids today are raised on MTV and *Sesame Street*, and long attention spans are not part of their makeup. If they do not like the book I am talking about at a given moment, they won't have to wait long for a change; I will soon be talking about another. Also, if the book I am discussing does not seem to grab the audience, I will move on even more quickly, go home and reassess what I could say about the book that might be more interesting, or abandon it altogether.

I have seen librarians do 15-minute booktalks on one book, going into the story in such detail that I lose all desire to read it. I want to be tantalized, to be intrigued, to have my appetite whetted. Booktalking for me does not mean rambling on and on about a good book I liked. A recommendation from a fellow reader is all that is necessary, not a huge plot description. Booktalking to me means telling people who may not be readers some of the reasons why a particular book will appeal to them.

I often show several books on one topic—the *Titanic*, science experiments, or Harriet Tubman—and allow children to pick the title that is at their reading level or that most appeals to them. The information in the books is pretty much the same, so the same booktalk suffices for all.

When booktalking, I often like to mention Gary Paulsen's book *Nightjohn*, a fiction book that describes a slave who teaches other slaves how to read and the horrible punishment he must endure as a consequence. One of the greatest ways to keep people from getting power is to prevent them from reading. If you want power, read. Tell your audience this. It may make an impression.

No, I do not read every word of every book I booktalk. Last year, I went into a ninth-grade classroom to talk about good books for just a few minutes. A friend of mine who is a travel editor at the *Washington Post* had assembled a list of recommendations of good books for her 14-year-old son. She had asked everyone she knew for suggestions and came up with an amazing list. Anyway, the top book, recommended by the book editor of the *Post* (who called it the best nonfiction book ever written), was *Endurance* by Alfred Lansing, about the Shackleton expedition to the South Pole. My husband is always in the market for good reading material, so I got the book for him. He could not put it down. I have never personally read *Endurance*, but he read aloud large chunks of it to me. Armed with a few of the amazing anecdotes from the book, I entered the classroom and told a few of the stories. As I don't work with junior high schoolers often, I was not sure it went all that well. This year the teacher called and wanted me back. She said I read the most wonderful story last year, and the kids were clamoring for my return. I had read no story. I had only told a little bit about one book, but everyone was interested in that book when I left. This experience also taught me that you do not always need a picture to leave students with a lasting image.

One of my big regrets in life is the picture I did *not* get. One of my favorite photos is of the mummy of an Italian monk, looking quite lifelike and in fairly good condition for someone who has been dead for a couple hundred years. The photo occupies almost all of a page in James Putnam's *Mummy*, and I have a color transparency of it. I feel I almost know this mummy. One day, while waiting in line in the supermarket before going to work, I perused the tabloid headlines. One was "Moses' Body Found on Mount Sinai!" The accompanying photograph was none other than that of my mummy! It was the same photograph from the Putnam book, but with a beard and a mustache drawn onto it. The next day I realized what an incredible statement that photo would make to any class I showed it to. I went back to the supermarket, but the tabloid was gone. Keep your mind open and your brain alert when you see such an opportunity, so you do not blow it the way I did.

Another thing I love to do with booktalks is to personalize them. I always ask myself if I have some information that will make the booktalk more interesting. My grandfather once paid for my father and my aunt to go up in an airplane in the 1920s. They were at a local fair, and pilots were barnstorming and taking passengers up for rides. The pilot who took my aunt on her ride was Charles Lindbergh! Recently, my mother told me that the first time she saw an airplane was at a different fair, when she was a small child. The fair featured a woman who walked on the airplane wings. Mom thought that was so scary, and she always remembered the woman's name: Ruth Law. I immediately sent her a copy of Don Brown's *Ruth Law Thrills a Nation*.

My dad also told us the story of the carnival that went through town in the 1930s with the exhibit of the body of John Wilkes Booth. He was skeptical that it was really the body of John Wilkes Booth, but it makes for a fascinating story, as does the story that Claudia Kennedy, the first three-star general in the history of the U.S. Army, told me. She was living in a house in Washington, D.C., that had once been a courthouse and prison. Not just any courthouse and prison, but the one where the Lincoln conspirators were imprisoned and tried. She swears that home is haunted by the ghost of Mary Surratt. You better believe I use *this* story. From that courthouse, the conspirators walked out to be hanged in an area that is now a tennis court—and that I stared at in mesmerized horror.

Finally, as a native of Walnut Grove, Minnesota (the little town where Laura Ingalls Wilder lived in *On the Banks of Plum Creek* and at the beginning of *By the Shores of Silver Lake*) I always tell the audience about my Wilder connection. I particularly love to booktalk *Searching for Laura Ingalls: A Reader's Journey* by Kathryn Lasky and Meribah Knight.

Have you visited places that are connected with the books you are booktalking? Tell your audience about them. I stood at the Civil Rights Museum in Memphis, once the Lorraine Motel, where Martin Luther King was assassinated. I couldn't stop crying. I saw, in the Museum of the Confederacy in Richmond, Virginia, newspaper ads that were placed by freed slaves 30 years after the Civil War ended, in which they were still looking for family members who had been sold away from them. I was in Louisiana in January of 1996, a bitterly cold month everywhere. When I read that many slaves in Louisiana never even had shoes to wear, I realized just what that might mean. It can be terribly cold in Louisiana. Kids are so interested when you can personalize a booktalk.

HOW TO PUT TOGETHER A BOOKTALK PROGRAM

How should your booktalks be ordered and organized? My best booktalk programs include at least one selection from every chapter in this book. I might start out with a description of one or more great disasters. Any disaster commands attention, as does your enthusiasm for the topic. Then I lighten up, read a poem or two from chapter 2 and have everyone try a couple of tongue twisters. Next I talk about a couple of fascinating people from chapter 6. If you can relate them to some of the history in chapter 7, that is all well and good, but I would probably talk about unrelated topics, so as to be almost certain of grabbing the interest of every person in the room.

I also like to demonstrate one of the science experiments from a Vicki Cobb book in chapter 5. If you can include a couple of kid volunteers, you'll keep attention and interest high. Show a picture of an animal from a book in chapter 3, and ask the kids some interesting questions. You cannot fail with bats or dinosaurs. Finally, I would end with an unsolved mystery or two from chapter 4. Everyone loves these, including me.

My specific suggestions for a booktalk include the following:

- Pick a good disaster. Mention the *Titanic* in passing but also include *Treasure Hunt: The Sixteen-Year Search for the Lost Treasure Ship Atocha*, *Shipwreck*, *Hidden Treasures of the Sea*, *Exploring the Bismark*, and other relevant disasters at sea.

- Sing a few of the poems from *Tyrannosaurus Was a Beast*, and ask the kids to name the songs. Then read a couple of the tongue twisters from *Fast Freddie Frog and Other Tongue-Twister Rhymes*, and ask the kids to try them with you.

- Describe the life of Elizabeth Cady Stanton and the legal status of women of her time, in *You Want to Vote, Lizzie Stanton?* Then tell the kids about some of the kids profiled in *Kids with Courage: True Stories About Young People Making a Difference*.

- Hold up *Gladiator* and describe how people got to be gladiators and some of the amazing gladiatorial events discussed in this book. Another, equally horrible life of danger is described in *The Underground Railroad*.

- Ask for volunteers to conduct a couple of experiments from *Bet You Can! Science Impossibilities to Fool You*. (My favorite is the one on page 87.)

- Show the kids a couple of photos from *My New Kitten* and tell them about *Rattlesnake Dance: True Tales, Mysteries, and Rattlesnake Ceremonies*, which starts with the author's true story of how, when she was a child, she was bitten by a rattlesnake.

- End with *Anastasia's Album* and a brief discussion of *Strange Mysteries from Around the World*.

Where do I do booktalks? Just about anywhere. I love to talk to anyone who will have me. In Anoka County, Minnesota, where I work, I am fortunate to be able to booktalk to many diverse audiences. I have booktalked to adult church groups and Rotary clubs. I have booktalked to prisoners in a state correctional facility and in a hospital lockup ward for disturbed teenagers. I booktalk to large and small groups of children, parent groups that want ideas, Title I parent/child combinations, and teachers. I particularly love booktalking to teachers, knowing how far-reaching the effects of my talk might be.

Every booktalk I give includes a library commercial tailored to the group. I find that giving adults some basic information about the library is highly effective (and welcome). Often, nonlibrary users are stunned at some of the basic information I give. Their jaws literally drop when I tell them they can call the library and find out how much their car is worth, or how large their monthly payments will be if they borrow X amount of money at X interest rate for X amount of time. I tell them we can get them recipes, addresses, poems for special occasions, sheet music, road maps, lake maps, travel guides, and much more. When I talk to parents, my theory is that I want to give them their own reason for coming to the library. Then they might also bring their children along.

I also do several booktalks outside the county where I work. It is an easy way to earn some extra income. I am in demand because my booktalks are *fun*.

A NOTE ABOUT US

I (Kathleen Baxter) am the Supervisor of Youth Services for the Anoka County Library, located in suburban Minneapolis, Minnesota. I also write a quarterly column for *School Library Journal* on booktalking nonfiction. I have an M.A.L.S. from the University of Minnesota. Although I have spent most of my career in Anoka County, my first job was working for the Queens Borough Public Library in New York City. I have done hundreds of booktalks on nonfiction, and I am a public speaker on several other topics as well.

When I was asked to write this book, I knew I wanted help. I tend to get overly enthusiastic. I go crazy with exclamation points! I needed someone to calm me down, someone I knew and respected. Marcia Agness Kochel immediately came to mind. Marcia is a book lover and fellow librarian who also has experience in the publishing business. We met in 1992 as we are both fans of children's author Maud Hart Lovelace. (If you have not read her Betsy-Tacy series, do so immediately!) We formed what eventually became the Maud Hart Lovelace Society, and Marcia edited and wrote our newsletter. She later left the Twin Cities to get her master's degree in library science at the University of North Carolina–Chapel Hill. She has been a middle school librarian and currently works as an elementary school librarian in Bloomington, Indiana. She is particularly interested in collaborating with teachers to integrate nonfiction books into the curriculum. Thanks to the Internet, we have done all of our work on this manuscript via e-mail.

Marcia and I love children's books and read them for pleasure even when we are not preparing a book. We are fanatics about quality books, and we bring different perspectives—one from a public library, one from a school library—to our work. We hope that this book will simplify your life, add some good ideas to your repertoire, and fill up your bag of tricks.

CHAPTER ———— 1

Great Disasters

Few booktalks can beat a booktalk about a disaster. *Disaster!* by Richard Platt is an excellent book to use for such a booktalk because it includes information about the most famous historical disasters as well some that are less well known. Beginning with "Vesuvius," each disaster rates a two-page spread. Read about the Black Death—the bubonic plague that killed so many people that the bodies were piled into mass graves. Or stare at the pictures of the 1666 Great Fire of London. Interestingly, when the Lord Mayor first was brought in to look at the fire, he did not think it looked like a big deal. "A woman could piss it out!" he said. He was horribly wrong. The Huang He (Yellow River) flood in 1935 was an unbelievable disaster as was the 1896 tsunami, the 80-foot-tall wave that rolled over northeastern Japan. As many as 900,000 people may have died as a result of the Huang He Flood, and about 27,000 died as a result of the 1896 tsunami. These numbers make many more famous disasters pale in comparison.

Other disasters covered in this book include the San Francisco Earthquake, the Blizzard of '88, the sinking of the *Titanic* (did you know that the ship's baker was able to stay alive for two hours in the icy water because he had been drinking whiskey?), and the *Hindenburg*. This colorful, oversize book provides an excellent introduction to some famous disasters and serves as a springboard for many of the booktalks that follow.

SHIPWRECKS AND DISASTERS AT SEA

One of the most fascinating disasters of all time is the sinking of the *Titanic*—rife with human interest stories, drama, wealth, poverty, and brutal injustices. Add pictures, and disaster stories like this are almost impossible to resist; photographs of the *Titanic* then and now will mesmerize your audiences. The 1997 blockbuster movie about the sinking ship sparked widespread interest in the disaster. Here is how you can describe it.

In 1912, the *Titanic* was the largest ship ever built, and word was out that it was unsinkable. It was expensive, beautiful, and packed with more than 2,200 passengers when it set sail from England to the United States. Guess what happened? It sank, sank on its first trip ever, sank several miles to the bottom of the ocean. How did this happen? It ran into an iceberg. If you do not know what an iceberg is, it is a mountain of ice floating in the ocean. Hitting the iceberg damaged the ship in such a way that it began to fill with water.

Now, as you know, an empty glass will float in a filled bathtub, but if water gets into the glass, it will soon sink. That is what happened to the *Titanic*.

But even after it hit the iceberg very few people believed it was going to sink. It was supposed to be unsinkable. When the ship's officers told passengers to board the lifeboats, many of them did not want to. It was nice and warm on the ship, and it was late at night and cold outside. When the people finally started getting into the lifeboats, the ship's officers followed the rules very strictly. Some books tell the story of John Jacob Astor, one of the richest men in America. He was returning from a honeymoon in Europe with his wife, who was going to have a baby. He made the decision to get into a lifeboat fairly early, but when he tried to climb aboard, he was informed that only women and children were allowed.

Boys invariably are horrified at this information. Inform the entire group that women were not even allowed to vote in 1912, so they did not have it so good either. What was really sad about Mr. Astor's story is that the lifeboat he tried to board was lowered into the water less than half full! John Jacob Astor's body was found floating in the water a few days later. He had frozen to death. Many of the passengers who died were wearing life preservers, allowing them to float. It took about an hour for them to freeze to death.

Survivors from the lifeboats have described how the *Titanic* sank, but there are no photographs. A great two-page color painting of the sinking appears on pages 26 and 27 of Robert Ballard's *Exploring the Titanic*. The ship ended up pointing almost straight up in the air before it sank, and when it went under, it created a whirlpool much as a bathtub drain does when you empty the water. Anyone near the ship would have been pulled down into that whirlpool, so those in the water tried to swim or row as far away from it as they could.

We now know that on its way to the bottom of the ocean, the ship broke into two pieces, but for 75 years no one knew what happened to it underwater or even exactly where it settled. Many people searched for the *Titanic*, but Robert Ballard led the expedition that finally located it in 1985. The incredible robot camera *Jason Junior* took photos of the shipwreck underwater, and Ballard's fascinating book compares the way it looks today with the way it looked when it set sail on its maiden voyage in 1912. The last photo in the Ballard book shows a pair of boots, now empty, at the bottom of the ocean. Once a person stood in those boots, but the fish and bacteria have since eaten everything but the leather. No one can swim around the *Titanic*; it is submerged too deeply for a human to survive.

More than 1,500 people—two out of every three passengers on board—died in the sinking of the *Titanic*. How many kids are in your room? Count out two-thirds of them and tell them that they would all be dead. The survivors were rescued the next morning by another ship, the *Carpathia*. Can you imagine what it might have felt like to watch the *Titanic* sink, knowing that your dad was in the cold water, dying if not already dead?

If you were on board the *Titanic* and were not a wealthy person, the odds increased that you would die, even if you were a woman or a child. Rich people in first class got aboard the lifeboats first. People in second class got on too, but there was little room for the poorest people, mostly immigrants who were coming to America to live. It is interesting to note that the owner of the *Titanic* did make it onto one of the lifeboats.

The Ballard book is a favorite with kids. Its photos and illustrations are enticing. But Judy Donnelly's *The Titanic: Lost . . . and Found* is much easier to read, and *On Board the Titanic: What It Was Like When the Great Liner Sank* by Shelley Tanaka is an appealing addition to the subject. It fictitiously describes the lives of two actual teenage boys who were on the ship, and it features photographs and some compelling color paintings by Ken Marschall. Marschall's fascinating paintings also fill Hugh Brewster's *Inside the Titanic*. His paintings will provide hours of fascination. *Polar the Titanic Bear* was written in 1913 by Daisy Corning Stone Spedden, who was herself on the *Titanic*. It tells the true story of a teddy bear that survived the disaster. This is a beautiful new edition with good illustrations and photographs. Always show your audiences some of the great pictures in these books.

Treasure Hunt: The Sixteen-Year Search for the Lost Treasure Ship Atocha by George Sullivan describes another interesting nautical disaster. In 1622 a ship loaded with South American gold on its way back to Spain sank in a storm. No one knew exactly where it sank, but it was common knowledge in the world of scholarly history that the ship was still out there, somewhere at the bottom of the ocean.

Mel Fisher, an American, read about the *Atocha* and decided to search for it. He started by asking the help of a close friend, Eugene Lyon, who could read Spanish fluently. He visited Spanish libraries, trying to read as much as he could and eventually targeted an area of the ocean not far from Miami. Even with Lyon's amazing research and much on-site searching, it took Fisher 16 years to succeed, and in the process, his own son drowned. When Fisher found the *Atocha*, it was heavy with gold that had been underwater for over 350 years.

Legal battles followed. Who actually owned the gold? Fisher eventually got a fortune's worth. What makes this astonishing story even more compelling to booktalk is that J.C. Penney stores hold *Atocha* gold sales every now and then. You can go to one and pick up a coin or handle a necklace worth $60,000. Be sure to booktalk this title if you see an *Atocha* ad in the newspaper!

A book for younger children that describes the *Atocha* and other ships is *Sunken Treasure* by Gail Gibbons. *The Search for the Atocha Treasure* by Fran O'Byrne-Pelham and Bernadette Balcer is another title that is considerably easier to read.

Richard Platt's *Shipwreck*, a beautiful Eyewitness Book, is jam-packed as always with great photos and interesting facts. For example, did you know that there are more than 2,000 wrecks in the English Channel, which is a fairly small body of water? Shipwrecks are very dangerous to other ships, so buoys are put up to mark them and warn other ships to stay away. On page 23 of *Shipwreck* is a photo of a traveler's chain from a Spanish Armada ship that sank in 1588. This gold necklace had another use: The links could be easily detached and used instead of money. Page 39 features a photo of a first-rate inflatable life raft. The people who died on the *Titanic* would have all lived if these had been available. The rafts include water bailers, fresh water, boarding ladders, ropes, a battery-powered lamp, and a roof to keep them warm in the cold and cool in the sun! Interesting information about the history of deep-sea diving appears on pages 44 and 45. Show the audience the photo of the "barrel diver" invented by John Lethbridge in 1715. Diving for wrecks inside the barrel made him a fortune. And don't leave out the section on shipboard life on pages 52 and 53. Here is a sample: "After just a few weeks at sea, drinking water became slimy and unpleasant, so every ship carried large quantities of wine, beer and spirits."

A good title to show in conjunction with books on the *Atocha* and other shipwrecks is *Aztec, Inca, & Maya* by Elizabeth Baquedano. This Dorling Kindersley title contains wonderful pictures and information about the three great Central and South American civilizations. Show the two-page spreads on pages 50-51, 54-55, and 62-63 to give children examples of the kind of treasure that ships like the *Atocha* were transporting to Spain. And for an excellent introduction to these cultures, recommend the title for its own sake.

A horrifying nautical disaster is the subject of *The USS Arizona* by R. Conrad Stein. The *Titanic* and the *Atocha* disasters happened a long time ago, but this disaster happened more recently. There are still people alive today who saw the *USS Arizona* go down in the 1941 Japanese attack on Pearl Harbor in Hawaii. The ship was bombed; then it burst into flames and sank. Many ships were sunk in World War II, but the story of this one resonates because the ship is still at the bottom of the harbor in Honolulu leaking oil, and a ceremony is held at the site every day.

This was not just another sinking. Eleven hundred seventy-seven men died. Air went to the bottom of the *USS Arizona*, formerly the top, so sailors trapped in the wreck were able to live for several days, tapping on the submerged hull and shouting for help. Servicemen on nearby vessels could hear the tapping and the shouting, which got weaker every day, but they were able to get only 32 men out. It was very hard to work underwater to cut through the hull of the ship. Everyone nearby heard men slowly dying, and those who were there are still haunted by it.

Robert Ballard is continually making new discoveries as he sails around the world in search of sunken ships. *Exploring the Bismarck* by Ballard and Rick Archbold describes the exploration of perhaps the most famous Nazi ship sunk in World War II. The *Bismarck* had been targeted by the British because its primary purpose was to sink merchant ships bringing supplies to Great Britain. Great Britain had been in the war for more than two years before the United States was bombed at Pearl Harbor and was very low on supplies for both the fighting men and the civilians. The Germans knew that a good way to fight the British would be to prevent supplies from getting to them.

This book tells what it was like to be on the *Bismarck* during both her glory days and her last battle—and what happened to some of the men who were rescued by the British. Interesting photos depict the sailors on the ship and one of them in the water, hoping to be rescued. But the British feared a German U-boat attack and saved only 115 men out of the 2,206 who were on board. One man whose arms had been blown off tried to grab a rescue line with his teeth!

Show your audience the picture of the *Bismarck* (pages 52-53) at the bottom of the Atlantic, with a huge swastika still painted on its deck, the poster on page 13, and another fine underwater illustration on pages 8 and 9.

Ballard and Archbold also co-wrote *The Lost Wreck of the Isis*. This book describes the search for and eventual discovery of a Roman merchant vessel that sank in the second half of the fourth century. Read aloud the second paragraph on page 16, which includes the information that:

> a ship almost never sinks in one piece. Even if it does, it leaves a field of debris as it goes down—pieces of the hull, pieces of the cargo, and so on. The main hull of the ship and the heaviest items tend to fall straight down. The lighter pieces drift as they fall, carried by underwater currents. You can usually find the main chunks of a wreck by following the debris trail from lighter to heavier objects.

Ballard and his colleagues named the ship the *Isis,* but no one today really knows what it was called. The book includes an illustrated fictitious hypothesis of what might have happened. Good pictures to show include the illustration of the storm and shipwreck on pages 46 and 47, and the incredibly well-preserved ancient artifacts on page 59.

Hidden Treasures of the Sea from National Geographic describes many shipwrecks and artifacts. Note the photo of the comb on page 49. One side is for combing hair, and the other side is for picking lice! Or show the two-page spread of gold and jewels found in shipwrecks on pages 68 and 69. Always stress that people who are looking for shipwrecks and buried treasure invariably start their quest by reading. You cannot look for anything without first acquiring basic information on where it is supposed to be. There would be no point in searching randomly for shipwrecks. The ocean is simply too large.

Buried in Ice by Owen Beattie and John Geiger tells the story of the *Franklin* expedition. The *Franklin* sailed through Arctic seas in 1845 attempting to find the Northwest Passage. People thought there had to be a way to get across the North American continent by water. (Pioneers made the arduous, hardship-filled journey across the plains, while wealthy people traveled by sea on a trip that took them all the way to the tip of South America.) No one ever returned alive from the *Franklin* expedition, and, for decades, no one knew what had happened to it. Finally, in 1984, researchers found not only remains of the ship but also human bodies. The bodies had been buried in ice and were perfectly preserved, looking not much different than they did the day they died 139 years earlier. Ice preserved those bodies, making it possible for us to find out what actually happened to the men on the *Franklin*.

Much of the food on the ship was canned food. People then did not know that lead poisoning was caused by eating food in tin cans. The sailors ate the food and got sick. To treat the sickness they were given more canned food. And if they ate enough of it, they died of lead poisoning! Show the picture on page 53. It's a grabber.

Cold was the biggest problem for Sir Ernest Shackleton in his 1914 attempt to reach the South Pole. His story has been brilliantly retold in *Endurance: Shackleton's Incredible Voyage* by Alfred Lansing, which some believe is the finest nonfiction book ever written. This title would work well for good middle school readers, but a more recent book by Jennifer Armstrong would also work well with middle school or upper elementary students. Armstrong uses compelling text and incredible photographs from the journey in her book *Shipwreck at the Bottom of the World: The Extraordinary True Story of Shackleton and the Endurance*. Michael McCurdy's *Trapped by the Ice! Shackleton's Amazing Antarctic Adventure* (figure 1.1) tells the story in much simpler language for younger children.

Fig. 1.1. *Trapped by the Ice! Shackleton's Amazing Antarctic Adventure* by Michael McCurdy

In 1914, when you went exploring, you were really alone. You could not contact anyone for help—there were no radios or any other ways to communicate, no airplanes to look for you and bring in supplies, and no really good warm clothing to block out the cold. Shackleton's voyage was an amazing triumph, but it must have felt like the biggest disaster he could imagine when he was in the middle of it.

Shackleton's ship, the *Endurance*, was trapped and crushed by huge blocks of ice, which eventually sank it. He and his crew were forced to live on the frozen Weddell sea, in tents, surviving on any food they could hunt. Penguins and seals grew scarce as the men ate any they could find. Nobody could have a bath, so everyone smelled disgusting. The crew used lifeboats to try to get to a whaling station 700 miles away, but conditions were horrible. One night when they set up their tents on an ice floe, the ice cracked in two in the middle of a tent—and one of the men went into the freezing water, still wrapped in his sleeping bag! Shackleton had to figure out a way to save his men, and what he did was both brilliant and courageous. Many people consider Sir Ernest Shackleton to be one of the greatest heroes of all time. Read this book to find out why.

FIRES, FLOODS, DISEASES, AND OTHER NATURAL DISASTERS

The eruption of Mount Vesuvius in A.D. 69 is one of the all-time greatest disasters. Volcanic ash and lava completely covered the two towns of Pompeii and Herculaneum, preserving them for almost 2,000 years. The study of these ruins has provided us with an enormous amount of information as to how people lived in ancient times. Actual loaves of bread were uncovered—81 loaves in one bakery oven! Photographs of the body casts that were made make fascinating visual aids in booktalks. As people and animals tried to escape from the fiery ash, their struggles were dramatically recorded as the ash engulfed them. Centuries later, modern researchers poured plaster into the impressions left after the bodies decayed, and they were able to get statues of people dying in agony. One particularly sad statue is of a dog that was tied up and could not get away.

Peter Connolly's *Pompeii*, large, colorful, and packed with illustrations, is a guaranteed crowd pleaser, as are almost any books about the eruption and subsequent excavation of Pompeii. Pictures guaranteed to impress an audience are the bodies cast in plaster on page 13 and the sponge stick, used then as we use toilet paper today, on page 67. (Kids adore bathroom anecdotes!) On page 36, we are informed that "The Pompeiians had little appreciation of hygiene. Open toilets are found either next to . . . or actually in the kitchen. They usually drained away into a pit. Only public toilets had a proper sewage system." Can you imagine what it would be like if you had to cook dinner in the bathroom? Aimed at grades six and up, this title includes much information about the actual excavations and the eruption itself. The illustration on page 9 of the pumice from the volcano falling is an impressive one to show, and the illustrations on the following page show the volcano as it probably looked then and as it looks today.

We are very fortunate to have an eyewitness account of this disaster, which happened so long ago. Pliny the Younger was on a boat and watched the eruption from a distance. He later wrote about it. His story is the oldest known eyewitness account of a natural disaster. Thanks to Pliny, we now know that Herculaneum, which was closer to Vesuvius, was buried under almost 10 yards of boiling mud; Pompeii, not quite so much. Talk about an unpleasant way to die!

The Secrets of Vesuvius by Sara C. Bisel includes a fictional account of what might have happened to some of the residents of Herculaneum. The author is a physical anthropologist who was asked by archaeologists to go to Italy in 1982 to examine several skeletons found there and to see what she could learn about them. She dedicates this book "to the Herculaneans of A.D. 79, who still have stories to tell. . . ." She learned some of the stories. Show your audience the colorful double-page spread of fire from the volcano raining down on the city on pages 44 and 45. Then show the picture on page 51 of the "ring lady," the skeleton with two rings still on her left hand, as well as two bracelets, a pair of earrings, and some coins by her side and the picture on page 55 of the skeleton of a young slave girl holding the baby who died in her arms. The fictional story in this book is about this slave girl, who worked very hard and was not well cared for.

Shelley Tanaka's *The Buried City of Pompeii: What It Was Like When Vesuvius Exploded* (figure 1.2) is another appealing account of the disaster. A great photo of the open crater of Vesuvius appears on page 5, and another fictionalized tale, this one of a steward in the House of Menander, is photographed and illustrated here. Also show the photo on page 12 of the little girl playing with the dog—the dog whose body cavity is later discovered. For some reason, this story of the dog that was tied up and thus could not escape seems to wrench more hearts than do the stories of the people who died. This book contains a fascinating quote worth sharing on page 12:

> At about 1 p.m., the mountain roared, and her summit cracked open. A huge column of pumice and ash shot up into the air like a rocket. When the column reached the height of 12 miles (20 kilometers), it spread out like a fountain. Ash and pumice began to fall to the ground."

Twelve miles! Imagine what that would look like.

Fig. 1.2. *The Buried City of Pompeii: What It Was Like When Vesuvius Exploded* by Shelley Tanaka

Ron and Nancy Goor's *Pompeii: Exploring a Roman Ghost Town* is another wonderful book, but its black-and-white photos put it at a disadvantage.

Add *Volcano & Earthquake* by Susanna Van Rose to your booktalk about Vesuvius. Its photographs are wonderful, and it is full of tantalizing pieces of information.

In 1902, one of the worst volcanic disasters of this century took place on the Caribbean island of Martinique. All but two residents of the city of St. Pierre were killed, one of whom was a condemned prisoner who survived only because his cell had thick walls and one tiny window that faced away from the volcano. Read about him on page 33. Find out how volcanoes and earthquakes happen and about the brave people who are always finding out more about them.

The photo of the skull on page 30 is riveting, and the photos on pages 28 and 29 of the plaster casts of the bodies in Pompeii are excellent.

Carole Garbuny Vogel's *Shock Waves Through Los Angeles: The Northridge Earthquake* describes a fairly recent catastrophe, the earthquake that shuddered through the Los Angeles area on January 17, 1994. Show children the photograph of the car falling into the crack in the freeway on page 5 (impossible as it may seem, the driver survived) and the photo of the Fillmore Hotel on page 7. How would you have felt if the front side of your house fell off? Imagine how it would feel to be sweeping a parking garage when the earthquake hit and having all the concrete above you fall on top of you. This happened to Salvador Peña. For a while it looked as though rescuers would have to amputate his legs to get him out. This book is loaded with great stories along with a good read-aloud explanation of earthquakes. Read this description on page 28:

> The planet is like a roughed-up chocolate-covered cherry. The crust (the chocolate coating) is broken into about a dozen large plates and several smaller ones. The plates float on the mantle, a layer of hotter, softer rock (the gooey syrup). Beneath the mantle lies the earth's hottest layer, its dense core (the cherry).

The shifting of the top plates causes earthquakes, and every single state in the United States is susceptible to an earthquake. Read the book to find out where the worst ones are likely to occur.

Patricia Lauber's *Flood: Wrestling with the Mississippi* includes breathtaking pictures both of the 1993 and the 1927 floods. The Mississippi River, which almost bisects the United States, is a powerful force. Any idea we had that we were in charge of the river instead of vice versa was completely disproved in 1993. This huge river is stronger than anyone who may seek to control it, and questions rage about how much the river should be controlled. The cover of the book makes a fine picture to show, as do the photos on pages 14 and 18.

Patricia Lauber also has written a book about hurricanes that is sure to please young weather enthusiasts. *Hurricanes: Earth's Mightiest Storms* tells the stories of two devastating hurricanes—one that hit Long Island in 1938 and a more recent hurricane that struck Miami, Florida, in 1992. Sandwiched between the stories is a good discussion of how hurricanes form, how scientists name and track them, and how hurricane-hunting planes fly into storms to measure and photograph them.

Tell your audience about the "monster storm" of 1938. At that time weather satellites did not exist, and no one knew how to track hurricanes. Consequently, no one knew that a hurricane was barreling toward New England, and so no one was prepared when the winds struck. Have your listeners close their eyes and imagine what it would feel like to be in the hurricane while you read aloud from page 8.

> In early afternoon, winds struck. Deck chairs and shutters swooped through the air like leaves. Roof shingles rippled and tore loose. Windows blew in, doors blew open. The sky turned black. Telephone poles snapped. Rain fell in sheets, sweeping through broken windows and open doors. Water crept up around houses. Then the sea struck.

Tell about the 40-foot storm surge, and pick up reading on page 10.

> Water swallowed houses. Roofs blew off. Pianos flew through the air. Birds, racing to escape, appeared to be flying backward. Rising water drove people from the first floor of their houses to the second to the attic. Then houses collapsed. Boats tore loose and crashed into other boats and bridges. Trees fell. Church steeples toppled. And through it all, the only sound that could be heard was the howl of the wind: sometimes a scream, sometimes a deep bass, but mostly a pulsing groan.

If you are booktalking to teachers, suggest that they use this passage when teaching about descriptive writing and action verbs. Kids can make a list of all the verbs that Lauber uses and imitate her style when writing descriptions of their own.

Patricia Lauber writes about another natural disaster in *Summer of Fire: Yellowstone 1988* (figure 1.3). This book answers the question "Are wildfires always disasters?" Sometimes it looks that way, but fire is a part of nature. As Lauber shows us in this fascinating book, sometimes it is a very helpful part of nature.

In 1988 it was hot and dry almost all over the United States. (If you remember specifics about this year in your area, relate them to your audience.) Forest fires in the West and Alaska burned 26 million acres, an area twice as large as the state of Delaware. Smoke from the fires could sometimes be seen in Minneapolis, well over 1,000 miles away.

The most famous fires ignited in Yellowstone Park, one of the most visited and beloved parks in our national park system. Yellowstone Park lies over a volcanic base, and that base is called magma. It causes all the unusual hot springs and geysers (like Old Faithful), which are so interesting to see. Flames spread as quickly as four or five miles a day, and one fire ran 14 miles in only four hours. Although 2,000 firefighters were battling the fires, it was impossible to keep up with them or put them out. One day more than 150,000 acres burned inside the park and the neighboring forests.

But Lauber explains why, although they seemed so awful at the time, the forest fires actually helped Yellowstone Park. Fire, she explains, frequently jumps over many things that would otherwise get burned. Actually, only about one percent of Yellowstone Park was turned to ashes. Fire, she tells us, adds desperately needed minerals to the soil, and not as many animals are killed as people often fear. Animals are smart enough to get out of the way when they see a fire coming. She tells us that only a few animals were killed, mostly by smoke inhalation.

Flip through the book to show your audience the beautiful photos. Any of them would work well in front of a group.

Fig. 1.3. *Summer of Fire: Yellowstone 1988* **by Patricia Lauber**

Pairing Lauber's book with *Wildfire* by Patrick Cone (figure 1.4) makes a good booktalk even better. Instead of concentrating only on the Yellowstone fires, (which he does include), Cone describes all sorts of wildfires.

Did you know that lightning starts most wildfires around the world? In the western United States, 65 percent of wildfires are caused by lightning. In the eastern part of the country, 90 percent of all wildfires are caused by humans! Fireworks alone cause nearly 50,000 fires a year in this country.

This colorful book is packed with interesting photos and information about wildfires. It describes the three different types—ground fires, surface fires, and crown fires—and features a great photo on page 24 of a firestorm, the most destructive type of crown fire. The book also provides facts about firefighting techniques.

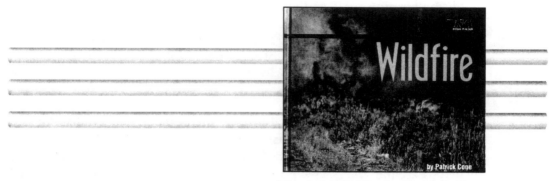

Fig. 1.4. *Wildfire* by Patrick Cone

Read to your audience one or two of the "Fascinating Facts" on page 45. Example: "In 1871, a wind-driven wildfire roared through the logging and railroad town of Peshtigo, Wisconsin, killing about 1,500 people. Some survived by standing neck-deep in the nearby river with their noses out of the water until the fire had passed."

The Great Fire by Jim Murphy highlights an American catastrophe, the infamous Chicago Fire of 1871. This book is a "must" booktalk for anyone who lives near Chicago, and it is interesting for the rest of us, too. *The Great Fire* is a Newbery Honor Book, and for good reason. It tells the fascinating story of an enormous disaster that could have been prevented if people hadn't kept on making mistakes.

Whenever something awful happens, one of the first things that people do is try to find someone or something to blame. It is easier to find one reason for a disaster, or to say that somebody goofed, than to search out all of the complicated causes that might exist.

So it was in Chicago. If you know anything at all about the Great Chicago Fire, it is probably that it started in Mrs. O'Leary's barn when her cow kicked over a lantern. That's not really true. This particular fire did start in the barn that belonged to the O'Learys, but probably not because a cow kicked over a lantern.

Tell students about Chicago in 1871. It was a city ready to burn. It boasted more than 59,000 buildings, most of them made of wood. It also had an elaborate system of 600 miles of dry, flammable, elevated wooden sidewalks connecting the city. It had barely rained since the summer, and by October, six fires were breaking out every day. When the big fire broke out on October 8, a series of fatal errors occurred that doomed the city to a fiery fate. Several people tried to alert the fire department, but the man who owned the drugstore with the alarm box stubbornly refused to call it in. A watchman scanning the sky mistook the new fire for the smoldering embers of the previous night's fire. When he finally realized it was a new fire, he sent fire engines to the wrong place. When someone on the scene went to turn in a second alarm, he made a mistake in the way he signaled and failed to indicate that this was a second alarm. Fueled by strong winds, the fire burned for 31 hours and spread across miles of the city, causing stampedes of people. In all, more than 100,000 people were forced to flee their homes. Read aloud this paragraph from page 60.

> As the fire burned and heated up an area (sometimes to 1500 degrees), the hot air rose and formed a column hundreds of feet tall. Oxygen-rich air was sucked into the column at the bottom of the base, where it mixed with the burning fuels and also rose, twisting and whirling around as it did. Sometimes giant bubbles of unburned gases rose within the column and then exploded high in the sky. The wind generated from such a column could reach out hundreds of feet and might attain hurricane-like speeds. At its fiercest, such a whirlwind could rip a roof off a house and pick up the building's contents.

The fire, which started on Saturday night, burned out of control for two days, until rain on Monday brought relief. Even on Tuesday, however, parts of the city were still burning. Murphy's book describes the true stories of the stampedes as frantic people rushed to escape, the boys who crossed a bridge carrying coffins, and a 12-year-old girl who was separated from her family in the rush. It's a great tale. You will want to read it for yourself before letting students have a chance at it.

Another famous fire is described in Shelley Tanaka's *The Disaster of the Hindenburg*. Imagine what it would be like to cross the ocean in a blimp. Most of us have seen blimps, sometimes at games, sometimes on TV, but not many of us have been lucky enough to ride in one.

Blimps are quiet, ride smoothly, and can stop almost noiselessly, making them a great place from which to look at whales. At one time, it was thought that blimps were the way most people would travel in the future. But that was before the *Hindenburg* disaster in 1937.

The *Hindenburg* was a huge blimp made in Nazi Germany. It was comfortable and easy to ride in, with great views, delicious food, and lots of good service. It carried passengers to many places, and everyone was excited when the *Hindenburg* made its first trip to the United States. Several kids were on the trip, and this book particularly tells the story of two teenagers, a cabin boy and a girl who was 16 years old.

There was one big drawback to the zeppelins, which was what blimps like the *Hindenburg* were called. They were filled with hydrogen gas, which was very flammable and quite dangerous. The crew took great care to make sure that no fire or sparks would occur, but there was always the possibility of an accident. There was a smoking room on the blimp, but it was tightly sealed.

The ocean crossing was expected to take only two days, but weather conditions delayed the arrival of the blimp into the Lakehurst airfield in New Jersey. When it finally started to land, the passengers looking down through the windows at the crew waiting below were startled to see people looking horrified and turning around and running away. What could have happened?

What had happened was that the *Hindenburg* suddenly caught fire, and in a flash it was a big fireball. People jumped out of the ship, and some landed in the arms of the onlookers below. Thirty-five of the 97 people on board died. No one knows how the fire started.

What was also unusual about the *Hindenburg* is that because many photographers had gathered to watch it land, many pictures were taken. No disaster before had ever been so well photographed. People who saw the pictures decided that they did not want to ride in a blimp—not ever. The era of the blimp had ended.

This book is loaded with interesting information about the zeppelin and what being in it was like. Show kids the cover, or the photo on pages 48 and 49, or the illustration of the teenage Irene getting ready to jump out of the burning ship on page 51 (she died).

Famous fires are interesting to read about, but what would it be like to be in a fire yourself? Not a famous fire, but a fire in which your home burned down and everything you owned burned up except your teddy bear and the clothes you were wearing when you went to bed? It does not sound like much fun, does it? What would you wear in the morning? *Fire! My Parents' Story* by Jessie Haas tells just such a story.

Jessie Haas's mother, Patty, was in a fire like that when she was eight years old, more than 50 years ago. It was awful. The house where she and her family lived burned to the ground, and they were able to save only a few of their possessions. What happened that night and what happened afterwards make for a fascinating story. Show your audience the picture of Patty holding her teddy bear on page 34.

For a lot of general information about firefighting, read *Fire!* by Joy Masoff. Do you know that 95 percent of all fires are caused by playing with matches? If you even start glancing through this book, you will be readily convinced that avoiding fires of all sorts is an excellent idea.

Fire is a fascinating subject, and everyone thinks firefighters are brave people with an interesting job. But this book will tell you many things you never even guessed about fires and firefighters. You'll learn some new words. Did you know that *flashover* describes what happens when all of the stuff in a room becomes so hot that everything suddenly bursts into flame in one huge explosion? One of the greatest fears of a firefighter is to be caught in a room when this happens. *Flash point* is the temperature at which a substance catches fire. Paper burns at 451 degrees Fahrenheit, but socks won't burn until the temperature reaches almost 600 degrees. Do you know that a PASS is a personal alert safety system? It detects when a firefighter stops moving, which usually means he or she is either hurt or trapped. The PASS makes a high-pitched noise to alert others to the fact that the firefighter needs help. The Jaws of Life is a "big, 50-pound can opener for a crushed car." (Show the picture on page 20.) In just 10 minutes a skilled firefighter can remove all four doors and the roof of a car using this tool.

This book includes information about people who fight fires and the history of firefighting. Small towns may have all volunteer fire departments, but cities employ firefighters. New York City firefighters go out on 350,000 calls a year! This book includes a list of the worst fears of firefighters, questions they get asked, and even a recipe that a firefighter cooks for the fire station. Show the audience a double-page spread or two from this fascinating book.

One of the worst disasters in American History is known as the Dust Bowl. What on earth was that? Have you ever heard of a dust storm? Most of us have never seen one, but in the 1930s they were very common in the Midwest, especially in an area of about 50 million acres in parts of Oklahoma, Texas, New Mexico, and Colorado. This area became known as the Dust Bowl, because there were so many dust storms, even though there were such storms in many other states as well. A dust storm could be as bad as a tornado, or any other kind of terrible storm.

On Black Sunday—April 14, 1935—a terrible black blizzard swept over the Great Plains, blotting out the sun and causing outdoor temperatures to drop as much as fifty degrees in only a few hours. During the summer of that year, the ceilings of some homes collapsed from the weight of all the dust that had accumulated in attics.

Why doesn't this happen much anymore, and why did it happen so often in the 1930s? When white settlers started living on the Great Plains, many tried to farm the land, with considerable success. But to farm it, they had to change much about it. They upset the ecology of the land, and they wore it out. On some maps, this area was known as "The Great American Desert," and by the late 1920s, rain had become very scarce. Hardly any rain fell for years. The land started to literally blow away, and this resulted in huge blizzards of dust. People got "dust pneumonia" from all of the dust in their lungs. Animals in fields got so much dust in their nostrils and mouths they could no longer breathe; some were even buried in the dust.

The Dust Bowl: Disaster on the Plains by Tricia Andryszewski tells us a lot about this fascinating time and of the hardships the people had to go through. Money and food were scarce, and people were very, very poor.

Some of the people in the Oklahoma panhandle were so poor that they could not make a living on the land. The story of these people is told in *Children of the Dust Bowl: The True Story of the School at Weedpatch Camp* by Jerry Stanley. Many of the "Okies," as they came to be called, lived on small farms and did not make much money even in good times. During the dust storms, families would sleep with wet washcloths or sponges over their faces to filter out the dust. But in the morning they would wake to find their pillows and blankets caked with dirt and their tongues and teeth coated with grit.

Farmers in California sent posters to the area advertising for farmworkers, and many people decided to sell their possessions, leave their farms, and move to California, a place they looked on as almost the promised land. Food and money were everywhere, they heard, and well-paying jobs were easy to find. They packed all of their belongings into their old cars or trucks and made the long, difficult journey west, often having very little to eat on the way. Children sometimes had to eat coffee grounds.

When they got to California, they found out that the stories were lies. There were no jobs. The jobs that did exist paid so little that people could not even buy enough food for their families, let alone pay for housing, clothing, or gas. People lived in their vehicles or in tents with no bathroom facilities, water, or food. To make matters worse, many people in California hated Okies and thought they were little better than animals.

Eventually, camps were set up for them, but the children were not allowed to go to the public schools. Their lives were miserable. Their clothes were ragged, they were uneducated, and their speech was not like the speech of the people in California.

But one man who wanted things to change made a big difference. That man was Leo Hart. He played with the kids at the camp, and he wanted them to have the same chances and the same education that the California kids had. He ran for superintendent of schools and did many things to make sure that the children of the camp would have a good school of their own, even if they had to build it themselves. How would you like to build your own school, grow and raise your own lunches, and even build a swimming pool—the first public swimming pool in the county? Read this fascinating book to find out how the children of Weedpatch Camp got what they so desperately needed thanks to one man who believed he could make a difference (figure 1.5).

Blizzards, heavy snow, and cold weather also can be disastrous. One of the most famous cold-weather disasters is an event in American history, detailed in *Snowbound: The Tragic Story of the Donner Party* by David Lavender.

In the spring of 1846, a small group of pioneers from Springfield, Illinois, decided to move west to California. They had a pamphlet written by a guide named Lansford Hastings that included a shortcut which he claimed would save time and distance. The Donner Party, so called because its leaders were men from the Donner family, got into trouble almost the minute they decided to take the shortcut. It was not a road, it went through barren desert, and the extra time it took meant that they were arriving in the dreaded Sierra Nevada mountains in time for the first snowfall; the Donners had taken the shortcut precisely to avoid snow.

They had little food, and soon there was none. They had to eat their dogs, their oxen, and their horses. They were living in pitiful shelters which were of little use against the bad weather. Rescue parties who attempted to reach them were also defeated by the snow. Starving people began to die, and therein lies our everlasting fascination with the Donner Party. The survivors began to eat the corpses of their friends. Eight of the fifteen people who had crossed what is now known as the Donner Pass died before rescuers finally reached the last seven. Some of the survivors lived long lives thereafter, and this book includes fine photographs of them. Of course no color photos exist, but this story is compelling enough to booktalk without them.

Fig. 1.5. *Snowbound: The Tragic Story of the Donner Party* **by David Lavender**

Terrible diseases are at least as horrifying as other disasters. James Cross Giblin's *When Plague Strikes: The Black Death, Smallpox, AIDS* describes three deadly pandemics. A pandemic is an epidemic, a fast-spreading disease that moves so quickly that much of the world is affected.

The first pandemic for which we have historic records is called The Plague of Athens, occurring in ancient Greece. But the one with which most of us are probably most familiar is called The Black Death, and it probably started in the Ukraine in the mid-1300s. The legend is that a group of Italian traders in the Black Sea area were blamed for the disease. They were Christians, while most in the area were Muslims. The Italians holed up in a fortress, but the natives got a horrible revenge. They catapulted dead bodies, riddled with the disease, into the fortress, and when the Italians went back to their own country, they carried the disease with them.

For a long time, people did not know that the sick people were not the main carriers of the disease. The true carriers were the black rats and the fleas that lived around and on them. Those rats and fleas spread the disease throughout Europe. The population of Venice was 130,000 when the plague broke out in December of 1347. Eighteen months later, almost half the people in the city were dead. In fact, it was estimated that almost one-third of the population in Europe died in this plague. Of course, someone had to be blamed, and as was usual in those times, the Jews were blamed for the plague and persecuted horribly.

The Black Death reappeared every now and then, even as recently as 1924 and 1925 in Los Angeles (the last outbreak in the United States), and as recently as 1994 in India. Modern medicine has found good ways to combat it, but it is not gone completely, as is smallpox, once the plague of the world.

Smallpox could kill you quickly, leave you blind, scar you for life, and cause many other tragic consequences. Smallpox killed more Native Americans in North and South America than any battles ever did. The native people had no defense or immune system against smallpox because they had never been exposed to it. They died horrible, painful deaths.

What saved the world from smallpox was an inoculation, or vaccination, that allowed patients to have a minor outbreak of the disease that would leave them immune to it in the future. Do you have a vaccination? Inoculations apparently started in Constantinople, what is now Istanbul, Turkey. In the 1700s, Europeans began to experiment with them. Read about what a horrible thing it was to be vaccinated when the procedure was new! How would you like to be bled for six weeks and then live in a stable for at least a week?

This book, which concludes with a section on our terrible modern epidemic, AIDS, will keep you riveted. The stories it tells will make anyone think about, and be grateful for, modern medicine.

The Black Death by Phyllis Corzine is a more detailed account of that plague with many illustrations. A booktalker might wish to use this in conjunction with the Giblin book for that reason.

BIBLIOGRAPHY

Andryszewski, Tricia. *The Dust Bowl: Disaster on the Plains.* The Millbrook Press, 1993. 64 p. ISBN 1-56294-272-7. Grades 4-7.

Armstrong, Jennifer. *Shipwreck at the Bottom of the World: The Extraordinary True Story of Shackleton and the Endurance.* Crown, 1998. 134 p. ISBN 0-517-80013-6 (trade); 0-517-80014 (lib. bdg.). Grades 4-up.

Ballard, Robert D. *Exploring the Titanic.* Edited by Patrick Crean. Illustrated by Ken Marschall. A Scholastic/Madison Press Book, 1988. 64 p. ISBN 0-590-41953-6; 0-590-41952-8 (pbk.). Grades 3-7.

Ballard, Robert D. with Rick Archbold. *Exploring the Bismarck.* A Scholastic/Madison Press Book, 1991. 64 p. ISBN 0-590-44268-6. Grades 3-7.

————. *The Lost Wreck of the Isis.* Archaeological and Historical Consultant Anna Marguerite McCann. A Scholastic/Madison Press Book, 1990. 64 p. ISBN 0-590-43852-2; 0-590-43853-0 (pbk.). Grades 3-7.

Baquedano, Elizabeth. *Aztec, Inca & Maya.* Photographs by Michel Zabé. Alfred A. Knopf, 1993. 63 p. ISBN 0-679-83883-X; 0-679-93883-4 (lib. bdg.). Grades 4-7.

Beattie, Owen, and John Geiger with Shelley Tanaka. *Buried in Ice.* A Scholastic/Madison Press Book, 1992. 64 p. ISBN 0-590-43848-4; 0-590-43849-2 (pbk.). Grades 3-7.

Bisel, Sara C. with Jane Bisel and Shelley Tanaka. *The Secrets of Vesuvius.* Historical Consultant Paul Denis. A Scholastic/Madison Press Book, 1991. 64 p. ISBN 0-590-43851-4 (pbk.). Grades 3-7.

Brewster, Hugh. *Inside the Titanic.* Illustrated by Ken Marschall. A Madison Press Book. Little, Brown, 1997. 32 p. ISBN 0-316-55716-1. Grades 4-6.

Cone, Patrick. *Wildfire.* Carolrhoda Books, 1997. 48 p. ISBN 0-87614-936-0 (lib. bdg.); 1-57505-027-7 (pbk.). Grades 4-6.

Connolly, Peter. *Pompeii.* Oxford University Press, 1979, 1990. 77 p. ISBN 0-19-917159-9; 0-19-917158-0 (pbk.). Grades 6-up.

Corzine, Phyllis. *The Black Death.* Lucent Books, 1997. 112 p. ISBN 1-56006-299-1. Grades 5-8.

Donnelly, Judy. *The Titanic Lost . . . and Found.* Illustrated by Keith Kohler. Random House, 1987. 47 p. ISBN 0-394-88669-0; 0-394-98669-5 (lib. bdg.). Grades 2-4.

Gibbons, Gail. *Sunken Treasure.* Thomas Y. Crowell, 1988. 32 p. ISBN 0-690-04734-7; 0-690-04736-3 (lib. bdg.). Grades 1-3.

Giblin, James Cross. *When Plague Strikes: The Black Death, Smallpox, AIDS.* Woodcuts by David Frampton. HarperCollins, 1995. 212 p. ISBN 0-06-025854-3; 0-06-025864-0 (lib. bdg.). Grades 5-8.

Goor, Ron, and Nancy Goor. *Pompeii: Exploring a Roman Ghost Town*. Thomas Y. Crowell, 1986. 118 p. ISBN 0-690-04515-8; 0-690-04516-6 (lib. bdg.). Grades 4-6.

Haas, Jessie. *Fire! My Parents' Story*. Greenwillow Books, 1998. 71 p. ISBN 0-688-15203-1. Grades 3-6.

Hidden Treasures of the Sea. National Geographic Society, 1988. 104 p. ISBN 0-87044-658-4; 0-87044-658-4 (lib. bdg). Grades 4-7.

Lansing, Alfred. *Endurance: Shackleton's Incredible Voyage*. Carroll & Graf, 1986. ISBN 0-88184-178-1. Grades 6-up.

Lauber, Patricia. *Flood: Wrestling with the Mississippi*. National Geographic Society, 1996. 64 p. ISBN 0-7922-4141-X. Grades 4-6.

———. *Hurricanes: Earth's Mightiest Storms*. Scholastic, 1996. 64 p. ISBN 0-590-47406-5. Grades 3-6.

———. *Summer of Fire: Yellowstone 1988*. Orchard Books, 1991. 64 p. ISBN 0-531-05943-X; 0-531-08543-0 (lib. bdg.). Grades 4-7.

Lavender, David. *Snowbound: The Tragic Story of the Donner Party*. Holiday House, 1996. 87 p. ISBN 0-8234-1231-8. Grades 5-7.

Masoff, Joy. *Fire!* Principal photography by Jack Reznicki and Barry D. Smith. Scholastic, 1998. 48 p. ISBN 0-590-97872-1. Grades 4-7.

McCurdy, Michael. *Trapped by the Ice! Shackleton's Amazing Antarctic Adventure*. Walker, 1997. 41p. ISBN 0-8027-8438-0; 0-8027-8439-9 (lib. bdg.). Grades 3-4.

Murphy, Jim. *The Great Fire*. Scholastic, 1995. 144 p. ISBN 0-590-47267-4. Grades 5-up.

O'Byrne-Pelham, Fran, and Bernadette Balcer. *The Search for the Atocha Treasure*. Dillon Press, 1989. 108 p. ISBN 0-87518-399-9. Grades 4-6.

Platt, Richard. *Disaster!* Illustrated by Richard Bonson. DK, 1997. 32 p. ISBN 0-7894-2034-1. Grades 4-8.

———. *Shipwreck*. Photographs by Alex Wilson and Tina Chambers. Alfred A. Knopf, 1997. ISBN 0-679-88562-5; 0-679-98562-X (lib. bdg.). Grades 4-6.

Spedden, Daisy Corning Stone. *Polar the Titanic Bear*. Illustrated by Laurie McGaw. A Madison Press Book produced for Little, Brown, 1994. 64 p. ISBN 0-316-80625-0. Grades 1-4.

Stanley, Jerry. *Children of the Dust Bowl: The True Story of the School at Weedpatch Camp*. Crown, 1992. 86 p. ISBN 0-517-58781-5; 0-517-58782-3 (lib. bdg.); 0-517-88094-6 (pbk.). Grades 4-7.

Stein, R. Conrad. *The USS Arizona*. Childrens Press, 1992. 32 p. ISBN 0-516-06656-0. Grades 4-6.

Sullivan, George. *Treasure Hunt: The Sixteen-Year Search for the Lost Treasure Ship Atocha*. Henry Holt, 1987. 150 p. ISBN 0-8050-0569-2. Grades 5-7.

Tanaka, Shelley. *The Buried City of Pompeii: What It Was Like When Vesuvius Exploded*. Illustrated by Greg Ruhl. Diagrams and maps by Jack McMaster. Historical Consultant Elizabeth Lyding Will. Photographs by Peter Christopher. A Hyperion/Madison Press Book, 1997. 48 p. ISBN 0-7868- 0285-5. Grades 4-6.

————. *The Disaster of the Hindenburg*. Historical Consultants Dennis Kromm, John Provan, and Dr. Douglas H. Robinson. A Scholastic/Madison Press Book, 1993. 64 p. ISBN 0-590-45750-0. Grades 4-7.

————. *On Board the Titanic*: *What It Was Like When the Great Liner Sank*. Illustrated by Ken Marschall. A Hyperion/Madison Press Book, 1996. 48 p. ISBN 0-7868-0283-9. Grades 4-6.

Van Rose, Susanna. *Volcano & Earthquake*. Alfred A. Knopf, 1992. 64 p. ISBN 0-679-81685-2. Grades 4-up.

Vogel, Carole Garbuny. *Shock Waves Through Los Angeles: The Northridge Earthquake*. Little, Brown, 1997. 32 p. ISBN 0-316-90240-3. Grades 4-6.

CHAPTER ——————————— 2

Fun Stuff—
Jokes, Gross Books, and Books That Will Make You Laugh

Those of us who love to read know that books can be fun. Children who grow up on authors like Dr. Seuss and Shel Silverstein know this, too. But as kids get older, they sometimes lose their love of books. Reading becomes a chore—an activity done only when absolutely necessary for a school assignment. Kids who aren't good readers get frustrated trying to read novels, and they don't even try to read nonfiction books. This chapter, dedicated strictly to fun stuff, is where you will find books to interest your most reluctant readers. Announce to your listeners that you are there to show them a good time. Tell a joke, read a funny poem, gross them out—whatever it takes to get them to pick up a book and start reading for fun.

PUZZLES, JOKES, AND FUN FACTS

A good way to grab your audience's attention is with a brainteaser or a puzzle. Middle school students will enjoy *Perplexing Lateral Thinking Puzzles* by Paul Sloane and Des MacHale. These puzzles are designed for use in a small group in which one person knows the answer and others try to figure it out by asking yes/no questions. The point is to get kids thinking creatively to come up with the answers. Here's one of the shorter puzzles: When Gertrude entered the plane she caused her own death and the deaths of 200 people. Yet she was never blamed or criticized for her actions. What happened? Give the kids one or two puzzles to work on, then let them check out the book and try to stump their friends. (The answer is that Gertrude, a goose, had been sucked into a jet engine.) If kids are hooked, let them know that Sloane and MacHale have written quite a few other books of lateral thinking puzzles, all available from Sterling Publishing Company, Inc.

David A. Adler's *Easy Math Puzzles* (figure 2.1) will be pretty easy for older kids but challenging and fun for children in the primary grades. An excellent puzzle to use is this: "This dog is on a leash. The leash is 4 feet long, but the dog can eat from a bowl 6 feet away. How is this possible?" Answer: No one is holding the leash. Gotcha!

Fig. 2.1. *Easy Math Puzzles* by David A. Adler

Kids also enjoy riddles, and Adler provides some good ones in *A Teacher on Roller Skates and Other School Riddles*. Holding up this book and reading or telling a few of the really stupid riddles about school will delight kids and make them want to read the book. Remember: A little stand-up comedy is happily welcomed in any booktalk. If you're lucky, even the teachers will be laughing.

We all love to torture ourselves with tongue twisters, so a good book chock-full of them can add a dash of spice to your booktalk. Try some from *Fast Freddie Frog and Other Tongue-Twister Rhymes* by Ennis Rees (figure 2.2) for an audience participation activity. Read aloud "Fast Freddie Frog," "Hairy Harry Hartley," and "My Wooden Whistle Wouldn't Whistle"—if you can!

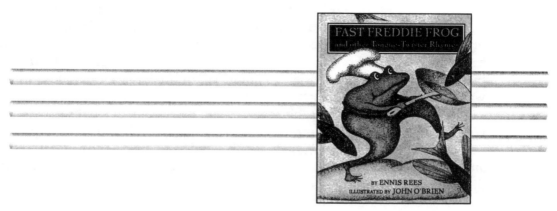

Fig. 2.2. *Fast Freddie Frog and Other Tongue-Twister Rhymes* by Ennis Rees

Go Hang a Salami! I'm a Lasagna Hog! and Other Palindromes by Jon Agee is guaranteed to get some interest. It's a book of crazy palindromes with clever cartoons to go along with them. This book can be presented as a puzzle. Show a few of your favorites (such as "Wonton? Not now" or "Did mom pop? Mom did") and ask kids to guess what the phrases have in common. When they finally figure out that they read the same backwards and forwards, they can't wait to look at the title of the book to see if the same holds true for it. Mention this book to language arts teachers who like to use creative language resources in their classrooms. Adults as well as middle school students will enjoy the humorous cartoons.

Students of all ages enjoy the tricks that their eyes play on them. *101 Amazing Optical Illusions: Fantastic Visual Tricks* by Terry Jennings contains many common illusions, but that does not make them any less enjoyable. Show the "Ghosts Before Your Eyes" double-page spread on pages 32 and 33. The "Into Perspective" section on pages 44 and 45 is also fun to use with a group. Optical illusions are great for reluctant readers and kids who don't read well.

Another popular book of illusions is *You Won't Believe Your Eyes!* by Catherine O'Neill. This is a big book, and simply showing pictures from it will create an immediate demand for this excellent, colorful title on optical illusions.

Show your audience the double-page spread on pages 4 and 5 and ask what is the matter. Almost everyone immediately decides that this is the scene of an earthquake. When you tell them no, that is not the case, sooner or later someone will figure out what is going on here. The explanation: The girl riding on a bicycle is pictured on a street so steep that it has steps instead of a sidewalk. People in front will then be able to see the steps. The photo, taken in San Francisco, has been cropped to make it look as though the houses, rather than the picture, are crooked. Demonstrate to the group how you could take a picture that would make everyone look as though they were about to fall down.

The double-page spread on pages 2 and 3 is also excellent. It shows what looks like a giant little girl staring into a house. It does not take long to realize it is an ordinary-sized girl looking into a doll house. Page 32 features a fine illusion—a photograph of a vase that has had its sides cut out to show the profiles of Queen Elizabeth II and Prince Philip. It may take more than a few seconds for some in the group to see this.

Everyday Mysteries by Jerome Wexler presents some photographic illusions that young children will enjoy. The photos show parts, surfaces, edges, and cross-sections of everyday objects such as a pineapple, a zipper, and a waffle. Readers guess what each item is, then check their answers at the end of each section. The full-page color pictures are ideal for showing to a small group. Just a few examples will make kids want to check out this colorful book.

Kids love fun facts, making one of the most popular books in any library *The Guinness Book of World Records*. It is published annually now in a large format with numerous photographs. This book hardly needs any introduction at all. Just open it to any page and read off some interesting world records. Boys especially seem to be drawn to this book year after year.

Kids are naturally attracted to *The Guinness Book of World Records*, and with a little encouragement, they will also be asking for *The World Almanac for Kids*, published annually. In addition to the usual facts about presidents and countries of the world, this book overflows with fascinating tidbits on subjects like the Internet, TV shows, children's books, holidays, sports and games, and hurricanes. Elementary school students love animals, so give them a quiz from the animals section: What is the world's largest animal? (blue whale) What is the largest land animal? (African bush elephant) What is the largest reptile? (saltwater crocodile) What is the largest snake? (anaconda) What is the fastest animal? (swift, a bird) What is the fastest land animal? (cheetah) What is the fastest insect? (dragonfly). They will guess some of these answers right, while others will stump them.

They will also be fascinated by some "Facts and Figures About the Body." For example, a newborn baby has 350 bones, but an adult's body has 206 bones. An adult's large intestine is about 5 feet long, and the small intestine is about 25 feet long. About 70 percent of the average-sized adult body is made up of water. It takes around 17 muscles to smile and around 43 to frown. You can just flip through the book and see what interesting facts you uncover. Or have a student pick a page number at random, and you can read the audience an interesting fact from that page. Of interest to kids studying weather will be the section detailing how hurricanes are named and giving a list of the year's upcoming hurricane names. Another interesting section tells how the U.S. states got their names. This book should appeal to students with a wide range of interests and abilities. The better you know your audience, the easier it will be to tailor your booktalk to their interests.

Kids will also love the quirky facts found in *Encyclopedia Brown's 3rd Record Book of Weird & Wonderful Facts* by Donald J. Sobol, especially the "Gender Gems" in chapter 1. Ask the audience to look at their fingernails. Observe how they do it, and then tell them that, according to the book, women usually extend their fingers palm down and men usually examine their nails by curling their fingers palm up. Then ask them to compare the lengths of their ring and index fingers. The ring finger is longer than the index finger on most men and shorter on most women. Ask them how they extinguish a match. According to Encyclopedia Brown, the average woman blows out a match, while the average man shakes it out. Share some of the other strange facts: Nearly 85 percent of the people killed by lightning are male; men have been noted to fall out of hospital beds twice as often as women; male lefties outnumber female lefties two to one. Kids will no doubt argue these findings, but they will be fascinated by the book. This is a good choice for reluctant middle school readers as the facts are funny and interesting, and the text is divided into short, readable paragraphs.

Amazing True Stories by Don L. Wulffson is another book with short, interesting tidbits that will grab kids' attention. Tell them about the $5,216 library fine (page 60) or the tidal wave of molasses that hit Boston (page 47). The chapter titled "The Unknown and Mysterious" has some particularly good stories to read aloud. "Message from the Grave" (pages 92-93) tells of a four-year-old boy who suddenly began to write in shorthand. When his writing was translated, it was a message from his dead father telling him and his mother to go to a certain bank in New York. There they found money and a life insurance policy that no one else had known about. "The Electric Lady" (pages 94-97) tells about an office building where all the lights unscrewed themselves and shattered, the photocopier did crazy things, and the phones rang for no reason. No one could find the cause until a young woman named Ann-Marie was questioned. When she began to answer police questions, the lights in the room started going off and on, and drawers opened by themselves. Somehow this woman gave off an electric charge that caused all these strange things to happen. Read a few of these stories, and your listeners will be intrigued enough to want to check out this book.

Another fun book of facts is *The Book of Lists for Kids* by Sandy and Harry Choron. This book contains 410 pages of lists on a wide assortment of topics. Some provide serious help for kids such as "9 Tips for Kids Who Live in Stepfamilies," "19 Things Kids Feel Peer Pressure About," or "12 Ways to Let Someone Know You Want to Be Their Friend." Many of the lists are just for fun. This book is the place to find out how to identify the flavors of fancy chocolates, the chronology of video game history, celebrities who have appeared on *The Simpsons*, and the first 100 Disney characters. With chapters on food, toys, books, TV, movies, and music, there is something in this book for everyone.

POETRY

Many adults think poetry is something that you study in English class and never read again. They can't imagine finding humor and delight in something so hard to understand. Fortunately, children don't have those preconceived notions—at least not if they've been exposed to the writing of poets like Shel Silverstein and Jack Prelutsky. Some of the funniest people around are writing poetry for children, and their books are included here. The poetry in this section is meant to be fun. Enjoy yourself as you read it and tell about it, and students will enjoy it along with you.

And the Green Grass Grew All Around: Folk Poetry from Everyone by Alvin Schwartz is one of the funniest books you will ever read. Browse through the book to find the poems or songs that delight you the most, and read or sing samples. Two that work wonderfully well are "Mary Had a Stick of Gum" on page 28 and "Ravioli" on page 16.

"Mary Had a Stick of Gum" is sung to the tune of "John Brown's Body." Memorize it and do it with appropriate actions. The last line will bring down the house, even if the house is all adults.

> Mary had a stick of gum.
> She chewed it long and slow.
> And everywhere that Mary went
> That gum was sure to go.
> It followed her to school one day
> Which was against the rule.
> And the teacher took the gum away
> And chewed it after school.

"Ravioli" can be sung to the tune of "Alouette."

> Ravioli, ravioli—
> Ravioli, that's the stuff for me.
> Do you have it on your sleeve?
> Yes, I have it on my sleeve.
> On your sleeve?
> On my sleeve.
> Ravioli, ravioli—
> Ravioli, that's the stuff for me.

Popcorn by James Stevenson contains some fun poems by one of our best-known authors. His poems are great to share—read just a couple to get kids interested in the book. Especially good are "The Bakery," "Crab Shell," and "At Last."

How does it really *feel* to play basketball? *Hoops* by Robert Burleigh (figure 2.3) describes it almost perfectly, and the pictures that go with it explain it even more. Show children almost any of the two-page spreads, but read the excerpt that starts with the line "Feel your throat on fire. . . ." Surely Michael Jordan must have felt like this when he played basketball.

Fig. 2.3. *Hoops* by Robert Burleigh

As with most humorous poetry books, the best booktalk is to hold up the book and read a poem or two or three. Try this with *Dinosaur Dinner (With a Slice of Alligator Pie): Favorite Poems by Dennis Lee*. Kids will laugh and love it. Read "The Dinosaur Dinner" on the first page, or "Big Bad Billy."

Nadine Bernard Westcott is the selector and illustrator of a collection of poems called *Never Take a Pig to Lunch and Other Poems About the Fun of Eating* (figure 2.4). Reading some of the poems from this funny book adds a lot to a booktalk, especially poems such as "It's Hot" (page 26) or "School Lunch" (page 12) or "Greedy Ned" (page 46). You'll be laughing as hard as the kids!

A greedy young fellow named Ned
Ate up before going to bed—
Six lobsters, one ham
Ten pickles with jam.
And when he woke up he was dead.
                                    —Anonymous.

Fig. 2.4. *Never Take a Pig to Lunch and Other Poems About the Fun of Eating* by Nadine Bernard Westcott

Oh, Grow Up! Poems to Help You Survive Parents, Chores, School and Other Afflictions by Florence Parry Heide and Roxanne Heide Pierce (figure 2.5) is one of those books that speaks to kids about their everyday lives. Read a couple of these funny poems for an excellent, easy booktalk. "Taking Out the Garbage" and "The Interrogation" are good ones to try.

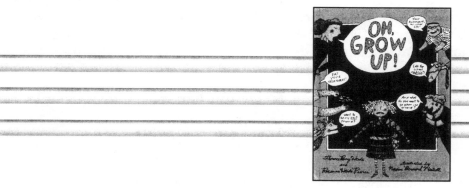

Fig. 2.5. *Oh, Grow Up! Poems to Help You Survive Parents, Chores, School and Other Afflictions* by Florence Parry Heide and Roxanne Heide Pierce

Dorothy M. Kennedy has selected a fun bunch of school poems in *I Thought I'd Take My Rat to School: Poems for September to June*. In this attractive collection, poets such as Russell Hoban, Nikki Giovanni, Gary Soto, and David McCord capture the good and bad sides of school. There are poems about math, English, and art class, as well as day-to-day topics like riding the bus, eating lunch, and yawning in class. Kids will especially like the poems about homework on pages 53-55. Their rhythm and humor can best be appreciated by reading them aloud. Elementary teachers wanting to make poetry a part of the school day will be glad to find this collection. Read a few poems aloud to teachers and recommend that they keep it on hand in the classroom. In addition to the high-quality poems, kids will love Abby Carter's energetic and funny drawings.

More school humor can be found in Carol Diggory Shields's *Lunch Money and Other Poems About School*. These funny poems make fun booktalks. Try "And the Answer Is…?" on page 11 or "Whew!" on page 30. If you are doing a booktalk for parents or teachers, the very last poem in this book, "Book Report," will crack them all up.

Jeff Moss, one of the original creators of *Sesame Street*, has written a wonderful collection of dinosaur verse called *Bone Poems*. Kids will be reminded of Shel Silverstein and Jack Prelutzky when they read Moss's whimsical poems. Some are short and to the point, like "Bones" (without them you'd be just a "big squooshy blob").

Others are longer and tell about the characteristics of various dinosaurs such as "Anatotitan" ("If ever he broke, cracked, or injured his teeth, Wonder of wonders, new teeth were beneath!"), "Apatosaurus" ("Each day he awoke in his dinosaur bed with a very big problem inside his small head: How could he keep his great body well fed?"), and "Ankylosaurus" ("All covered with armor the "Ankylosaurus" moved with a clunk and a Clankylosaurus."). Some of Moss's funniest poems are the really short ones with long titles like "What You Should Answer If Some Scientist Comes Up to You and Says, 'What Do All Proboscideans Have in Common?' " (The answer: noses like hoses.)

Kids will love these poems and will learn a great deal about dinosaurs at the same time. Show this book to teachers—it makes an excellent addition to a unit on dinosaurs.

Another book of dinosaur poems, *Tyrannosaurus Was a Beast: Dinosaur Poems*, comes from Jack Prelutsky. The great thing about this collection is that every poem in the book can be sung to an old song. If you are not afraid to sing in front of your audience, this can be a huge crowd pleaser. Ask the kids to guess which tune the poem is being sung to. They will want one more, just one more—repeatedly. Teachers swear that kids will memorize these poems just to be able to sing them. These songs work quite well for the poems:

"Tyrannosaurus"	"Mary Had a Little Lamb"
"Brachiosaurus"	"On Top of Old Smokey"
"Leptoterygius"	"The Streets of Laredo"
"Stegosaurus"	"When Johnny Comes Marching Home"
"Deinonychus"	"Grandfather's Clock"
"Ankylosaurus"	"99 Bottles of Beer on the Wall"
"Diplodocus"	"Pop Goes the Weasel"
"Coelophysis"	"Yankee Doodle"
"Triceratops"	"Solomon Levi"
"Corythosaurus"	"Skip to My Lou"
"Allosaurus"	"Row, Row, Row Your Boat"
"Iguanadon"	"O Christmas Tree"
"Quetzacoatlus"	"The Daring Young Man on the Flying Trapeze"
"Seismosaurus"	"Twinkle, Twinkle Little Star"

As in *Tyrannosaurus Was a Beast*, the poems in *The Dragons Are Singing Tonight* by Jack Prelutsky can be put to music. See if any children can figure them out, or encourage them to do so. Some that work are:

"I'm an Amiable Dragon"   "The Yellow Rose of Texas"
"Nasty Little Dragonsong"   "My Darling Clementine"
"My Dragon Wasn't Feeling Good" "Battle Hymn of the Republic"
"A Dragon Is in My Computer"   "My Bonnie Lies Over the Ocean"
"I Am Boom!"   "I Am the Very Model of a Modern
                                  Major General"

Read *For Laughing Out Loud! Poems to Tickle Your Funnybone*, and you will not have to wonder why Jack Prelutsky is one of the most popular poets and collectors of funny poetry. His choices and his own work never fail to delight an audience. Read, on page 17, "I Love to Do My Homework."

I love to do my homework,
It makes me feel so good.
I love to do exactly
As my teacher says I should.

I love to do my homework,
I never miss a day.
I even love the men in white
Who are taking me away.
                    —Anonymous

For another real groaner, try "Mary Had a Little Lamb" on page 27.

Mary had a little lamb,
You've heard this tale before;
But did you know
She passed her plate
And had a little more?
                    —Anonymous

Richard Michelson has developed a host of fun and useful animals in his collection *Animals That Ought to Be: Poems About Imaginary Pets*. These imaginative poems with eye-catching illustrations are great fun to share, and these pets would be fantastic to have. For instance, whose life wouldn't be simpler with The Roombroom? A few other great pets to have around the house are the Channel Changer, the Nightmare Scarer, the Talkback Bat, and the Leftover Eater. By the time you're ready to leave the room, the children will be making up their own "animals that ought to be." This could lead quite naturally into a creative writing project for the classroom or library.

What to Do When a Bug Climbs in Your Mouth and Other Poems to Drive You Buggy by Rick Walton is a collection of poems that will delight readers and lead right into the next section on "Gross Stuff." The title poem of this fun collection makes for a gross booktalk—one that will delight your audience and leave them wanting more.

GROSS STUFF

Body Noises by Susan Kovacs Buxbaum and Rita Golden Gelman is a great little surprise for any booktalk. Hold the book behind your back, and tell your audience that you have in your hands a book about something that everyone wonders about, but no one talks about. As they look at you, bewildered, pull it out and show them the title. Everyone will laugh and, at the first opportunity, run to pick up the book and look through it.

You will find some gross recipes in *Creepy Cuisine* by Lucy Monroe. Just reading some of the recipe titles to your audience will guarantee circulation of this funny book. What would you like to make? Gory Gorilla Tonsils? Strained Eye Balls? Ear Wax Weiners on Cotton Swabs? Pus Pockets? Wild Lice? Bloody Bug Juice? The recipes are for normal foods, but presented with excellent, and revolting, serving suggestions. Show audiences some of the fun sketches as well.

Another book of gross recipes was inspired by the books of Roald Dahl, a favorite among kids. *Roald Dahl's Revolting Recipes* is a real cookbook that tells you how to make such delicacies as stink bugs' eggs, fresh mudburgers, and candy-coated pencils for sucking in class. Each recipe is based on foods Dahl wrote about in his popular books for kids. Quentin Blake's funny drawings, put together with photographs of the food, make this book inviting and appealing. Just read from the recipe list on page 61, and kids will be anxious to see for themselves what these concoctions look like.

Yuck! A Big Book of Little Horrors by Robert Snedden (figure 2.6) has a catchy title and some eye-catching photographs as well. Just holding up the hugely magnified pictures from the book and asking the audience what they depict is a surefire way to add sparkle and laughter to any booktalk. Favorites include the dust mite on the second two-page spread, the toothbrush on the third, bread dough on the fourth, and the potato on the fifth. Give clues if you feel like it. For example, this is a food that we all eat regularly and almost everyone likes.

Then flip to the second-to-the-last two-page spread and ask the audience to guess what these photos show. The clue: All of these things are on human bodies, including yours. The amazing microscopic photos show hairs growing from a human scalp (this shows all too clearly where dandruff starts), the tongue, perspiration, and split ends. Audiences of all ages love it.

Fig. 2.6. *Yuck! A Big Book of Little Horrors* **by Robert Snedden**

Yikes! Your Body, Up Close! by Mike Janulewicz has exactly the same format as its equally gross predecessor, *Yuck!* All of the photographs are of objects enlarged many times, and each photograph is of a part of the human body or of parasites that live on the human body. Showing a group a selection of the photographs and asking them to guess what they are seeing is great fun.

Be sure to ask if anyone knows what most dust is made of. The answer may freak you out—mostly human skin! Let kids know that dead skin cells are dropping off their heads right now, even as you speak.

A similar title, but with more details and information, is *Discover Hidden Worlds: The Home* by Heather Amery and Jane Songi. This book shows close-ups of everyday household objects, like Velcro, compact discs, and bread mold. The magnified picture of an ant holding a microchip is a good one to show (pages 20-21), as is the big red grain weevil on page 25.

A Medieval Castle by Fiona Macdonald tells what it was like to live in a castle in the Middle Ages. You probably would not expect to find this book in a chapter on gross stuff, but the double-page spread on pages 8 and 9 makes for one of the most effective (and gross) booktalks around.

Children love bathroom habits. Show the castle part of the spread, then point out the man on the right-hand side using the lavatory. Note the particulars of the drawing. The man is going to the bathroom into a long chute which descends into a moat under construction.

Have any of you ever been to a castle? If you have, you may know that a moat was a common feature in castles. Human waste went into the moat. So now you know why no one ever wanted to go swimming in the moat! How do you suppose it looked? How do you suppose it *smelled*? What do you think it smelled like inside the castle?

Inevitably, someone will ask about toilet paper. Tell them there was no toilet paper. People in the Middle Ages in Europe didn't even have paper! Yes, kids, Robin Hood did not have toilet paper! This book will help you imagine what it was like to live in those times.

Another book about history that can make for an effective and gross booktalk is *Mummies* by Joyce Milton. This simple-to-read account of how mummies were made and, later, discovered and disinterred is very appealing. Read this definition on page 10: "A mummy is a body that has been dried out like a raisin. It will not rot away." Good pictures to show are the spreads on pages 18 and 19 of the mummy being wrapped, and the one on pages 40 and 41 of a mummy being unwrapped by Victorian travelers, who were remarkably uninterested in historical preservation.

A fun look at mummies is found in *How to Make a Mummy Talk* by James M. Deem. Start your booktalk by reading the "Mummy Mythology Test" on page 11. It is a real eye-opener. Did you know that mummies have been found on every inhabited continent, including North America? When we hear the word *mummy*, a lot of us think of only Egyptian mummies. This book will open up your mind! It tells us about accidental mummies, as well as mummies that were deliberately made.

The Scythians, a group of tribes who lived in Southern Russia more than 2,000 years ago, mummified their dead kings. Herodotus, a Greek writer, described what every man in the tribe had to do when he saw the body. "[He had to] sever a piece of his ear, cut his hair short, make a cut all the way around his arm, make a hole in his fore-head and nose, and finally, as if this weren't enough, drive an arrow completely through his left hand." And that was just the first year! Wait until you read what happened the second year (page 64), and be thankful that you are not a Scythian!

You will be astounded at what you learn when you read this book. For instance, did you know that a mummy of a 36,000-year-old bison was discovered in Alaska in 1979? Scientists were able to discover a great deal about it. If you want to be an expert on a topic that fascinates nearly everyone, read this book.

Mummy by James Putnam, an attractive title from Dorling Kindersley, is a sure-fire hit on a popular topic. Show the audience the photo of the monk mummy on page 62. It is astoundingly lifelike and does not fit with most people's concept of what mummies look like. This is an Italian monk mummy, well over 100 years old. It is in a church in a city in Palermo, where it became fashionable to embalm all sorts of people as mummies. The mummy was placed in a hinged coffin, also pictured on page 61, so that people could come visit with the dead person and, perhaps, hold his hands while talking with or praying for him. Now all of these mummies are seen by many tourists, and the monks who still work in the church where they are entombed vacuum them all at least once a year.

That is just one kind of mummy. Show audiences the pictures of the 500-year-old Inuit (Eskimo) mummy on page 7, the cat mummies on pages 46 and 47, and the mummy bundle on page 53. Then flip through the book to show some of the great photos of the mummies with which we are most familiar, the Egyptian mummies.

For an appealing booktalk, group *Mummy* with the following books described in chapter 5: *Cat Mummies; Iceman; Discovering the Iceman: What Was It Like to Find a 5,300-Year-Old Mummy?; Frozen Man*; and *Discovering the Inca Ice Maiden: My Adventures on Ampato*. You could also use *Mummy* to perk up an audience by using it with a group of titles on disparate subjects. If you want to include some humor in your booktalk, try using *Mummy Riddles* by Katy Hall and Lisa Eisenberg.

JUST PLAIN FUN

Some children, usually boys, are interested in almost nothing you have to show them until you pull out a high-interest book from Capstone Press. The following titles from this publisher are particularly popular with students in grades three through seven: *Motorcycles* and *Super Sports Cars* by Jackson Jay, *BMX Bicycles* by Barbara Knox, *Monster Trucks* (figure 2.7) and *Pickup Trucks* by James Koons, *Motocross Cycles* and *Racing Cars* by Jeff Savage, and *Big Rigs* by Jay Schleifer. Flip through them, and show them some of the colorful pictures. The topics are guaranteed to snare the interest of even the most reluctant readers.

Fig. 2.7. *Monster Trucks* **by James Koons**

Face painting is so popular that any book on the topic is a cinch to booktalk. The directions in *The Most Excellent Book of Face Painting* by Margaret Lincoln are clear and precise. Part of the goal of a booktalk is simply to let children know that the library has materials such as this. Showing the wonderfully spooky face on page 6 or the spotted leopard on page 16 or the creature from space on page 21 will get your audience thinking. The hand designs on page 31 are a real bonus. This book is recommended for children of all ages.

Making Shaped Books by Gillian Chapman and Pam Robson inspires a fun activity for kids. A shaped book is a book in the shape of something else (e.g., a hat, a boot, a train). Show both the front cover and pages 14, 16, and 17. The book is large, so the book alone will work well in front of a small group. Everyone will want to make their own shaped books!

There are games that everyone would like to know how to play, and many of them are described in *Marbles: 101 Ways to Play* by Joanna Cole and Stephanie Calmenson and *Dominoes Around the World* by Mary D. Lankford (figure 2.8). A lot of kids already know how to play marbles and dominoes, but these titles are full of fun information and ideas for the many, many games you can play with them.

Both dominoes and marbles have been played for thousands of years. Dominoes were even discovered in King Tut's tomb! Dominoes also resemble the tiles used in a popular Chinese game called Mah-jongg.

Fig. 2.8. *Dominoes Around the World* **by Mary D. Lankford. © 1997 Morrow Junior Books.**

As for marbles, we know that the ancient Romans played with them; we can see some of the ones they used in museums. Marbles got their name because they were once made from the stone called marble, but it was very expensive. In 1846, a German glassmaker finally figured out how to make marbles cheaply and effectively. He heated strips of glass, clipped globs the right size off with a special pair of scissors, and made marbles that worked very well and that people could afford to buy.

One decision you must make before you play marbles is whether to play friendlies or keepsies. If you play friendlies, no matter if you win or lose, you get to keep your marbles. If you play keepsies, the winner keeps all of the marbles. It is always a good idea to play friendlies when you are first learning the game!

Marbles: 101 Ways to Play not only tells you how to play a lot of games but teaches you how to shoot a marble and how to start your own marble collection.

Bryan Iguchi's *The Young Snowboarder* features DK Publishing's appealing photographs of kids performing an increasingly popular sport. What do you suppose "riding goofy" means? It means you prefer to lead with your right foot. Pictures of equipment, safety precautions, positions, tricks on the ground and in the air, and addresses to which you can write for more information add up to a winning title. Just showing your audience any of the two-page spreads will move the book right out of your library.

Everyone loves to come home and find something in the mail for him or her. Kids often have the frustration of leaving the mailbox empty-handed, but they can change that if they seek out some of the offers in *Free Stuff for Kids*. Here they will find out how to send for free items such as key chains, bookmarks, posters, friendship bracelets, bumper stickers from sports teams, and more. To really impress your audience, send away for a few neat freebies and show them off during your booktalk. Kids will have fun while they learn to write letters, follow directions, and make creative use of their free time. *Free Stuff for Kids* is published annually by Meadowbrook Press. Be sure to have the latest edition on hand, because offers are honored only during the year of publication.

Cross Your Fingers, Spit in Your Hat: Superstitions and Other Beliefs is a compilation of superstitions collected by folklorist Alvin Schwartz. This enormously fun book from 1974 still makes good booktalk material today. Start out by asking your listeners if they know what superstitions are. Then ask if they are superstitious about anything. Inform them of any superstitions of your own. Then read the selection of school superstitions on pages 58-60, emphasizing to the group that the book contains many other superstitions as well.

You can also use this book as an opportunity to teach a fun almanac lesson. Tell kids that there are superstitions about days on which to be born. Most people won't know what day of the week they were born on, but they can find out by using the perpetual calendar found in *The World Almanac and Book of Facts*. Help them find out the day of the week on which they were born. Then let them know which days are lucky (see page 73). At the same time you can also tell them about lucky days for haircuts and cutting their fingernails.

Schwartz has another fun book of folklore called *Telling Fortunes: Love, Magic, Dream Signs, and Other Ways to Learn the Future*. Kids are always fascinated with predicting the future, and this book tells all kinds of ways to find out what's in store. Schwartz tells about various omens (shoelace knots mean trouble ahead, dropping a knife means a quarrel is on the way) and ways to predict your future love life. He even gives detailed instructions for making a cootie catcher and a list of dream signs and their meanings. Remind kids that, while all these methods have been used throughout history, none of them has been proven to work. Recommend this book for slumber parties, camp outs, and any time a group of kids needs something to keep them busy.

We take cameras for granted, but they weren't always around. Find out all about how they came to be in *Snapshot: America Discovers the Camera* by Kenneth P. Czech (figure 2.9).

Imagine having to sit perfectly still for five minutes while someone took your picture. That's what it used to be like back when cameras were first invented. Sitting still like that is so hard to do that many photographers used head clamps to keep people's heads from moving! (See the photo on page 7.) And no wonder no one smiled. Have your group start smiling and see how they look after 10 seconds. *Snapshot* is a lot of fun and loaded with interesting information about all the differences that photographs have made in our lives.

Fig. 2.9. *Snapshot: America Discovers the Camera* by Kenneth P. Czech

Bubblemania: A Chewy History of Bubble Gum by Lee Wardlaw will prove to kids that history can be fun. In spite of its title, this book is really a history of all gum, not just bubblegum. And it is great fun to read or browse through and share with kids.

Many human beings love to chew gum. In fact, humans are the only beings on Earth who chew it. According to dental scientist Carl Kleber, you can get monkeys to chew gum for a couple of minutes, but then they just take it out and stick it in their hair. Even in the Stone Age people chewed resin, a gummy substance found in certain pine trees. Today Americans spend about $500 million a year on the stuff, and theories are that it feels good to chew and that it relieves stress and tension.

This book tells us how gum got to be so popular and the story of the men who had the idea they could make money selling it. Did you know that General Santa Anna, the man who led the defeat at the Alamo, is involved in the history of chewing gum? But probably the most famous chewing gum salesman of all time is William Wrigley. We still buy his gum in vast quantities today, and he got so rich he bought his own baseball team and built Wrigley Field for them. He also built his own skyscraper, one of the most famous and most beautiful in Chicago. Wrigley was a great innovator. He was one of the first businessmen to heavily use advertising to increase sales, and did it ever work!

The first man to really invent a workable bubble gum was William Diemer. He worked for the Fleer Corporation, and his bubble gum (Double Bubble) is still one of the most popular brands. Bubble gum became so popular that soldiers took it with them when they were in World War II. Not only did they introduce it to kids all over the world, they used it to repair things and fix holes in rafts! Gum was included in soldiers' rations. In 1965, two astronauts smuggled the first gum into space. (Show their picture on page 73. They don't *look* like smugglers.)

Chapters describe the making of bubble gum balls; gum ball machines; bubble gum cards and comics; a museum called Bubble Gum Alley, which is covered with wads of chewed gum; and a recipe for making your own chewing gum. One chapter even describes an annual bubble-blowing contest. Be sure to read the tips from the pros on page 128. These include:

- Flatten the gum on the roof of your mouth, or between your tongue and your teeth. Part your teeth a bit, then breathe out s-l-o-w-l-y until a bubble forms.
- Chew at least five sticks or five chunks of bubble gum, combined with a teaspoon of peanut butter.
- Chew the gum for a minimum of five minutes to dissolve most of the sugar.
- Experiment with different brands. Extra-soft bubble gum tends to work best for some bubblers; others prefer a stiffer chew.

Circus: An Album by Linda Granfield is a fun book for browsing. Everyone loves a circus—clowns, wild animal acts, acrobats, tightrope walkers, the ringmaster, the tent, the food! But how did circuses start, and how did they get to be what they are today?

We know that acrobatic and animal acts date back more than 4,000 years. The ancient Romans had something called circuses, but they were more like gladiator fights, with to-the-death battles (for a book about gladiators, see chapter 7).

The book tells us that in the Middle Ages it is estimated that the average person saw no more than 100 people in his or her entire life time (while the average person today has seen hundreds of people before his or her first birthday!). The arrival of small shows of traveling entertainers going from village to village was very exciting to people who hardly ever saw anyone different.

Circuses as we know them began in England about the time of the American Revolutionary War. Just having menageries of animals was a big hit. People had never seen many animals, and it was a real thrill to see an elephant or a giraffe.

Probably the most famous circus person ever was P. T. Barnum. He started out in the business by buying a slave named Joice Heth, who was supposed to be 161 years old and had once been the nursemaid of George Washington. When she died, doctors said there was no way she was more than 81 years old—much younger than Washington.

Take a look at this fun book, filled with interesting information. Just flipping through it in front of your audience should attract readers. Every two-page spread has eye-catching illustrations or photographs.

Fireworks are another favorite of kids, and *Fiesta Fireworks* by George Ancona is an easy sell. Every town in Mexico has a patron saint who is honored each year with a fiesta. Almost every fiesta has fireworks, but the town of Tultepec is perhaps the most famous of them all for its wonderful fireworks.

The photographs show Caren and her family preparing for the celebration, getting ready huge puppets full of fireworks and building castles of fireworks. The photo of Caren holding the bull puppet she has made above her head is delightful. Show your audience members a variety of photographs—they will all want to go to Tultepec.

BIBLIOGRAPHY

Adler, David A. *Easy Math Puzzles*. Illustrated by Cynthia Fisher. Holiday House, 1997. 32 p. ISBN 0-8234-1283-0. Grades K-3.

————. *A Teacher on Roller Skates and Other School Riddles*. Illustrated by John Wallner. Holiday House, 1989. 64 p. ISBN 0-8234-0775-6. Grades 1-4.

Agee, Jon. *Go Hang a Salami! I'm a Lasagna Hog! And Other Palindromes*. Farrar, Straus & Giroux, 1991. 70 p. ISBN 0-374-33473-0. Grades 4-up.

Amery, Heather, and Jane Songi. *Discover Hidden Worlds: The Home*. Western, 1994. 39 p. ISBN 0-307-15662-1; 0-307-65682-9 (lib. bdg.). Grades 4-7.

Ancona, George. *Fiesta Fireworks*. Lothrop, Lee & Shepard Books/Morrow, 1998. 32 p. ISBN 0-688-14817-4 (trade); 0-688-14818-2 (lib. bdg.). Grades 1-3.

Burleigh, Robert. *Hoops*. Illustrated by Stephen T. Johnson. Harcourt, Brace, 1997. 32 p. ISBN 0-15-201450-0. Grades 2-up.

Buxbaum, Susan Kovacs, and Rita Golden Gelman. *Body Noises*. Illustrated by Angie Lloyd. Alfred A. Knopf, 1988. 56 p. ISBN 0-394-85771-2. Grades 4-6.

Chapman, Gillian, and Pam Robson. *Making Shaped Books*. The Millbrook Press, 1995. 32 p. ISBN 1-56294-560-2 (lib. bdg.). Grades 2-up.

Choron, Sandy, and Harry Choran. *The Book of Lists for Kids*. Houghton Mifflin, 1995. 410 p. ISBN 0-395-70815-X. Grades 5-8.

Cole, Joanna, and Stephanie Calmenson with Michael Street. *Marbles: 101 Ways to Play*. Illustrated by Alan Tiegren. A Beech Tree Paperback Book, 1998. 127 p. ISBN 0-688-12205-1. Grades 4-6.

Czech, Kenneth P. *Snapshot: America Discovers the Camera*. Lerner, 1996. 88 p. ISBN 0-8225-1736-1. Grades 5-8.

Deem, James M. *How to Make a Mummy Talk*. Illustrated by True Kelley. A Yearling Book, 1995. 185 p. ISBN 0-440-41316-8. Grades 4-6.

Free Stuff for Kids. Meadowbrook Press. Grades 4-7. (Published annually.)

Granfield, Linda. *Circus: An Album*. DK Ink/DK, 1997. 96 p. ISBN 0-7894-2453-3. Grades 5-8.

The Guinness Book of World Records. Guinness Media. Grades 4-up. (Published annually.)

Hall, Katy, and Lisa Eisenberg. *Mummy Riddles*. Illustrated by Nicole Rubel. Dial Books for Young Readers, 1997. 48 p. ISBN 0-8037-1846-2; 0-8037-1847-0 (lib. bdg.). Grades 1-3.

Heide, Florence Parry, and Roxanne Heide Pierce. *Oh, Grow Up! Poems to Help You Survive Parents, Chores, School and Other Afflictions*. Illustrated by Nadine Bernard Westcott. Orchard Books, 1996. 32 p. ISBN 0-531-09471-5; 0-531-08771-9 (lib. bdg.). Grades 3-5.

Iguchi, Bryan. *The Young Snowboarder*. DK, 1997. 37 p. ISBN 0-7984-2062-7. Grades 4-7.

Janulewicz, Mike. *Yikes! Your Body, Up Close*. Simon & Schuster Books for Young Readers, 1997. 28 p. ISBN 0-689-81520-4. Grades 3-6.

Jay, Jackson. *Motorcycles*. Capstone Press, 1996. 48 p. ISBN 1-56065-366-3. Grades 3-7.

———. *Super Sports Cars*. Capstone Press, 1996. 48 p. ISBN 1-56065-367-1. Grades 3-7.

Jennings, Terry. *101 Amazing Optical Illusions: Fantastic Visual Tricks*. Illustrated by Alex Pang. Sterling Publications, 1996. 96 p. ISBN 0-8069-9462-2. Grades 4-6.

Kennedy, Dorothy M., comp. *I Thought I'd Take My Rat to School: Poems for September to June*. Illustrated by Abby Carter. Little, Brown, 1993. 62 p. ISBN 0-316-48893-3. Grades 3-6.

Knox, Barbara. *BMX Bicycles*. Capstone Press, 1996. 48 p. ISBN 1-56065-369-8. Grades 3-7.

Koons, James. *Monster Trucks*. Capstone Press, 1996. 48 p. ISBN 1-56065-371-X. Grades 3-7.

———. *Pickup Trucks*. Capstone Press, 1996. 48 p. ISBN 1-56065-372-8. Grades 3-7.

Lankford, Mary D. *Dominoes Around the World*. Illustrated by Karen Dugan. Morrow Junior Books, 1998. 40 p. ISBN 0-688-14051-3 (trade); 0-688-14052-1 (lib. bdg.). Grades 4-6.

Lee, Dennis. *Dinosaur Dinner (With a Slice of Alligator Pie): Favorite Poems by Dennis Lee*. Selected by Jack Prelutsky. Illustrated by Debbie Tilley. Alfred A. Knopf, 1997. 32 p. ISBN 0-679-87009-1 (trade); 0-679-97009-6 (lib. bdg.). Grades 3-5.

Lincoln, Margaret. *The Most Excellent Book of Face Painting*. Illustrated by Rob Shone. Copper Beech Books. 1997. 32 p. ISBN 0-7613-0551-3. Grades 4-6.

Macdonald, Fiona. *A Medieval Castle*. Illustrated by Mark Bergin. Peter Bedrick Books, 1990. ISBN 0-87226-340-1. 48 p. Grades 3-up.

Michelson, Richard. *Animals That Ought to Be: Poems About Imaginary Pets*. With paintings by Leonard Baskin. Simon & Schuster Books for Young Readers, 1996. 24 p. ISBN 0-689-80635-3. Grades 3-up.

Milton, Joyce. *Mummies*. Illustrated by Susan Swan. Grosset & Dunlap, 1996. 48 p. ISBN: 0-448-41326-4 (GB); 0-448-41325-6 (pbk.). Grades 1-3.

Monroe, Lucy. *Creepy Cuisine*. Illustrated by Dianne O'Quinn Burke. Random House, 1992. 80 p. ISBN 0-679-84402-3 (pbk.). Grades 2-5.

Moss, Jeff. *Bone Poems*. Illustrated by Tom Leigh. American Museum of Natural History/Workman, 1997. 78 p. ISBN 0-7611-0884-X. Grades 2-6.

O'Neill, Catherine. *You Won't Believe Your Eyes!* National Geographic Society, 1987. 104 p. ISBN 0-87044-611-8; 0-87044-616-9 (lib. bdg.). Grades 4-7.

Prelutsky, Jack. *The Dragons Are Singing Tonight*. Illustrated by Peter Sis. Greenwillow Books, 1993. 40 p. ISBN 0-688-09645-X (trade); 0-688-12511-5 (lib. bdg.). Grades 2-6.

———. *Tyrannosaurus Was a Beast: Dinosaur Poems*. Illustrated by Arnold Lobel. Greenwillow Books, 1988. 32 p. ISBN 0-688-206442-6 (trade); 0-688-06443-4 (lib. bdg.). Grades K-6.

Prelutsky, Jack (selector). *For Laughing Out Loud! Poems to Tickle Your Funnybone*. Illustrated by Marjorie Priceman. Alfred A. Knopf, 1991. 89 p. ISBN 0-394-82144-0 (trade); 0-394-92144-5 (lib. bdg.). Grades 4-6.

Putnam, James. *Mummy*. Photographed by Peter Hayman. Alfred A. Knopf, 1993. 64 p. ISBN 0-679-83881-3; 0-679-93881-8 (lib. bdg.). Grades 4-up.

Rees, Ennis. *Fast Freddie Frog and Other Tongue-Twister Rhymes*. Illustrated by John O'Brien. Caroline House/Boyds Mills Press, 1993. 32 p. ISBN 1-56397-038-4. Grades 3-6.

Roald Dahl's Revolting Recipes. Illustrated by Quentin Blake. Photographs by Jan Baldwin. Recipes compiled by Josie Fison and Felicity Dahl. Viking, 1994. 61 p. ISBN 0-670-85836-6. Grades 4-6.

Savage, Jeff. *Motocross Cycles*. Capstone Press, 1996. 48 p. ISBN 1-56065-370-1. Grades 3-7.

———. *Racing Cars*. Capstone Press, 1996. 48 p. ISBN 1-56065-368-X. Grades 3-7.

Schleifer, Jay. *Big Rigs*. Capstone Press, 1996. 48 p. ISBN 1-56065-373-6. Grades 3-7.

Schwartz, Alvin. *And the Green Grass Grew All Around: Folk Poetry from Everyone*. Illustrated by Sue Truesdell. HarperCollins, 1992. 195 p. ISBN 0-06-022757-5. All ages.

———. *Telling Fortunes: Love Magic, Dream Signs, and Other Ways to Learn the Future*. Illustrated by Tracey Cameron. J. B. Lippincott, 1987. 128 p. ISBN 0-397-32132-5; 0-397-32133-3 (lib. bdg.). Grades 4-up.

Schwartz, Alvin, comp. *Cross Your Fingers, Spit in Your Hat: Superstitions and Other Beliefs*. Illustrated by Glen Rounds. J. B. Lippincott, 1974. 162 p. ISBN 0-397-31530-9; 0-397-31531-7 (pbk.). Grades 4-up.

Shields, Carol Diggory. *Lunch Money and Other Poems About School*. Illustrated by Paul Meisel. Dutton Children's Books, 1995. 40 p. ISBN 0-525-45345-8. Grades 3-5.

Sloane, Paul, and Des MacHale. *Perplexing Lateral Thinking Puzzles*. Sterling, 1997. 95 p. ISBN 0-8069-1769-5. Grades 6-8.

Snedden, Robert. *Yuck! A Big Book of Little Horrors*. Simon & Schuster Books for Young Readers, 1996. 30 p. ISBN 0-689-80676-0. All ages.

Sobol, Donald J. *Encyclopedia Brown's 3rd Record Book of Weird & Wonderful Facts*. Illustrated by Sal Murdocca. William Morrow, 1985. 134 p. ISBN 0-688-05705-5. Grades 5-7.

Stevenson, James. *Popcorn*. Illustrated by James Stevenson. Greenwillow Books, 1998. 64 p. ISBN 0-688-15261-9. Grades 3-6.

Walton, Rick. *What to Do When a Bug Climbs in Your Mouth and Other Poems to Drive You Buggy*. Illustrated by Nancy Carlson. Lothrop, Lee & Shepard Books, 1995. 32 p. ISBN 0-688-13658-3; 0-688-13659-1 (lib. bdg.). Grades 2-5.

Wardlaw, Lee. *Bubblemania: A Chewy History of Bubble Gum*. Illustrated by Sandra Forrest. Aladdin Paperbacks, 1997. 144 p. ISBN 0-689-81719-3. Grades 4-up.

Westcott, Nadine Bernard (selector). *Never Take a Pig to Lunch and Other Poems About the Fun of Eating*. Illustrated by Nadine Bernard Westcott. Orchard Books, 1994. 64 p. ISBN 0-531-06834-X. Grades 3-5.

Wexler, Jerome. *Everyday Mysteries*. Dutton Children's Books, 1995. 38 p. ISBN 0-525-45363-6. Grades K-3.

The World Almanac and Book of Facts. World Almanac Books. All ages. (Published annually.)

The World Almanac for Kids. World Almanac Books. Grades 3-6. (Published annually.)

Wulffson, Don L. *Amazing True Stories*. Illustrated by John R. Jones. Cobblehill Books/Dutton, 1991. 128 p. ISBN 0-525-65070-9. Grades 5-8.

CHAPTER 3

Animals

Ask elementary school librarians what nonfiction books are always in demand, and they will tell you—animal books. Kids love reading about animals, and so much can be learned by studying their behaviors, habitats, and characteristics. Many books about animals have been published, some of them very ordinary and others decidedly different. The books included in this chapter are out of the ordinary. Some have exceptional illustrations or photographs, some provide unusual and interesting tidbits, and some offer a different twist on an old topic. All of them encourage readers to think about animals in new and different ways. Sample these books and see what you find intriguing, then share that information with the kids to whom you booktalk. You can never go wrong with books about animals.

CREATURES OF THE AIR

Flying is an amazing thing, and scientists still do not completely understand how it works. The incredible information in *The Secrets of Animal Flight* by Nic Bishop will grab your attention (figure 3.1). Do you know what is the only mammal that flies? It is the bat. And bats fly a lot differently than birds or insects do. Did you know that, ounce for ounce, the muscles in the thorax of an insect's body, in its midsection, are the most powerful muscles known in nature? That those muscles can cause wings to flap about 200 times a second? Did you know that bees suck nectar from many flowers, so many that each bee probably visits about 100 flowers every time it leaves its nest? Did you know that some birds can travel up to 2,000 miles without stopping?

This book explains the differences between the many kinds of animal flight and illustrates those differences in superb photographs. Maybe after reading this book you will turn out to be one of those scientists who learns about the mystery of flight.

Fig. 3.1. *The Secrets of Animal Flight* **by Nic Bishop**

Puffins are called the "clowns of the sea" because of their bright bills and the awkward way in which they fly and land. In *Nights of the Pufflings* (figure 3.2), author-photographer Bruce McMillan shows us how kids help these animals when they first learn to fly. Every year, millions of them return to an island off the coast of Iceland to lay their eggs and raise their chicks, called pufflings. Puffins return to the same burrows every year, and children love to watch them as they fish in the ocean to feed themselves and their babies.

By August, the baby pufflings are ready to fly, but they are not very good at it. However, they must learn quickly, for soon they will leave for their winter at sea. They start from a high cliff. Some of the birds make it safely to the ocean, but others crash-land in the village where the children live.

The children, equipped with boxes and flashlights, search the village to find these birds before they are eaten by other animals or run over by cars and trucks. They put the birds in boxes, then take them to the beach in the morning and release them for their first flight. The picture on page 17 is a good one to show. Tell your listeners to read the book to see all of the great photos of these interesting birds and the kids who help them.

Fig. 3.2. *Nights of the Pufflings* **by Bruce McMillan**

Even if you are not much of a bird-watcher, you will enjoy *Watching Water Birds* by Jim Arnosky (figure 3.3). Did you know that a loon can dive down to depths of 200 feet and easily outswim a trout? Did you know that birds that feed on the surface of the water have legs set midway in their body while birds that dive underwater have legs that are set far back? Show the two-page spread that illustrates where a water bird's wings go when the bird is not spreading them. Then show the picture of the hooded mergansers, with and without their crests fully raised. Arnosky's enthusiasm for his subject is contagious. The next time you go near a body of water, you will see the birds there with new eyes.

Fig. 3.3. *Watching Water Birds* by Jim Arnosky

In her book *Hawk Highway in the Sky: Watching Raptor Migration* (figure 3.4), Caroline Arnold gives this description of raptors (page 8):

> Hawks, eagles, and falcons are predatory birds called raptors. Raptors have strong grasping feet, sharp talons, a hooked upper beak, and excellent vision—qualities that make them superb hunters. Owls are raptors too, but they specialize in flying and hunting at night whereas hawks, eagles and falcons are active by day.

The author was intrigued by the Hawk Watch team in the Goshute Mountains of Eastern Nevada. There, scientists and volunteers watch the raptors migrate, count them, trap a few, band their legs, and take measurements so we can learn more about raptor behavior.

Thirty-one different species of hawks, eagles, and falcons live in North America. Scientists still have much to learn about them. Many questions about migration remain to be answered, including how birds find their way on long journeys, sometimes thousands of miles long. We do know that they follow routes where food is available and where they can find safe perches for the night, and that migrating hawks travel on an average 100 to 150 miles a day. But some birds fly more than 300 miles a day! They usually fly directly north or south, but they sometimes change direction to take the shortest route across or around a large body of water or a barren desert. If they were to fly over these areas, it would be dangerous, for there is no food or place to rest. Many raptors die of starvation during migration.

Arnold tells us how the raptors are captured for a short time and banded, and how we can help scientists with this project. The photos in this fascinating book are wonderful. A great picture to show is on page 13, but there are many others as well in this colorful book.

Fig. 3.4. *Hawk Highway in the Sky: Watching Raptor Migration* **by Caroline Arnold**

A wood thrush is a beautiful songbird, but like most songbirds today, it is in grave danger as its habitats continue to diminish. Whenever people cut down woods or forests to build houses or make pastures, or just to harvest the trees, the songbirds have fewer places to live. They need lots of space, and they need to keep safe from other animals that will harm them or eat them, such as cats and raptors.

Flute's Journey: The Life of a Wood Thrush by Lynne Cherry (figure 3.5) is the story of one wood thrush who is born in Maryland and migrates to Costa Rica. Cherry tells how Flute lives and how he is able to migrate. In one day he travels 600 miles! Then, after the winter is over, he must travel back home and face new dangers.

Whether or not you know much about songbirds and the dangers they face, this book is great reading, and it includes ideas for things that kids can do to help them. The illustration of Flute's mother feeding her babies a worm is a good one to show.

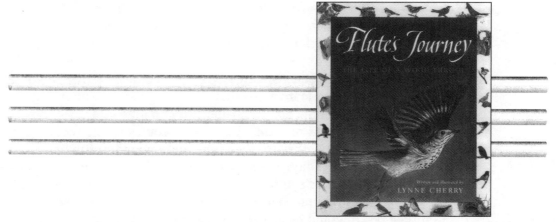

Fig. 3.5. *Flute's Journey: The Life of a Wood Thrush* **by Lynne Cherry**

Wild Flamingos by Bruce McMillan tells some little-known facts about a beautiful bird. Did you know that flamingos get their beautiful coloring because of the food that they eat? Did you know that if they stop eating that food, their feathers will turn back into the dullish gray color that they were when they were very young? This book has beautiful photographs of flamingos that live in the wild.

Another creature of the air—the bat—is described in Diane Ackerman's *Bats: Shadows in the Night.* Have you ever heard of Bracken Cave, near San Antonio, Texas? In that cave is the largest concentration of warm-blooded animals in the world. There, 20 million Mexican free-tailed bats hang by their toes, coming out at dusk to feed. At that time of day, people who live in San Antonio are rarely more than 70 feet from a feeding bat. It is an amazing sight, as you can see from the photographs in this book.

Bats scare a lot of people for no good reason. They are actually fascinating creatures, and Ackerman supplies great information about them. Did you know that the biggest bats are called flying foxes, and that their wingspans can be up to six feet wide? Or that bats give birth to only one baby bat at a time? Or that bats live to be 15 years old, on average, but that some bats live as long as 34 years? Or that bats send out streams of clicks when they fly? When they listen for the echoes of those clicks, bats can tell where things are, how big they are, and how fast they are moving.

The informative and beautiful photographs in the book are great to show groups. Show them the photo of the tiniest bat, the bumblebee bat, on page 27, or the bat in flight on page 5 or page 8.

Outside and Inside Bats by Sandra Markle is an excellent book to use in conjunction with the Ackerman book. Along with many of the same facts stated in the Ackerman book, Markle supplies additional information about the anatomy of a bat. Bats, for instance, feed on blood for about eight minutes, and that may equal 60 percent of the bat's body weight. How much do you weigh? How would you feel if you ate 60 percent of your body weight at one meal? Because a bat eats so much, it must get rid of some of the waste almost immediately. Imagine having to go to the bathroom two minutes after you finished eating to get rid of a lot of what you ate!

Excellent photos include those on pages 19 and 29.

CREATURES OF THE WATER

Although about 240 kinds of land turtles exist, there are only 8 kinds of sea turtles. *Sea Turtles* by Gail Gibbons (figure 3.6) introduces us to them. Sea turtles were alive at the time of the dinosaurs, and they were big. Scientists found the fossil of one they named Archelon. If Archelon were alive today, a car could park between its flippers!

Sea turtles have flippers so strong that they are powerful swimmers. Some of them can swim as fast as 20 miles an hour. They swim long distances, too. Scientists found one turtle that swam 4,000 miles after being tagged in Brazil.

The biggest sea turtle of all is the leatherback; show your audience the illustration of it on page 13. It does not have a shell, yet it weighs more than 1,000 pounds. Its back is leathery, and it can dive as deep as 1,300 feet—almost a quarter of a mile.

Sea turtles return to the same beach where they were born to lay their eggs. This instinct does not always serve them well, for many beaches now have houses on them and are not good spots in which to lay eggs. But people can help. If you live near a sea turtle beach, maybe you can help too. Read this fascinating book to find out how.

Fig. 3.6. *Sea Turtles* **by Gail Gibbons**

The Octopus: Phantom of the Sea by Mary M. Cerullo tells about an animal that is even more interesting than it looks, which is pretty amazing. This 1997 ALA Notable Book starts out with a true story that is a real attention-grabber. An octopus in an aquarium, restless at night after the staring crowds are gone, explores its tank, looking for a way out. It finds a small rip in the screen covering and squeezes its entire "sixty pounds of boneless body" through the two-inch hole. "It slides around behind-the-scenes like animated Jell-O, searching for other aquarium specimens to eat. The next morning, a surprised aquarist finds the fugitive in another tank, nestled among the shells of its former neighbors" (page 2).

Many different types of octopi exist, but the biggest, and the one on which this book concentrates, is the giant Pacific octopus, which may reach a length of 20 feet. Its eyes are not like ours, for they have horizontal, not round, pupils (show your audience the photos on pages 12 and 13). An octopus is a real loner. The only time it wants to be with any other octopus is during the mating season. An octopus is so antisocial that it will eat any octopus smaller than it is.

An octopus is a cephalopod, which means a "head-footed animal," because its appendages grow directly out from the head (show the photo on page 16). Octopi can change color and camouflage themselves very quickly, and they also squirt out ink which can confuse predators. Their arms have up to 240 suction cups each, for a total of nearly 2,000 suckers! An arm that is amputated by a predator will grow back. A fine picture on page 27 shows an octopus with the webs between its arms open, enabling it to float like a parachute and also to close around its prey like an umbrella.

Scientist have done much testing on the octopus and have learned that it is an incredibly intelligent animal. One octopus used to sneak out of its aquarium each night, crawl into nearby tanks to eat fish, and then return to its own tank before researchers arrived back at work the next morning.

Patricia Lauber's *An Octopus Is Amazing* brings the same subject to younger children. Did you know that an octopus can change color in a flash? Color changes help them escape enemies. They can even have spots or stripes, or be half one color and half another. Scientists say that an angry octopus turns dark red while a frightened octopus turns pale. Did you know that a female octopus lays as many as 200,000 eggs at one time? She guards the eggs for four to six weeks until they hatch, and then she dies. This well-illustrated little book will introduce young children to the truly amazing octopus.

Manatees are an endangered species. Although they are water animals, they are distant relatives of elephants, and what is making their survival hard today is that their habitats are changing so rapidly. To quote from page 8 in *A Safe Home for the Manatees* by Priscilla Belz Jenkins, "Your home is your habitat. There you have the food, water, air, space, and shelter you need to live. Imagine what it might be like if one of these things was missing." It sounds pretty horrible, doesn't it?

Adult manatees need to eat about 100 pounds of plants a day. People are disturbing their habitats, making it very hard for them to live. People are filling in lagoons to make more land, and they disturb and injure manatees with their speedboats. Today, scientists estimate that there are only about 3,000 Florida manatees. Read this book to find out about them and how you and your class can help them to survive.

Harp seals are beautiful animals named because a pattern on their fur looks like a harp. They live in the North Atlantic Ocean, where it is so cold that the ocean freezes in the winter. Even though they are used to living in the cold, harp seals are actually warm-blooded mammals like dogs or monkeys or human beings. They are sort of like large dogs that have learned to live in the sea.

Harp Seal Pups by Downs Matthews (figure 3.7) tells how harp seal pups are born and grow up. Their mothers go to one of four places where it is slightly warmer and where their enemies, the polar bears, cannot find them. Several excellent photos show a harp seal's claws, which help it crawl on slippery ice, and its eyes, which run with tears continuously to keep them free of salt and sand. A harp seal can hold its breath for a very long time; it can stay underwater for as long as 15 minutes and dive more than 800 feet to find food.

Baby seals are born, only one to each mother, in less than a minute. They are about 15 pounds and about two feet long. Their mother feeds them so often that they gain about five pounds a day. By the 12th day, the baby weighs about 80 pounds, and the mother stops feeding it. But all of her blubber keeps the baby fed until it can find its own food.

A great photo to show is the one of the baby seal and its mother touching noses right after the birth; another excellent example is the full-page photo of the harp seal about six pages from the end.

Fig. 3.7. *Harp Seal Pups* by Downs Matthews

Did you know that some animals can actually *walk* on water? Really! No tricks! How is this possible? Patricia A. Fink Martin not only explains how it is possible but gives us some experiments to do that tell us how it is done in her book *Animals That Walk on Water*.

Lots of people do know that there is a sort of a skin on water, a skin that can keep some objects afloat. Some animals and insects walk on this layer of water. Other creatures use other methods. All of them are fun to read about in this colorful book. The rove beetle, about as big as a grain of rice, almost jet skis across the water. The water measurer insects almost row across it. The water strider, the one we would be most likely to see, actually walks on the water. The fisher spider is able to catch and kill fish three times its size while lounging around on the water, and the birds called western grebes run across a stretch of water as long as 66 feet in their courtship ritual. But perhaps the most amazing water walker of all is the basilisk lizard. Mexicans call this amazing animal the "Jesus Christ" lizard because it can walk on water. Show the audience the photo of the lizard on page 17 (also on the cover) and the one of the spider eating a much larger fish on page 34. Read this book to learn some great new information.

ANIMALS AROUND THE WORLD

Some of the most fascinating animals in the world are in Africa, and *African Animals* by Caroline Arnold tells us about several of them. What do you think is the heaviest of all of the land animals? (Show the photo of the elephant on page 15.) Some adult elephants weigh as much as 14,000 pounds—as much as a medium-sized truck. What do you think is the fastest land animal? The cheetah (page 29) can run as fast as 75 miles per hour. And what do you think is the biggest bird? Ostriches (page 21) may grow to be eight feet tall and weigh as much as 300 pounds. The great photographs in this book will seduce your audience.

A unique animal that lives in Eastern Africa is exposed in *Naked Mole Rats* by Gail Jarrow and Paul Sherman. This fascinatingly ugly mammal lives underground in a complex tunnel system. Like some insects, the naked mole rat colony has a queen who is in charge of giving birth, as shown in the photograph on page 39. Strangely enough, this mammal's body temperature changes with the temperature of its surroundings, much like a reptile. Tell the kids about the "bossy lady" (page 36-39) and how she is the only known mammal to increase in length after reaching adulthood. Can you believe that she can give birth to more than 900 pups in her life time? The fantastic photographs in this award-winning book will both fascinate and disgust audiences of all ages.

Take another African journey by reading *The Chimpanzee Family Book* by Jane Goodall. Kids love primates, and they will be drawn to this book by its many color photographs of chimpanzees. Provide some background about Jane Goodall—how she has lived and worked among chimpanzees for more than 30 years and how she has named all of the chimpanzees she knows. For this book, Goodall tracked some chimpanzees for a day and described their behaviors and interactions. Quite a few of the photographs are large enough to show to a group, which will be fascinated by them. Show pictures of the chimps and point out how similar they are to humans.

Jumbo by Rhoda Blumberg tells the story of an African animal that moved to Paris, and then London, and later traveled all over North America. Currently, we use the word *jumbo* to mean something big, but in the 1800s, it was a meaningless word. Blumberg's book tells the story of the elephant whose name became a word in the English language.

In the mid-1800s a baby elephant was captured in the African jungle and taken to a zoo in Paris. He was small and scrawny, so he was sold to a zoo in London. There, he was given the name Jumbo because zoo officials thought it sounded African. Jumbo was well cared for by trainer Matthew Scott, and he grew by leaps and bounds until he became the largest animal in captivity in the world. Fearing that he might become dangerous, the zoo sold Jumbo to American showman P. T. Barnum, whose circus also featured the "most tattooed person in the world" and "the smallest midget in the world." An interesting picture toward the middle of the book shows Jumbo in a huge crate being lowered by a crane onto a ship. Jonathan Hunt's illustrations are beautiful, and Blumberg's storytelling ability gives life to the hype that surrounded the world's most famous elephant. This book reads like a story and will be enjoyed by young elementary school students.

A good companion to *Jumbo* is *The Giraffe That Walked to Paris* by Nancy Milton. This giraffe lived in the 1800s and belonged to the pasha of Egypt. She was given to King Charles X of France as a gift, and so she traveled by ship across the Mediterranean Sea. The people of Paris had never seen a giraffe and were very anxious to see her, but the winter was cold in Paris and the giraffe stayed by the sea in Marseilles for a few months. Finally, it was time to bring her to Paris, but how could her handlers move the giraffe such a long distance? They decided to walk her to Paris, and all along the route people turned out to see her. Eventually, she reached her new home in the Paris zoo where she was loved and cared for and visited by thousands of people.

This picture book has numerous illustrations that will please a younger audience. Perhaps the most interesting tidbits of information are found on the final pages, where we learn the details of this giraffe's life. Tell the students that the giraffe lived to be 21 years old, and when she died she was stuffed and put in a museum. She can still be seen today in La Rochelle, France (show the picture of the stuffed giraffe on the final page of the book).

Komodo dragons live on Komodo Island in the middle of Indonesia. Although people have been fascinated by them for centuries, they are just now being studied in great detail, and they are described in *Komodo Dragon: On Location* by Kathy Darling. Komodo dragons are meat eaters and can reach almost 11 feet in length, a fact that kept most people off that island throughout much of history. Two pages provide information guaranteed to intrigue readers: The dragon's scaly skin is made of keratin, which is the same material your fingernails are made out of (see page 13), and the dragon lays an egg not much bigger than a chicken's egg but contains in it a baby dragon 18 inches long! (Show the life-size drawing on page 34.)

National Geographic magazine sent Jim Brandenburg to Ellesmere Island, near the Arctic Circle, to photograph animals. But Brandenburg has always loved wolves, and he kept watching one wolf pack. He called one of the wolves Scruffy, because, frankly, he looked so scruffy. In his book *Scruffy: A Wolf Finds His Place in the Pack*, (figure 3.8) he tells about this poor wolf. Scruffy seemed to have low status in the wolf pack. All of the other wolves bossed him around, and he had to eat after everyone else had eaten. Brandenburg did not know why Scruffy was able to stay in the pack, because all wolves must be of value to the pack, or they will die. After extensive observation, Brandenburg found Scruffy's talent. He was a great babysitter who taught wolf pups how to behave. And the wolf pups seemed to think he was pretty cool!

Take a look at the fine photos in this colorful book. The one on the title page clearly indicates why Brandenburg chose the name Scruffy, as do the ones of Scruffy waking up after his nap and being dive-bombed by a bird. The photo labeled "Scruffy, the hero of the pups, sometimes felt like a king" is a guaranteed kid-pleaser.

Fig. 3.8. *Scruffy: A Wolf Finds His Place in the Pack* **by Jim Brandenburg**

Imagine what it would be like to live in Alaska. For most of us, it sounds like a very exciting place. *Orcas Around Me: My Alaskan Summer* by Debra Page tells the true story of a boy named Taiga, who was raised in Alaska with his mom, dad, and little brother. Taiga's family makes money in the summer by fishing for salmon which they sell to fine restaurants and grocery stores around the world.

But what is it like to fish for salmon? It sounds easy, but it is not. It involves a lot of work, and the salmon must be cleaned immediately, which is *really* hard work, so that it stays very fresh. Taiga often sees otters, sea lions, and other animals. Once, as in the book's title, three orca "killer" whales surrounded the family's fishing boat. They were afraid that this time the fishermen would get eaten by the whales!

A full-page color painting appears on each two-page spread, and many are worth sharing with the group. In particular, show your audience one of the pictures of the orcas approaching the family boat.

Fig. 3.9. *Orcas Around Me: My Alaskan Summer* **by Debra Page**

Dawn to Dusk in the Galapagos: Flightless Birds, Swimming Lizards, and Other Fascinating Creatures by Rita Golden Gelman is a beautiful book about a fascinating place. Tell your students about the 13 Galapagos Islands located right on the equator off the coast of Ecuador. This book is really a photo essay, and almost every page includes a picture worth showing to an audience. Kids will especially like the photographs of the iguanas, lizards, and tortoises. The book has no page numbers, but be sure to show them the picture near the end of marine iguanas. Look closely to see the unbelievable number of lizard-like creatures sprawled out on the warm rocks. You can tie this book in with booktalks about endangered species by telling students about Lonesome George, the only tortoise left in the world of his species (see chapter 1 of *And Then There Was One: The Mysteries of Extinction*, found later in this chapter).

The entire series of "Babies" books by Kathy Darling is enormously appealing. Just showing the children the photographs of the different animals will make them want to take the books home. Show them the lemur (pronounced, helpfully, LEE mer, in a brief but very useful sidebar) found in *Desert Babies*. Be sure to show the children pictures of it standing on its hind legs, allowing them to see how lemurs got their name, which means "ghosts." Lemurs can jump up to 30 feet forward, sideways or backwards. Wonderful color pictures illustrate this enticing book.

Children recognize many animals, so it is particularly fun to show them ones with which they are not so familiar. Other books in the series include *Rain Forest Babies*, in which the photos of the marmoset, the orangutan wearing a leaf hat, and the sloth are among the most delightful; *Seashore Babies*, in which all of the animals are quite familiar, but in which the photos of the baby pelican, penguin, sea lion, and dolphin are irresistible; and *Arctic Babies* (figure 3.10), which has lovely photos of a baby lynx, fox, and seal. The baby porcupine looks so soft and cuddly! *Desert Babies* includes great shots of a baby camel, caracal, gemsbok, quokka, coyote, and emu.

Fig. 3.10. *Arctic Babies* by Kathy Darling

Kathy and Tara Darling must have found lemurs intriguing, for they wrote a whole book about them. *Lemurs: On Location* informs us that lemurs are found only on the island of Madagascar, which long ago was once part of Africa. When it broke away millions of years ago, the animals there developed differently from the animals in other places.

Lemurs don't just *look* like ghosts, they sound a lot like them, too. Renowned for their leaping, a "nine-foot sifaka could spring up and sit on a ten-foot-high basketball hoop. (Michael Jordan, eat your heart out!)." Although their leaps are incredible, they are not very good at walking Their hind legs are so long that some of them cannot walk at all, but have to hop. The brown lemurs smell horrible to humans. All lemurs use their sense of smell more than any other sense. These unique animals are great fun to read about.

The picture on page 9 of Kathy Darling feeding the four curious lemurs, who sit up almost like cats around her, will make you want to go to Madagascar immediately. Other good photos to show are on pages 15, 18, and 19.

CREEPY-CRAWLY CREATURES

Show a few pictures from *Blood-Feeding Bugs and Beasts* by L. Patricia Kite, and kids will be squirming in their seats. Hold up a picture of the conenose assassin, which occasionally bites sleeping people around the mouth, or show the magnified picture of a flea. The photographs of leeches and ticks are equally disgusting, and kids may not know that people used to use leeches routinely in medicine. A short booktalk should be all it takes to get kids interested in this book.

Another close-up look at bugs can be found in *Amazing Bugs* by Miranda Mac-Quitty. This is one of DK Publishing's "Inside Guides," which feature intricate three-dimensional models that show how everything fits together and works. It is packed with great photos and cross sections of bugs, as well as information about insect anatomy and behavior.

The cover of this book is a booktalk in itself. Showing it to your audience will bring an enthusiastic and loud reaction. Flip the book open to page 15, and show the model of a mosquito biting human skin. Did you know that there are more than 3,000 kinds of mosquitoes? Show the model of the horsefly's head on pages 20 and 21. Flipping through this book in front of a group will make many sales!

Doug Wechsler's *Bizarre Bugs* pairs well with *Amazing Bugs*. Although the pictures in Wechsler's book are of real bugs, not models (as are many in the MacQuitty book), these two books complement each other.

Did you know that there are at least one million species of insects—and maybe even as many as *30 million* species? Wechsler tells us that not all insects are really bugs, but that a lot of people call all insects bugs.

Right away, he shows us two fascinating pictures of the peanuthead bug (and yes, its head really does look like a peanut). Show the pictures on pages 2 and 3. The one on page 5 shows the peanuthead bug flashing its eyespots, and it certainly looks bigger and more threatening that way than it does normally. This is a great example of camouflage. Another fine example is on page 4. Ask the kids if they can find the camouflaged mantis in this picture. It's one thing to look for it when you know it is there. If you didn't know it was there and just glanced, do you think you would even see it at all?

The book tells us how insects protect themselves in many unusual and interesting ways. It also tells us about a bug with ears on its legs and another with jaws almost as long as the rest of its body. It's a fun read, with a lot of interesting facts to share with your friends.

Those Amazing Ants by Patricia Brennan Demuth tells about ants and their behavior in a way that younger children will enjoy. The book starts off with an interesting fact: All the ants you see walking around are females. And all the ants live to serve their queen. The fourth-page spread shows a nice drawing of a queen ant and her attendants, who wait on her, feed her, rub her back, and even bathe her. Demuth tells how ants "smell" with their feelers, leave trails of chemicals to guide others to food, and lift chunks of food 10 times their weight. In the end you will find the answer to the question you've been asking: Where are all the male ants? They are the ants with wings who have only one job: to mate with the queen. Afterward, they die. First through third graders will enjoy this look at some surprisingly interesting creatures.

Just showing the children a few double-page spreads and briefly describing the bugs is guaranteed to attract readers to Lucille Recht Penner's *Monster Bugs*. This book answers questions we had not thought to ask—and the answers are intriguing. Did you know that the "stinkiest, smelliest bug" is a stinkbug, depicted on page 14? The longest bugs are Australian walking sticks. Did you know that a praying mantis will eat anything smaller than itself? Even a baby bird that falls from its nest. After eating, the mantis washes its face like a kitten. Show the picture on page 19. An assassin bug can squirt poison that turns the inside of a caterpillar to mush (pages 34 and 35). The book does not go into much detail. In fact, it does not even always mention where all of these amazing insects live. But it is great fun and worth promoting to your listeners.

Take a Look at Snakes by Betsy Maestro is a good introduction to the world of snakes. Did you know that there are more than 2,700 kinds of snakes in the world? The biggest are more than 30 feet long (measure this distance in your library or classroom) and weigh more than 400 pounds (how many students would it take to weigh this much?). And did you know that there are no snakes in Iceland, Ireland, and New Zealand? Maestro tells how snakes move, shed their skins, and unhinge their jaws. Page 40 is a "Did you know that . . . ???" list of fun facts you can share with children. Filled with information, this book may be appreciated by your more squeamish readers because it is illustrated with drawings rather than photographs.

Pairing Alexandra Parsons's *Amazing Snakes* with Mavis Smith's *A Snake Mistake* results in an amazingly effective booktalk. Start by showing the picture of the egg-eating snake on pages 14 and 15 of *Amazing Snakes*. Explain that an egg-eating snake can swallow an egg twice the size of its head, and ask if people can do that. Of course not, but why not? And how does a snake do it?

Demonstrate with your hands the difference between our jaws, which are hinged, and snake jaws, which are not. Then explain that when a snake eats a whole egg, the snake moves its head down, pushing the egg up against a row of sharp spikes that stick down from the back of its throat to cut a slit in the eggshell so that the insides can come out. Later, the snake uses its muscles to crush the shell and spit it out.

Now, pull out *A Snake Mistake*. Explain that this book is based on a true story about a farmer in Florida who read somewhere that chickens will lay more eggs if you put fake eggs in their nests. The farmer decided to put some old lightbulbs in his chickens' nests, and it worked.

One night, a snake came into the henhouse, and guess what it ate! Let the children guess; they will know. Not just one, but *two* lightbulbs! As children have already learned, through Parsons's book, what happens to an egg inside the snake's body, they can link that knowledge with this new information. Things do not look good for Jake the snake.

The farmer felt bad when he found the snake, and he must have been a very kind-hearted man, for he took the snake to the veterinarian, who took an X-Ray (show the two-page spread) and performed surgery to rid the snake of the lightbulbs. Children will want you to read the book on the spot, but, if you do not, they will rush to check it out.

One more book worth mentioning is *The Snake Book* by Mary Ling and Mary Atkinson. The huge fold-out photo of the reticulated python is a big crowd pleaser.

Rattlesnakes! Everyone loves to hear about them. Younger kids will enjoy *All About Rattlesnakes* by Jim Arnosky. Did you know that some rattlesnakes can grow to be *seven feet long*? And that a rattlesnake gets a new segment on its rattle every time it sheds its skin, at least twice a year? Why do you suppose the rattlesnake sheds its skin? How many kinds of rattlesnakes are there? Are there any in the area where you live? Did you know that we human beings are the rattlesnake's greatest enemies? Or that roadrunners kill a lot of rattlesnakes? All of this information and more is included in this fascinating book.

Show your audience the picture of the roadrunner and the rattlesnake on the second to the last two-page spread, or, in fact, any of the book's colorful pictures.

Jennifer Owings Dewey was bitten by a rattlesnake when she was a child. In *Rattlesnake Dance: True Tales, Mysteries, and Rattlesnake Ceremonies* (figure 3.11), she describes that amazing experience.

As a nine-year-old living in New Mexico, Dewey loved to ride her horse, usually alone, in the hills. One day she climbed up a cliff face and reached for a grip on a ledge. She felt a horrible pain. A rattlesnake had bitten her hand.

She was terrified, but she knew what to do. Although she heard the snake rattle, she was relieved that her horse did not. She got back on her horse and made the 20-minute ride home, afraid she might die on the way. Read the following from page 11:

> Ten minutes into the twenty-minute ride my stomach backed up and I started feeling dizzy. I was afraid of falling off the horse. The earth and sky rotated. Blue mountains in the distance reeled and rolled. My vision began to cloud over. Black shadows moved across my eyes until all I could see was a tiny pinpoint of light. I wondered if I'd make it home before I died.

Clearly, she did make it home and she did not die, but she was sick all summer and had to receive skin grafts to repair the skin that had been destroyed by the snakebite.

This book is full of fascinating information about rattlesnakes, who live in pits and are also called pit vipers. Eight thousand people a year are bitten by pit vipers in North America, but only about 10 to 15 of these people die. The book features an excellent map showing which kinds of snakes are found in each state. Maine is the only state free of pit vipers.

Dewey has seen two male rattlesnakes dance and fight with each other, and she describes it as more of a wrestling match than a fight to the death. She has also seen the incredible Hopi Snake Ceremonies. To find out more information about rattlesnakes, read this delightful book. The picture of the rattlesnake dance on page 40 is a good one to show.

Fig. 3.11. *Rattlesnake Dance: True Tales, Mysteries, and Rattlesnake Ceremonies* **by Jennifer Owings Dewey**

The incredibly disgusting photo on the cover of *Those Amazing Leeches* by Cheryl M. Halton works well with small groups. Most of us have heard of leeches and sort of know what they are. Some of us may even know that leeches were once used in medicine for sucking out blood from people (known as "bleeding" a patient). This may sound like a really stupid thing to do, but many doctors today still use leeches for that purpose! The reason we get bruises, for instance, is that blood gathers under the skin. Putting a leech on a spot can stop a bruise from forming. And some of you may remember that Laura Ingalls and Nellie Oleson of the "Little House" books both got leeches on themselves when they went wading in Plum Creek. Use this book in a booktalk about the Ingalls family, as the two topics tie together so well because of this.

Most leeches are only one to two inches long, but some are much smaller, and some leeches grow to be as long as 18 inches. Locate the photo, on page 10, of a small crocodile with a huge leech attached to its back. The caption informs us that a leech this big can easily kill a small animal.

Leeches are parasites that live off of other creatures, including people. Soldiers throughout history have had terrible problems with leeches. When the famous general Napoleon's army marched from Egypt to Syria 200 years ago, the soldiers drank water anyplace they could find it. Consequently, they swallowed many tiny leeches. But when the leeches started sucking their blood inside their mouths, noses, and throats, many soldiers died from blood loss or suffocated when the leeches, swollen with blood, blocked their air passages. Leeches start out tiny, but they become huge when they drink blood. Read this book with its amazing photographs to find out more!

A lot of kids are crazy about chameleons, and they can read about them in *Chameleons: On Location* by Kathy Darling. The way chameleons change colors is exciting and interesting. A chameleon cannot control its color changes any more than you can control the fact that you blush. When a chameleon is angry or upset, it changes its colors. But the green skin is a protective coloration. Green skin is the best color to have, for many chameleons rely on their color to hide them and protect them from danger. The meanest chameleons change color more times than any of the others! The color chart "How to 'read' Chameleon" on page 13 is fun:

- Green means calm and peaceful;
- Tan means sleepy, cold, tired, or sick;
- Yellow means surrender;
- Bright stripes means angry;
- Black means *REALLY* angry; and
- Black with orange dots means pregnant.

Show the photo of an angry male pardalis on page 19, and the photo of the parsonii—the heaviest of all 128 species of chameleon—on page 6.

Lots of kids really like salamanders, and no wonder. They are interesting-looking, fascinating animals, and younger children will enjoy reading about them in Emery and Durga Bernhard's *Salamanders* (figure 3.12).

This book tells us that of the 360 kinds of salamanders in the world, more than 100 live in North America. These types include newts. Many male newts sport bright colors. The red eft is one whose bright red skin gives off a poison that burns the mouth of animals that bite it (show the picture on page 18). Giant salamanders are usually from 12 to 29 inches long—but in China and Japan they can grow more than five feet in length and weigh as much as 50 pounds! How would you like to see one of those? (You can see a picture of one on page 20.)

Another interesting thing about some salamanders is that their tails sometimes break off and wiggle about when they are being chased by a predator. The enemy tries to catch the tail while the salamander escapes. Then the salamander grows a new tail in a process called regeneration. One of the reasons scientists study salamanders is to find out why this happens.

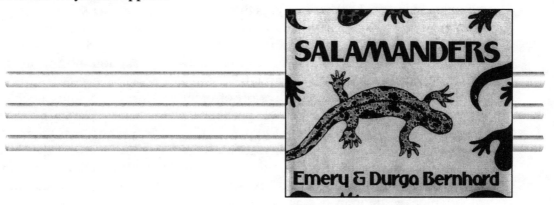

Fig. 3.12. *Salamanders* **by Emery and Durga Bernhard**

PETS

How would you feel if a big dog started barking at you and looked like he was going to attack you? Would you be scared? Almost everybody is scared of a dog like that, and that is one reason why dogs are such good partners for police officers. A police dog who starts barking at a burglar, for instance, will usually make the burglar put his hands in the air and surrender. No one wants to be attacked by a dog.

Sammy, the hero of *Sammy: Dog Detective* by Colleen Stanley Bare, is a family pet, but he is also a partner in a K-9 unit. His partner, Andy, is not only a police officer but is also the father of the family to which Sammy belongs. Like every other family dog, he sleeps with people, slobbers on the newspaper when he brings it in, and likes to play.

But Sammy also has a job—a job that he loves. Five days a week, eight hours a day, he works for the police department. This fun book shows how he was trained and explains that his parents were both police dogs too. The photo on page 7 is a fun one to show audiences.

You will meet another dog with a job in *Rosie: A Visiting Dog's Story* by Stephanie Calmenson (figure 3.13). Like Sammy, Rosie is a pet dog with a day job. Her job is to cheer up people who are sad or sick or lonely. Rosie was a gentle and friendly puppy, and she had to go through a lot of training to become qualified to be a visiting dog. She needed to trust people, to get along with other dogs, to be comfortable with children as well as old people, and to be obedient. Rosie also had to be a good traveler so she could ride on trains, buses, and airplanes. When she was finally certified as a visiting dog, Rosie visited a children's hospital and a nursing home. Tell your audience about her visit with Bill (page 42). Bill was a lonely old man who hadn't spoken in weeks. But when Rosie came in, Bill began talking again.

With photos on every page, this book is great to show to groups of kids. A couple of particularly good photos are of Rosie and a sick child, on page 26, and of Rosie with an older woman, on page 38.

Fig. 3.13. *Rosie: A Visiting Dog's Story* **by Stephanie Calmenson**

Would you like to have a kitten? Doesn't everyone think kittens are cute? Young readers will love *My New Kitten* by Joanna Cole (figure 3.14). Showing your audience a few of the lovely photos in this book will guarantee its immediate circulation.

Fig. 3.14. *My New Kitten* **by Joanna Cole. © 1994 Morrow Junior Books.**

Those same listeners will also eat up Joanna Cole's *My Puppy Is Born*. Ask if anyone in the group likes puppies (brace yourself for a chorus of excited affirmations). Tell the kids that this book tells about how a puppy is born and grows up. Show the audience the picture of Dolly, at four weeks old, strong enough to sit and stand, and be sure to show the picture of Dolly eating her first solid food. This delights audiences of any age.

Puppies, a DK Publishing book by Carey Scott, is also an easy sell. Pairing it with *My Puppy Is Born* makes for an irresistible combination. Show your audience almost any of the photos, although the big pictures on pages 18-19, 26-27, and 30-31 are particularly appealing.

Another book by Joanna Cole, *Riding Silver Star*, will appeal to kids who dream of having their own horse. Showing your audience just a photo or two from this book will sell it to them. Show the double-page spread of Star about to make a jump and the photo of Abigail giving him his bath.

A more unusual pet is described in Elaine Landau's *Your Pet Iguana*. Have you ever thought it would be fun to have a pet iguana? Would it be neat to own a pet that looks like a small dragon?

If you are interested in iguanas, this book not only tells you a little bit about where they come from and what they are like, but it tells you how to take care of one and how to select the right one at a pet store. Iguanas are not the easiest pets to own, and they can get sick fairly easily. Also, they are not at all cuddly or loving. Many people do not take good care of their pet iguanas, and the iguanas die as a result. Even if you would not like to own one, this book makes for good reading. Show your audience the pictures on pages 4, 7, and 43. For a view of iguanas in the wild, show the photo of iguanas on the rocks in *Dawn to Dusk in the Galapagos* (see the section "Animals Around the World" earlier in this chapter).

A book about unusual pets for older kids is *The Tarantula in My Purse and 172 Other Wild Pets* by Jean Craighead George. George, author of *Julie of the Wolves*, and other children's classics, wrote this book from her family's experiences over the years with 173 wild pets. Each chapter, full of action and excitement, is a captivating story, made even more fascinating by the fact that the stories are true. Tell the kids about their pet crow named Crowbar, who lived with George's family for two and a half years before a flock of crows kidnapped him (chapter 12). Chapter 13, which describes feeding a rat to a pet boa constrictor, is also a good one to mention.

Recommend this book to teachers as a great read-aloud for a fourth- or fifth-grade class. The chapters are short, interesting, and teach many lessons about ecology, biology, and living with nature.

AMAZING ANIMAL FACTS

Skeletons: An Inside Look at Animals, by Jinny Johnson, tells us a lot about the insides *and* the outsides of animals. Here are just a few of the many interesting facts from this book.

- Most birds have light bones, so they can fly more easily, but penguins' bones are much heavier. The added weight helps them dive below the surface of the sea. Whale bones, however, are light. That is why, even though a whale has a big body, the water is able to support it.
- Moose grow new antlers every year. Their old antlers fall off, and new ones grow with more branches than the old ones. Antlers grow a half inch a *day*.
- A full-grown Atlantic cod is normally four feet long and weights about 25 pounds, but fishermen have reported seeing cod as long as six feet!
- A Nile crocodile measures about 16 feet in length. That is longer than most cars.
- An elephant seal weighs about 5,000 pounds. That is the same as a full-grown rhinoceros!
- A baby kangaroo lives in its mother's pouch for more than a year. When it is born, it is no bigger than an adult human's thumb, but when it is full-grown, a red kangaroo is taller than many humans.
- Three-toed sloths usually hang upside down. In fact, when they are what we would consider right-side up, they have a hard time moving and have to drag themselves.
- Human beings cannot do a lot of things as well as some animals, but they do most things that animals can do pretty well. That is one reason they have survived so long.

Any of the skeleton pictures in this oversize book are fun to show.

Take a look at *What Do You Do When Something Wants to Eat You?* by Steve Jenkins (figure 3.15). Just paging through this book and sharing a few of the amazing defense mechanisms used by animals will guarantee an attentive audience. This is a very simple book, but one with large, colorful illustrations. Showing it will perk up a booktalk and add variety to your presentation. Here are a few examples of defense mechanisms that kids find fascinating:

- A threatened octopus squirts black ink into the water to confuse its attacker.
- Pangolins roll up into an armor-plated ball.
- A gliding frog, as its name would indicate, can glide up to 50 feet to get from one tree to another.
- The flying fish can spread its wing-like fins and glide as far as 1,000 feet over the water.

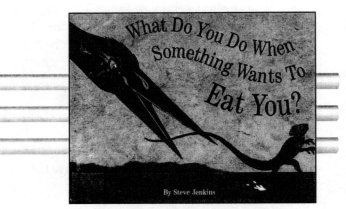

Fig. 3.15. *What Do You Do When Something Wants to Eat You?* **by Steve Jenkins**

As the above examples show, animals can ride the wind. Air is a very real environment, with currents that help both plants and animals to move. *Ride the Wind: Airborne Journeys of Animals and Plants* by Seymour Simon describes some of the ways in which animals and plants move through the air.

Animals migrate in many amazing ways, but the Arctic tern migrates farther than any other animal. Every year, the adult terns fly from the Arctic to the Antarctic and back again. This is an almost 25,000-mile trip! The small wading bird, the golden plover, also travels a long distance—almost 12,000 miles round trip from northern Canada to Argentina. One amazing fact about their journey is that young plovers travel a different route from their elders. Scientists still don't understand this completely, but it is clear that the route the plover must take changes with the age of the bird.

Monarch butterflies migrate at such regular times that towns on their route have festivals and celebrations when they arrive.

Locusts are one of the most feared migratory insects. They swarm and eat everything they can find. Swarms as huge as 50 billion insects can eat 3,000 tons of crops in one day. Farmers dread them. Show the picture of the arrival of locusts—it looks like an alien invasion.

Greylag geese in Siberia migrate to their winter home in India starting in late August. At this time, the geese cannot fly, because they are growing new tail feathers. So they *walk* for the first 100 miles! This is very dangerous, as human and animal hunters kill them easily during this time.

> After two weeks, their feathers grown in, the geese take flight to the south. If they had waited only two weeks to begin their journey, the greylags could have flown the first hundred miles in a few hours. Yet each year, they migrate in the same strange way. No one knows why.

Animal behavior never fails to fascinate, and you will learn a lot by reading Margery Facklam's *Bees Dance and Whales Sing: The Mysteries of Animal Communication.* Have you ever seen an endless trail of ants heading toward a food source? How do they find their way? Facklam tells us that they leave a trail of chemicals, called pheromones, to signal other ants. Scientists use this knowledge to catch insects by using pheromones as bait. Chapter 2 tells about dancing bees. Rather than leave pheromones as a trail, bees dance for each other to indicate the location of food. Scientists have learned how to interpret their dances and have used a tiny electronic honeybee to "talk" to a hive of bees. In one experiment the robot bee convinced 300 bees to follow its directions! Also tell your audience about Koko, the young chimpanzee who learned American Sign Language (pages 41-45).

This high-quality book with its intricate pencil drawings is not flashy, and so it might take some encouragement to get kids to check it out. But it is well worth the effort. It truly is a fascinating book that will make readers think about animals and how closely related they are to human beings.

The Really Fearsome Blood-Loving Vampire Bat and Other Creatures with Strange Eating Habits by Theresa Greenaway is a DK Publishing book with great pictures and great animal facts. Here are a few fascinating tidbits about some really yucky creatures:

- A vampire bat with a full stomach will vomit up blood to feed a hungry relative.
- Many cockroaches have stink glands that produce a disgusting smell when the insects feel threatened.
- A tsetse fly can drink three times its own weight in blood in one gulp.

Any photos in this book make for great viewing, but be sure to show the "Good Grub" spread that features grubs, maggots, and larvae. Kids will like this book for its entertainment value, but they can't help but learn a lot at the same time.

Another DK Publishing book with interesting facts is *Animal Homes* by Barbara Taylor. Intricate 3-D models show a variety of habitats from a wasp nest to a compost heap to a rotting log. "Under the Sand" (pages 30 through 32) is a particularly interesting model of life just beneath the sand. Kids will never see the beach in the same way after they find out how many creatures are beneath their feet. "Animal Lodgers" on pages 38 and 39 is also interesting. It shows how many animals find refuge in human homes. Does your house have bats in the attic, moths in the closet, bloodsucking bedbugs, and bookworms? Before you answer, read this book to find out what other creepy-crawlies might be hanging around the house.

DINOSAURS

Keeping up with all of the news about dinosaurs can be difficult. Scientists are continually making new discoveries, finding new fossils, and extending their research. We know much more about dinosaurs today than we did even five years ago. For this reason, make sure the books you present are up-to-date. When booktalking dinosaur books, you might also want to mention two fun books of dinosaur poetry: *Tyrannosaurus Was a Beast* by Jack Prelutsky and *Bone Poems* by Jeff Moss (see also chapter 2).

Some of the fun facts you will learn when you read *The New Book of Dinosaurs* by David Unwin include these:

- Tyrannosaurus Rex was "so heavy it would be badly hurt or possibly killed if it fell over while running at more than 20 mph. But Tyrannosaurus Rex didn't need to run fast—there was nothing to run from and prey could always be ambushed and killed with a single bite" (page 17).

- For about 20 years, scientists argued about how pterosaurs moved on the ground. Now, well-preserved tracks found in France and the United States in the early 1990s show that these bat-like creatures were flat-footed and walked on all fours.

- Recently, huge numbers of dinosaur eggs containing complete and well-preserved embryos at various stages of development have been discovered in central China. Discoveries like this greatly aid scientists in their studies.

- It has long been thought that sauropods ate stones and kept them in their gizzard to help grind up food. New discoveries on the Isle of Wight in Britain show that this was indeed the case.

The Dinosaur Question and Answer Book by Sylvia Funston lets us in on some more of the latest news about dinosaurs. Examples are:

- "Did dinosaurs sit on their eggs to hatch them? If you weighed more than two fat hippos, would you sit on your eggs?" (page16). The answer is no. It seems that many dinosaurs buried their eggs in bowl-shaped mounds.

- "How large were dinosaur eggs?" (page17). A nonfossilized hypselosaurus egg would have been large enough to make scrambled eggs for 36 people!

- "How much would it hurt if a plant-eating dinosaur bit you? Being bitten by parasaurolophus would hurt as much as if you stuck your fingers in an automatic food grinder. These dinosaurs didn't just have a single set of dentures. They had interlocking rows of teeth that formed a continuous grinding surface. First they'd bite, then they'd grind. Ouch!" (page 20).

- Blue whales, alive today, are the biggest animals that ever lived.

- The smallest dinosaur was the compsognathus, which "would be able to stare a rooster in the eye without bending down" (page 24).

A great way to start a booktalk is to ask the listeners how they would feel if they were walking down the street and saw a dinosaur with a paper bag over its head coming toward them. Would they be able to tell whether it was a plant-eater or a meat-eater? The answer is on page 34. Most dinosaurs that ate plants walked around on four feet. Most that ate meat walked around on two. There are, of course, a few exceptions, and it is possible that someone in the group may be aware of them, which creates a fun diversion.

This book is full of colorful pictures. Just flipping through a few of them is fun, but be sure to point out the photo on page 43, a fossil of archaeopteryx, the oldest known bird, which clearly had feathers.

Raptors! A lot of us had never heard of them until we saw *Jurassic Park*. They sure were scary in that movie. Believe it or not, it was Steven Spielberg, the movie's director, who suggested to Don Lessem that he write *Raptors! The Nastiest Dinosaurs*.

The first raptors were discovered only 80 years ago. Scientists learned that they came in many different sizes. Some of them were as small as ostriches, while others were as big as trucks. From page 6:

> Raptors are most easily recognized by their killer claws, fearsome weapons on their inside fingers and toes. Long, curved and narrow, these blades could be pulled up off the ground while the animal was moving. And, like switchblades, they could be snapped down and forward when the animal wanted to leap and slash at its victims.

While digging, one scientist found what he thought was a rib, but it turned out to be a claw of what is the biggest raptor yet discovered, the utahraptor. It was "longer than a station wagon and as heavy as a polar bear."

All raptors had long tails. They needed them so that they could keep their balance when they were attacking other animals. Not only did they kill plant-eating dinosaurs, but scientists have found evidence that raptors fought with and killed each other.

This book is crammed with interesting information about dinosaurs of all sorts and the scientists who research them. One scientist, Dr. Philip Currie, is so expert that he can identify any meat-eater from a single tooth. Another intriguing fact: More dinosaur skeletons have been found in Alberta, Canada, than in any other place on Earth.

Be sure to show the audience the illustration of the fossils of a velociraptor fighting with a protoceratops, which were found in the Gobi Desert in Mongolia, and the illustration on page 15 of the two velociraptors engaged in combat.

Kids who are really into dinosaurs are the natural audience for *How Dinosaurs Came to Be* by Patricia Lauber. While not flashy, this book is full of solid information and numerous color drawings of the earliest dinosaurs. Unlike other books about dinosaurs, this one focuses on the little-known ancestors that lived in the Permian and Triassic Periods. Along the way, Lauber gives information about paleontology—including how scientists know what they know from fossils and how they have divided time into eras and periods. Some of the animals pictured are very strange looking. It would be worth showing these to children. Half the battle is pronouncing the unfamiliar names (such as eryops and procompsognathus). You could make up a transparency of some of the names and have the kids try to figure out how to pronounce them. Then ask your audience to try to match up pictures of early dinosaurs with their names.

Dinosaurs! Strange and Wonderful by Laurence Pringle (figure 3.16) gives a basic introduction to dinosaur types and characteristics. The drawings by Carol Heyer are vivid and look sort of like graphics from a video game. The book describes many kinds of dinosaurs and gives some interesting facts. Did you know that the smallest known dinosaur, compsognathus, was the size and shape of a skinny chicken? Or that velociraptor was about the size of a wolf? And you may have thought that the front legs of the mighty tyrannosaurus were weak, but bones discovered in Montana have proven that its short arms had big muscles. Each arm was probably strong enough to lift up your mother or father! We know a lot about dinosaurs from studying fossils, but we may never know what colors they were and what sounds they made.

Fig. 3.16. *Dinosaurs! Strange and Wonderful* **by Laurence Pringle**

A book that puts dinosaurs into perspective for younger readers is *How Big Were the Dinosaurs?* by Bernard Most (figure 3.17). Every page shows a different dinosaur and a comparison of its size to something that little kids can easily understand. For example, Tyrannosaurus Rex had teeth as big as your toothbrush. Stegosaurus was so big that the plates on its back were larger than a school crossing sign. Can you believe that Diplodocus was so big it was as long as a basketball court? Playful and colorful drawings help illustrate these amazing comparisons. Once you get started, kids will want you to read the whole book to them aloud.

Fig. 3.17. *How Big Were the Dinosaurs?* **by Bernard Most**

Some kids will want more detailed dinosaur information, and they can find it in Jinny Johnson's *Prehistoric Life Explained: A Beginner's Guide to the World of Dinosaurs*. This extremely attractive book comes filled with facts and colorful illustrations and explanations. It not only tells about dinosaurs and other reptiles from the past, it explains how dinosaurs spread throughout the world, how fossils are formed, how dinosaurs might have gone extinct, and how dinosaur bones were first discovered. Show any of the colorful pictures from this book, and recommend it to inquisitive kids.

Funston, Sylvia. *The Dinosaur Question and Answer Book.* Little, Brown, 1992. 64 p. ISBN 0-316-37736-1. Grades 4-6.

Gelman, Rita Golden. *Dawn to Dusk in the Galapagos: Flightless Birds, Swimming Lizards, and Other Fascinating Creatures.* Photographs by Tui De Roy. Little, Brown, 1991. 48 p. ISBN 0-316-30739-4. Grades 4-6.

George, Jean Craighead. *The Tarantula in My Purse and 172 Other Wild Pets.* Illustrated by Jean Craighead George. HarperCollins, 1996. 134 p. ISBN 0-06-023626-4; 0-06-023627-2 (lib. bdg.). Grades 4-7.

Gibbons, Gail. *Sea Turtles.* Holiday House, 1995. 32 p. ISBN 0-8234-11915. Grades 1-3.

Goodall, Jane. *The Chimpanzee Family Book.* Photographs by Michael Neugebauer. Picture Book Studio, 1989. 64 p. ISBN 0-88708-090-1. Grades 3-6.

Greenaway, Theresa. *The Really Fearsome Blood-Loving Vampire Bat and Other Creatures with Strange Eating Habits.* DK Publishing, 1996. 18 p. ISBN 0-7894-1029-X. Grades 1-3.

Halton, Cheryl M. *Those Amazing Leeches.* Dillon Press, 1989. 120 p. ISBN 0-87518-408-1. Grades 3-6.

Jarrow, Gail, and Paul Sherman. *Naked Mole Rats.* Carolrhoda Books, 1996. 48 p. ISBN 0-87614-995-6 (lib. bdg.); 1-57505-028-5 (pbk.). Grades 3-6.

Jenkins, Priscilla Belz. *A Safe Home for the Manatees.* Illustrated by Martin Classen. HarperCollins, 1997. 32 p. ISBN 0-06-027149-3; 0-06-027150-7 (lib. bdg.); 0-06-445164-X (pbk.). Grades 1-3.

Jenkins, Steve. *What Do You Do When Something Wants to Eat You?* Houghton Mifflin, 1997. 32 p. ISBN 0-395-82514-8. Grades 1-3.

Johnson, Jinny. *Prehistoric Life Explained: A Beginner's Guide to the World of Dinosaurs.* Consultant Professor Barry Cox. Henry Holt, 1996. 69 p. ISBN 0-8050-4871-5. Grades 4-6.

————. *Skeletons: An Inside Look at Animals.* Illustrated by Elizabeth Gray. Reader's Digest Kids, 1994. 46 p. ISBN 0-89577-604-9.

Kite, L. Patricia. *Blood-Feeding Bugs and Beasts.* Millbrook Press, 1996. 48 p. ISBN 1-56294-599-8. Grades 4-6.

Landau, Elaine. *Your Pet Iguana.* Children's Press, 1997. 47 p. ISBN 0-516-20387-8 (lib. bdg.); 0-516-26267-X (pbk.). Grades 1-3.

Lauber, Patricia. *How Dinosaurs Came to Be.* Illustrated by Douglas Henderson. Simon & Schuster Books for Young Readers, 1996. 48 p. ISBN 0-689-80531-4. Grades 4-6.

————. *An Octopus Is Amazing.* Illustrated by Holly Keller. HarperCollins, 1990. 32 p. ISBN 0-690-04801-7. Grades 1-3.

Lessem, Don. *Raptors! The Nastiest Dinosaurs*. Illustrated by David Peters. Scientific Adviser Dr. Philip Currie. Little, Brown, 1996. 32 p. ISBN 0-316-52119-1. Grades 4-6.

Ling, Mary, and Mary Atkinson. *The Snake Book*. Photographs by Frank Greenaway and Dave King. DK, 1997. 28 p. ISBN 0-7894-1526-7. Grades 4-6.

MacQuitty, Miranda. *Amazing Bugs*. DK, 1996. 44 p. ISBN 0-7894-1010-9. Grades 4-6.

Maestro, Betsy. *Take a Look at Snakes*. Illustrated by Giulio Maestro. Scholastic, 1992. 40 p. ISBN 0-590-44935-4. Grades 1-4.

Markle, Sandra. *Outside and Inside Bats*. Atheneum Books for Young Readers, 1997. 40 p. ISBN 0-689-81165-9. Grades 1-5.

Martin, Patricia A. Fink. *Animals That Walk on Water*. Franklin Watts, 1997. 64 p. ISBN 0-531-20297-6 (lib. bdg.); 0-531-15896-9 (pbk.). Grades 3-5.

Matthews, Downs. *Harp Seal Pups*. Photographs by Dan Guravich. Simon & Schuster Books for Young Readers, 1997. 34 p. ISBN 0-689-80014-2. Grades 2-5.

McMillan, Bruce. *Nights of the Pufflings*. Photo-illustrated by Bruce McMillan. Houghton Mifflin, 1995. 32 p. ISBN 0-395-70810-9. Grades 1-3.

————. *Wild Flamingos*. Photo-illustrated by Bruce McMillan. Houghton Mifflin, 1997. 32 p. ISBN 0-395-84545-9. Grades 2-4.

Milton, Nancy. *The Giraffe That Walked to Paris*. Illustrated by Roger Roth. Crown, 1992. 32 p. ISBN 0-517-58132-9 (trade); 0-517-58133-7 (lib. bdg.). Grades 2-4.

Most, Bernard. *How Big Were the Dinosaurs?* Harcourt Brace, 1994. 30 p. ISBN 0-15-236800-0. Grades 1-2.

Page, Debra. *Orcas Around Me: My Alaskan Summer*. Illustrated by Leslie W. Bowman. Whitman, 1997. 40 p. ISBN 0-8075-6137-1 Grades 2-4.

Parsons, Alexandra. *Amazing Snakes*. Photographs by Jerry Young. Alfred A. Knopf, 1990. 32 p. ISBN 0-679-80225-8; 0-679-90225-2 (lib. bdg.). Grades 1-4.

Patent, Dorothy Hinshaw. *Back to the Wild*. Photographs by William Muñoz. A Gulliver Green Book/Harcourt Brace, 1997. 69 p. ISBN 0-15-200280-4. Grades 4-6.

Penner, Lucille Recht. *Monster Bugs*. Illustrated by Pamela Johnson. Random House, 1996. 48 p. ISBN 0-679-86794-3 (pbk.); 0-679-96974-8 (lib. bdg.). Grades 1-3.

Pringle, Laurence. *Dinosaurs! Strange and Wonderful*. Illustrated by Carol Heyer. Boyds Mills Press, 1995. 30 p. ISBN 1-878093-16-9. Grades 1-4.

Scott, Carey. *Puppies*. DK, 1997. 37 p. ISBN 0-7894-2133-X. Grades 3-6.

Simon, Seymour. *Ride the Wind: Airborne Journeys of Animals and Plants*. Illustrated by Elsa Warnick. Browndeer Press/Harcourt Brace, 1997. 40 p. ISBN 0-15-292887-1. Grades 2-5.

Smith, Mavis. *A Snake Mistake*. HarperCollins, 1991. 32 p. ISBN 0-06-026909-X (lib. bdg.); 0-06-107426-8 (pbk). Grades 1-3.

Taylor, Barbara. *Animal Homes*. DK Publishing, 1996. 44 p. ISBN 0-7894-1012-5. Grades 4-7.

Unwin, David. *The New Book of Dinosaurs*. Illustrated by Richard Rockwood and Rob Shone. Consultant Dr. Michael Benton. Copper Beech Books, 1997. 32 p. ISBN 0-7613-0568-8 (lib. bdg.); 0-7613-0589-0 (pbk.). Grades 4-6.

Wechsler, Doug. *Bizarre Bugs*. Photographs by Doug Wechsler. Cobblehill Books/Dutton, 1995. 35 p. ISBN 0-525-65181-0. Grades 4-6.

CHAPTER

4

Unsolved Mysteries

Who doesn't love hearing about mysteries? Who doesn't enjoy the tantalizing idea that the sleuth who someday fills in the missing pieces could be them? All the booktalks in this chapter have an element of mystery to them. Do UFOs exist? What happened to Amelia Earhart? Is there such a thing as Bigfoot? When you tell about the titles discussed in this chapter, emphasize the mysteries involved and the fun of trying to solve them. Remind kids that reading is the first step in solving any mystery or problem in life.

MISSING PERSONS AND DISAPPEARANCES

There she stands, an impish little girl sticking out her tongue and making a face at the camera. Her dress is a bit old-fashioned and elaborate, but except for that, she could be any little girl almost anywhere.

What do you suppose she grew up to be? Actually, she did *not* grow up. She was executed by a firing squad instead.

What crime had she committed? None. Her name was Anastasia, and she was a princess in Russia before the Russian Revolution. Her father was the tsar, or king, and her only crime was being his daughter. She and her parents and brother and sisters were marched to a cellar in the house where they had been imprisoned and were then shot—suddenly, cruelly, and brutally. The executioners said the bullets flew around the room, bouncing off the jewels in the women's dresses. Their bodies were dragged out and buried secretly in the night, but two of the bodies were never found. One of the missing bodies is that of one of the four princesses, perhaps Anastasia's. The other missing body is that of their only brother. He was their little brother, and he was the tsarevich—the heir to the throne.

The fascinating *Anastasia's Album* by Hugh Brewster (figure 4.1) doesn't give every detail surrounding these mysteries, but a good booktalker can certainly introduce them to an eager crowd. Just be prepared for the inevitable barrage of questions and have some other books on the Russian Revolution handy as well.

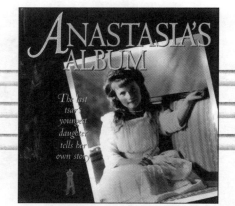

Fig. 4.1. *Anastasia's Album* by Hugh Brewster

Sky Pioneer: A Photobiography of Amelia Earhart by Corinne Szabo is one of many biographies of the most famous woman aviator of all time. Other flyers may have been as skilled as she, others in this era flew farther and did more, but her life is shrouded in mystery, and we all love a good mystery.

Amelia Earhart started out as a lucky little girl in Atchison, Kansas. Although she was born more than 100 years ago, her parents were ahead of their time and encouraged her and her sister to be inventive, independent, and imaginative. She saw her first airplane in 1905, at the Iowa State Fair.

By the time Amelia was 21, she volunteered to be a nurse's aide in Toronto, where she was visiting a friend. There was a desperate need for people to help in hospitals, for many young men were wounded and returning from World War I. She became friendly with some of the wounded pilots and watched her former patients practice flying. By the time she was 25, she owned her own airplane.

Amelia had many interests and did a lot of good things with her life, but her passion was flying. In 1932, five years after Charles Lindbergh became the first pilot to cross the Atlantic alone, Amelia became the first woman pilot to do so.

But what everyone remembers about Amelia is her disappearance. We still do not know what happened in 1937, when she and her navigator, Fred Noonan, set out on an expedition to fly around the world. By June 29, they had traveled for almost six weeks and covered 22,000 miles. But the most dangerous part of the trip was ahead of them—flying 2,556 miles over the Pacific Ocean to Howland Island, which was very tiny and hard to find. On July 2, she talked several times to a U.S. Coast Guard cutter, and then there was silence. No one has ever found a trace of the plane or of Amelia or Fred.

Read this interesting book, packed with photos, to find out more—and find out what experts think might have happened. You may be surprised!

A Picture Book of Amelia Earhart by David A. Adler is much shorter, as it is meant for younger children. Show them the cover of the book and mention that it is easier to read. Amelia is a fascinating character to children and adults of all ages.

Maybe you have been to Los Angeles, and, if so, maybe, in a very busy part of town, you have passed something called the La Brea Tar Pits. Have any of you ever seen them or heard of them? You can read about them in *Death Trap: The Story of the La Brea Tar Pits* by Sharon Elaine Thompson (figure 4.2).

Thanks to the La Brea Tar Pits, we know a lot about prehistoric life in California. The pits are full of seeping oil, or asphalt, commonly called tar. In prehistoric times, animals would sometimes get stuck in the sticky asphalt and be unable to get out. The pits were not deep, but just two inches of tar could cause an animal to get stuck. Even today, the people who work at the sites can get stuck in the tar. No one has ever gotten permanently stuck, but their shoes have!

When an animal got stuck in the tar, it became a sitting duck. Any meat-eating animals looking for a meal could see one right in front of them—one that could not run away. But the animals who went to eat it might get stuck too. Even birds who wanted to eat might get in trouble if the asphalt got in their feathers.

What all of this led to is a magnificent site where paleontologists can discover all sorts of information about what kind of animals lived in California. What were their lives like? What did they eat? Did they migrate, or did they live in one place all of their lives? Because the oil has preserved animal bones—and some DNA—wonderfully, many of these mysteries have been solved, but other questions remain unanswered. One big mystery that remains unsolved is the partial skeleton of La Brea Woman, who died about 9,000 years ago. How did she get to be in the pit? She appears to have been buried there. Wouldn't you like to solve the mystery?

Fig. 4.2. *Death Trap: The Story of the La Brea Tar Pits* **by Sharon Elaine Thompson**

Like the tar pits, peat bogs can preserve living things from the past. Find out about them in *Bodies from the Bog* by James M. Deem (figure 4.3). A bog is an area that was once a shallow lake. Centuries ago, the lake lost its water source and became a stagnant pool. The reeds growing around the lake decayed, falling in the pool and eventually filling up the lake. Sphagnum moss began to grow and build up its own layers of peat. Sphagnum moss is an amazing substance, one that was used for bandages as recently as World War I. It prevents the growth of bacteria. When bacteria do not grow, bodies do not decay the way they normally would.

Over the centuries many preserved bodies have been found in the peat bogs of Britain and northern Europe. Some of the bodies are thousands of years old, with parts of them still in good condition. Show your audience the frontispiece of the Tollund man. The bodies were usually found by workers who were digging up the peat, which is used for fuel. Some of the bodies were at first mistaken for people who had died fairly recently.

Scientists believe that most of the bodies in the bogs were thrown in as human sacrifices. Tollund man, who looks so peaceful, was hanged, as the rope still wrapped around his neck proves. We do not know enough about the people who made the sacrifices to know how people were selected to be sacrificed or why they were sacrificed.

We do know that it is unlikely that any more peat bodies will be found. Machines are now doing the work once done by human beings, and by the time a body is discovered it has been cut into many, many pieces.

Read this fascinating book with its incredible photos to find out more about other objects that have been found in the bogs.

Fig. 4.3. *Bodies from the Bog* by James M. Deem

Several books describe one of the most famous mysteries in American history, one that still tantalizes us today. To get kids interested in the "Lost Colony," use *The Roanoke Missing Persons Case* by Anita Larsen or *Roanoke: The Story of the Lost Colony* by Peter I. Bosco. What, we wonder, became of the Roanoke colony? It was a colony of English settlers in America, founded in 1587 on Roanoke Island, off the coast of what is now North Carolina. It consisted of a group of almost 100 colonists, and their timing was awful. They did not have enough food to last the winter, and it was too late in the season to plant new crops. Despite the fact that his daughter, Eleanor Dare, was one of the colonists, and his granddaughter, Virginia Dare, was the first white child born in an English colony in America, Governor Edward White left them to return to England for supplies. Unfortunately, circumstances prevented him from returning before three years had passed, and when he returned, the people were gone. Vanished! Yes, there were traces, but they did not reveal much. The fort where the colonists had lived was undamaged, with no signs of a struggle. White had instructed them to carve a cross someplace if there was ever any trouble, but no cross was carved. They had taken the time to bury three chests he had left behind for safekeeping.

The biggest clue was a word—CROATAN—carved on a tree. Croatan was a small island nearby, but there were no settlers there. What on earth could have happened? Were the colonists killed by Native Americans? Did they go live with the Native Americans? Rumors of blue-eyed people among the natives persisted for centuries. Could the Spaniards, with whom the English were at war at this time, have killed them? Read about this intriguing story and decide what *you* think must have happened.

People are reported missing at sea fairly frequently. Perhaps the most famous missing sailors are the crew of the *Mary Celeste*. In 1872, a British ship in the middle of the ocean spotted a strange-looking ship. Some of its sails were missing, and no one could be seen on board. Three sailors decided to investigate.

Although the ship was in fine shape, it had obviously been abandoned in great haste by its crew, who left even their pipes and tobacco on board. Only the lifeboat was missing. But *why*? There were no signs of a struggle. Did a giant sea monster attack and destroy the crew? Did pirates attack the ship? Could aliens have abducted the crew? No one knows. When will we ever find out? Both this mystery and the next one are discussed in several books, including Seymour Simon's *Strange Mysteries from Around the World* and Catherine O'Neill's *Amazing Mysteries of the World*.

Another intriguing disappearance involves something that is almost certainly *there*—but no one can get at it. Oak Island, off the coast of Nova Scotia, is the site of a mystery that has eluded the most intrepid of detectives for more than 200 years.

In the late 1700s, a teenage boy discovered a sunken pit underneath a huge oak tree that had the remains of a pulley on one of its branches. Certain that pirates must have buried treasure there, Dan McGinnis returned the next day with two of his friends to dig. At 10 feet down they found a platform. At 20 feet down and 30 feet down they found more platforms. In fact, there was a platform every 10 feet! They dug for nine years before they formed a company. When they reached 95 feet down, the pit flooded. And it has done so ever since. Every new attempt at finding whatever is down there fails because the hole floods, no matter how creative and inventive the searchers are about constructing and managing the digging.

For 200 years people have been digging, planning, and investing in trying to find out what is at the bottom of what has become known as "The Money Pit." Franklin Delano Roosevelt invested in the project. Five men have died trying to find out what is in the pit. No one seems to be any closer to finding out what is down there than they were 200 years ago. Theories range from pirate treasure (unlikely, as the engineering involved, including the construction of an artificial beach on the island, is too sophisticated), to the French crown jewels, the treasure of the Knights Templar, proof that Frances Bacon was Shakespeare, and the Holy Grail. Who will ever figure out a way to retrieve what is buried there? Will it be you? Or someone else in this room?

Simon's book also includes chapters on "The Big Bang in Siberia" (which many now think was a meteorite crash), fire walking, and the mysterious Crystal Skull (pictured on the book's front cover, and a fine and perturbing skull it is).

If you have ever been interested in seeing or finding lost treasures, *The Children's Atlas of Lost Treasures* by Struan Reid is the book for you. Some of the treasures described have been found, but the locations of many others remain a mystery. We believe or even know that treasures are missing, but we do not know where to find them.

Take a look at the Scythian tomb on page 21. This was a truly amazing discovery. In 1929, Russian archaeologists went to look at a burial mound in eastern Russia. Burial mounds, by the way, are raised areas in the ground. They have often been an excellent source of treasure. This mound, in Siberia, proved to be difficult to open. The archaeologists had to use boiling water to get through the frozen earth. The bad news: The tomb they found had already been robbed, probably shortly after the mound had been made, more than 2,400 years before. The good news: Those robbers had left holes in the roof of the tomb. Water had poured in and promptly frozen solid, preserving everything there, including a Persian carpet— the oldest carpet ever discovered. An excellent cutaway drawing shows the tomb.

You never know when you might accidentally find treasure. In Britain, a farmer found some metal objects sticking out of the earth as he was plowing. Eventually, he and his helper found 34 pieces of ancient Roman silver, the most incredible Roman treasure hoard ever found in Britain. Read about the Treasures of Mildenhall on page 40.

Of course, pirate treasure is always worth looking for. It seems that many pirates were good at hiding the things they stole. The treasure of the ship *Mary Dear* is supposedly buried on Cocos Island off the coast of Panama. Why hasn't anyone ever been able to find it, or to find the treasure of Captain Kidd?

Almost half of the ships in the famous Spanish Armada sank in the terrible naval battle off the coast of England, but few have been recovered. Wouldn't it be great to be the person who found one? Reid's book also talks about one of the most famous mysteries of all, the mystery of the lost city of Atlantis, and some mysterious treasures in the United States, as well.

Wouldn't everyone like to find these buried treasures? *How to Hunt Buried Treasure* by James M. Deem (figure 4.4) tells you how to get started. Do you know the best place to start? *In the library!* No one is going to find any buried treasure by simply starting to dig. You have to have a rough idea of what you are looking for and where it might be. The best way to find that out is by reading about it. What treasures, real or imaginary, are undiscovered? Pirate treasure? Ransom money? What treasures do we know are missing? The library can tell you where to start. This book gives you step-by-step techniques for finding treasure, and it also tells the true story of the Oak Island buried treasure.

Fig. 4.4. *How to Hunt Buried Treasure* by James M. Deem

Strangely enough, sometimes whole civilizations can disappear, leaving modern people to wonder what happened to them. The Mayans, who lived in southern Mexico and Central America, once had a civilization that rivaled the achievement of the ancient Egyptians and the ancient Greeks. But they left behind a mystery. What happened to that civilization? Scientists and archaeologists are learning more all the time, but many questions remain unanswered. Find out about the disappearance of the Mayans in *The Mystery of the Ancient Maya* by Carolyn Meyer and Charles Gallenkamp.

Much of the exploration of the ruins of the Mayan cities began in 1839 with two interested adventurers, an Englishman, Frederick Catherwood, and an American, John Lloyd Stephens. Their first discovery was of the ancient city of Copan. They *bought* it! They bought the whole city for $50, and that was just the beginning of their discoveries. Many others were to follow and to find much, much more.

A great deal of what we know about the Mayans came from a man who hated them. This man was a bishop, one of the Spanish monks who was sent to live in the Mayan area in 1549. He wrote a long account of their traditions and history, while, at the same time, burning many of their written accounts of that tradition and that history. But even today we rely on what he knew.

We know the Mayans believed in human sacrifice, and some of the mysteries we still want to solve concern that. Some of the ways they sacrificed people were brutal and horrifying in any age.

Read this absorbing book to find out more about these people, whose descendants are still alive—and still live in homes much like the homes of their Mayan ancestors.

Find out about the disappearance of another group of people in Susan E. Goodman's *Stones, Bones, and Petroglyphs: Digging into Southwest Archaeology*. A lot of people would like to go on an archaeological dig. Who knows what you might dig up? Or what you might learn about the place where you were digging? Wouldn't it be great if your whole class could help on an archaeological dig? This is what happened to an eighth-grade class from Hannibal, Missouri. They spent a week in Colorado studying the people who lived in the pueblos and helping the archaeologists who were excavating the cliff dwellings. The Pueblo people used to be called Anasazi, but it is a word that means "enemy of our people" and was given to them by the Navajo. So descendants of the Pueblo people do not like that word.

The eighth graders learned a lot, including that many mysteries remain. Some, perhaps, may one day be solved—but not yet. The people who lived in the cliff dwellings went to enormous lengths to construct them, but they lived there for only a few years before they disappeared. What happened to them? Did they leave voluntarily? Were they forced to leave? No one knows, although there are many theories. This book is colorful and fun to look through. The cover itself is good to show a group.

Disappearances such as the ones highlighted in this section are fascinating to young and old alike. Kids who read these books and want to learn more might like to read *Vanishings*, part of a Time–Life series called the "Library of Curious and Unusual Facts." While not specifically written for children, *Vanishings* would be appropriate for middle or high school students. It contains 127 pages of short stories of true disappearances. Many of the vanishings described are of human beings, but the book also tells about the millions of packages that the U.S. Postal Service can't deliver, a dog that swallowed a Rolex watch, and a postcard sent during World War I that was delivered in 1981. One chapter of the book tells how magicians perform their most famous tricks, and another deals with extinction.

UNEXPLAINED PHENOMENA

ESP, UFOs, ghostly lights, alligators in sewers, Bigfoot, living dinosaurs, giant squid, spontaneous human combustion. . . . These are just some of the unexplained phenomena of the world that fascinate children (and adults) and can be a lot of fun to read about. Although they may circulate frequently, children's books about these topics sometimes are not of the highest quality. This can be frustrating when kids really want to know the facts. Look to the books in this section for truthful and entertaining accounts of unexplained phenomena.

An authoritative source of information about a wide range of unexplained happenings is a three-volume set published by UXL (an imprint of Gale Research). *Strange & Unexplained Happenings: When Nature Breaks the Rules of Science* edited by Jerome Clark and Nancy Pear deals with physical (as opposed to psychic) phenomena. It calls them anomalies and defines them as "human experiences that go against common sense and break the rules that science uses to describe our world."

This very thorough set of books deals with an amazing range of topics. Volume 1 covers UFOs, interplanetary communication, other worlds, government cover-ups, vanishings, light shows, strange showers from the sky, and unusual weather events. Volume 2 deals with unexpected and misplaced animals, shaggy two-footed creatures (Bigfoot, Yeti, and others), living dinosaurs, and other fantastic creatures. Monsters of the deep, living folklore, and other strange events are discussed in Volume 3.

This set will appeal to middle school kids with a strong interest in the unexplained. The size of the books won't intimidate them if they are truly fascinated by the subject. After they have read all the library books about Bigfoot (or UFOs, etc.), point them to these books for even more information. Each one includes a glossary, a table of contents covering the whole set, and numerous illustrations.

Children of all ages are fascinated by UFOs and the idea of life forms on other planets. *The Mystery of UFOs* by Judith Herbst starts out by telling us about the only official landing strip for flying saucers. It is a long, straight highway in Nevada, and four big signs along the road invite any aliens who may be in the vicinity to land there.

All throughout history, and in legends from many lands, people have wondered about and recorded the strange things they saw in the skies. We still do not know what it was they saw, and we certainly are not sure what people who believe they see aliens or alien spacecraft are seeing today. Maybe there really are aliens. Maybe a lot of people have been kidnapped by them. We just don't know.

Some of the more famous UFO incidents, such as the one reported in Roswell, New Mexico, are retold here in a fun and interesting fashion. If you are interested in UFOs (and face it, who isn't?), you'll have a good time reading this one.

Herbst's book features several large color illustrations. Fun ones to show include the second double-page spread and the second-to-the-last double-page spread.

Another good UFO book, this one aimed at older children, is *ETs and UFOs: Are They Real?* by Larry Kettelkamp. This book presents well-documented encounters with UFOs and extraterrestrial beings and lets the reader determine their authenticity. The NASA photo of a large human face on the surface of Mars (page 10) is an eye-catcher, and makes a good introduction to the book.

Kids probably will be most fascinated by the tales of alien abduction in chapter 3 of Kettelkamp's book. Read or tell them what happened to teenagers Michael and Janet on pages 54-59. The two camp counselors were watching the sunset from a boat dock when a series of bright lights began to zigzag across the sky. The UFOs came closer, and inside they saw small childlike figures with large heads, long necks, and eyes extending beyond the sides of their heads. A bright light shone down, and Michael and Janet felt themselves floating upward. Their next memory was of lying on the dock. It wasn't until five years later that Michael recalled what happened in the UFO. Under hypnosis both Michael and Janet reported similar details of their abduction. Read this story, and it just might make a believer out of you!

Michael and Janet's story is also told in *How to Catch a Flying Saucer* by James M. Deem. This book doesn't have flashy pictures to show, but like other books by the author, it is loaded with information and is great fun to read. Deem makes it clear that although UFOs exist, they are not necessarily from outer space. They are simply unidentified objects seen in the sky. Read this book and you will learn about UAPs (unidentified atmospheric phenomena), IFOs (identified flying objects), and TRUFOs (real unidentified flying objects or "True UFOs").

We've all heard of close encounters of the third kind, but do you know what a close encounter of the first, second, or fourth kind is? Read chapter 4 (page 47) of *How to Catch a Flying Saucer* to find out. Michael and Janet's experience was a close encounter of the fourth kind, and their story begins on page 55. This book also tells kids how they can become a UFOlogist (the first step is to read all the UFO books you can find). Readers who enjoy this book will enjoy the other books by James Deem, including *How to Read Your Mother's Mind*, *How to Find a Ghost*, and *How to Hunt Buried Treasure*.

The Loch Ness Monster by Elaine Landau tells about a mysterious creature reported to be seen in Scotland. The Scottish word for "Lake" is "Loch." Loch Ness is a huge lake in Scotland, about a mile wide by 24 miles long. It is so deep that you could fit three times as many men, women, and children as live *in the world* inside it!

Now, finding something that lives in a lake that big is not an easy thing to do. But for centuries, stories have circulated that a very strange and very large creature lives in that lake. No one knows for sure if those stories are true!

There are a lot of theories about what the Loch Ness monster might be. About 12,000 years ago, there was an Ice Age, and Scotland was flooded. Sea animals swam everywhere. When the ice melted, some of those animals might have stayed in the lakes that were formed, and perhaps some of them were able to survive in those lakes. If it does exist, the "monster" that lives in Loch Ness today might very well be a descendant of those sea animals, perhaps of plesiosaurs, water-dwelling dinosaurs. Could Nessie, as the Loch Ness monster is called, be a dinosaur?

However, some people think it is just an otter. And some people think it is just a lie.

Lots of people have photographed what they thought was the monster. Some of the photos were mistakes. What was photographed could easily be explained and was not a monster. Other photographs were better—but might have been faked. (People might have faked them with computers in the last few years.) Scientists have studied the lake but feel no certainty that a monster exists, although there are some indications that it might. The most famous photo ever taken of Nessie is on page 30, and a color sketch of Nessie on page 9 is also fun to show.

Read this fun book to find out the theories so that you can decide for yourself.

Sasquatch: Wild Man of North America and *Yeti: Abominable Snowman of the Himalayas*, both by Elaine Landau, can be easily paired together, for the mysteries involved are remarkably similar. In every single state but Rhode Island and Hawaii, mysterious sightings of strange beasts have been reported, and equally mysterious sightings have been reported in the Himalayan mountains in Asia.

What do people see? Usually a giant hairy being, maybe eight feet tall, that seems almost human. In North America, it is called Sasquatch, a Native American name taken from a creature in Native American legends. It is also called Bigfoot because footprints have been found that are at least one and one-half times the size of normal human feet. In the Himalayas, it is called Yeti or, in a garbled version of what the natives there call it, the Abominable Snowman.

A man named Albert Ostman was hunting for gold near Vancouver Island in 1924 and set up a campsite. One night he was astounded to realized that someone or something was dragging his sleeping bag along the ground—with him in it! He figured he was dragged along rocky ground for about 25 miles. When he was let out, he was surrounded by a Sasquatch family—a father, mother, son, and daughter.

He escaped after six days. The Sasquatch family never threatened or harmed him, but he was so afraid people would make fun of him that he kept his story a secret for 33 years. In 1957, he swore before a justice of the peace that his story was true—and people who knew him said he was an honest man.

Many people claimed to have seen Sasquatches in the 1970s, and one very famous photograph of them was taken. Show this photo (page 33) to your audience. A lot of people think the photograph and the stories are fake, and no real proof exists that Sasquatches are real. However, a lot of reliable, honest people claim to have seen them. Read this book and see what you think.

Stories of the Yeti have been told in the Himalayas for centuries. Parents would tell their children that the Yeti might get them if they were not good. In 1921, a group of British mountain climbers saw big tracks. The natives who were helping them told them the tracks belonged to the "Wild Man of the Snows." This was incorrectly translated into English as the "Abominable Snowman."

In 1938, an explorer claimed to have been rescued and cared for by a Yeti. As in the case of the Sasquatch, Yeti footprints have been found (show the photo on page 33), but also like the Sasquatch sightings, no one has been able to prove anything. Still, some scientists think Yetis might really exist. What do you think?

Wouldn't you just love to know what your mother is thinking? *How to Read Your Mother's Mind* by James M. Deem (figure 4.5) has an intriguing title and an eye-catching cover—just showing the book will delight your audience.

What the book is really about is extrasensory perception, or ESP. Maybe you have it. Did you ever know who was calling you before you picked up the phone? This book offers a fun look at what ESP is and is not, and gives several interesting tests to see if you or your friends have ESP.

Deem's book also describes some true stories involving ESP. Read the one in the box on page 55 about the pilot who was practicing some maneuvers in the air. She kept having a feeling that something was wrong on the ground. Finally, she stopped practicing and gave in to her instinct. She flew 70 miles off course until she saw a car that had gone off a deserted road. She landed the plane, ran to the car, and pulled an unconscious woman from behind the wheel. As she dragged the woman away, the car burst into flames. She laid the woman down and only then realized that the woman was her mother. Read this intriguing book to find out more.

Fig. 4.5. *How to Read Your Mother's Mind* by James M. Deem

In 1922, Howard Carter made one of the most incredible discoveries of all time. He found the tomb of an Egyptian pharaoh, a tomb that had been almost undisturbed for thousands of years.

Why was this incredible? Well, ever since pharaohs were buried with wonderful, expensive goods all around them, robbers had been stealing the treasure. Robbers were very good at getting into supposedly sealed tombs and taking whatever they wanted. Not much was left for explorers to find. But this tomb had barely been disturbed. Almost all of the beautiful treasures were still there. The mummy was that of a young pharaoh named Tutankhamen.

The world went mad for "King Tut," and one of the things that so interested everybody was that many believe a series of very strange events followed the opening of that tomb. They say that 30 people directly or indirectly involved with opening that tomb died within the next 10 years, many in very mysterious ways. People began to wonder if there was a curse in that tomb, if the people who opened it were cursed!

Read *The Curse of Tutankhamen* by Elaine Landau to find out the amazing theories of how that could happen. Perhaps the very walls of the tomb were poisoned. Be sure to show the group the color pictures on pages 16 and 17 of some of the beautiful treasures.

The Magic Detectives: Join Them in Solving Strange Mysteries! by Joe Nickell presents a different approach to unsolved mysteries—it solves them! Many mysteries discussed in other books are explained here. The question is: Do you agree with the explanations? Read almost any section aloud to your audience. (The sections are brief, usually two or three short pages.) Then flip the book over to read the explanation at the end.

Some mysteries discussed are those of the Holy Shroud, Uri Geller, Bigfoot, UFO Creatures, the Amityville Horror, and Ancient Astronauts. Kids will definitely have fun with this book.

GHOSTS AND URBAN LEGENDS

Do you believe in ghosts? Lots of people would rather not! But many people believe that ghosts exist. Find out more about them in Elaine Landau's book *Ghosts*.

Ghosts are spirits of people who have died. Believers feel that they are somehow blocked from reaching their final destination, be it heaven or someplace else. Some ghosts are thought to be people who were brutally murdered, or whose bodies were either never buried or were buried improperly, and some are thought to be people who were genuinely evil when alive. Theories abound as to why dead people become ghosts.

This book tells many stories about people who have seen ghosts. It includes a chapter about poltergeists (ghosts that move things around and make loud noises) and even information about ghost hunters who have actually talked to ghosts! Show the color photo from the movie *Poltergeist* on page 21.

Many people throughout the ages have tried to find ways to bring the dead back to life. In *Raising the Dead*, Daniel Cohen tells about such attempts, and he lists his top 10 favorite horror movies on the subject.

Maybe the most famous dead person of all is Frankenstein's monster, although many people just call him plain old Frankenstein. Mary Shelley wrote the story that became so famous, but there really is a Castle Frankenstein, and who knows what happened there? Some people think that Shelley based her story on the life of Konrad Dippel, who according to legend, did all sorts of amazing things.

Cohen's book also tells about the mummy's curse; small people who reportedly were grown in the 1700s; people who found the secret (or were cursed with the secret) of everlasting life; and some very talented embalmers who were able to make dead people last a long time, looking almost normal. He describes the "Resurrectionists," grave robbers who stole freshly buried corpses so that medical students could dissect and study them.

Maybe the most mysterious dead people of all are the zombies. There does seem to be some scientific basis for people being turned into zombies to be slaves to others. Cohen gives us some theories as to how this could happen. What do you think? Read it and decide for yourself. This book has a fine cover to display to the group.

Probably the person who has been "seen" the most times since his death is Elvis Presley, who died in 1977. Read about him in *The Ghost of Elvis and Other Celebrity Spirits* by Daniel Cohen. Cohen describes some strange encounters that people believe they had with him or his ghost, and he includes stories about other famous people who also were "seen" after they died.

You will enjoy the story of a man who picked up a hitchhiker who turned out to be Elvis in 1980 (Is it true or not? You decide), the story of the appearance of Elvis's face in a pantry door, and other good tales. Celebrity ghosts besides Elvis include Mary Surratt, who was hanged for being involved in the assassination of President Lincoln, although a lot of people felt she was not guilty; Edgar Allan Poe, who supposedly haunts the streets of Baltimore and the churchyard where he is buried; and George Reeves, who played Superman on television. There are great stories about Mark Twain, Harry Houdini, and General Patton. Patton believed in reincarnation and did some startling things that show he may have lived centuries before. It's a fun read! Make up your own mind—are ghosts real or not?

Cohen, a prolific writer of ghost tales, has published numerous books that appeal to young readers. Has a ghost ever warned you that something terrible was about to happen? In fact (or in fiction at least) warnings seem to be among the most frequent remarks of ghosts. Find out about some of these warnings in *Ghostly Warnings* by Daniel Cohen. Learn about "the fetch"—a fetch is *you*, or at least your ghostly double. Seeing a fetch is not usually a good thing because a fetch has usually come to fetch you, but seeing your own double can also be very helpful. There is a story in this book about a man who saw his double twice, and both times his double saved him and the people he was with from being killed.

A good selection to read to a group is a very brief retelling of the legend "An Appointment in Samarra," on pages 62 and 63. The stories in this book are short and fairly easy to read, and the appealing topic should attract readers.

Kids who are interested in ghosts might want to do some ghost hunting on their own. Find out how in James M. Deem's *How to Find a Ghost*. Deem tells about the six most common types of ghosts and the best places to look for them. He says that the best place to start is a haunted house. The second best place to start searching is at your library in the local history room. Deem's book is full of tips and suggestions, lists of equipment, and even instructions on how to write a ghost report. This book is great fun to read and will certainly encourage curious young people to look for ghosts of their own.

Many ghost stories are actually folklore, and have been told for hundreds of years in various forms. Another type of folklore, one that is wildly popular with adolescents, is the urban legend. Urban legends are modern-day stories that people tell around campfires, at slumber parties, and at work or school. Tellers of urban legends usually claim that they are true and that they happened to a friend of a friend, or someone in a nearby town. Scholars say that they reflect our culture's deepest fears, but kids like them because they are scary or gross or funny. Daniel Cohen has collected these stories in *Southern Fried Rat & Other Gruesome Tales*. Introduce your middle school audience to any of these stories. Kids will especially love the food stories on pages 9-15. Read about the boy who found a decomposed mouse in his soda or the finger that got ground up with hamburger meat. The book is full of good read-alouds and attention-getting stories. Tell some urban legends that you have heard yourself and ask if kids know of any of these stories. If you like this book, Cohen has another collection of urban legends called *The Headless Roommate and Other Tales of Terror*. These books are excellent choices for middle or high school students who don't normally choose to read.

BIBLIOGRAPHY

Adler, David A. *A Picture Book of Amelia Earhart*. Illustrated by Jeff Fisher. Holiday House, 1998. 32 p. ISBN 0-8234-1315-2. Grades 2-4.

Bosco, Peter I. *Roanoke: The Story of the Lost Colony*. The Millbrook Press, 1992. 72 p. ISBN 1-56294-111-9. Grades 4-8.

Brewster, Hugh. *Anastasia's Album*. Hyperion Books for Children, 1996. 64 p. ISBN 0-7868-0292-8. Grades 4-7.

Clark, Jerome, and Nancy Pear (editors). *Strange & Unexplained Happenings: When Nature Breaks the Rules of Science*. UXL (an imprint of Gale Research), 1995. 372 p. (in three volumes). ISBN 0-8103-9780-3 (set); 0-8103-9781-1 (vol. 1); 0-8103-9782-X (vol. 2); 0-8103-9889-3 (vol. 3). Grades 6-up.

Cohen, Daniel. *The Ghost of Elvis and Other Celebrity Spirits*. G. P. Putnam's Sons, 1994. 100 p. ISBN 0-399-22611-7. Grades 4-6.

———. *Ghostly Warnings*. Illustrated by David Linn. Cobblehill Books, 1996. 64 p. ISBN 0-525-65227-2. Grades 4-6.

———. *The Headless Roommate and Other Tales of Terror*. Illustrated by Peggy Brier. M. Evans, 1980. 128 p. ISBN 0-87131-327-8. Grades 6-up.

———. *Raising the Dead*. Cobblehill Books/Dutton, 1997. 151 p. ISBN 0-525-65255-8. Grades 4-8.

———. *Southern Fried Rat & Other Gruesome Tales*. Illustrated by Peggy Brier. M. Evans, 1983. 128 p. ISBN 0-87131-400-2. Grades 6-up.

Deem, James M. *Bodies from the Bog*. Houghton Mifflin, 1998. 42 p. ISBN 0-395-85784-8. Grades 4-6.

———. *How to Catch a Flying Saucer*. Illustrated by True Kelley. Houghton Mifflin, 1991. 192 p. ISBN 0-395-51958-6. Grades 5-7.

———. *How to Find a Ghost*. Illustrated by True Kelley. Houghton Mifflin, 1988. 137 p. ISBN 0-395-46846-9. Grades 5-7.

———. *How to Hunt Buried Treasure*. Illustrated by True Kelley. Houghton Mifflin, 1992. 192 p. ISBN 0-395-58799-9. Grades 4-7.

———. *How to Read Your Mother's Mind*. Illustrated by True Kelley. Houghton Mifflin, 1994. 192 p. ISBN 0-395-62426-6. Grades 4-7.

Goodman, Susan E. *Stones, Bones, and Petroglyphs: Digging into Southwest Archaeology.* Photographs by Michael J. Doolittle. Atheneum Books for Young People, 1998. 48 p. ISBN 0-689-81121-7. Grades 4-6.

Herbst, Judith. *The Mystery of UFOs.* Illustrated by Greg Clarke. Atheneum Books for Young Readers, 1997. 32 p. ISBN 0-6893-1652-6. Grades 2-4.

Kettelkamp, Larry. *ETs and UFOs: Are They Real?* Morrow Junior Books, 1996. 86 p. ISBN 0-688-12868-8. Grades 5-8.

Landau, Elaine. *The Curse of Tutankhamen.* The Millbrook Press, 1996. 48 p. ISBN 0-7613-0014-7. Grades 3-6.

————. *Ghosts.* The Millbrook Press, 1995. 48 p. ISBN 1-56294-544-0. Grades 3-6.

————. *The Loch Ness Monster.* The Millbrook Press, 1993. 48 p. ISBN 1-56294-347-2. Grades 3-6.

————. *Sasquatch: Wild Man of North America.* The Millbrook Press, 1993. 48 p. ISBN 1-56294-348-0. Grades 3-6.

————. *Yeti: Abominable Snowman of the Himalayas.* The Millbrook Press, 1993. 48 p. ISBN 1-56294-349-9. Grades 3-6.

Larsen, Anita. *The Roanoke Missing Person's Case.* Illustrated by James Watling. Crestwood House, 1992. 48 p. ISBN 0-89686-619-X. Grades 4-6.

Meyer, Carolyn, and Charles Gallenkamp. *The Mystery of the Ancient Maya.* Revised edition. Margaret K. McElderry Books, 1995. 179 p. ISBN 0-689-50619-8. Grades 6-up.

Nickell, Joe. *The Magic Detectives: Join Them in Solving Strange Mysteries!* Illustrated by Joe Nickell. Prometheus Books, 1989. 115 p. ISBN 0-87975-547-4 (pbk.). Grades 4-7.

O'Neill, Catherine. *Amazing Mysteries of the World.* National Geographic Society, 1983. 104 p. ISBN 0-87044-497-2 (trade); 0-87044-502-2 (lib. bdg.). Grades 4-7.

Reid, Struan. *The Children's Atlas of Lost Treasures.* The Millbrook Press, 1997. 96 p. ISBN 0-7613-0219-0. Grades 5-8.

Simon, Seymour. *Strange Mysteries from Around the World.* Morrow Junior Books, 1997. 58 p. ISBN 0-688-14636-8. Grades 4-6.

Szabo, Corinne. *Sky Pioneer: A Photobiography of Amelia Earhart.* National Geographic Society, 1997. 64 p. ISBN 0-7922-3737-4. Grades 4-7.

Thompson, Sharon Elaine. *Death Trap: The Story of the La Brea Tar Pits.* Lerner, 1995. 72 p. ISBN 0-8225-2851-7. Grades 4-6.

Vanishings. Time-Life Books, 1990. 127 p. ISBN 0-8094-7687-8; 0-8094-7688-6 (lib. bdg.). Grades 6-up.

CHAPTER 5

Science and Fun Experiments to Do

EXPERIMENTS AND ACTIVITIES

If you're looking for science experiments and activities, start with Vicki Cobb's books. She has written numerous fun titles that will get kids (and booktalkers) experimenting. Some of her best include *Bet You Can! Science Possibilities to Fool You* and *Bet You Can't! Science Impossibilities to Fool You* (both co-written with Kathy Darling), *Magic . . . Naturally! Science Entertainments & Amusements*, and *Wanna Bet? Science Challenges to Fool You*.

These four books are loaded with fun scientific tricks, many of which can be used in front of almost any audience. Try some of these from *Bet You Can!* On page 18 you will find directions for hanging a spoon on the end of your nose, complete with an assurance that some people can "hang spoon" for several hours. This is particularly effective just before lunchtime. Page 30 gives directions for balancing a sheet of newspaper on its edge, and page 41 tells how to stuff a full glass of water with cotton balls—and not spill any water. Page 74 explains how you can keep a Ping–Pong ball in the air for an hour . . . with no hands! The answer is pretty easy:

Use a hair dryer. Directions on page 102 explain how to pass your body through a three-by-five-inch card. All of these are great fun, but for a guaranteed crowd pleaser, you cannot top the trick on page 87.

Here's what you do: Ask a volunteer from the audience to come up front and sit facing you, and sideways to the audience, on a chair. The chair should fit the volunteer, so if only adult-size chairs are available, pick a tall child. Tell the child to sit straight up, back against the chair, feet flat on the floor, and hands in lap. Then, gently pressing your finger against his or her forehead, tell him or her to stand up. Your volunteer will not be able to do it, although many will try to cheat by moving the back, the hands, or the feet. The reason:

> Your friend is now a prisoner at your fingertip. In a resting position, the center of gravity of the body (the point at which all weight seems to be centered) is located over the place where it rests (the base). In a seated position the center of gravity is in the seat. In order to stand, the center of gravity must shift to the feet. The head must move forward to make this shift. The slight pressure against the forehead is just enough to keep your friend sitting tight.

Advise the children that this is a great trick to do on anyone who is bigger than they are. Then watch them try it on each other!

In *Bet You Can't!* a similar trick is on page 19, with one minor difference. Instead of pressing a finger against the volunteer's forehead, ask the volunteer to fold his or her hands across the chest. Again, the old center of gravity law kicks in. The volunteer can't get up.

Pages 56 and 57 offer a couple of fun tricks to use with a funnel. Try to blow a candle out through a funnel and try to blow a Ping-Pong ball out of the funnel.

Page 111 describes an interesting example of the powerlessness of the ring finger, demonstrated to people who work with children on a regular basis whenever "Where is Thumbkin?" is sung. If you hold a penny between your two ring fingers, as demonstrated in the sketch on the same page, it is impossible to slide your fingers apart and drop the penny.

Some good number tricks begin on page 115, starting with "Bet you can't write this number down! Get a pencil and paper. You have ten seconds. Ready? Write this number . . . eleven thousand, eleven hundred, and eleven." Answer: 12,111. Read the book to find out why.

A great favorite is the one on page 75: "Bet you can't fold a sheet of paper in half more than nine times!" Challenge the kids to do this, but make sure they fold it *in half*, not just over and over. It truly is impossible. By the seventh fold, you are working with 128 separate sheets, almost like folding a book.

Magic . . . Naturally! presents some tricks that you can do in front of an audience. There is a certain kind of child who will pore over this title. Many of the tricks presented can be set up in advance and done with small groups on the spur of the moment. The very simple "Writhing Snake" trick on pages 74-76 is wonderfully effective, as are the electrostatic tricks on pages 90-94. "Quick Money," which tests reaction time, may require a small amount of practice but works well. Neither "The Clinging Cup" on pages 40-43 nor "Drag Race" on pages 48-50 requires much preparation, and "Intelligent Eggs" on pages 58-62 is great fun. A trick like one of these can really spice up a booktalk.

Showing the children these tricks and promising more great ideas in the books is a great way to get kids interested in reading and in science.

Wanna Bet? Science Challenges to Fool You includes, on page 17, directions for a simple way to get rid of a red nose in the winter. All you have to do is rub your ears!

> Your nose becomes colder than the rest of your face because it sticks out. Blood rushes in to warm it up, making it red. Rubbing makes blood rush to your ears. They steal the nearest blood, which, when you're cold, happens to be in your nose. Someone should have told Rudolph.

On page 18 are directions for a trick you can easily do in front of a classroom—leaning against a wall with your head, you will be unable to stand up if you follow the directions. Page 22 offers another good trick to use in front of a room—balance a yardstick on your two hands and then slowly move them apart. One hand won't move. Try it! Kids love the bionic arm trick on page 45—one kid sits on the floor with an open hand on top of his or her head. Another tries to lift him or her up by the arm. It cannot be done. The last trick in the book is fun too—bet you can draw a triangle with three right angles! Sound impossible? Not if you draw it on a balloon!

Fun & Games: Stories Science Photos Tell, also by Vicki Cobb, has some grand photographs which will add a lot of color to your science booktalks. Show your listeners the photo of the football being kicked on page 10, and encourage them to read the explanation of what happens. You may never have envisioned a football looking quite like that! "The foot is traveling at about fifty-five miles an hour when it meets the football. It stays in contact with the ball for .008 seconds" (page 11).

Look at the photo of astronaut Ron McNair, who died in the *Challenger* disaster, breaking a thick concrete slab with his hand while doing a karate chop. How can this be? How does this happen? Read and find out. This book is great fun to look through. The photographs are fascinating, and the explanations painlessly provide a lot of scientific information.

Let's face it. We all find volcanoes fascinating. As popular author Janice Van-Cleave says, scientists have known for a long, long time that inside the earth it is hot, because so many hot things come out of the earth. In *Volcanoes: Mind-Boggling Experiments You Can Turn into Science Fair Projects*, VanCleave gives us 20 experiments having to do with volcanoes, measuring volcanoes, and finding out more about volcanoes. Most of the experiments can be done at home, usually in the kitchen, but at least one requires you to go outside because an explosion might result! This book even tells you how to make your own model of an erupting volcano. This is a great book to pair with books on volcanic disasters, such as the ones on the eruption of Vesuvius found in chapter 1 of this book.

Have you ever thought about all of the ways you use electricity? Name some! Maybe you thought that Ben Franklin discovered electricity, but that is not really true. *The Ben Franklin Book of Easy and Incredible Experiments* will tell you more about this fascinating man. What Ben Franklin did was prove that lightning and electricity are the same thing. He went out in a field with a kite during a thunderstorm. Near the end of the kite string, he tied a ribbon with a key on it. He did not want to tell anyone what he was doing, because he was afraid they might make fun of him if he was wrong. When he touched his knuckle to the key after a thundercloud passed over, there was a spark—and he knew that he was right, but that was more than 250 years ago. No one really knew what you could do with electricity. Ben Franklin at least had a sense of humor about it. He once suggested that there could be a picnic on the river where the turkey would be "killed by electric shock"!

Ben Franklin was one of the greatest Americans who ever lived, and he could do so many things. If you are looking for some neat ideas or projects for your next science fair, or if you, too, would like to be an inventor and a discoverer, this book is a great place to start.

The Science Chef Travels Around the World: Fun Food Experiments and Recipes for Kids by Joan D'Amico and Karen Eich Drummond is a fun book loaded with more than 50 science experiments you can do with food, interesting facts about foods and eating around the world, and a lot of delicious-sounding recipes. Have you ever thought, for instance, of making peanut soup? Does that sound good to you? If it does, you might want to try the recipe from West Africa on pages 142 and 143.

Just reading some of the information on the various countries is fascinating. Do you know which country has the biggest land area in the western hemisphere? It is Canada! Do you know there are stores in Mexico called tortillerias—stores that sell only tortillas? Did you know that pizza did not originally come from Italy? It probably came from Egypt. Experiments such as "What makes orange soda fizz?" "What makes peanut butter smooth?" and directions for doing things with food, such as eating with chopsticks, make this book worth a closer look. You'll get hungry reading the recipes, which come with clear, simple directions, and you'll want to try some of the experiments.

Super Science Concoctions: 50 Mysterious Mixtures for Fabulous Fun by Jill Frankel Hauser is a perfect book for kids who like hands-on fun. Did you ever want to make your own watercolors? How about making watery ghosts in a glass? How many pennies can you put into a full glass of water? (You will be surprised. The water amazingly forms a skin across the surface to prevent itself from overflowing—see pages 102 and 103.) How can you form a hole in the water? Easy, see page 107. Make your own bubble brew (page 115), gelatin worms (page 124), or lava (pages 52 and 53). The many interesting experiments and projects will entice everybody in your audience.

Even more fun concoctions can be made using *Lotions, Potions, and Slime: Mudpies and More!* by Nancy Blakey. Some are pretty obvious, but kids will enjoy hearing about the concoctions and ideas described here. This is also a good book to use with parents, as many of the ideas presented here are designed for families. Among the biggest crowd pleasers: boiling water in a paper cup (page 14) and making a one-fisted egg (a real winner found on page 34), marbled milk (page 12), carbon dioxide balloons (page 31), an Oobleck (pages 16 and 17), homemade icebergs (page 24), an underwater volcano (page 25), Kool-Aid dye (page 58), and fake blood (page 105). Crash cookies (page 76) are great to make on a day when you feel the need to punch something!

Homemade Slime & Rubber Bones! Awesome Science Activities by William R. Wellnitz has several fun activities, including making an egg bounce (pages 4 and 5). Note that this activity requires some preparation. The egg must first be soaked in quite a bit of vinegar for a few days, but it's worth the effort. An egg that bounces will impress almost anyone. Another popular demonstration is sticking a balloon to the wall without using tape. How? You use static electricity. Rub the balloon across your shirt or hair 10 to 20 times, then stick the rubbed side to the wall. It will stay there for five to ten minutes. Using the same basic principle, you can also move a soft drink can by holding a balloon over it. Activities like these are fun and easy to do in front of a group, but also promise your audience such delights as a recipe for making slime and a solution that will make dull pennies shine.

For more fun in the kitchen, try *Soda Science: Designing and Testing Soft Drinks* by Bernie Zubrowski. The very title of this book is so appealing that it alone will probably sell the book to the kids.

Just about everybody loves soda pop, and almost everyone has a favorite flavor. But what if you knew how to make your own soda pop? Follow the step-by-step directions in the book, which include information on everything from making soda gas with yeast to adding food coloring and deciding what flavors to put in your invention. The book even includes directions for doing a scientific taste test—asking others to rate your soda on flavor, sweetness, color, and fizz. Who knows? You might have to patent your invention. And you might create the next soft drink sensation!

Any discussion of soft drinks brings up an interesting question: What do you call it? Soda or pop? Why? Why do you call it a soft drink? The answer lies in *Wrapper Rockets & Trombone Straws: Science at Every Meal* by Ed Sobey. Soft drinks are so called to differentiate them from hard drinks, such as liquor, and those who call it "pop" got the word from the popping sound the bubbles make.

The real novelty of this book is the sensational ideas for activities to do while you are waiting for dinner to be served, especially in restaurants. Here can be found a way to explode a straw, histories of favorite foods, and more. It's great fun for browsing.

Have you ever wanted to be a detective? What kinds of skills does it take to be a detective, and what kinds of things should you know? *Detective Science: 40 Crime-Solving, Case-Breaking, Crook-Catching Activities for Kids* by Jim Wiese is full of great ideas for experiments and projects. Show the audience the lip prints on page 24. Did you know that each of us has a unique lip print, and sometimes criminals are caught because they might have left their lip print on a glass? Look at the five different common lip print patterns. Which one most resembles yours?

Sometimes criminals are identified through teeth impressions. A fun experiment in the book tells you how to get teeth impressions from your friends. After you have them all, ask a friend to bite into a piece of cheese—and see if you can match up that bite to the teeth impressions you have collected.

Another fun picture to show is that of the sketch of the dollar bill on page 109. Ask the kids to test their powers of observation and name the 12 mistakes (really only 11 now) on the bill.

A teacher might also enjoy using the "Mystery Box" experiment on page 9 as a classroom exercise.

A good detective needs excellent powers of observation. (You may be appalled at how bad yours are!) *Detective Science* offers suggestions for how anyone can improve his or her powers of observation.

For a change of pace, try *How Math Works* by Carol Vorderman. This appealing compendium of math information and experiments is not a book that kids will be likely to read from cover to cover. But it is jam-packed with fun information for browsing, and much of the text will work wonderfully well in booktalks.

Take a look at some of the experiments, games, and activities you can do in this fun book. Do you know what tare weight is? See page 33. It will show you a simple way to weigh your pet (weighing a cat by itself, for instance, might be tricky to do).

Have you ever heard of Sissa's reward (page 49)? A king told Sissa to choose his reward, and he asked for rice. He put one grain of rice on the first square of a chessboard and told the king he wanted double the amount on each succeeding square. The king could not believe he asked for such a small thing. But was it small? How much rice do you think Sissa ended up with?

Try some of the puzzles in the book. A friend tells you that on his birthday, his mother is three times as old as he is, but in 15 years she will be only twice as old as he. How old is your friend, and how old is his mother on that day? Could you figure this one out? (See page 70.)

Do you know what a golden section is (page 58)? Have you ever seen one? How can you find out the volume of your hand (page 102)? Would you like to know how good your reaction time is (page 109)? Would you like to make and use a pinhole camera (page 123)? Do you know what tangrams are? Do you know what you can do with them (page 130)? If you are on a train and you jump in the air, will you travel backward on the train by the time you land (page 172)? A good puzzle to use with a group is the one about the fox, the hen, and the grain on page 176. Merely flipping through this book in front of your audience will create a demand.

INVENTIONS AND ACCIDENTS

In *Guess Again! More Weird & Wacky Inventions*, Jim Murphy tells us right off the bat that "Americans have produced more than four million patented inventions over the past 200 years, one of the greatest outpourings of practical creativity in history. The list is endless, but includes such well-known items as the safety pin, telephone, elevator, screw-top jar, baseball glove, airplane, barbed wire, and record player."

What this book provides is a guessing game that is great fun. Show your favorite illustrations in the book. Each is of a particular invention, and below it are three explanations for what the invention is. Have your audience guess which is the correct one. Then show them the explanation page, with an illustration of the invention in use. Not only is this activity hilariously funny, but it is educational and an enticement to check out the book. You will have a great time with this one, which works equally well for adult, older elementary, and middle school audiences

A lot of us think it would be really great to invent something someday. Get started by reading *Put a Fan in Your Hat! Inventions, Contraptions, and Gadgets Kids Can Build* by Robert S. Carrow.

You wear a hat to protect yourself from the summer sun, but you end up sweating. Wouldn't it feel great to have a fan in your hat? This book gives directions on how to do it and how to make such things as a battery. Read the tips for inventors in the introduction to the book on pages x and xi. The most important one to share with kids is number seven—inventors read and write. Famous inventors must be able to read and write well. (They won't become famous if they can't document their work.) Reading can give you a basic understanding of practically everything. Whether you read books, magazines, or the newspaper, you are learning and getting ideas.

You don't have to be grown-up to be an inventor. *The Kids' Invention Book* by Arlene Erlbach (figure 5.1) tells about things that have been invented by kids. Earmuffs, for example, were invented by a young boy named Chester Greenwood. Chester lived in Farmington, Maine, and his ears got cold in the winter. In 1873, when he was 15 years old, he came up with the idea of putting some cloth pads on the ends of a piece of wire, and—abracadabra—he had earmuffs. Kids today have lots of ideas too, and this book describes some of them, with photographs of the inventors.

Do you love your cat but hate having to deal with the icky spoon after dishing out its food from the can? Suzanna Goodin, only six years old, came up with the idea of making an edible spoon. You would never have to clean it; you could just let your cat eat it! Other kids have invented an automatic fish-feeding machine, a two-door mailbox, gummy worms to catch fish with, and an all-in-one washer-dryer.

The author gives excellent tips for designing your own inventions, includes a list of invention contests, and explains how to patent your invention (warning, it is not cheap). She also tells you how to join—or invent your own—inventors club. The front cover of this book is an appealing one to show.

Fig. 5.1. *The Kids' Invention Book* by Arlene Erlbach

Girls & Young Women Inventing: Twenty True Stories About Inventors Plus How You Can Be One Yourself by Frances A. Karnes and Suzanne M. Bean also tells about kids who have had great ideas for inventions. This book not only tells the stories of 20 young inventors, it tells girls how they can be inventors, too. The young women featured in the book all created inventions in response to their own observations about how things could be done differently. Inventions include the pocket diaper, the electro-lock, the asthmameter, and the kiddie stool. Descriptions of the inventions are given in the words of the young inventors. Tell kids about Emily Meredith Tucker's ice blades (page 81), which are ice skates that can be turned into in-line skates. Explain how she came up with an idea, made a prototype, modified the design, and finally had a successful invention. The photos of each girl aren't large enough to show to a class, but kids will enjoy seeing them up close.

If you have time for an activity, ask the kids to think of something they would like to see invented. Use the questions on page 129 to spark discussion: "I wish I had a better way of . . ." "The products I would like to see improved are . . ." "My life would be easier if . . ." Kids can sketch out their ideas, and some might even want to create a prototype.

A fun look at inventions is found in Don L. Wulffson's *The Kid Who Invented the Popsicle and Other Surprising Stories About Inventions*. What is the most popular indoor game in the world? (Answer: the crossword puzzle.) When and why was the fly swatter invented? What about the postage stamp? Why on earth is Scotch tape called Scotch tape? (No, it was not made in Scotland.) When do you think that people started wearing underwear? Did you know that the first hair dryers were vacuum cleaners? Why is ice cream with syrup or fruit on it called a sundae? This book is jam-packed with fun information like this. Booktalkers can just mark some of the more interesting chapter headings and summarize these stories.

Get an interesting perspective on inventions by reading *Nature Got There First* by Phil Gates. Did you know that a wrench is just a mechanical version of a crab's claw? Or that a parachute is much like a dandelion seed? Or that a burglar alarm functions like a rattlesnake rattle? You will see things differently when you learn all the ways that nature inspires humans to invent things. This colorful book will make you think twice about everyday objects and how they came to be.

"The Earth Is Flat"—and Other Great Mistakes by Laurence Pringle is a fun book of true stories that prove the old saying "To err is human." Pick a few of the famous mistakes to discuss. Students who are struggling to learn keyboarding will appreciate "Muddling Along with QWERT." Tell them that their poor typing may not be their fault—the arrangement of letters on a keyboard was deliberately made to slow typing. In addition, the QWERT keyboard encourages errors and causes fatigue. Let them think about how they would design a better keyboard.

Students will also enjoy hearing about "The Dumb Kid" (page 36) who turned out to be Albert Einstein and the "Wrong-Way Run" (page 64) that sent professional football player Jim Marshall on a 66-yard run to the wrong end zone. This book could also be used as a lead-in to a booktalk on disasters (see chapter 1), as some disasters are the result of human error (see pages 51 and 52 for a short summary of the *Titanic* shipwreck).

A similar book presented in a more eye-catching format is *Shocking Science: 5,000 Years of Mishaps and Misunderstandings* by Steve Parker. Parker tells of scientific blunders throughout history—some with negative results and others with fortunate consequences. Kids will be shocked at the medical mistakes found on pages 34 and 35. Tell them about the process of trephining (drilling holes in the head) and the medieval practice of bloodletting. Then share this fact from the bottom of page 35:

> In ancient India, doctors were supposed to look at the inside of the body as part of their training. Yet the law did not let them use knives on dead bodies. So instead, they would leave the dead body in water. After a week, it was so soggy that it could simply be pulled to bits!

With hundreds of colorful illustrations and quirky facts, this book will be enjoyed by upper elementary and middle school students.

Not all mistakes are unfortunate, as you'll see if you browse through *Accidents May Happen*. Charlotte Foltz Jones has put together 50 lively anecdotes about the origins of foods, clothing, toys, and other everyday objects. Tell listeners that Corn Flakes were just overbaked wheat (page 2), and that Wheaties cereal was a mistake, too. Then tell them how ether and nitrous oxide, used by dentists to control pain, were originally used for entertainment at parties (page 32). Explain that before the 1800s, when people had surgery, they had several options. They could be frozen, beaten senseless, asphyxiated, pumped full of alcohol, or given a piece of wood to bite down on. We can be glad that dentist Horace Wells decided to experiment with nitrous oxide!

Some of the stories in this book are legends; we are not certain they happened as described. For instance, a goatherd near the Red Sea watched his goats eat some berries growing on bushes. Suddenly, they seemed very energetic. When the goatherd tried eating some of the berries himself, he too became very energetic. What had he discovered? Coffee! Did you know that four out of every five adult Americans drink coffee?

And did you know that the yo-yo started out as a weapon? Or that dry cleaning is really wet? The only thing "dry" about the process is that it does not use water. Read this fun book to find out how many things we use every day came into existence.

Have you ever gone for a walk outside and returned home covered with cockleburs? Didn't they drive you nuts? Wasn't pulling them off a real pain? If you were the kind of a person described in *Lucky Science: Accidental Discoveries From Gravity to Velcro, with Experiments* by Royston M. Roberts and Jeanie Roberts, you might have started thinking about cockleburs and what on earth makes them so sticky. You might have gotten out a magnifying glass and looked at them closely. As a result of examining them, you might have invented Velcro! That is precisely what Georges DeMestral did more than 50 years ago, and Velcro, as most would agree, is an excellent invention.

Many famous and useful things were discovered more or less by accident. It is one thing to discover a fact by accident and another thing altogether to figure out what to do with it. Because the scientist Luigi Galvani saw a leg cut from a dead frog twitching, the battery eventually was invented. Because Alexander Fleming was a very observant man, one who remembered small details, he discovered penicillin, an antibiotic that has saved countless lives. Because a worker forgot to turn off a whipping machine when he took his lunch hour, a type of soap was made which had more air in it than any other soap—so much air that it floated. The soap: Ivory soap.

Who would have thought of making safety glass? Do you know what safety glass is? It is glass that pretty much sticks together, even if it is broken. The need for safety glass became obvious when people started driving and riding in automobiles. More people were hurt because of broken glass than because of any other reason. It took a scientist to figure out how to keep broken glass together. Not only does this interesting book recount fascinating stories, it also tells about related experiments that can be done at home or at school.

Engineers are a special kind of inventor, and their mistakes can prove to be disastrous. *Catastrophe! Great Engineering Failure—and Success* by Fred Bortz will appeal to kids with scientific minds. The book begins with an explanation of Murphy's Law (if something can go wrong, it will), then discusses several well-known engineering disasters. Bortz describes hotel skywalks collapsing in a Hyatt Regency hotel, the failure of the Tacoma Narrows Bridge, the space shuttle *Challenger* explosion, and several other accidents. The notable thing about this book is its thorough explanation of why disaster struck. The details may be too complex for some readers, but future engineers will be fascinated. The book contains several interesting photographs that would be worth showing. Pages 13, 20, and 76 are particularly good.

THE WORLD AROUND US

The world is full of amazing things—including volcanoes, earthquakes, thunderstorms, lightning, and changing seasons. Find out how continents move around on the face of the earth in *Our Patchwork Planet: The Story of Plate Tectonics* by Helen Roney Sattler. With the help of many colorful photographs and illustrations, Sattler tells the history of Earth's landmasses, how they were formed, how they move around, and what happens when they move. Show the picture on page 33 of the California lettuce field's displaced rows to illustrate what an earthquake can do. This book is packed with good information—recommend it to teachers as well as students.

Find out about some fascinating forces in the world by reading *Shake, Rattle, and Roll: The World's Most Amazing Volcanoes, Earthquakes, and Other Forces*. Spencer Christian (of *Good Morning America* fame) and Antonia Felix have written a highly informative and fun book dealing with plate tectonics, earthquakes, volcanoes, geysers, and other geological wonders.

The book contains some easy experiments to try. You'll find out how to make your own volcano, of course, but you'll also find a neat experiment with shock waves, using a candle and a salt container (page 50), and a chocolate lava lesson that uses fudge brownies (page 77). Tell kids some of the "Bizarre Things Animals Do Before an Earthquake" (page 57). Rats panic and readily approach people, cockroaches scramble around, pet goldfish swim frantically, and freshwater fish jump wildly. Chapter 6, "Killer Quakes and Exploding Mountains," describes some of the greatest disasters of all time. Use this chapter to tie the book in with the other great disaster books found in chapter 1 of this book.

Spencer Christian and Antonia Felix have written another book with a title that asks an interesting question: *Can It Really Rain Frogs? The World's Strangest Weather Events*. The answer is yes. It really can rain frogs—and snails, fish, and snakes, among other things. This fun book tells how it can happen and is filled with other amazing weather facts that readers can share with friends and family. Do you know that the windiest place on earth is Commonwealth Bay in Antarctica? Or that the rainiest place on earth is in Hawaii? Or that the largest hailstone ever recorded—about the size of a grapefruit—was in Kansas? Or that the most powerful wind ever recorded was in New Hampshire—231 miles per hour on the top of Mount Washington? Now *that* is windy. Did you know that lightning can indeed strike twice in the same place? The Empire State Building has been struck by lightning as many as a dozen times in *one storm!*

Spencer Christian gives us lots of facts, as well as some tips on making our own fog and rain, and on performing many experiments.

Do any of you know why so many weather vanes have roosters on them? Would you like to guess? The answer (on page 95) will probably surprise you!

More weather information can be found in Franklyn M. Branley's *Down Comes the Rain.* Have you ever wondered about hail? How can ice fall out of the sky on a hot summer day? Sometimes great big pieces of ice fall. Once, in Kansas, hail as big as softballs fell on the ground.

This fun book describes how rain and hail occur. Where do they come from? How do they get there? What makes rain? Why does hail form? The book even tells us how we can very easily change water vapor into water—something all of us have done many times but didn't know that was what we were doing. Very colorful, large illustrations make it easy to entice a young audience.

For some dramatic weather photos, try *Lightning* by Seymour Simon. This book will perk up even the most bored listener. The first page starts off with some startling facts. Did you know that more than 100 lightning bolts strike the earth every second of every day? That makes 10 million lightning bolts per day! Did you know that lightning bolts travel 6,000 times faster than the fastest spaceship? If you happen to live in Florida, mention that you're living in the "lightning capital of the United States," where you get three times the number of lightning strikes of any other place in the country.

How many people do you think are hit by lightning each year? According to Simon, 100 people in the United States are killed by lightning, and another 250 people are struck but survive. The second-to-last page in the book tells what to do if you are caught in a lightning storm. See what kids think they should do, then read that page to them. They probably didn't know the part about becoming "a basketball with legs." Show any of the fabulous photographs to get your audience interested in this dramatic and colorful book.

For more great pictures of storms, try *Eye of the Storm: Chasing Storms with Warren Faidley* by Stephen Kramer. Warren Faidley is a storm chaser who makes his living by photographing lightning, tornadoes, and hurricanes. Does that sound like an interesting career? Faidley's photographs are incredible, and so are the stories of how he got those particular shots. Show the pictures of tornadoes on the cover and on page 28. Or show any one of the dramatic lightning photographs. Follow Warren Faidley on his journeys, and you will learn a lot about all kinds of weather.

Wherever you live, the changing seasons affects you. Award-winning author Seymour Simon has written a beautiful series of books explaining the natural processes of nature throughout the year. The photographs in *Spring Across America* will delight an elementary school audience. Show the male hyla's puffed-up throat or the two black bear cubs in the tree. Take time to read aloud segments from these books, which are as well written as they are beautiful. *Winter Across America* ends with some poetic words about winter:

> It is the sound of the wind blowing through the dark shapes of leafless trees outlined against the white ground. It is a film of ice needles on a pond or stream. It is the silence of glittering stars on a frosty night. Winter brings rest and renewal. It is a pause in the great, eternal cycle of the seasons.

Also in the series is *Autumn Across America*, with equally beautiful photographs and pages colored in the reds, golds, and oranges of autumn.

You can read about some very strange natural happenings in *The Case of the Mummified Pigs and Other Mysteries in Nature* by Susan E. Quinlan (figure 5.2). Here's one mysterious case. In 1944, scientists released 29 reindeer on Saint Matthew Island in the Bering Sea. The island had a lot of food that reindeer like to eat and no predators, or enemies, of reindeer. The scientists thought the reindeer herd would grow quickly. And they were right. In 19 years the reindeer herd on the island grew to almost 6,000. But two years after that, scientists who visited found only a few live reindeer and hundreds, or maybe thousands, of reindeer skeletons. What had gone wrong?

This book is about what the famous scientist Aldo Leopold called "the land organism," and about ecology, the science that studies it. What made the tips of the songbird called the cedar waxwing change colors? Why did the bodies of dead baby pigs turn into mummies when they were kept in a certain kind of cage where insects could not get in?

The book gives one interesting example after another of how all of the plants and animals in nature interact with each other. It's a great read—pick it up to find out what happened to the reindeer and the baby pigs.

Fig. 5.2. *The Case of the Mummified Pigs and Other Mysteries in Nature* **by Susan E. Quinlan**

DEAD BODIES
(ARCHAEOLOGY AND ANTHROPOLOGY)

Some scientists concern themselves with dead bodies. Yikes! This statement will get kids' attention and will lead you into some captivating booktalks. Who wouldn't want to hear how murders are solved, why cats were made into mummies, or how a 5,000-year-old frozen man was found? Share some of these books with your audience, and you will be introducing them not only to some fascinating topics, but to some careers they probably have not ever considered.

What on earth is a forensic anthropologist? *The Bone Detectives: How Forensic Anthropologists Solve Crimes and Uncover Mysteries of the Dead* by Donna M. Jackson (figure 5.3) uses a great story to describe what forensic anthropologists do. A man from Finland found a skull in a boy scout camp in Missouri. It took him a while, but eventually he told the police about it. Investigators sifting through the ground found several pieces of evidence, most notably a button that said "Texwood" on it. Forensic anthropologists were called in and were able to learn a lot about the victim just by examining the bones. One of the anthropologists, a specialist, was able to reconstruct her head (show page 35) by piecing together the information gleaned from examining her bones. What the police found out was her approximate age, the fact that she was a fairly young woman who had children, and that she was Asian. This photo was published in the newspapers, and police asked that anyone who knew anyone who looked like that—and who had not been seen recently—call the police department.

Some people saw the photo and thought it looked a lot like the wife of a friend of theirs. They had not seen her for some time, for her husband told them that she had left him and moved back to her original home: Thailand. The Texwood button the police had found was from a pair of jeans made in Thailand. Guess what had happened to her!

Several other cases involving bone detectives are described near the end of the book: Lucy, the three-million-year-old fossil skull found in Ethiopia; bones which almost certainly belong to Custer's half-Indian scout, Mitch Boyer, found on the battlefield of the Little Big Horn; and some of Jesse James's bones, found in Missouri. An exceptional discovery is that of the world's oldest mummy, "The Iceman." This prehistoric man was found in the Alps in 1991, complete with intact tissue, making it an absolutely stupendous discovery.

The book is loaded with good color photographs, which have enormous child appeal. Be sure to flip through the book so that the audience can see how many there are.

Fig. 5.3. *The Bone Detectives: How Forensic Anthropologists Solve Crimes and Uncover Mysteries of the Dead* **by Donna M. Jackson**

Charlotte Foltz Jones writes about a similar subject in *Fingerprints and Talking Bones: How Real-Life Crimes Are Solved.* Crime is always an interesting topic, and this book gives all kinds of information about how crimes get solved. It explains how detectives use bullets, fibers, glass shards, fingerprints, bite marks, car tracks, and all sorts of other evidence to reach conclusions. It's full of real-life examples of crimes and how they were solved, and just reading some of them would make for a good booktalk.

The whole book is captivating, but a particularly interesting section begins on page 70. It explains how forensic entomologists study insects on dead bodies to determine the actual time of death. Tell kids about the different bugs that find their way to corpses in a certain order. First are the blowflies that lay the eggs that become the maggots that are the best indicator an entomologist can use to determine time of death. Then come numerous other flies and beetles, depending whether the body is in the city, country, or underwater. Bugs can even give clues about drugs that the victim had been taking. If you have time, read aloud pages 70 through 73. The grisly details speak for themselves.

Discovering the Iceman: What Was It Like to Find a 5,300-Year-Old Mummy? by Shelley Tanaka (figure 5.4) tells the fascinating story of a mummified man preserved in ice. In September 1991, two tourists discovered a body in the Alps. At least 200 or so mountain climbers die there every year, so the presence of a body was not considered unusual, but this body was different. It looked strange, wrinkled, almost like a mummy. When the body was examined by scientists, they almost immediately realized that it was at least 4,000 years old; in actuality, it turned out to be almost 5,300 years old. This man had lived more than 2,300 years before Jesus Christ or Julius Caesar.

How did a body last so long? How was it preserved so well that the people who found it thought it had been dead just a few days? What was the significance of the clothing that the man had on and of the objects that were found near him?

This book makes guesses as to what the life of the Iceman was like and features excellent color photographs and intriguing color illustrations. A discovery like that of the "Iceman" makes it a lot easier for us to learn about how people used to live. Show the photo of the body on page 40 and the illustration of the man stuffing his shoe with grass on page 35. Other good books about the Iceman include *The Iceman* by Don Lessem and *Frozen Man* by David Getz.

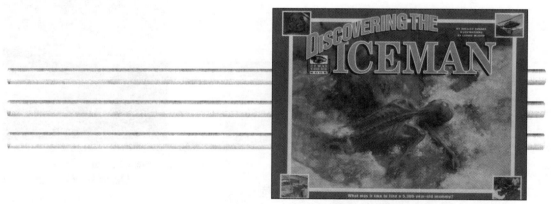

Fig. 5.4. *Discovering the Iceman: What Was It Like to Find a 5,300-Year-Old Mummy?* by Shelley Tanaka

Another fascinating mummy was found in South America in 1995. This one was a 500-year-old frozen Inca girl. Johan Reinhard has written about his findings in the National Geographic Society's book *Discovering the Inca Ice Maiden: My Adventures on Ampato.* This book is a real winner, with great photographs, a good adventure story, an erupting volcano, and a melting mummy. Show the photograph on page 19 of the climber holding the Inca maiden. You will also want to show other photographs of "Juanita" (the name given the mummy), such as the ones on pages 35 and 45. The aspect of this story that will most interest kids is that this young Inca girl was a victim of human sacrifice. Due in part to discoveries such as the Ice Maiden, anthropologists have pieced together how Incas carried out human sacrifice rituals. Read about it on pages 36 and 38, and tell students in your own words what happened to Juanita 500 years ago.

In 1888, an Egyptian farmer was digging a hole when he made an incredible discovery: thousands and thousands of mummified cats. Show the picture of a cat mummy from *Mummy* by James Putnam as well (described in chapter 2). *Cat Mummies* by Kelly Trumble (figure 5.5) tells us why the ancient Egyptians, who went to a lot of trouble to make mummies of human beings, considered it well worth their time to make mummies of cats as well.

This book is loaded with interesting information. Cats, as well as several other animals, were considered sacred animals and were accorded high honors. No one could harm a cat, and once the people killed a Roman soldier who accidentally killed one. Egyptians suffered one of their worst military defeats when their Persian enemies captured as many cats and other sacred animals as they could and released them right at the start of the battle. This caused the Egyptians to become paralyzed. They couldn't fight against the Persians, because they might kill or injure a cat accidentally, and so the army fled from the field (show the accompanying picture on page 37). Read this fascinating story to find out how cats came to be sacred animals and what happened to all those cat mummies.

Fig. 5.5. *Cat Mummies* by Kelly Trumble

Kids might also be interested in a career that involves digging up old bones and treasures. A good introduction to the field is found in *Archaeologists Dig for Clues* by Kate Duke. Being an archaeologist is a challenge. Lots of people would love to dig up the treasure archaeologists find, but alas, most archaeologists don't find treasure. What they do find, what really helps them learn about other times and other people is—garbage!

Your garbage tells a lot about you. Think of the wastebaskets in your home. Would your birthday cards tell other people when your birthday is? Would a lot of candy wrappers show that you like candy a lot and maybe eat too much? Would your school tests indicate whether you are a good or a bad student?

Archaeologists look for dirt that is darker than the rest of the dirt around it. It is darker "because people have walked on it, cooked on it, spilled things, burned things, spit, peed, thrown up. . . ." (page 6). The pictures on pages 16 and 17 or page 22 are fun to show an audience. This is an eye-opening book to share.

Some other interesting archeological finds are described in Caroline Arnold's *Stone Age Farmers Beside the Sea: Scotland's Prehistoric Village of Skara Brae* (figure 5.6). The Orkney Islands, off the coast of Scotland, are beloved by archaeologists. People have lived there for more than 5,000 years, and there are many prehistoric monuments. Perhaps the most amazing is Skara Brae, a real village, in remarkable condition. The reason it is in remarkable condition is pretty amazing too.

In 1850, huge storms battered the Orkneys, and the Laird of Skaill (*Laird* is the Scottish word for "Lord") went out to inspect the damage. A high dune had almost blown away, and that dune had been covering up the remains of a village for more than 4,000 years. That village was Skara Brae, and its miraculous preservation has helped archaeologists understand much about life in ancient times. Skara Brae had circular buildings and thick walls. It was a community of several families, families who farmed and could walk from house to house under covered walkways. It marked a big change from the times when people lived in isolation from one another.

This book has great photos of the village and gives an idea of what it might have been like to live there. It also gives us an idea of how archaeologists learn from the artifacts they find. Read it and wonder if you would have liked to have lived in Skara Brae.

Fig. 5.6. *Stone Age Farmers Beside the Sea: Scotland's Prehistoric Village of Skara Brae* **by Caroline Arnold**

Sometimes people think that everything there is to discover on earth has already been discovered, but this is not so! *Painters of the Caves* by Patricia Lauber starts out with a story that proves that theory is wrong. In December 1994, three friends went exploring in France. They were looking for caves, especially ones with prehistoric cave paintings. They explored near Avignon, in southeast France, where many cave paintings have been found.

It was a great day for them, and for art and science, for they found a cave that had been unvisited by human beings for thousands of years. It had more than 300 paintings of animals that lived more than 32,000 years ago. That cave was named the Chauvet cave, after one of the explorers.

During the Ice Age, probably about 100,000 years ago, the first modern humans spread out of Africa, where they had first appeared. These were called Cro-Magnons, and they lived for some time in existence with another group of human beings, the Neanderthals. Apparently, they lived together peacefully but did not have much to do with each other. Cro-Magnons were creative and inventive and intelligent, much more so than the Neanderthals. They made tools and improved hunting methods, and even made needles. Consequently, they did not have to spend all of their time hunting for food. Unlike the Neanderthals, they had free time, so they began to create art.

Wonderful art, full of handprints, appears in the caves. It clearly carries messages, but as this book states, they are not messages for us. They were messages for people we do not completely understand, who lived 32,000 years ago, and we just don't understand those messages today.

This book is fun to read and loaded with fascinating pictures. Show the one on page 37, or the one of the rhinoceroses on page 38. The two-page spread of cave paintings on pages 42 and 43 is distinctive. Also, the computer-produced image of a young Neanderthal on page 12 is fun to show.

THE HUMAN BODY

Take a look inside the human body (and many other animal bodies) in Richard Walker's *The Visual Dictionary of the Skeleton*. This Dorling Kindersley title is full of fascinating information and fabulous photography. It would help any student needing to learn the names of bones, and it will appeal to kids of all ages. It is especially interesting to see how similar human skeletons are to other animals. The pullout of the human skeleton (pages 9-16) is excellent to show an audience.

Introduce Seymour Simon's *The Heart: Our Circulatory System* by reading from the final page.

> Within each of us flows a river unlike any river on planet Earth. This river of blood flows past every part of the body on an incredible sixty-thousand-mile voyage, enough to travel two and a half times around the world. It is a journey as strange and wonderful as any journey to the stars.

This book will prove to you that the heart is an amazing creation. Ask kids to guess how many times a human heart beats in a year (30 million times) and in the average lifetime (2,000 million times). Flip through this book to show off some of the stunning illustrations, such as the close-ups of blood cells taken with a scanning electron microscope and computer-enhanced photographs of the heart in motion.

A book for younger readers on the same topic is *Blood* by Anna Sandeman. This engaging look at the circulatory system comes with colorful photographs and easy-to-read text. Pages 28 and 29 contain good booktalk material in the form of "Did you know?" questions. Did you know that some insects have green blood? That the capillaries in your body could encircle the world two and a half times? That an elephant's heart weighs about 44 pounds?

Anna Sandeman has written several other books for children in her series of "Body Books." *Skin, Teeth & Hair* is loaded with great information. Can you think where the skin on your body is the thinnest? (Your eyelids.) The thickest? (The palms of your hands and the soles of your feet, because they are subject to such hard use.) Do you know why people get wrinkles? It is because our skin grows with us and stays the same size when we are young, up to about age 25. After that, it is not as elastic. Skin changes constantly—in just one minute, you may lose as many as 40,000 skin cells! "Your blood vessels, hairs, and sweat glands work together to make sure your body does not get too hot or too cold" (page 12). How does that happen? Do you know? And that's just some fun stuff about skin—imagine how much you could learn about your teeth and your hair.

Brain, another Anna Sandeman book in this fun series, informs us that a brain looks like a "soft, pinkish-gray wrinkled sponge. More than three quarters of it is water. Without a skull to support and protect your brain, it would sag like jelly" (page 8). The brain controls our movements, both voluntary and involuntary. Can you think of any examples of either one of those? A good example of involuntary movement happens when we pick up something hot. We either drop it or put it down in a big hurry. What other movements might you make without thinking about them? The brain controls our memory, too. What did you have for lunch one week ago today? Can you remember? Why or why not?

Other "Body Books" by Sandeman include *Eating, Bones, Breathing*, and *Babies*.

For a fascinating look at how humans try to heal the body, take a look at *Medicine* by Steve Parker. This "Eyewitness Science" book has some incredible photographs. Show the skull with three holes in it on page 9. This person lived more than 4,000 years ago, and we know he survived having holes drilled in his skull because the bone shows signs of healing. Scientists think the holes may have been intended to release evil spirits believed to cause mental illness. Aren't you glad you're alive today instead of back then? Show your audience some of the tools on pages 26 and 27, especially the surgical saw and the small saw for amputating fingers and toes. Then show the cautery iron on pages 22 and 23 and explain how it was heated like a branding iron and applied to amputation stumps. Finally, turn to pages 54 and 55 for a look at mechanical hands through the ages. This book will captivate readers of all ages.

For another fascinating look at how the science of medicine has changed over the years, read *Just What the Doctor Ordered: The History of American Medicine* by Brandon Marie Miller. For a long time, medicine in America was a chancy business. Men who wanted to be doctors could buy a license saying that they were doctors for only $20. No training was necessary. White men found that Native Americans had some fine remedies, but the Native Americans had no medicines that could cure the diseases that the white men brought to them, diseases like smallpox and measles.

When white people first settled in America, disease and famine killed many of them quickly. Even with help from the Native Americans, of the 105 people who founded the Jamestown colony in May 1907, half were dead by September. By January, only 38 of the colonists were left. Medical breakthroughs happened slowly. Cures that had been used for years, such as bleeding patients with leeches, were popular. No one washed their hands or considered it necessary to do so. Trash and sewage were thrown in the streets. If a patient did not get better when treated, the list of the possible causes included: "the patient did not cooperate; the patient proved unreasonable, the patient refused to pay the doctor; or sin caused the sickness, which ultimately had to be cured by God" (page 23).

When the same contagious disease struck many people, the sick people were often taken to pesthouses. These were horrible, filthy places where the sick people were not cared for. They were simply taken there so other people would not catch the disease! By the late 1700s, real progress began to be made as doctors and scientists learned more and more about health and hygiene and bacteria. But reading this interesting book will make you very happy that you live today, and not even 100 years ago!

BIBLIOGRAPHY

Arnold, Caroline. *Stone Age Farmers Beside the Sea: Scotland's Prehistoric Village of Skara Brae*. Photographs by Arthur P. Arnold. Clarion Books, 1997. 48 p. ISBN 0-395-77601-5. Grades 4-6.

The Ben Franklin Book of Easy and Incredible Experiments. Illustrated by Cheryl Kirk Noll. John Wiley & Sons, 1995. ISBN 0-471-07639-2; 0-471-07638-4 (pbk.). Grades 4-6.

Blakey, Nancy. *Lotions, Potions, and Slime: Mudpies and More!* Illustrated by Melissah Watts. Tricycle Press, 1996. 110 p. ISBN 1-883672-21-X (pbk.). Grades 4-6 (younger with adult guidance).

Bortz, Fred B. *Catastrophe! Great Engineering Failure—and Success*. Illustrated by Gary Tong. W. H. Freeman, 1995. 80 p. ISBN 0-7167-6538-1. Grades 6-up.

Branley, Franklyn M. *Down Comes the Rain*. Illustrated by James Graham Hale. HarperCollins, 1997. 32 p. ISBN 0-06-025334-7; 0-06-025338-X (lib. bdg.); 0-06-445166-6 (pbk.). Grades 1-3.

Carrow, Roberts. *Put a Fan in Your Hat! Inventions, Contraptions, and Gadgets Kids Can Build*. Illustrated by Rick Brown. McGraw-Hill, 1997. ISBN 0-07-011657-1; 0-07-011658-X (pbk.). Grades 4-6.

Christian, Spencer, and Antonia Felix. *Can It Really Rain Frogs? The World's Strangest Weather Events*. John Wiley & Sons, 1997. 121 p. ISBN 0-471-15290-9 (pbk.). Grades 4-7.

————. *Shake, Rattle, and Roll: The World's Most Amazing Volcanoes, Earthquakes, and Other Forces*. John Wiley & Sons, 1997. 122 p. ISBN 0-471-15291-9 (pbk.). Grades 4-7.

Cobb, Vicki. *Fun & Games: Stories Science Photos Tell*. Lothrop, Lee & Shepard Books, 1991. 32 p. ISBN 0-688-09315-9 (trade); 0-688-09316-7 (lib. bdg.). Grades 4-6.

————. *Magic . . . Naturally! Science Entertainments & Amusements*. Illustrated by Lionel Kalish. HarperCollins, 1993. 150 p. ISBN 0-06-022474-6; 0-06-022475-4 (lib. bdg.). Grades 4-6.

Cobb, Vicki, and Kathy Darling. *Bet You Can! Science Possibilities to Fool You.* Illustrated by Stella Ormai. Avon Camelot, 1983. 112 p. ISBN 0-380-82180-X (pbk.). Grades 4-6.

————. *Bet You Can't! Science Impossibilities to Fool You.* Illustrated by Martha Weston. Lothrop, Lee & Shepard, 1980. 128 p. ISBN 0-688-41905-4; 0-688-51905-9 (lib. bdg.). Grades 4-6.

————. *Wanna Bet? Science Challenges to Fool You.* Illustrated by Meredith Johnson. Lothrop, Lee & Shepard, 1993. 128 p. ISBN 0-688-11213-7. Grades 4-6.

D'Amico, Joan, and Karen Eich Drummond. *The Science Chef Travels Around the World: Fun Food Experiments and Recipes for Kids.* Illustrated by Tina Cash-Walsh. John Wiley & Sons, 1996. 177 p. 0-471-11779-X (pbk.). Grades 4-6.

Duke, Kate. *Archaeologists Dig for Clues.* HarperCollins, 1997. 32 p. ISBN 0-06-027057-8. Grades 2-4.

Erlbach, Arlene. *The Kids' Invention Book.* Lerner Publications, 1997. 64 p. ISBN 0-8225-2414-7. Grades 4-6.

Gates, Phil. *Nature Got There First.* Kingfisher, 1995. 80 p. ISBN 1-85697-587-8. Grades 4-6.

Getz, David. *Frozen Man.* Illustrated by Peter McCarty. Henry Holt, 1994. 68 p. ISBN 0-8050-3261-4. Grades 3-5.

Hauser, Jill Frankel. *Super Science Concoctions: 50 Mysterious Mixtures for Fabulous Fun.* Illustrated by Michael Kline. Williamson, 1997. 160 p. ISBN 1-885593-02-3. Grades 4-6.

Jackson, Donna M. *The Bone Detectives: How Forensic Anthropologists Solve Crimes and Uncover Mysteries of the Dead.* Photographs by Charlie Fellenbaum. Little, Brown, 1996. 48 p. ISBN 0-316-82935-8. Grades 5-8.

Jones, Charlotte Foltz. *Accidents May Happen.* Illustrated by John O'Brien. Delacorte Press, 1996. 86 p. ISBN 0-385-32162-7. Grades 4-6.

————. *Fingerprints and Talking Bones: How Real-Life Crimes Are Solved.* Illustrated by David G. Klein. Delacorte Press, 1997. 131 p. ISBN 0-385-32299-2. Grades 5-8.

Karnes, Frances A., and Suzanne M. Bean. *Girls & Young Women Inventing: Twenty True Stories About Inventors Plus How You Can Be One Yourself.* Free Spirit, 1995. 168 p. ISBN 0-915793-89-X (pbk.). Grades 5-8.

Kramer, Stephen. *Eye of the Storm: Chasing Storms with Warren Faidley.* Photographs by Warren Faidley. G. P. Putnam's Sons, 1997. 48 p. ISBN 0-399-23029-7. Grades 4-7.

Lauber, Patricia. *Painters of the Caves.* National Geographic Society, 1998. 48 p. ISBN 0-7922-7095-9. Grades 4-6.

Lessem, Don. *The Iceman.* Crown, 1994. 32 p. ISBN 0-517-59596 (trade); 0-517-59597-4 (pbk.). Grades 4-6.

Miller, Brandon Marie. *Just What the Doctor Ordered: The History of American Medicine.* Lerner Publications, 1997. 88 p. ISBN 0-8225-1737-X. Grades 5-8.

Murphy, Jim. *Guess Again! More Weird & Wacky Inventions.* Bradbury Press, 1986. 92 p. ISBN 0-02-767720-6. Grades 4-7.

Parker, Steve. *Medicine.* Dorling Kindersley, 1995. 64 p. ISBN 1-56458-882-3. Grades 5-up.

————. *Shocking Science: 5,000 Years of Mishaps and Misunderstandings.* Illustrated by John Kelly. Turner, 1996. 63 p. ISBN 1-57036-269-6. Grades 4-7.

Pringle, Laurence. *"The Earth Is Flat"—and Other Great Mistakes.* William Morrow, 1983. 72 p. ISBN 0-688-02466-1; 0-688-02467-X (lib. bdg.). Grades 4-7.

Quinlan, Susan E. *The Case of the Mummified Pigs and Other Mysteries in Nature.* Illustrated by Jennifer Owings Dewey. Boyds Mills Press, 1995. 128 p. ISBN 1-878093-82-7. Grades 4-7.

Reinhard, Johan. *Discovering the Inca Ice Maiden: My Adventures on Ampato.* National Geographic Society, 1998. 48 p. ISBN 0-7922-7142-4. Grades 4-up.

Roberts, Royston M., and Jeanie Roberts. *Lucky Science: Accidental Discoveries from Gravity to Velcro, with Experiments.* John Wiley & Sons, 1995. 110 p. ISBN 0-471-00954-7. Grades 4-7.

Sandeman, Anna. *Blood.* Illustrated by Ian Thompson. Copper Beech Books, 1996. 31 p. ISBN 0-7613-0477-0 (lib. bdg.). Grades 1-3.

————. *Brain.* Illustrated by Ian Thompson. Copper Beech Books, 1996. 31 p. ISBN 0-7613-0490-8. Grades 1-3.

————. *Skin, Teeth & Hair.* Illustrated by Ian Thompson. Copper Beech Books, 1996. 31 p. ISBN 0-7613-0489-4. Grades 1-3.

Sattler, Helen Roney. *Our Patchwork Planet: The Story of Plate Tectonics.* Illustrated by Giulio Maestro. Lothrop, Lee & Shepard, 1995. 48 p. ISBN 0-688-09312-4; 0-688-09313-2 (lib. bdg.). Grades 5-8.

Simon, Seymour. *Autumn Across America.* Hyperion Books for Children, 1993. 30 p. ISBN 1-56282-467-8 (trade); 1-56282-468-6 (lib. bdg.). Grades 3-6.

————. *The Heart: Our Circulatory System.* Morrow Junior Books, 1996. 30 p. ISBN 0-688-11407-5 (trade); 0-688-11408-3 (lib. bdg.). Grades 3-7.

————. *Lightning.* Morrow Junior Books, 1997. 28 p. ISBN 0-688-14638-4 (trade); 0-688-14639-2 (lib. bdg.). Grades 3-7.

————. *Spring Across America.* Hyperion Books for Children, 1996. 30 p. ISBN 0-7868-0069-0 (trade); 0-7868-2056-X (lib. bdg.). Grades 3-6.

————. *Winter Across America.* Hyperion Books for Children, 1994. 30 p. ISBN 0-7868-0019-4 (trade); 0-7868-2015-2 (lib. bdg.). Grades 3-6.

Sobey, Ed. *Wrapper Rockets & Trombone Straws: Science at Every Meal.* Illustrated by Carol Chapin and Charles J. Nappa. Learning Triangle Press/McGraw-Hill, 1997. 139 p. ISBN 0-07-021745-9. Grades 4-6.

Tanaka, Shelley. *Discovering the Iceman: What Was It Like to Find a 5,300-Year-Old Mummy?* Illustrated by Laurie McGaw. A Hyperion/Madison Press Book, 1996. 48 p. ISBN 0-7868-0284-7. Grades 4-6.

Trumble, Kelly. *Cat Mummies.* Illustrated by Laszlo Kubinyi. Clarion Books, 1996. 56 p. ISBN 0-395-68707-1. Grades 4-6.

VanCleave, Janice. *Volcanoes: Mind-Boggling Experiments You Can Turn into Science Fair Projects.* John Wiley & Sons, 1994. 90 p. ISBN 0-471-30811-0. Grades 4-6.

Vorderman, Carol. *How Math Works.* The Reader's Digest Association, 1996. 192 p. ISBN 0-89577-850-5. Grades 3-8.

Walker, Richard. *The Visual Dictionary of the Skeleton.* Dorling Kindersley, 1995. 64 p. ISBN 0-7894-0135-5. Grades 4-up.

Wellnitz, William R. *Homemade Slime & Rubber Bones! Awesome Science Activities.* TAB Books, 1993. 116 p. ISBN 0-8306-4093-2; 0-8306-4094-0 (pbk.). Grades 4-7.

Wiese, Jim. *Detective Science: 40 Crime-Solving, Case-Breaking, Crook-Chasing Activities for Kids.* Illustrated by Ed Shems. John Wiley & Sons, 1996. 118 p. ISBN 0-471-11980-6 (pbk.). Grades 4-7.

Wulffson, Don L. *The Kid Who Invented the Popsicle and Other Surprising Stories About Inventions.* Cobblehill Books/Dutton, 1997. 114 p. ISBN 0-525-65221-3. Grades 4-6.

Zubrowski, Bernie. *Soda Science: Designing and Testing Soft Drinks.* Illustrated by Roy Doty. Morrow Junior Books, 1997. 92 p. ISBN 0-688-13917-5. Grades 4-6.

CHAPTER 6

Fascinating People

Every year teachers assign book reports on biographies and send students to the library to check out books. Many children look for biographies of popular sports stars, actors, or musicians. Once those books are checked out, the rest of the kids are lost. They want to read about someone familiar to them, and they haven't even heard of most of the people in the library's biography section. This is when a good nonfiction booktalk can work wonders. Libraries are full of high-quality books about all kinds of interesting and inspiring people. What could be more interesting than the real-life adventures of people throughout history?

SCIENTISTS, ARTISTS, MUSICIANS, AND WRITERS

Leonardo da Vinci by Diane Stanley is a lovely book about an extraordinary human being. Stanley's appealing illustrations are complemented by actual notebook drawings done by da Vinci and by color reproductions of da Vinci paintings.

Leonardo da Vinci was born on April 15, 1452 in Vinci, a village near Florence. Because his parents were unmarried, da Vinci had little education, and his illegitimacy forbade him access to many professions. However, the parish priest did teach him reading, writing, and simple arithmetic, and he was beloved by his uncle Francesco. When da Vinci showed a talent for drawing, he was apprenticed to a famous artist, Antonio de Verrochio, who became very fond of his pupil and realized his incredible skill.

Da Vinci started his first true commission when he was accepted into the painters' guild, but he abandoned that partially completed project as he was to abandon many projects throughout his life. No one is sure why this happened, but a possibility is that he became bored quickly.

All of his life he sought patrons to sponsor him and pay him, and he did many different jobs for them. He worked for them as an engineer, a painter, a weaponmaker, and a pageant and entertainment designer, among many other tasks. He was left-handed, and the many notebooks he kept were written in mirror writing. He kept thousands of pages of notebooks, of which an estimated 6,000 have disappeared. The ones that remain show his amazing intelligence—his designs for inventions including the contact lens, the tank, the door closer, a submarine, and pliers. He made extensive studies of human anatomy. He was the first to realize that sound and light travel in waves through the air and to conclude that light waves travel faster than sound waves.

Da Vinci was a truly astounding man who never married and was never wealthy, although he died in the employ (and perhaps the arms) of the King of France in 1519. He was 67. His most famous painting is the *Mona Lisa*, and almost as famous is *The Last Supper*. Some of the horrors the latter painting has been through are detailed in this book. Although primarily known as an artist, da Vinci, as this book shows, was a brilliant man in many ways:

> For three hundred years the public knew Leonardo only as an artist. His lifetime of scientific research and his marvelous inventions bore no fruit because his notebooks remained in the hands of collectors, and few other people knew about them before 1800. It is frustrating to imagine how the development of science and technology might have been advanced if only his work had been published. In just two examples: Leonardo worked out the first law of motion before Newton, and one hundred years before the first telescope was built, while making a study of optics, he wrote a note to himself to "make glasses to see the moon large."

A Picture Book of Thomas Alva Edison by David A. Adler (figure 6.1) tells about the most famous inventor who ever lived. Edison was born in Ohio in 1847, and from the time he was a small boy, he loved to experiment. He was experimenting with fire inside his father's barn once, and the barn burned down. His father punished him by spanking him right in the center of town.

Edison's career as an inventor really took off when he became a telegraph operator and worked on improving what could be done with the telegraph. He loved to experiment so much that even on his wedding day, he went to his shop to work on an experiment.

Edison's most famous invention was probably the lightbulb. Imagine what our lives would be like without electric light. He also invented the phonograph, moving pictures, a copy machine, a cement mixer, and lots and lots of other things.

Fig. 6.1. *A Picture Book of Thomas Alva Edison* **by David A. Adler**

Most well-known scientists of the past were men, but you can learn about a woman scientist in Leonard Everett Fisher's book *Marie Curie*. Madame Curie, who is one of the most famous women who ever lived, was born Marya Skodowska in 1867 in Warsaw, Poland. She was the youngest of five children, and she was always very, very smart.

At that time, Poland was under the rule of the Russian tsars, and when Marya was only 10 years old, she saved her teachers and the head of her school from going to prison. A Russian inspector had come to the school to see if the children were speaking Polish and being taught Polish history, which was against the law. They were, but Marya was so smart that she was able to answer all of his questions about Russian history in perfect Russian. As a result, he could not prove that the school was doing anything against the law!

Marya would be a heroine in many ways all of her life. Although she was often poor, sometimes hungry, and frequently sick, she pursued her interest in science no matter what. She went to the Sorbonne University in Paris and was the first and only woman there. Later, she married Pierre Curie, to whom she had been introduced because he had his own laboratory where she could do research. She became fascinated by some glowing rays seen in uranium by a colleague, Henri Becquerel, and was eventually able to isolate radium, a material that made X rays possible. She became the first woman to win a Nobel Prize in 1903, when she shared the award with her husband and Becquerel.

Her life is fascinating to read about. In spite of all the odds against her, Madame Marie Curie, as she came to be known, was triumphant. Find out more by reading this book.

The best nonfiction books about people inspire readers to dream big dreams—to say, "Hey, I could do something like that!" *Black Stars in Orbit: NASA's African American Astronauts* by Khephra Burns and William Miles is one of those books. It tells the little-known story of how African Americans came to be part of NASA and eventually to be space shuttle astronauts. They faced a great deal of prejudice in the early years of the space program but persevered to earn their place as astronauts.

An interesting story is found on pages 37-41. In 1976 NASA began to recruit astronauts for the new space shuttle program. They wanted women and minority applicants, but after a year they had only 100 women and 35 minority applicants. They ended up hiring Nichelle Nichols, the actress who played Lieutenant Uhura on the TV series *Star Trek*, to convince women and minorities that NASA was serious about recruiting them. Thanks to her public relations work, NASA received 1,649 applications from women and more than 1,000 from minorities. From those applicants came the first shuttle astronauts, including three African Americans, one Asian American, and six women. The photo on the cover of the book shows the first three African American astronauts. Read this book to find out what happened to these pioneering astronauts.

Mark Twain must be one of the most appealing people who ever lived. Well over 100 years after first publishing his work, his books continue to delight us. Read about him in *A Brilliant Streak: The Making of Mark Twain* by Kathryn Lasky.

Mark Twain's real name was Samuel Langhorne Clemens. He was born in 1835, on the night when Halley's Comet streaked across the sky in a small town called Florida, Missouri. Seventy-five years later, when that comet came back, Mark Twain died. Clemens loved telling stories and making things up.

> Sam's excited imagination led him to become a truth stretcher, a manipulator of facts, and on occasion an outright liar. He was the first to admit it, claiming that although he couldn't remember his first lie, he told his second when he was nine days old and pretended that a diaper pin was sticking him.

When he was a kid, Clemens was good at playing hooky, and he loved to go swimming naked in Bear Creek, near Hannibal, the town where he grew up. He always had a great sense of humor, no matter what happened to him, and his early life influenced the writing of his great books, *The Adventures of Tom Sawyer* and *The Adventures of Huckleberry Finn*.

Find out how Sam Clemens turned into Mark Twain, and what made him a man who is remembered with great fondness almost 100 years after he died. This book is guaranteed to make you laugh. Show your audience the picture on page 4 of Clemens pretending to be sick.

Kathleen Krull has written a series of books that includes these titles: *Lives of the Artists: Masterpieces, Messes (and What the Neighbors Thought)*; *Lives of the Musicians: Good Times, Bad Times (and What the Neighbors Thought)*; and *Lives of the Writers: Comedies, Tragedies (and What the Neighbors Thought)*. These charming and informational mini-biographies of famous people are delightful to booktalk. Each biography features a full-page color picture that is excellent to show a group. Try a question-and-answer format to booktalk these books, using some of the fun facts they contain. Here are some samples:

From *Lives of the Artists*: What famous Mexican artist, married to an artist almost equally famous, was so big that he could not find underwear to fit? His wife had to make it for him in bright pink cotton. (Answer: Diego Rivera who was married to Frieda Kahlo. By the way, Madonna owns many of Kahlo's paintings.) Who became famous for painting soup cans? (Answer: Andy Warhol.) Which great artist "lived in a small, dark house in an alley. . . decorated with cobwebs and his drawing of a man carrying a coffin. He seldom bathed or even took off his dog-skin boots. When he did remove them, sometimes bits of his feet came off, too, as he didn't believe in buying socks"? (Answer: Michelangelo.) Which artist painted 200 paintings the year he was 90 years old? (Answer: Picasso, who refused to meet his grandchildren, another interesting fact.) What great American artist said, "I'm frightened all the time. But I've never let it stop me," and among other things, killed a lot of rattlesnakes by chopping off their heads with a hoe? (Answer: Georgia O'Keefe.)

From *Lives of the Musicians*: Which French composer stood outside bare-chested one winter night, caught severe bronchitis, and spent three months in bed because he did not want to serve in the military? When he died, his brother was the first stranger to come to his apartment after 27 years—and there he found many, many umbrellas. (Answer: Erik Satie.) An African American wrote "Maple Leaf Rag," the first piece of sheet music to sell more than one million copies. Who was he? (Answer: Scott Joplin.) Which Russian American composer, usually considered the most influential of the twentieth century, wrote a piece called "Do Not Throw Paper Towels in Toilet" as well as a polka for 50 elephants wearing ballet tutus? (Answer: Igor Stravinsky.) Then, read this passage from page 41:

> When Clara Wieck was a little girl, a student of her father's used to tease her with scary stories. He would wait till the room got dark and then dress up as a ghost, making shapes in the dim light. The man was Robert Schumann, and when Clara grew up, she married him.

From *Lives of the Writers*: Which famous American writer was the first person in the world to have a private telephone in his home? (Answer: Mark Twain.) Which famous English woman writer lost all of her teeth? (Answer: Charlotte Brontë. She was only 38 when she died.) Which book was the first in the English language to have a child as its hero? (Answer: *Oliver Twist* by Charles Dickens.) What famous fairy tale writer was afraid that he might be accidentally buried alive and consequently put a sign next to his bed that said "I am not really dead"? (Answer: Hans Christian Andersen.) What famous writer was not afraid of spiders—so unafraid that he once let hundreds of them hatch and build webs on top of his dresser? (Answer: E. B. White.)

Duke Ellington by Andrea Davis Pinkney tells about this famous musician (figure 6.2). Duke Ellington was born Edward Kennedy Ellington, but he told people to call him Duke. As a child, playing the piano was not what he wanted to do. He much preferred to play baseball and thought piano practice was really boring.

Then one day Ellington heard a new kind of music. They called it ragtime, and he liked it so much that he decided he had better learn to play the piano so he could play ragtime too. By the time he was 19 years old he was having a great time playing the piano for money. Ellington eventually became one of our great American composers. He had his own band and was famous throughout the land. Read this interesting story of how he became one of the all-time jazz greats.

The colorful illustrations in this book are great fun to show an audience. The front cover and the illustration of people dancing at the Cotton Club in Harlem are particularly appealing. Also, this would be a great booktalk to use with a tape recorder; play a sample of ragtime and then a sample of Ellington's music (his most famous piece probably is "Sophisticated Lady").

Fig. 6.2. *Duke Ellington* **by Andrea Davis Pinkney**

Read about a famous dancer in *Martha Graham: A Dancer's Life* by Russell Freedman. "I did not choose to be a dancer," Martha Graham frequently said. "I was chosen." Have you ever felt that way about something? You want to do it and you *love* doing it so much that you feel you have no choice but to do it.

Martha Graham is considered one of the greatest dancers and choreographers of all time. But she did not know when she was young what she would do with her life. She was already in her twenties when she started dancing seriously, an age that even now is considered much too late to start becoming a dancer. But it was all she wanted to do, and she was willing to live in poverty to do it. More than once she walked away from well-paying and secure work to do what she felt she needed to do. What she ended up doing was making a tremendous impact on dance all over the world.

If you want to do things your way, if you need to do your own thing and no one else's, this is a great person to read about. Martha Graham was a fascinating woman, and when you start reading this book, you will find it hard to put down.

Show the photos on pages 13 and 49 to your audience.

AMAZING WOMEN

Have you ever heard of a female pirate? Well, once upon a time there was a very famous pirate who was a woman. Her name was Grania O'Malley, and you can read about her in *The Pirate Queen* by Emily Arnold McCully. She was born in about 1530 in Ireland to a family that lived by the sea. Her family was made up of sailors who, as often as not, were pirates when they got the chance.

From the time she was a little girl, O'Malley wanted to go to sea. Her mother said it was "no life for a girl," but little Grania cut her hair like a boy's and won the right to go to sea.

She was brave and seemingly felt no fear. Her crew, all men, respected her. She married, and the day after her first baby was born, her mates came running down to ask her to help defend the ship against Turkish pirates. She did, and they won!

O'Malley had a life full of adventure. She married twice, had four children, and spent time in prison. Finally, in her middle age, she met another kind of queen—the Queen of England, Elizabeth I, and showed *her* a thing or two just like she showed people all of her life.

Show your audience almost any of the pictures in this book; the colorful spreads are very appealing.

Grania O'Malley wasn't the only woman in history to dress as a man to do a man's job. Everyone knows that men and women serve in today's military, but did you know that during the Civil War more than *400* women, on both sides, fought in the war dressed as men? *Behind Rebel Lines: The Incredible Story of Emma Edmonds, Civil War Spy* by Seymour Reit tells the true—and absolutely fascinating—story of one such woman. Emma Edmonds not only disguised herself as a man and enlisted in the army, she went on to volunteer for spy missions that took her into dangerous enemy territory to learn Confederate secrets. Edmonds spent two years as a man in the Union army and took on 11 different spy missions behind rebel lines. She always disguised herself before sneaking into enemy territory. Her favorite disguise was to color her face black, put on a wig, and pretend she was Cuff, a runaway slave. She also disguised herself as a middle-aged Irish woman peddler and as an African American woman. Imagine it—a white woman disguised as a white man disguised as an African American woman! Recommend this book to reluctant middle school readers, both male and female. It is full of action and intrigue, and is short and easy to read.

Imagine a time when women were not allowed to vote. It wasn't very long ago, as a matter of fact. Many women did not think it was fair or right. You can learn about those times in Jean Fritz's book, *You Want Women to Vote, Lizzie Stanton?*

The Declaration of Independence stated that all *men* are created equal. Clearly, the words meant just that, for only white men were really created equal in the eyes of the signers. When Elizabeth Cady was born in 1815, almost 40 years later, women had almost no rights at all. Their fathers told them what to do when they were young, and when they married, their husbands controlled all their property and expected them to obey. Most women received little education.

Elizabeth fell in love with an abolitionist, Henry Stanton, and married him. Women and abolitionists could agree on some things some of the time. The abolitionists wanted to get rid of, or abolish, slavery, and they wanted ex-slaves to have rights. Women wanted women and ex-slaves to have rights. Elizabeth and Henry Stanton went to London to a world anti-slavery convention, and there she met and became friends with Lucretia Mott, a Quaker who believed strongly in women's rights. Stanton became a leader of that movement, and in 1848 she became involved with the first Women's Rights Convention in Seneca Falls, New York.

Stanton got in trouble all of her life, but she had a lot of fun too. She knew a lot of the great people of her time, and she was never afraid to do anything—however outrageous—that might advance her cause. Read about her trip to Kansas, where she hated sleeping in the homesteaders' beds because they never changed their sheets, not even for company!

The work that Elizabeth Cady Stanton and her friends did set the groundwork for the 19th Amendment, passed in 1920, 18 years after her death. Finally, women were allowed to vote.

In 1909, 22-year-old Alice Ramsey and three of her women friends decided to drive across America. "So what's the big deal?" you might say. It was a big deal in 1909, because no woman had ever done that. There were no road maps of most of the country, and, in fact, there were few roads. You can read about their trip in Don Brown's *Alice Ramsey's Grand Adventure*. Ramsey had to measure the gasoline with a stick, and she had to light the headlamps with a match. The only bridge across the Platte River, which she had to cross, was a railroad bridge, and Ramsey had to keep moving, for if she stopped, her wheels would get caught between the railroad ties. This is a fun picture book that is perfect to share with young listeners.

Can you imagine being adventurous enough to climb into a barrel and go over one of the largest waterfalls in the world? In 1901 a woman named Annie Edson Taylor did just that. Doreen Rappaport's *Living Dangerously: American Women Who Risked Their Lives for Adventure* tells about Taylor and several other women who did courageous things. Annie Taylor, adventurous throughout her life, was out of money and wanted to become famous, so she had a special barrel made with a harness and padding, climbed into it backwards, and had the lid sealed. She was then pushed over Niagra Falls. Read about how she survived the falls and show the photo of her on page 15. What's most amazing about this story is that, at the time of her adventure, Annie Taylor was 63 years old!

This book also tells about a mountain climber, a diver, a triple amputee who competed in a marathon, and an elephant hunter. These women will amaze and inspire you.

Later in this chapter you will read about Queen Elizabeth I of England, also known as Queen Bess. Strangely enough, there is another very different woman known as Queen Bess. This woman was an African American who was a pioneer of the twentieth century. She was Bessie Coleman, and she has the distinction of being the first African American woman to earn a pilot's license. Most students have heard of Amelia Earhart, but many have not heard of Bess Coleman. *Up in the Air: The Story of Bessie Coleman* by Philip S. Hart (figure 6.3) is a 75-page biography of this little-known woman. She did many amazing things in her life, and she never let herself be stopped by the fact that she was an African American woman. This book is a great choice for a middle school student wanting to learn more about a little-known American heroine.

Fig. 6.3. *Up in the Air: The Story of Bessie Coleman* by Philip S. Hart

What on earth would a person have to do to be called "The Most Dangerous Woman in America"? Mother Jones did it, and she was one tough cookie. Find out about her by reading *Mother Jones: Fierce Fighter for Workers' Rights* by Judith Pinkerton Josephson (figure 6.4).

For much of American history, working conditions for most people were horrible. Even children were forced to work in mines and factories to help support their families. Children worked 14 hours a day for $3 or less a week. Many were paid not in real money but in "company money," which could be spent only in the company store. When workers got their pay, they also got their bill for food and necessary items from the store. This bill was often higher than their paycheck. Because they owed the company money, they could never quit. Dangerous conditions existed everywhere, especially in the mills and the mines. If you were injured on the job (many children had their hands cut off in machinery), it was your fault, and you got fired. People lived in cold, flimsy shacks without running water or toilets.

Mother Jones hated all of that, and she dedicated her life to changing it. She came to America from Ireland, got married, and had children. Her husband and her children were all killed in a yellow fever epidemic in Memphis, Tennessee, and she decided to fight for people everywhere. She traveled all over the United States organizing unions and standing up for workers, no matter what country they came from or what race they were. She made speeches. She got put in jail. She got run out of town and ordered never to come back. (She almost always came right back, though.) She drove officials crazy, and she made a difference in a lot of people's lives. Even when she was an old woman, in her 80s and 90s, she was running around causing all sorts of trouble. She was a fascinating lady, and this book tells you her amazing story.

Fig. 6.4. *Mother Jones: Fierce Fighter for Workers' Rights* by Judith Pinkerton Josephson

Women Inventors by Linda Jacobs Altman is one of those books that doesn't look very interesting but is, in fact, fascinating to read. When booktalking this book, you can have the satisfaction of knowing that readers probably would not have chosen it if you hadn't gotten them interested in it.

Historically, women have had a much more difficult time achieving recognition, even when they worked as hard and were as brilliant as men. *Women Inventors* starts with the story of Carrie Jacobs, who invented the vacuum canning process that made food taste better, last longer, and be much more nutritious. This process has been in use for more than 125 years! Other fascinating women include Sara Josephine Baker, who made incredible, lifesaving changes in the way people took care of their babies.

She saved thousands and thousands of lives, working in New York City with poor people. Her ideas were so good that people everywhere started using them.

Ida Rosenthal invented the Maidenform bra, which set the standard for bras everywhere. She was a Russian immigrant who came to America in 1905, at the age of 21, and she was very poor at first. By the time she died she was a multi-millionaire! Ruth Handler invented the Barbie doll, because she was convinced that little girls wanted to play with dolls who looked like grownups. She named it after her daughter Barbara, and when fans wrote her telling her that Barbie doll needed a boyfriend, she named him after her son Ken.

But Madame C. J. Walker perhaps had the toughest road to travel. Born in a slave shack to ex-slaves two years after the Civil War ended, she grew up in an environment of poverty and prejudice. She married young, at age 14, but her husband was killed a few years later, and she had to support herself and her child. She did laundry, working very hard and gradually acquiring many customers. One day she went to hear Mrs. Booker T. Washington speak. She thought Mrs. Washington looked so immaculate and so wonderful that she felt all women should try to look like that.

Her own hair never looked very good. She decided to try to create a formula that would make her hair easier to manage and look great. It took her a long time, and the formula that eventually worked came to her in a dream. Her family and friends tried it, and everyone loved it. Read the amazing story of how she marketed the product nationwide, always hiring African Americans, treating them well, and paying them a fair wage, which almost no one did at that time.

The year before she died, C. J. Walker built a beautiful mansion on the Hudson River. Show the picture of the shack where she was born and the mansion in which she died 52 years later. What an amazing woman! No wonder the U. S. Postal Service created a postage stamp in her honor.

Read about another fascinating African American woman in *Princess of the Press: The Story of Ida B. Wells-Barnett* by Angela Shelf Medearis. In 1876, when Ida Wells was 14 years old, her parents died in an epidemic. Luckily, Wells was not afraid of work; in fact, it seems as though she wasn't afraid of anything. She decided to take care of her brothers and sisters, and got a job teaching school in a place where some of her students were older than she was.

Wells wasn't a slave (although her parents had been born slaves), but the late 1800s was still a tough time to be an African American. Although African Americans had won rights after the Civil War, those rights were slowly taken away from them. Wells first caused trouble when she refused to move from the nice railroad car for white people into the dirty, crowded one for others. She sued the railroad company and won $500. The railroad company countersued, and she ended up losing money. But the experience made her ready to start fighting for her rights.

Ida Wells went into journalism, and before too long she owned her own newspaper. She spent her whole life fighting for the rights of women and African Americans. She was renowned for her writing against lynching. Mobs of angry whites would hang, burn, or otherwise kill African Americans. When one of her best friends was lynched, Wells went into action. Before long the whole country started hearing about these atrocities.

Loaded with fascinating information, *The Smithsonian Book of the First Ladies: Their Lives, Times, and Issues* edited by Edith P. Mayo is a real crowd pleaser. With its many photographs and essays on the status of women throughout U.S. history, it is both attractive and thought-provoking. A fun way to booktalk it is to ask some questions and give some information. Do you know which first lady was the only one to be both the wife of one president and the mother of another? (Answer: Abigail Adams.) Which woman was the wife of one president and the *grandmother* of another, but never got to be first lady? (Answer: Anna Harrison, who died before her husband became president.) Which first lady was the first one to ever hold a job outside of the home? (Answer: Abigail Fillmore, who was a schoolteacher for almost seven years in her twenties.) Which first lady was the first one to graduate from college? (Answer: "Lemonade" Lucy Hayes, so-called because she would not serve liquor in the White House.) Which first lady had electricity installed in the White House? (Answer: Caroline Harrison, in around 1890.) Which first lady had sudden epileptic seizures? (Answer: Ida McKinley. When she had one, her husband "would calmly reach into his pocket for a large handkerchief that he placed over her face, meanwhile continuing whatever conversation he might be engaged in. As soon as he sensed that she had recovered from her spell, he removed the handkerchief, still without giving any sign of being the least perturbed. This peculiar response to Ida's epilepsy was characteristic of how such illnesses were treated at the time.") Which first lady was the last one to keep a cow on the White House lawn? (Answer: Nellie Taft, around 1912.) This book is appropriate for students in grades 5 and up. Increase interest in the subject by linking your booktalk with a school unit on American presidents.

ATHLETES

Wilma Unlimited: How Wilma Rudolph Became the World's Fastest Woman by Kathleen Krull tells about a woman who overcame amazing obstacles. Wilma Rudolph was born in 1940 in Clarkson, Tennessee, the twentieth child out of 22 born to a poor African American family. She weighed only four pounds at birth and was sickly as a child; she caught every disease her siblings had, usually worse than they did. Only one doctor in Clarksville would treat African Americans, and doctors were an expensive luxury, so Rudolph was nursed at home.

But at age five, Rudolph got polio, a disease only the doctor could treat. She was told she would never walk again. But that doctor did not know Wilma Rudolph and her family. Twice a week Wilma and her mother took the bus to Nashville, 50 miles away, to the nearest hospital that would treat African American patients. She exercised and eventually got a brace. With the brace she was able to go to school, and out of sheer determination she was able to stop using that brace. She started playing basketball and eventually received a full scholarship to Tennessee State University. Within eight years of mailing the brace back to the hospital, Wilma won three gold medals for running in the 1960 Olympics. She was the fastest woman in the world.

You will be hard-pressed to read *Lou Gehrig: The Luckiest Man* by David A. Adler without wanting to cry at the end (figure 6.5). Some people think that Lou Gehrig was the greatest baseball player ever, and he is still a hero today. Gehrig worked hard at everything he did. He never missed one day of school from first through eighth grade—and when he became a baseball player, he set a world record for never missing a game. He played 2,130 games without missing one.

Gehrig was a Yankee, and with his teammate Babe Ruth and a group of outstanding players, he helped make the Yankees the best team in baseball. Gehrig considered himself a really lucky guy, even when he became unable to hit, started feeling sick, and kept falling down in the locker room. Finally, the doctors told him he had a terrible disease, and Gehrig knew he couldn't play his beloved game anymore. Read all about it in this wonderful book about a really wonderful man.

Fig. 6.5. *Lou Gehrig: The Luckiest Man* by David A. Adler

Jim Thorpe: 20th-Century Jock by Robert Lipsyte is the story of a famous athlete with an interesting background. Jim Thorpe is the name he is known by, but he had another name, Wa-tho-huck, Bright Path.

Born in 1887 in Indian Territory, soon to be Oklahoma, Thorpe had at least 18 brothers and sisters. It was not a good time to be a Native American. According to Lipsyte, "most whites were conditioned to believe that Indians were a subhuman species who would die out because their time was over." At one time, there were $500 rewards for each "buck Indian's scalp" captured in Arizona (pages 16 and 17).

Thorpe was sent away to "Indian schools" to learn how to be a white person. Sometimes children were sent away for years, forbidden to speak in their native language. When they went home, they could no longer speak to their parents, for they had forgotten their own language. Thorpe went to a school called Haskell, and he turned out to be an excellent football player. Eventually, he ended up at the Carlisle Indian School in Pennsylvania, where he became one of the most outstanding athletes of all time. Two other Native Americans on his team were All-Americans—the only time in history three players from the same team achieved that status.

One summer, he played semi-pro baseball in North Carolina. This was common at the time, but it was to have tragic consequences for Thorpe. After he won two gold medals at the Olympics, it was discovered that he had once been paid to play sports in North Carolina, and he was stripped of his medals.

Thorpe excelled at almost every sport he ever tried. Many think he was the greatest American athlete ever. Read this book to find out more about his fascinating story.

Kathleen Krull's *Lives of the Athletes: Thrills, Spills (and What the Neighbors Thought)* gives an intriguing glimpse into the lives of some famous athletes.

The most popular soccer player in the history of the game started out as a very poor child. A grapefruit was his first soccer ball, and his second was "an old sock stuffed with newspapers." He quit school in fourth grade to play soccer. Who was he? (Answer: Pele.) Which famous runner was hated by the Nazis because he was living proof that at least one African American could beat any Nazi—and everyone else in the world too? Nazis believed that African Americans were inferior. Jesse Owens certainly proved them wrong. But life for an African American was not so great at home either. When times were toughest, he raced against horses for money. Which famous baseball player liked to eat pickled eels with chocolate ice cream between games, and once had to be hospitalized when he ate twelve hot dogs and drank eight bottles of soda? (Answer: Babe Ruth.) Which Olympic gold medal skating champion finished in last place at her first Olympics, when she was only 11 years old—but ended up winning the gold medal in the next three Olympics? (Answer: Sonja Henie.)

Ask the kids in your audience if they can believe that there was ever a time when African Americans were not allowed to play professional sports with white people. Most of them will be surprised when you tell them that this was not so very long ago.

Teammates by Peter Golenbock (figure 6.6) tells the story of the first African American to integrate professional sports. His name was Jackie Robinson, and, wow, could he play baseball. He was a star player in the Negro Leagues, and Branch Rickey, the manager of what was then the Brooklyn Dodgers, decided to take a chance and hire him. Rickey knew that a lot of people would hate any African American for playing with white people. Robinson, he felt, was special, so he gave him a chance.

"Mr. Rickey told him, 'I want a man with the courage to not fight back!' Jackie Robinson replied, 'If you take this gamble, I will do my best to perform.' " Robinson knew that his behavior would affect the future of all African American athletes in America. If he did well, doors would open to them.

But it was terribly hard. People yelled at him, were cruel to him, and called him names. Some of the players tried to hurt him. The Ku Klux Klan threatened him. He had to stay in a separate hotel from the rest of the team because African Americans were not allowed to stay in the same hotels as white people.

A teammate of Robinson's named Pee Wee Reese, considered to be one of the world's greatest shortstops, did something very special to show the world that he thought Jackie Robinson deserved to be on the team. Read this book to find out what it was.

Fig. 6.6. *Teammates* **by Peter Golenbock**

HISTORICAL FIGURES

To introduce *Good Queen Bess: The Story of Elizabeth I of England* by Diane Stanley and Peter Vennema, ask your listeners if there has ever been a female president of the United States. How about a vice president? Have them guess how long it will be before a woman will be elected to such a position. Then tell them that as long as 400 years ago, a woman ruled England—a woman who was one of the greatest leaders in history. Students may have heard of Henry VIII, who married numerous times and killed several of his wives. Tell them that at that time families wanted to have sons to carry on the family name. Elizabeth was, unfortunately, a daughter, and this did not make her father, Henry VIII, happy. When Elizabeth's mother, Anne Boleyn, failed to have a son, Henry had her killed, and then he married four more times.

Elizabeth became queen at age 25 and ruled for 45 years until her death in 1603. She was intelligent, brave, and beautiful. She was especially admired for her willingness to meet with the people of her land. When her army was camped on the coast of England, braced for an attack from Spain, Elizabeth herself rode up on a horse wearing steel armor.

Although it is in picture book format, this book contains excellent historical information and would be useful for middle school students. The illustrations by Diane Stanley are detailed and elaborate, and capture the spirit of the Elizabethan age.

Just about everyone has heard of Betsy Ross. But what do most of us know about her? Probably only that she sewed the "first" American flag. But what did that look like? Do you have any idea? *Betsy Ross: Patriot of Philadelphia* by Judith St. George will tell you about this misunderstood figure in American history.

This lively book tells us about Ross, who lived an interesting life and was greatly affected by the Revolutionary War. She was born in and lived near Philadelphia all of her life. She was a Quaker, a member of a peaceful religious group, who left her church when she was 21 to marry John Ross. Together they opened an upholstery and sewing shop. John helped the Revolutionary effort by working as a citizen guard, but he was killed in an explosion in 1776.

Many things, as we all know, were happening in 1776. One day Betsy Ross was amazed when George Washington walked into her shop and asked her to sew a new flag he had designed. She ended up making lots of flags. If you have heard that maybe Betsy Ross really did *not* make the flag, read the end of the book to find the reasons why most people believe that she did. And it was not really the first flag, it was the first stars and stripes flag. As the flag is something we all see every day, it is fun to know some of its history.

Another interesting American is described in *Bill Pickett: Rodeo-Ridin' Cowboy* by Andrea D. Pinkney. Bill Pickett's parents were slaves, brought to Texas from South Carolina by their masters in 1854. There they learned how to work the land and care for the animals. Pickett's father, Thomas, was only 11 at the end of the Civil War. He married and settled in Jenks-Branch, a freed slave community just north of Austin, Texas. He and his wife, Mary, had 13 children. Their second child was Willie, called Bill, a feisty boy who grew up listening to the stories of his trail-driving horsemen cousins. He decided that he wanted to do the same work when he grew up.

Pichett was straddling the gate one afternoon when he saw an eye-popping sight. A bulldog was holding a restless cow's lower lip in its teeth. He began to wonder why he couldn't do the same thing. He tested his idea a few days later, holding with his teeth a cow that was to be branded. It worked, and the trick made Bill Pickett's career. Although he worked as a ranch hand, he was able to tame broncos and practice "bull-dogging," which he named after the dog he saw biting the bull. Eventually, he was able to do his work in rodeos throughout the west. He married in 1890 and became the father of nine children. He suffered from prejudice because he was an African American but ultimately worked with the 101 Ranch Wild West Show, which played Madison Square Garden, Mexico City, Canada, and South America, and he even performed for the King and Queen of England in 1914!

A Boy Called Slow: The True Story of Sitting Bull by Joseph Bruchac tells about a famous Native American and his courageous acts. In 1831, the first boy in the family of "Returns Again" of the Hunkpapa band of the Lakota Sioux was born. Every child was given a childhood name, and that name frequently described the way the child acted. This child's cousin was named "Hungry Mouth" because he ate so much. But the son of Returns Again did not eat too much, or move quickly. He took his time in all that he did, so his family called him "Slow." (An excellent classroom exercise might be to ask the children in the room to describe themselves. If you were to be named after what people saw you doing, what would your name be?)

"Slow" did not much like his name, but until he earned a new one it could not be changed. A child earned a name by having a powerful dream or by doing some brave or special deed. He envied his father, whose full name was "Returns Again to Strike the Enemy." This was a good name, a brave name, a name other people would wish to have for their own.

The boy named Slow was given his own name when he, too, did something courageous. His new name is a name we all know, even today, for he became one of the most famous Native Americans who ever lived. To find out who he was and how he got his name, read this book.

Show audiences almost any of the beautiful illustrations as you page through the book.

Another story about Native Americans is told in *Plains Warrior: Chief Quanah Parker and the Comanches* by Albert Marrin. Quanah Parker was born in interesting times. His very birth was interesting, for his mother was Cynthia Ann Parker, a white woman who had been captured as a child by the Comanches. When she became old enough to marry, a warrior who became famous chose her for his wife. Quanah was their first child, probably born around 1845. Cynthia loved the Comanche life, and when she was recaptured by the white people several years later, she was miserable. She ended up starving herself and dying of grief and starvation because she wanted to go back to the life she loved.

This book tells not only the story of Quanah Parker and his family, but also describes what life was like for the plains people before and after the arrival of the white man. Major changes took place long before white settlers actually came to the plains, for the arrival of the horse, brought by the Spaniards decades earlier, had dramatically altered the way the Native Americans lived. It is fascinating to read about their life and how the land they lived on affected them.

Quanah Parker ended up being the only Comanche chief. He was a practical man who realized that the ways of the Native Americans were doomed. He ended up living in Fort Sill, Oklahoma, in a frame house with his seven wives. In his old age, he was thrilled to see a photograph of his mother. Be sure to show audiences that photograph on page 87 and the photograph of Quanah on page 98.

To most people, Crazy Horse is noteworthy for his participation in the battle of Little Big Horn, the only battle in which Native Americans completely and thoroughly defeated white settlers. A year after that battle, the mighty victor was dead, killed by the white people he is renowned for having defeated. Read about what happened to him in Russell Freedman's *The Life and Death of Crazy Horse.*

Crazy Horse was an extraordinary warrior. No photographs of him exist, and no one knows where he was buried. Most of the knowledge we have of him is based on some 1930 interviews with his relatives and surviving warriors. Prior to that time, published accounts of his life were almost exclusively based on the accounts of white men who fought against him.

Crazy Horse was probably born in 1841, and he died at the age of about 36. He resisted white men all his life and never signed a treaty with them. He did not wear war paint or take scalps, and he refused to boast about his brave deeds. Faithful to a vision he had as a boy, he rode into battle with a single hawk's feather in his hair, a small brown stone tied behind one ear, and a few hailspots painted on his body. He was victorious in battle, but treachery and deceit led to his violent death at Camp Robinson.

Among the many wonderful features of this book are the pictures of Sioux life drawn by Amos Bad Heart Bull, born in 1869. He drew the pictures of Sioux life in a ledger book, and they are authentic.

Two fascinating historical figures are brought to life in Becky Rutberg's *Mary Lincoln's Dressmaker: Elizabeth Keckley's Remarkable Rise from Slave to White House Confidante.* Elizabeth Keckley was an unlikely person to be a personal friend to Abraham Lincoln's wife. She was a former slave who bought her freedom and worked as a seamstress for the most renowned people of her generation. She not only became Mary Lincoln's dressmaker, she became her closest confidante and best friend at a time when white and African American people were not usually friends. She was there when the Lincolns' son Willie died, when Mary Lincoln became jealous of other women being near her husband, and the day that Abraham Lincoln died. She raised money to help the widowed Mrs. Lincoln, defended her against criticism, and later wrote a book about her experiences with the Lincolns. Unfortunately, that book so angered Mary Lincoln that she never spoke to Elizabeth Keckley again. Rutberg includes many interesting details about the Lincolns and their personal lives, as well as photographs of notable people of the time. Booktalk this title to teachers as well as students—anyone with an interest in American history will be intrigued.

Andrea Warren's *Orphan Train Rider: One Boy's True Story* (figure 6.7) describes how poor or homeless children in New York City were put on the "orphan trains" and sent West. At every stop, the children were herded off the train cars, inspected by the people from the local community, and taken into new homes. Some children were lucky and found wonderful homes with loving parents. Others were selected primarily for labor and wound up working in almost slave-like conditions. As Lee, the hero of this true story, gets on a train with his little brother, his father hands him a piece of paper with the father's address on it. He tells Lee to write him when he finds a new home so that the father can eventually come and bring his boys back to live with him. In a scene right out of Charles Dickens (or Stephen King) the woman in charge of the group sees the paper and tears it up, telling the children they will not need it anymore. The boys never saw their father again. This brief introduction is sufficient to sell Warren's book to an eager audience. But also tell them that Lee did find two of his other brothers when he was more than 60 years old.

The picture of Lee on the front cover is a good one to share with your audience.

Fig. 6.7. *Orphan Train Rider: One Boy's True Story* by Andrea Warren

KIDS' FAVORITE AUTHORS AND ILLUSTRATORS

Everybody has heard of Walt Disney. Not only did he produce some favorite movies and create Mickey Mouse, he also built Disneyland and Disney World. Learn more about him by reading *Walt Disney: His Life in Pictures* edited by Russell Schroeder.

This is a fun book to look at, because it is loaded with excellent photographs of Walt Disney throughout his life. He was a big ham, and many of the photos reflect that.

Born in Chicago, Disney spent much of his childhood on the family farm in Marceline, Missouri. When the United States entered World War I in 1917, Disney lied about his age and joined an ambulance unit. He always said that it was a good thing for him because being on his own made him more self-reliant.

When he came home, he was determined to become an artist. He got a job in animation in Kansas City, and with the first money he made he bought a moving picture camera. He started out by making "Alice" comedies, but he hit it big when he invented and started making short films about a character called Mickey Mouse. In the late 1930s he made his first full feature-length film. Can you guess what it was? Probably most of you have seen it. It was called *Snow White and the Seven Dwarfs*, and it was a huge hit. In fact, it made the most money of any movie ever made up to that time.

In spite of the Depression and some financial setbacks, Disney and his company continued to thrive. By the 1950s Disney decided to start his own amusement park. He called it Disneyland, and to advertise it, he started a TV show.

Now, more than 30 years since his death, the Disney organization is one of the most influential in the world. Read about the man who created it in this fun biography.

Show your audience the photo on page 44 of Walt Disney holding Mickey.

Packed with humor and hundreds of drawings, *Bill Peet: An Autobiography* will also appeal to young artists (figure 6.8). Ask students if they are familiar with the artwork of Bill Peet. Chances are they won't be. Then ask them if they have seen the animated Disney movies *Snow White, Pinocchio, Fantasia, Dumbo, Peter Pan, Song of the South, Cinderella, 101 Dalmatians, Sleeping Beauty,* and *The Jungle Book*. If they have seen any of them, then they have seen Bill Peet's artwork. They also may be familiar with Peet's children's books such as *Chester the Worldly Pig, Huge Harold,* and *Randy's Dandy Lions*. Show them the autobiography and flip through some pages for them. Show them the monsters on page 89 and ask if they have seen them before. When they say no, tell them why: Peet drew these monsters to be part of *Pinocchio,* but Walt Disney didn't like them and cut them from the story. Then show listeners pages 124 and 125. These are preliminary sketches of the mice that made it into the movie *Cinderella*. Another interesting aspect of the book is the insight into Walt Disney's personality. The man who created an empire based on children's movies and family entertainment wasn't always a nice guy. In fact, one of his artists considered him to be an "insensitive, uncultured, illiterate clod" (page 98).

Fig. 6.8. *Bill Peet: An Autobiography* by Bill Peet

Another favorite author/illustrator is Dr. Seuss. *Oh, the Places He Went: A Story about Dr. Seuss* by Maryann N. Weidt (figure 6.9) gives a lively overview of his life. Kids may not know that his real name was Theodor Geisel, and that he sometimes wrote under the name Theo LeSieg (Geisel spelled backward). A few tidbits to share with your audience: His fan letters at one time averaged between 1,500 and 2,000 a week. He wrote in verse for so long that he used to dream in rhyme and had trouble writing a letter without the words rhyming. He continued to write books until he died at age 87. He never had any children of his own. Middle to upper elementary school children will enjoy this biography.

Fig. 6.9. *Oh, the Places He Went: A Story about Dr. Seuss* by Maryann N. Weidt

Most kids are familiar with Roald Dahl, creator of favorites such as *Charlie and the Chocolate Factory, James and the Giant Peach,* and *Matilda.* In *Boy: Tales of Childhood* Dahl gives readers an understanding of how he came to write the books he wrote. Several incidents center around candy, which might explain the inspiration for *Charlie and the Chocolate Factory.* A good section to read aloud begins on page 33. Dahl describes the sweet shop that was the center of his life when he was a boy. Unfortunately, the woman who owned the shop was, in his words, a horror—a "small skinny old hag with a mustache on her upper lip and a mouth as sour as a green gooseberry." Read the gruesome description of Mrs. Pratchett beginning on page 33 and ending on page 34. The final paragraph of the chapter is a great teaser:

> So you can well understand that we had it in for Mrs. Pratchett in a big way, but we didn't quite know what to do about it. Many schemes were put forward but none of them was any good. None of them, that is, until suddenly, one memorable afternoon, we found the dead mouse.

You can leave it at that, or tell the kids that Dahl and his friends put the dead mouse in Mrs. Pratchett's jar of gobstoppers. They will have to read the book to find out what happened next. This 174-page book has a few photos and drawings, but is mainly text and is most appropriate for middle school students or elementary school students with good reading skills.

Probably the most famous children's author of recent years is R. L. Stine, creator of "Goosebumps" and "Fear Street" books. Kids will love his biography called *It Came from Ohio! My Life as a Writer*, which looks distinctly like a "Goosebumps" book. Stine, who used to be a humor writer, makes his life story entertaining and interesting to kids. He includes lots of photos of himself and his family, and numerous anecdotes about how he gets his ideas for horror stories. Just show the cover of this book, with its colorful, shiny optical illusion sticker, and "Goosebumps" fans will be clamoring to read it.

Small Steps: The Year I Got Polio by Peg Kehret (figure 6.10) tells the story of a popular children's author who overcame great adversity at a young age. Peg Schulze, who lived in Austin, Minnesota, was 12 years old in 1949 when she was afflicted with three kinds of polio at once. The disease paralyzed her from the neck down and made it practically impossible for her to breathe. She was a very lucky girl, however, because she got better.

Kehret, who fell ill the day of the homecoming parade, was taken first to the Sheltering Arms Hospital and then to the University Hospital. Frantic and terrified, she suffered even more because her parents were not allowed to see her for the first few days. Not only was she deathly ill, she was also alone. But one day her leg itched, and to her own astonishment, her hand scratched it. It was the first major sign that she was on the road to some sort of recovery. At the University Hospital, she went through Sister Kenny's treatment, for which she is still grateful, and roomed with an eight-year-old boy in an iron lung. Eventually she was able to move to the Sheltering Arms Hospital, where she had four roommates, all of whom were in worse condition than she was and whose parents were either very poor or lived far away and almost never came to see them. Peg realized how blessed she was. Her own parents came every Sunday, no matter what, and brought a seemingly endless supply of gifts and goodies, taking care of Peg's roommates, as well.

Kehret details her various therapies and reveals the grit and determination that got her through. The book ends seven months after it starts, as she returns to school in Austin, on crutches, but with the cheers of her classmates. She was the only person in Austin to get polio that year, and everyone was rooting for her. Kehret eventually married and had children and wrote many children's books, including *Cages, Danger at the Fair, Earthquake Terror,* and *Nightmare Mountain.*

Fig. 6.10. *Small Steps: The Year I Got Polio* **by Peg Kehret**

"If at first you don't succeed, try, try again" is a saying we have all heard. Helen Lester, who writes funny and fun books for kids, tells us how true it is in her book *Author: A True Story* (figure 6.11).

Even when she was three years old and the only person who could read what she wrote, Lester considered herself an author. She always liked to write, and after she had taught school for several years, she decided to write a book for kids. She thought it was a good one, and she sent it to a publisher. The publisher said "no thanks." Lester tried again. The publisher still said "no thanks." It took Helen a lot of trying and a lot of work before she finally got her first book published. But she did succeed.

Sometimes we think that good things come easily to other people, just not us. This book proves that is not true. And you will laugh when you are reading it. When book-talking this book, be sure to show some of Lester's other books, including *Tacky the Penguin, Three Cheers for Tacky*, and *A Porcupine Named Fluffy*.

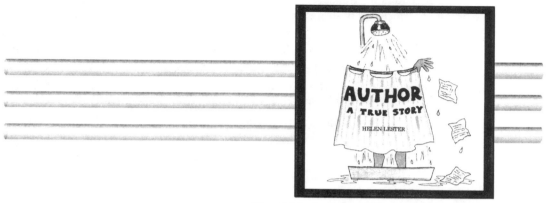

Fig. 6.11. *Author: A True Story* by Helen Lester

Imagine what it would have been like to be a pioneer, to travel West, settling the new land, seeing wild animals, and meeting Native Americans. Laura Ingalls Wilder did this, as did many others, but what was special about Laura is that she wrote about what it was like. In her beloved "Little House" books, she describes growing up in Wisconsin and moving to Kansas, Minnesota, and South Dakota. Her stories were fiction, based on the truth, but not always perfectly true. She left out some things, such as the death of her little brother. *Laura Ingalls Wilder* by Alexandra Wallner (figure 6.12) is a nonfiction account of her life and how she learned "to make pictures with words" for her sister, Mary, when Mary lost her sight. Show audiences the first full-page color picture of the interior of the little house in the Big Woods and the picture of Pa playing his fiddle while the family listens.

Fig. 6.12. *Laura Ingalls Wilder* by Alexandra Wallner

The World of Little House by Carolyn Strom Collins and Christina Wyss Erickson is not only a biography of Laura Ingalls Wilder and her family, but describes her books one by one, comparing them with the real life of the Ingalls family. It features actual photographs of the people who were characters in the books; Laura's recipe for gingerbread and other foods she loved, such as pulled molasses and town party lemonade; and directions for crafts and games mentioned in the books. Best of all are floor plans for each of the houses Laura lived in, as well as Almanzo's *Farmer Boy* home.

If you wish to visit the places where Laura lived, refer to the book's directory, which includes addresses. You can also write for further information. This book will appeal to adults as well as children, so be sure to booktalk it to parents and teachers.

Searching for Laura Ingalls: A Reader's Journey by Kathryn Lasky and Meribah Knight is the delightful true story of Meribah Knight, who lives in Boston and who loves Laura Ingalls. Knight's mom was a writer of children's books, and her dad was a fine photographer, and they decided to take a family trip to some of the places where the Ingalls family lived. They flew to Minneapolis and rented a camper, then they drove to Pepin, Wisconsin, where Laura and her family lived in *Little House in the Big Woods*. Next they visited Walnut Grove, Minnesota, where they lived in *On the Banks of Plum Creek*. Knight particularly wanted to swim in Plum Creek, so she did—and guess what? She got a leech on her just like Laura once did. Show the photo of Knight with the leech on her foot. (You might want to use this as a lead-in to a booktalk of *Those Amazing Leeches*, discussed in chapter 3.) The family's last stop was De Smet, South Dakota, which was *The Little Town on the Prairie*, and the setting for *By the Shores of Silver Lake*, where the Ingalls family spent *The Long Winter* and where Laura married Almanzo in *These Happy Golden Years*.

Meribah Knight's dad took some wonderful pictures of the places where Laura lived, and flipping through the book while telling about the trip is a good way to sell it to audiences. But the photo of Knight wearing her Laura Ingalls bonnet is a good one to use, as is the one of her and the leech.

Grace McCance was another real pioneer girl, about 15 years younger than Laura Ingalls. She grew up in Nebraska and lived to be more than 100 years old. Her story, told in *Pioneer Girl: Growing up on the Prairie* by Andrea Warren, is a fine one. Grace McCance was one tough lady. When she was elderly, one of her daughters suggested that they go out to lunch and shop. McCance was not in the mood. She announced that she would rather kill rattlesnakes, and they killed quite a few that day.

McCance grew up in a "soddy"—a house of bricks made from soil. Sod houses were very difficult to keep clean, and Nebraska was not always the finest place in which to make a good living. Droughts were common, many farmers barely made enough to feed their families, and children often died at a very young age. But for city people in hopeless situations, owning and farming their own land was an incredible opportunity.

McCance's story was written by her daughter in 1963. Andrea Warren, who also lives in Nebraska, retells it here. She lets us know what it was like living in a soddy, knowing hard times, and being a kid at a time when a lot of kids had to work hard to help the family. You'll be glad you read it.

Sid Fleischman, author of *The Abracadabra Kid: A Writer's Life*, must be one of the neatest guys around. Do you know what he does when he visits a school? He asks kids to volunteer, because he wants to cut one of them in half! Then he cuts the kid in half with a red ribbon, so, he says, that the blood won't show.

Fleischman has written some really good books. One of them, *The Whipping Boy*, won the Newbery Medal. But he did not start out by wanting to be a writer. He wanted to be a magician and do magic shows. He started practicing when he was very young and did shows for money when he was just a teenager. He considers himself lucky that one of his friends was the widow of Harry Houdini, who was probably the most famous magician who ever lived. She liked to help and encourage young magicians.

The Abracadabra Kid is funny and fun to read. After you read about his life and adventures, you will wish Sid Fleischman would come to visit your school so that you could meet him (and maybe even get cut in half).

Show the photo of Sid, age three, on page 5. The caption is great. Be sure to read it: "A characteristic pose of me looking forward, as usual. Here I am looking forward to my fourth birthday. Notice my trend-setting haircut, which finally caught on in the 1990s." Another great caption appears with the last photo, on page 195: "I notice that quite often authors' public photographs show them thirty years earlier, in the prime of youth. Here I am, taken ten minutes ago."

HEROES AND HEROINES

The first Africans in what is now the United States arrived in Jamestown, Virginia, on a Dutch ship in 1619. They came as indentured servants, agreeing to work for a set period of years in order to be set free. As was common later in our history, not all of the promises were kept. Many indentured servants were forced into slavery.

Despite their hardships, African Americans triumphed in all sorts of ways. *African Americans Who Were First* by Joan Potter and Constance Claytor tells us many of the ways in which they were first—and some of those ways will probably surprise you. The first person to make a clock in the American colonies was an African American named Benjamin Banneker, who later became famous for helping design the capitol building in Washington, D.C. He carved his clock entirely out of wood and figured out how to do it by examining a pocket watch, a picture of a clock, and a geometry book. His clock ran for 40 years. Do you think you could do that?

The first African American senator was Hiram Rhoades Revels, elected from Mississippi in 1870. It was more than 100 years before an African American woman was elected to the senate—Carol Mosely-Braun, from Illinois, in 1992. The first African American governor of any state was not elected until 1990—L. Douglas Wilder from Virginia.

The first African American to have his picture on a postage stamp was Booker T. Washington. You have probably heard of him, but there are other African Americans on postage stamps who may not be so famous. If you do not know who Benjamin Davis or Bessie Coleman or Madame C. J. Walker are, you can find out here.

African Americans have done some pretty amazing things. The first man to perform open-heart surgery, in 1893, was Daniel Hale Williams. The inventor of the automatic traffic light and the gas mask, the first doctor to successfully separate twins joined at the head, the first person to reach the North Pole, the first to set up a blood bank, the first to win the world heavyweight champion title three times—all were African Americans! In fact, during the famous attack on Pearl Harbor, one African American, Dorie Miller, ran to a machine gun and shot down *four* enemy planes.

If you are interested in people who did great things despite adversity, this is the book for you.

The man who became known as Nelson Mandela is one of the most amazing people who ever lived. Read about him in Floyd Cooper's book, *Mandela: From the Life of the South African Statesman*. His father was the chief of a South African village, but he lost his position and had to leave his home when the English rulers who had taken over South Africa disagreed with a decision he had made. The white people forced the natives of South Africa to obey them in all things and had made life very hard for them.

When Nelson was a small child, everyone called him Buti, but he received the name Nelson when he went to school at age 7. The English teacher gave all of the children English names. How would you feel if your teacher decided to change your name to anything she wanted?

Mandela's father believed in justice and fairness, and he taught his son to stand up for what was right. He also believed that it would be good for Mandela to get as much education as possible. Mandela did both. He eventually went to live in a terribly poor area of Johannesburg, the capital of South Africa. The place where he lived had no running water, no electricity, and no heat. Most black people were forced to live in places like these and take low-paying jobs, but nothing could stop Mandela from getting more education and becoming a lawyer.

Mandela was horrified at the unfairness with which his people were treated, so he became a leader, someone who wanted conditions to change, because that was fair and right. Many, many times Mandela was sent to jail because he tried to change things in South Africa. In 1963 he went to jail and was sentenced to do hard labor, for 27 years! But even in prison he continued to work for what he felt was fair and right, and finally, Nelson Mandela was released from prison and became the president of South Africa.

Read about this wonderful man who was willing to suffer to make things change. Show children almost any of the lovely pictures in this oversize book to illustrate your booktalk and pique their interest.

Did you know that an airplane pilot was once one of the most famous people in the country? Today we are very used to media celebrities, but in 1927, the idea of them was quite new. Charles Lindbergh was one of the most famous of them all, but his fame did not bring him much happiness. You can find out what made him so famous in *Charles A. Lindbergh: A Human Hero* by James Cross Giblin (figure 6.13).

Charles Lindbergh was the first person to fly across the Atlantic Ocean, from New York to Paris, and he did it alone. He was only 25 years old, he had no desire to be famous, and he loved to fly. His flight was terrifying to many. Several people had already died trying to make the trip, and there was not even a front window for him to see out of the plane! His fuel was so heavy he was not even sure he would be able to get up off the runway. He brought along five sandwiches to eat, water to drink, and a jar in which to go to the bathroom. He was cold, and he had to stay awake for two days. He knew if he fell asleep, he would die.

When he completed the feat, he became an instant hero. The press and the public would not leave him alone, and five years after the trip his baby was kidnapped and killed. Lindbergh always blamed the press for part of his problems.

Charles Lindbergh was a fascinating man whose story continues to interest us more than 25 years after his death. Show kids the photo on page 42 and the picture of the women holding the Lindbergh doll on page 97. Remind them that we can all see the tiny plane in which Lindbergh made his famous flight at the Smithsonian Institution in Washington, D.C.

Fig. 6.13. *Charles A. Lindbergh: A Human Hero* **by James Cross Giblin**

Have you ever wondered what it would be like to save the lives of dozens of people? Kate Shelley was a heroine who lived more than 100 years ago, and you can read about her in *Kate Shelley: Bound for Legend* by Robert San Souci.

Fifteen-year-old Kate Shelley was an Iowa farm girl in 1881. She lived close to a railroad bridge, and she knew every train that passed through her area.

During a huge rainstorm, she and her mother heard a crash as a "pusher" engine went over the bridge and fell into the water. Do you know what a pusher engine is? It is an engine that helps other trains go up steep hills.

Shelley knew what was going to happen next. Hundreds of passengers going to Chicago would be on the midnight train, due to cross that bridge in less than an hour, and now there was no bridge! She told her mother she would try to get to the nearest station to get the telegraph man to send a warning, but if she could not make it in time, she planned to flag down that train herself. How could she do it in the dark of a fierce storm with only a lantern? And what if she did not make it to the station? How can anyone stop a speeding train alone in the dark? Read Kate Shelley's story to find out what happened.

Leon's Story by Leon Walter Tillage tells about a young man who became involved in the Civil Rights Movement. Tillage grew up in the "Jim Crow" era in North Carolina. What he lived through as a child is horrifying to read about. He accepted it as normal because, to him, it was normal—it was the way people had to live. Tillage's father could neither read nor write. He worked as a sharecropper, which meant that he did an enormous amount of work for a white farmer but could never get out of debt. The family lived in a shack with no running water, no electricity, and no indoor toilet. They, like all of the African Americans in the area, lived in constant fear. They were used to it. It was the way things were, and most people thought they could do nothing to change it.

Tillage's dad thought learning to read and write was not important, but his mother thought it was *very* important, so Tillage helped her learn to read. As they learned to read, they began to realize that things might not always have to be the way they were. And when a man named Martin Luther King Jr. came to town and got people excited about the nonviolent way they might be able to make changes, Leon Tillage decided he wanted to help too.

For a riveting booktalk, read aloud the section on pages 66-69 about the death of Leon's father. It will break hearts.

FASCINATING KIDS

Vicki Van Meter is living proof that kids can do anything they set out to do. At the age of 10 she began taking flying lessons, and shortly thereafter she became the youngest girl ever to fly across the country. The day after finishing sixth grade she took off to pilot a plane across the Atlantic. *Taking Flight: My Story* is Van Meter's account of how she accomplished so much at such a young age. It includes photos of her with Al Gore, Jay Leno, Conan O'Brien, and other celebrities. It tells in her own words how she found the courage to do such brave things at a very young age.

Kids with Courage: True Stories About Young People Making a Difference by Barbara A. Lewis is full of inspiring read-aloud stories. The book is divided into four sections: Kids Fighting Crime, Kids Taking Social Action, Heroic Kids, and Kids Saving the Environment. Any one of the stories would make a good booktalk—choose one that coincides with a unit of study or an item in the news. A particularly riveting story, found on page 91, deals with guns in the schools. Ruben Ortega, a high school student, became a hero when another student held his class hostage at gunpoint. It was an ordinary day at school until Jeff came into class with a rifle. He ordered the teacher to leave the room and demanded that pizzas be delivered. The class sat in terror until Ruben Ortega bravely came to the front of the room, wrestled Jeff to the floor, and pushed the barrel of the gun toward the ceiling just as it fired. Thanks to Ruben Ortega, no students were injured, and Jeff received the help he needed. The book includes photographs of all the young heroes, and is a good choice for reluctant middle school readers.

Phillip Hoose's book *It's Our World, Too! Stories of Young People Who Are Making a Difference* is a similar title, full of stories about kids doing remarkable things. The preface tells about kids throughout American history who made a difference: young men who fought in the Revolutionary War, young women who protested poor factory conditions, children who led slaves to freedom, newspaper boys who went on strike for better wages, and young civil rights workers. The rest of the book profiles modern kids who are fighting crime and racism, saving the earth, and helping others. Pick any one of these chapters to share with students. The photographs of the kids are rather small and dark, but the stories speak for themselves and will leave your listeners wanting to take some action to solve a social problem.

BIBLIOGRAPHY

Adler, David A. *Lou Gehrig: The Luckiest Man.* Illustrated by Terry Widener. Gulliver Books/Harcourt Brace, 1997. 32 p. ISBN 0-15-200523-4. Grades 1-3.

————. *A Picture Book of Thomas Alva Edison.* Illustrated by John Wallner and Alexandra Wallner. Holiday House, 1996. 30 p. ISBN 0-8234-1246-6. Grades K-3.

Altman, Linda Jacobs. *Women Inventors.* Facts on File, 1997. 118 p. ISBN 0-8160-3385-4. Grades 5-up.

Brown, Don. *Alice Ramsey's Grand Adventure.* Illustrated by Don Brown. Houghton Mifflin, 1997. 32 p. ISBN 0-395-70127-9. Grades 1-3.

Bruchac, Joseph. *A Boy Called Slow: The True Story of Sitting Bull.* Illustrated by Rocco Baviera. Philomel Books, 1994. 32 p. ISBN 0-399-22692-3. Grades 1-3.

Burns, Khephra, and William Miles. *Black Stars in Orbit: NASA's African American Astronauts.* Gulliver Books/Harcourt Brace, 1995. 72 p. ISBN 0-15-200432-7. Grades 5-8.

Collins, Carolyn Strom, and Christina Wyss Erickson. *The World of Little House.* Illustrated by Deborah Maze and Garth Williams. HarperCollins, 1996. 150 p. ISBN 0-06-024422-4; 0-06-024423-2 (lib. bdg.). Grades 3-up.

Cooper, Floyd. *Mandela: From the Life of the South African Statesman.* Philomel Books, 1996. 40 p. ISBN 0-399-22942-6. Grades 1-3.

Dahl, Roald. *Boy: Tales from Childhood.* Puffin Books, 1984. 176 p. ISBN 0-14-031890-9. Grades 5-8.

Fisher, Leonard Everett. *Marie Curie.* Macmillan, 1994. 32 p. ISBN 0-02-735375-3. Grades 3-5.

Fleischman, Sid. *The Abracadabra Kid: A Writer's Life.* Greenwillow Books, 1996. 198 p. ISBN 0-688-14859-X. Grades 5-up.

Freedman, Russell. *The Life and Death of Crazy Horse.* Illustrated by Amos Bad Heart Bull. Holiday House, 1996. 166 p. ISBN 0-8234-1219-9. Grades 5-up.

————. *Martha Graham: A Dancer's Life.* Clarion Books, 1998. 176 p. ISBN 0-395-74655-8. Grades 6-up.

Fritz, Jean. *You Want to Vote, Lizzie Stanton?* Illustrated by DyAnne DiSalvo-Ryan. G. P. Putnam's Sons, 1995. 88 p. ISBN 0-399-22786-5. Grades 4-6.

Giblin, James Cross. *Charles A. Lindbergh: A Human Hero.* Clarion Books, 1997. 212 p. ISBN 0-395-63389-3. Grades 4-up.

Golenbock, Peter. *Teammates.* Illustrated by Paul Bacon. Gulliver Books/Harcourt Brace Jovanovich, 1990. 32p. ISBN 0-15-200603-6. Grades 1-4.

Hart, Philip S. *Up in the Air: The Story of Bessie Coleman.* Carolrhoda Books, 1996. 80 p. ISBN 0-87614-949-2 (lib. bdg.); 0-87614-978-6 (pbk.). Grades 5-8.

Hoose, Phillip. *It's Our World, Too! Stories of Young People Who Are Making a Difference*. Little, Brown, 1993. 166 p. ISBN 0-316-37241-2. Grades 5-8.

Josephson, Judith Pinkerton. *Mother Jones: Fierce Fighter for Workers' Rights*. Lerner Publications, 1997. 144 p. ISBN 0-8225-4924-7. Grades 5-up.

Kehret, Peg. *Small Steps: The Year I Got Polio*. Whitman, 1996. 181 p. ISBN 0-8075-7457-0. Grades 4-7.

Krull, Kathleen. *Lives of the Artists: Masterpieces, Messes (and What the Neighbors Thought)*. Illustrated by Kathryn Hewitt. Harcourt Brace, 1995. 96p. ISBN 0-15-200103-4. Grades 4-6.

———. *Lives of the Athletes: Thrills, Spills (and What the Neighbors Thought)*. Illustrated by Kathryn Hewitt. Harcourt Brace, 1997. 96 p. ISBN 0-15-200806-3. Grades 4-6.

———. *Lives of the Musicians: Good Times, Bad Times (and What the Neighbors Thought)*. Illustrated by Kathryn Hewitt. Harcourt Brace, 1993. 96 p. ISBN 0-15-2480102. Grades 4-6.

———. *Lives of the Writers: Comedies, Tragedies (and What the Neighbors Thought)*. Illustrated by Kathryn Hewitt. Harcourt Brace, 1995. 96 p. ISBN 0-15-248009-9. Grades 4-6.

———. *Wilma Unlimited: How Wilma Rudolph Became the World's Fastest Woman*. Illustrated by David Diaz. Harcourt Brace, 1996. 42 p. ISBN 0-15-201267-2. Grades 2-4.

Lasky, Kathryn. *A Brilliant Streak: The Making of Mark Twain*. Illustrated by Barry Moser. Harcourt Brace, 1998. 42 p. ISBN 0-15-252110-0. Grades 4-6.

Lasky, Kathryn, and Meribah Knight. *Searching for Laura Ingalls: A Reader's Journey*. Photographs by Christopher G. Knight. Macmillan, 1993. 48 p. ISBN 0-02-751666-0. Grades 2-5.

Lester, Helen. *Author: A True Story*. Houghton Mifflin, 1997. 32 p. ISBN 0-395-82744-2. Grades 1-3.

Lewis, Barbara A. *Kids with Courage: True Stories About Young People Making a Difference*. Free Spirit, 1992. 173 p. ISBN 0-915793-39-3. Grades 5-8.

Lipsyte, Robert. *Jim Thorpe: 20th-Century Jock*. HarperCollins, 1993. 103 p. ISBN 0-06-022988-8 (trade); 0-06-022989-6 (lib. bdg.). Grades 4-7.

Marrin, Albert. *Plains Warrior: Chief Quanah Parker and the Comanches*. Atheneum Books for Young Readers, 1996. 200 p. ISBN 0-689-80081-9. Grades 5-up.

Mayo, Edith P. (editor). *The Smithsonian Book of the First Ladies: Their Lives, Times, and Issues*. Henry Holt, 1996. 302 p. ISBN 0-8050-1751-8. Grades 5-up.

McCully, Emily Arnold. *The Pirate Queen*. G. P. Putnam's Sons, 1996. 32 p. ISBN 0-399-22657-5. Grades 3-5.

Medearis, Angela Shelf. *Princess of the Press: The Story of Ida B. Wells-Barnett*. Lodestar Books/Dutton, 1997. 48 p. ISBN 0-525-67493-4. Grades 4-6.

Peet, Bill. *Bill Peet: An Autobiography*. Houghton Mifflin, 1989. 190 p. ISBN 0-395-50932-7. Grades 4-7.

Pinkney, Andrea D. *Bill Pickett: Rodeo-Ridin' Cowboy*. Illustrated by Brian Pinkney. Gulliver Books/Harcourt Brace, 1996. 32 p. ISBN 0-15-200100-X. Grades 1-3.

Pinkney, Andrea Davis. *Duke Ellington*. Illustrated by Brian Pinkney. Hyperion Books for Children, 1998. 32 p. ISBN 0-7868-0178-6 (trade); 0-7868-2150-7 (lib. bdg.). Grades 3-5.

Potter, Joan, and Constance Claytor. *African Americans Who Were First*. Cobblehill Books/Dutton, 1997. 116 p. ISBN 0-525-65246-9. Grades 4-7.

Rappaport, Doreen. *Living Dangerously: American Women Who Risked Their Lives for Adventure*. HarperCollins, 1991. 117 p. ISBN 0-06-025108-5; 0-06-025109-3 (lib. bdg.). Grades 5-8.

Reit, Seymour. *Behind Rebel Lines: The Incredible Story of Emma Edmonds, Civil War Spy*. Harcourt Brace, 1988. 114 p. ISBN 0-15-200424-6. Grades 5-8.

Rutberg, Becky. *Mary Lincoln's Dressmaker: Elizabeth Keckley's Remarkable Rise from Slave to White House Confidante*. Walker, 1995. 166 p. ISBN 0-8027-8224-8; 0-8027-8225-6 (reinforced). Grades 6-8.

St. George, Judith. *Betsy Ross: Patriot of Philadelphia*. Illustrated by Sasha Meret. Henry Holt, 1997. 118 p. ISBN 0-8050-5440-5. Grades 3-6.

San Souci, Robert D. *Kate Shelley: Bound for Legend*. Illustrated by Max Ginsburg. Dial Books for Young Readers, 1995. 32 p. ISBN 0-8037-1289-8. Grades 3-6.

Schroeder, Russell (editor). *Walt Disney: His Life in Pictures*. Disney Press, 1996. 64 p. ISBN 0-7868-3116-2 (trade); 0-7868-5043-4 (lib. bdg.). Grades 3-6.

Stanley, Diane. *Leondardo da Vinci*. Morrow Junior Books, 1996. 48 p. ISBN 0-688-104371. Grades 3-6.

Stanley, Diane, and Peter Vennema. *Good Queen Bess: The Story of Elizabeth I of England*. Illustrated by Diane Stanley. Four Winds Press, 1990. 40 p. ISBN 0-02-786810-9. Grades 3-6.

Stine, R. L., with Joe Arthur. *It Came from Ohio! My Life as a Writer*. Scholastic, 1997. 140 p. ISBN 0-590-36674-2. Grades 4-7.

Tillage, Leon Walter. *Leon's Story*. Illustrated by Susan L. Roth. Farrar, Straus & Giroux, 1997. 107 p. ISBN 0-374-34379-9. Grades 4-6.

Van Meter, Vicki, with Dan Gutman. *Taking Flight: My Story*. Viking, 1995. 134 p. ISBN 0-670-86260-6. Grades 5-8.

Wallner, Alexandra. *Laura Ingalls Wilder*. Illustrated by Alexandra Wallner. Holiday House, 1997. 32 p. ISBN 0-8234-1314-4. Grades 1-3.

Warren, Andrea. *Orphan Train Rider: One Boy's True Story*. Houghton Mifflin, 1996. 80 p. ISBN 0-395-69822-7. Grades 4-6.

————. *Pioneer Girl: Growing Up on the Prairie.* Morrow Junior Books, 1998. 94 p. ISBN 0-688-15438-7. Grades 4-6.

Weidt, Maryann N. *Oh, the Places He Went: A Story about Dr. Seuss—Theodor Seuss Geisel.* Illustrated by Kerry Maguire. Carolrhoda Books, 1994. 64 p. ISBN 0-87614-823-2 (lib. bdg.); 0-87614-627-2 (pbk.). Grades 4-6.

CHAPTER 7

Our Wonderful, Terrible Past

Face it—librarians and teachers are interested in history. But convincing kids that it is fascinating stuff can be difficult indeed. The phenomenal success of the movie *Titanic*, however, proves that kids *can* learn to like history, quickly and painlessly. We just need to encourage them. Don't concentrate on the facts and the statistics. Instead, introduce them to some of the many books that are filled with the kinds of information they love. Search for those nuggets of information that will intrigue and entice—or gross out and appall. Seek human interest stories that will kindle empathy and increase understanding.

The categories for this chapter were chosen for several reasons. First, there is a fabulous selection of materials on these topics. If you do not have access to the particular titles we select, others are readily available. Second, the topics are inherently interesting, and important for children to know about. Finally, some of our favorite books fall into these categories, and the best booktalks stem from true enthusiasm about good books.

ANCIENT HISTORY

Materials on ancient history proliferate. Many are colorful and accessible—a relatively recent phenomenon. Most older titles were unappealing, containing lots of text and a few black and white photographs. Today we are fortunate to have many attractive titles, and kids love being exposed to them. If asked, most kids would never say they had an interest in ancient civilizations or world history. But introduce them to some of the following books and they will be mesmerized. History is full of disasters, horrors, gross stuff, and bloody battles—all of high interest to kids. In this section you will find a wide variety of books dealing with ancient civilizations and times past.

Rebecca Stefoff's oversize book *Finding the Lost Cities* is tantalizing and full of enticing photos. Flipping the book open to the magnificent two-page color photo of the ruins of Troy on page 93, you can't help but start looking for more. Lost cities! The romance! The splendor! Who lived there? Why did they leave? How did we find them today? Can I go visit? May I help with the digging?

Surely the story of the rediscovery of Troy is one of the best ever. Heinrich Schliemann found a city that hardly anyone else really believed existed. For centuries, people thrilled to the story of the beautiful city; of Helen, the most beautiful woman in the world; Achilles, the guy with the famous heel; Hector; Priam; Paris; Ulysses; and many other famous names. All of these people were characters in the epic poems *The Iliad* and *The Odyssey* by Homer. Many books and movies center on the Trojan War, but most people believed it was just a story, something that never really happened.

But Schliemann loved to read, and the more he read *The Iliad* and *The Odyssey*, the more certain he was that Troy and the Trojan War were real and that Troy could still be found—if you guessed correctly about where to start digging.

The photography in Stefoff's book is stunning, and the text is full of amazing facts. For example, there are no free-standing buildings in Petra, in Jordan (see the photo on pages 12 and 13); all are carved out of the canyon walls within which the city stands. Every ancient city has a wonderful story, both about the city itself and about how it was discovered in modern times.

Other popular books about ancient times focus on Pompeii and the eruption of Vesuvius. (See chapter 1 for several titles on this intriguing disaster.)

The Roman News by Andrew Langley and Philip de Souza is jam-packed with fascinating information in a format that reminds you of eating peanuts. Once you start, you can't stop. Fun items to read aloud include the information on gladiators on page 9 (Did you know that at one point women fought as gladiators?), the good slave guide on page 11 (Children born into slavery will be good slaves, because they do not know any other life.), and the ads for the baths on page 25.

Gladiators—everyone has heard about them, but who were they, and what did they do? Find out about them in Richard Watkins's book, *Gladiator* (figure 7.1).

The first gladiatorial combat in Rome was held at a funeral more than 2,000 years ago. Three pairs of slaves fought to the death because the heirs of the dead man thought that such a sacrifice would please the gods. This idea caught on, and other people started doing it too. Fifty-two years later, *60* pairs of slaves fought to the death at a funeral. Everybody loved seeing those fights, and by the time Julius Caesar became emperor, he had realized that putting on gladiator fights helped make him popular with the people. Two hundred thirty-eight years after the first Roman gladiator fight, the emperor Augustus decided that the only gladiator games allowed would be his gladiator games. No one else could sponsor them.

Gladiators were captured warriors, slaves, men who were hoping to earn money and fame, or criminals. They went to special schools to learn how to fight well. If you could not fight well, you would bore the crowds. Take a look at the pictures of the different types of gladiators on pages 20-26 and read about the animals that attacked them and other, more helpless, people. Did you know that many people, such as the Christians, were tied to posts on carts and wheeled out so that the animals could kill them?

The biggest gladiator shows of all were sea battles with ships. Special big lakes were built, and sometimes sharks would be brought in. If a gladiator fell in the water, a shark would probably get him. People just loved to watch these shows. They would stand in line for days to get a good place. But the people who watched the shows had to be careful too. One particularly nasty emperor, Caligula, ordered a whole group of audience members to be thrown to the wild animals because he thought they were laughing at him!

You won't believe some of the true stories that are in this book. Ask kids if they can think of anything we do today that resembles those gladiator shows.

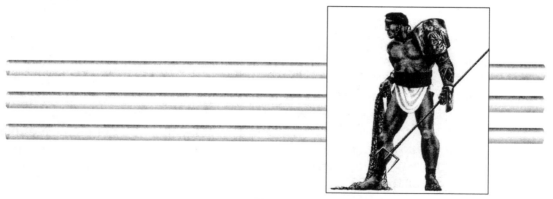

Fig. 7.1. *Gladiator* by Richard Watkins

Kids who like gladiators might also enjoy *A Soldier's Life: A Visual History of Soldiers Through the Ages* by Andrew Robertshaw. Color photographs illustrate what various soldiers wore through the ages, what they ate, and what weapons they used. Look at the different types of shoes. Which do you think would be the best suited for long marches? Why do you think soldiers wear dog tags? This is a fascinating look at a world that boys especially find interesting.

The Great Wall of China is one of the most incredible structures in the world. It is 30 feet high and thousands of miles long, and it was so wide that many people lived on it and worked in it to help defend the borders of China. Why would anyone need to build a wall thousands of miles long?

The Great Wall by Elizabeth Mann (figure 7.2) tells the story with great illustrations. It opens with an incredible incident that happened in 1449, when the young Chinese emperor who had led his army into a hopeless battle sat down on the ground and waited for it to end. Hours later, a Mongol prince rode up and saw him sitting there, surrounded by the dead bodies of his guards, and led him away (show this picture on pages 4 and 5).

China, which was a wealthy and successful country, had always had problems with invaders. Many small walls were built over the centuries to try to keep them out. Although the building of the Great Wall was never completely organized, at one time it spanned most of the borders of the country. Now most of it is gone—eroded and ruined. (Show the four-page fold-out spread on pages 28 through 31.) Spend some time with this fascinating book to find out more.

Fig. 7.2. *The Great Wall* **by Elizabeth Mann**

Another ancient structure that intrigues children is described in *The Great Pyramid* by Elizabeth Mann. Most of us saw *The Ten Commandments*, and, if we didn't learn it there, we surely heard it elsewhere: The pyramids were built by slaves. Not according to this entertaining and enlightening book. The pyramids were built by free, paid laborers who volunteered for the honor of doing the backbreaking work required to create the most studied buildings of all time. But who got the idea of building the first pyramid? Colorful, big pictures, including foldouts, make it easy to show this book to an eager audience. (For other books on mummies and ancient Egypt, see the titles listed chapter 5.)

CUSTOMS AND COSTUMES THROUGHOUT THE AGES

It may come as a surprise to kids that people haven't always eaten with silverware. In fact, for most of human history, the main utensils for eating were the fingers. *From Hand to Mouth, or, How We Invented Knives, Forks, Spoons, and Chopsticks & the Table Manners to Go with Them* by James Cross Giblin is a fascinating book that proves that history does not have to be about wars and politics and dates to memorize. Describe the meal at a duke's castle in France in 1200 (pages 19-21). There are no plates, only slabs of four-day-old bread called trenchers. Diners help themselves to food with their bare hands and place it on the trenchers. Every two people share one bowl of soup. Some guests bring their own sharply pointed knives with which to spear meat. No one uses forks because they have not yet been introduced to Western Europe.

Now jump forward a few hundred years. Europeans are feeling ashamed of their history of bad table manners. Plates and eating utensils have become commonplace, and people decide it is time to teach children how to eat in a civilized fashion. A man named Erasmus publishes a book on manners—full of new rules for eating. Read the following list of rules (pages 31 and 32), and ask kids to imagine what meals must have been like at that time.

- Take care to cut and clean your fingernails before dining. Otherwise dirt from under the nails may get in the food.
- Don't be the first to reach into the pot; only wolves and gluttons do that. And don't put your whole hand into it—use only three fingers at most.
- Take the first piece of meat or fish that you touch, and don't poke around in the pot for a bigger one.
- Don't pick your nose while eating and then reach for more food.
- Don't throw bones you have chewed back in the pot. Put them on the table or toss them on the floor.
- Don't clean your teeth with your knife.
- If your fingers become greasy, it is not polite to lick them or wipe them on your coat. Bring a cloth along for this purpose if your host does not provide one. Or else wipe them on the tablecloth.

This well-researched and detailed book is probably most appropriate for middle school students who are at least somewhat familiar with the Middle Ages, the Renaissance, and world history in general.

Not only have table manners changed throughout the ages, so has the food that people eat. Can you name five foods that ancient Romans or medieval knights or ancient Egyptians or Africans never ever ate? Tomatoes, potatoes, corn, beans, peppers, peanuts, squash, pineapple, vanilla, avocados, and chocolate are possible answers. These foods came from North or South America, and until Europeans visited these continents, they did not have access to these wonderful delicacies. Imagine life without baked potatoes, or French fries, or baked beans, or hot chocolate, or corn on the cob, or catsup, or popcorn! Find out about the history of these foods in *Tomatoes, Potatoes, Corn, and Beans: How the Foods of the Americas Changed Eating Around the World* by Sylvia A. Johnson.

When these foods were first brought to the Old World, many people were suspicious of them. In fact, in 1620 someone wrote that potatoes cause a terrible disease called leprosy.

Filled with interesting information and lots of illustrations, this is a fun book to browse through and read.

Laurie Lawlor deals with social history in a similar way in her book *Where Will This Shoe Take You? A Walk Through the History of Footwear* (figure 7.3). The book, written for middle school students, traces footwear from earliest times through the present, and features some interesting photographs. Show the picture on pages 52 and 53 and talk about how shoes can show status. This shoe was worn by wealthy men in fourteenth-century Europe. Obviously, with shoes this long they couldn't be doing much except trying to keep from falling on their faces. Also show Elton John's platform shoes on page 62 and compare them with the 300-year-old shoes on page 69. It seems that the more things change, the more they stay the same.

Fig. 7.3. *Where Will This Shoe Take You? A Walk Through the History of Footwear* **by Laurie Lawlor**

Another book about clothing, appropriate for younger readers, is *Bloomers!* by Rhoda Blumberg. This picture book tells how several famous women defied fashion rules of the 1850s and began to wear the ballooning trousers known as bloomers. They were laughed at and sometimes humiliated, but these women's suffrage leaders carried on and paved the way for numerous freedoms that women enjoy today.

Have you ever wondered how eyeglasses came to be invented? *Eyeglasses* by Margaret J. Goldstein explains how they came to be and how they work. The way they bend light rays is quite interesting, and finding out the history of eyeglasses makes for a good read.

Almost all old people need glasses, but there was not always a great need for them. In olden times, many people could not read at all, and most people didn't live to be very old, either. But sometime in the late 1200s, someone somewhere, probably in Italy, made the first pair of spectacles. No one really knows (yet) who got the idea.

These spectacles were much different from the ones we know today. There were no temples—the part of the glasses that hangs on the ears. People had to be creative to come up with ways to keep their glasses on. The book contains a picture of a man who made straps that looped around his ears. Some people attached their glasses to their hats but ran into trouble when they had to take their hats off. Only people with a fair amount of money could afford glasses anyway.

Through the centuries, different styles of glasses were invented. Benjamin Franklin made the first pair of bifocals, and they looked a lot like the ones that people still use today. The book is full of fun photographs. Show your audience the cover.

When was the last time you took a bath or a shower? How would it feel if you could *never* take a bath or a shower? Imagine living in a home where people relieved themselves anywhere they felt like it—in the corners, on the steps, on the floors, or in the halls; or imagine walking in a street filled with sewage. Imagine watching someone lean out an upstairs window and yell at everyone to duck as she empties out a bowl of raw sewage. If you do not think bathrooms are important, read *Toilets, Bathtubs, Sinks, and Sewers: A History of the Bathroom* by Penny Colman.

For a long, long time, most people had no idea that it was a healthy and a good thing to keep clean. Queen Isabel, who financed Columbus's trip to what turned out to be America, was proud of the fact that she had only taken two baths in her whole life! Isabel lived during one of the dirtiest times ever. The living quarters of many ancient people had plumbing, drains, or baths. (The Romans even had some bathtubs attached to ropes, so you could swing and bathe at the same time.) But by the Middle and late Middle Ages, hardly anyone took baths anymore. Saint Francis of Assisi said that one sign of a holy person was dirtiness.

Later, some people began to like baths. Ben Franklin even liked to read in his bathtub. By the 1830s, people began to realize that keeping clean was a good thing and essential to staying healthy. Bathrooms, so popular in ancient Rome, became popular again.

This history of bathrooms around the world will delight you and give you a lot of interesting facts to tell your friends. For instance, do you know where the phrase "the wrong end of the stick" comes from? Can you guess? (The answer is on page 30.)

Death is not a comfortable subject for most of us, but it can be an intriguing topic, especially to kids. Penny Colman's *Corpses, Coffins, and Crypts: A History of Burial* describes funeral and burial customs all over the world. Here are some examples: Did you know that in India, traditional Hindu rituals required the widow of a dead man to burn herself to death on her husband's funeral pyre? This custom has been outlawed since 1929 but is still continued in some places. The Vikings, in the Dark and Middle Ages, had the same custom. But if a man died before he was married, they let him celebrate his marriage after his death—by burning a young woman with his body.

Some coffins were made with drop bottoms so that a body could be dropped out of it into the grave and the coffin reused. Today many people use the words *coffin* and *casket* interchangeably, but they are really not the same. A casket is the rectangular container that most of us are familiar with, while a coffin is a wedge-shaped, simple container for a corpse.

This book contains some interesting stories. Read the story of the Hiller caskets that begins on the bottom of page 83. Mrs. Hiller set up her casket in her parlor, and she frequently climbed in it to show her friends how she would look after she died!

Another grisly story is that of the ossuary near Kutna Hora in the Czech Republic. Ossuaries were built to house the bones of plague victims. This one held the bones of 30,000 people who died in a plague in 1318. The Schwarzenberg family acquired the ossuary, and in 1870 they commissioned a designer to arrange the bones in a decorative manner. Pictures of a chandelier and family crest built entirely of bones are on pages 104 and 105.

Although the author tells of many customs from other times and places, and informs us that a lot of customs in America have changed, one has stayed the same for centuries. When someone dies, people always bring food to the home or the family of the deceased person. Just about everyone in the room has probably experienced this.

Near the end of the book are some interesting inscriptions from gravestones. One particularly fine one, on page 184, reads, "I told you I was sick."

THE AMERICAN SPIRIT

All history is full of great stories, but American history is full of *our* stories. Why did our country turn out the way it has? What made us the way we are? People complain that today's young people do not know American history. Read some of the following books, and you will have to agree it is not because there are no interesting books on the subject. The American spirit, exemplified in the diverse people who settled this country and who live here today, is alive and well, and with some encouragement, kids will want to learn more. Many books have been written about the history of our country, some of which can be found in chapters 1 and 6, and others of which can be found here. The following is a selection of some favorite books, with topics ranging from pioneer days to engineering feats to female sports stars.

A title that will get kids thinking about their own history is David Weitzman's *(The Brown Paper School Presents) My Backyard History Book*. This book is old but still in print, and so jam-packed with fun projects and thought-provoking questions that it makes an irresistible book to use with kids. Teachers will find it a superb resource. Warning: You will have to update some of the questions, but many work well at any time.

The time line of your own life (pages 18 and 19) features memory-jogging questions such as "Write in all of the events of your life that you can remember. The very first thing you remember happening. Your first toys. The first book you read by yourself. When you met your best friend. When your first tooth fell out," and so on. Or on pages 16 and 17: "Where (town, state, or country) and when (year at least) were all of your grandparents born? What are (or were) the occupations of all of your grandparents? From which country did your father's family come originally? (Unless you are a Native American, they came from someplace else.) From which country did your mother's family come originally? When did your ancestors (on both sides) come to this country? Where did they land when they arrived in this country?" and so on.

Included are tips for finding out about the history of your town and for completing oral history projects. People with an interest in the past, their own family's or their community's, will be attracted to this book.

The nineteenth century was a time of rapid expansion for the United States. It seems that people were always searching for a better life over the horizon. Pioneers, westward expansion, and the American West are subjects that have an air of mystique about them, and the following books will get kids interested in the adventures of American explorers.

It would be a lot like going to Mars. There were no maps. No one knew for certain what was out in the west. But the brand-new American nation, under the leadership of President Thomas Jefferson, needed to find out what was on the rest of the continent. In *The Incredible Journey of Lewis and Clark*, Rhoda Blumberg tells of an amazing adventure.

Thomas Jefferson chose his 28-year-old personal secretary, Meriwether Lewis, to head an expedition whose purpose was not only to explore and discover, but also to find a direct water route that would go all of the way across North America. Almost everyone believed that such a route existed. Most people thought that the Missouri River probably connected with the Columbia River and that it was just a matter of finding out where. Once the direct water route was discovered, boats could be sent across the continent.

In turn, Meriwether Lewis picked a good friend, William Clark, to co-lead the expedition. Their "corps of discovery" numbered about 40 men, and what an adventure they had! They received training in all sorts of things including medicine, collecting plant and animal specimens, and dealing with Native Americans. Jefferson had some particular tasks for them. He had heard that there was a salt mountain in the west 180 miles long and 45 miles wide. He was hoping they would find that.

Lewis and Clark set off on May 14, 1804, heading up the Missouri River from St. Louis. They were going to see the Pacific Ocean, visit and greet Native American peoples along the way, and learn as much as they could. No one thought they would be gone long, as no one had a good idea of how far it actually was to the Pacific Ocean, and hardly anyone knew how huge the Rocky Mountains along the way were going to be. It was an amazing trip, and Blumberg's book is an excellent introduction to it.

Martin W. Sandler's book *Pioneers: A Library of Congress Book* tells the sweeping story of westward expansion in words and pictures. Packed with photographs, this book is particularly good for browsing. Two excellent photos are worth showing to a group: one on page 9 of the men cutting down a redwood tree, and another on page 72 of a horse and rider jumping off a high dive. Tell kids that there were no radios, movies, or television, and so people invented spectacular live entertainment.

People of the West by Dayton Duncan introduces 15 different people who struggled to make a home in the West. Based on a PBS documentary, the book is illustrated with more than 100 photographs and contains stories from American settlers, Native Americans, Chinese immigrants, and others. A particularly interesting segment begins on page 86 with the life of Emmeline Wells. A Mormon woman who was the wife of several polygamous men, she strongly supported the practice of polygamy and equal rights for women. Show students the portraits on page 87 of Brigham Young and a few of his wives. Wells worked for women's suffrage and encouraged women to join the workforce and make a living for themselves. She lived to age 93, long enough to see the U.S. Constitution amended to grant women the right to vote.

For a glimpse of some real people of the frontier, try *Prairie Visions: The Life and Times of Solomon Butcher* by Pam Conrad.

Solomon Butcher came to Nebraska and set up a photography studio, but his main business was as a traveling photographer capturing the lives of the pioneers, the homesteaders who came to the prairie looking for land and hope. They did not have much, and most of them lived in sod houses. These houses were built of "Nebraska brick"—pieces of sod cut into bricks, which kept the home somewhat cool in summer and somewhat warm in winter but leaked horribly when it rained (mud rained down *inside* the house!). And, of course, snakes and animals lived in the sod houses, too.

Look at the great photographs in this book and imagine what the lives of the people were like. Almost all of the photographs are of people sitting in front of their soddies, sometimes showing prized possessions as well. In the photo opposite the table of contents, the family brought their prized organ out of the house but were *not* shown in front of the house because the mother insisted that Butcher photograph only the things she was proud of.

Read the story of the "Snowbank Suicide" on pages 23 and 24, and show the photo on page 21. Butcher accidentally damaged a negative, and to cover it up, he drew in a picture that he said was of a turkey on the roof. It had to have been a monster albino mutant turkey the way it looks, but apparently the farmer accepted the story and paid for the photo anyway! On page 81, Pam Conrad describes her meeting with John Carter, an expert on Solomon Butcher. She asked him what one question he would ask if he could step into one of those photographs. His answer was immediate. "Where are the outhouses?" he asked.

Being a pioneer wasn't easy for anyone, but women had a particularly hard life. Children who enjoy the Laura Ingalls Wilder books might like to read *Buffalo Gals: Women of the Old West* by Brandon Marie Miller to get a taste of frontier life for women. Ask them if they know what state first allowed women to vote. They may be surprised to know that in 1870 Wyoming women turned out at the polls to vote. It took 40 more years before all American women had this right.

People may not realize that many African American women also helped settle the West. William Loren Katz's *Black Women of the Old West* covers this little-known historical fact and presents many pictures of these courageous women. African Americans moved west under a variety of circumstances. One little-known fact is that many were slaves to Native Americans. They practiced a less brutal form of slavery than did white people, but slavery by its very nature is inhumane. Slaves, most famously Dred Scott and his strong wife, Harriett, did everything they could to be free, including suing, which sometimes actually worked.

This book is full of pictures of African Americans in their new homes in the new land. Although many laws were passed that made their lives very difficult, they persevered, some with outstanding success. The last governor of Mexico's California before the Americans took over was part-African American. Here in these pages are photos of some extraordinary people—the first African American graduate of Oberlin College, Cathy Williams, who passed herself off as a man named William Cathy; mail order brides who went west to marry whatever man had paid for their train fare; and May B. Mason who struck gold in the Yukon.

One woman who really had a hard life in the West was Olive Oatman. The front cover of *The Ordeal of Olive Oatman: A True Story of the American West* by Margaret Rau is startling (figure 7.4). It is a photograph of a beautiful young woman, whose face is disfigured by a tattoo running from her lower mouth to her chin. This is Olive Oatman, who, starting at age 12, spent six years as a slave to Apache and Mohave Indians in the 1850s.

Oatman's family, including her mother, father, and seven other children, were traveling west in a covered wagon. They had left the other people in the wagon party when they encountered several hostile Apaches who massacred most of the family but captured Olive and her six-year-old sister, Mary Ann. The girls became slaves and were eventually sold to the Mohaves, to be slaves for them as well.

This is the true story of what happened to them, of how the tattoos were painfully applied to their faces to indicate their status as slaves, of how only Olive survived the captivity, and of her rescue and discovery that she was not the only one of her family to have survived.

Fig. 7.4. *The Ordeal of Olive Oatman: A True Story of the American West* **by Margaret Rau**

Leonard Everett Fisher's book *The Oregon Trail* tells about the wagon trains of the 1840s and 1850s that traveled thousands of miles to reach Oregon and California. It was a grueling journey, and the emigrants created an expression to describe the very worst possible conditions. Starving to death, dying of cholera, or drowning in quicksand was "seeing the elephant." About 35,000 people died trying to make this journey. That's one person every 17.5 miles. One strength of this book is the full-page spreads of photographs. Talk about the hardships of the journey, and show children the Henry Smith family on pages 32 and 33 or the emigrant family on pages 8 and 9.

No discussion of western pioneers would be complete without some mention of the California Gold Rush of 1849. *The Gold Rush* by Liza Ketchum tells of the individual men, women, and children who traveled to California, and of the Native Americans and Spanish-speaking Californios whose lives were affected by the thousands of miners who poured into the area. Based on a PBS television series, this book is filled with photographs and quotes that help bring the time period alive. Another book on the same subject is *The Great American Gold Rush* by Rhoda Blumberg. Students might like to hear a little bit about "law and order" in a mining camp. Read them the five popular types of punishment from page 91: banishment, cutting off ears, branding, flogging, and hanging.

You will learn a lot about some interesting women by reading *Gold Rush Women* by Claire Rudolf Murphy and Jane G. Haigh. Did you know that one in ten of the people who raced to the Klondike to look for gold in 1897 was a woman? Not many of them, it turned out, found gold—but many became wealthy or at least comfortable in other ways. Women came mainly because so many men were searching for gold. Wherever there were that many men, cooks, seamstresses, laundresses, and housekeepers were in great demand. So were hotels and boardinghouses.

Some of the women of the Gold Rush were Native Americans, born right where it happened. Many of them were teenagers who married much older miners, and many of their stories ended sadly. The women who came in from outside the Klondike had to follow the rules set up by Canadian authorities. Afraid that people would come into the cold country without adequate supplies, they made a law that said that anyone coming in had to bring 1,400 to 2,000 pounds of food, tools, and clothing. You could not carry that alone! People had to hire help or do their carrying in relays, going back and forth.

And when they finally did get to the Klondike, there weren't many comforts. Ethel Berry, who was one of the women who struck it rich (show her picture on the book's cover) said, "When I got there the house had no door, windows, or floor, and I had to stand around outside until a hole was cut for me to get in." Klondike Kate was a show-girl, who made and lost a lot of money. Lucille Hunter was African American. Josephine Earp and her husband, Wyatt, the famous western lawman, also came to the Gold Rush. Interesting pictures and incredible stories make this book a fun read.

Nothing symbolizes the Old West like the image of rugged, hard-living cowboys. Surprisingly, the cowboy era lasted only about 20 years, but as Linda Granfield's *Cowboy: An Album* shows, the cowboy image survives. Granfield explains in words and pictures the nitty-gritty of cowboy life: their lingo, their underwear, their food, their domino games, and their tobacco spitting. She goes on to detail how the cowboy myth grew through westerns and rodeos, and how the West lives on today.

Most people don't realize that many cowboys were African Americans. *Black Frontiers: A History of African American Heroes in the Old West* by Lillian Schlissel tells their story. She writes that of the 38,000 working cowboys in the southwestern United States between 1870 and 1885, about one in four was an African American man. She tells about Nat Love, who tried to lasso a cannon, and Bill Pickett, the great rodeo rider (see chapter 6 for a biography on Pickett). She also writes about the Buffalo Soldiers who fought in the Civil War, prominent African American women of the West, and the relationship between African Americans and Native Americans.

A fascinating book for older readers deals with medicine on the frontier. *Frontier Fever: The Scary, Superstitious—and Sometimes Sensible—Medicine of the Pioneers* by Elizabeth Van Steenwyk (figure 7.5) describes medical practices from 1607 to 1890. Doctors routinely practiced phlebotomy (bloodletting), in addition to purging, blistering, and induced vomiting. Settlers faced malaria, cholera, scurvy, and numerous other diseases, not to mention wounds from guns and arrows. Page 69 tells of Andrew Broadus, who shot himself in the arm and encouraged a friend to amputate it with a handsaw and a razor. The wound was dressed with tar, and Broadus healed completely. Civil War enthusiasts will want to read chapter 10, titled "When Beans Killed More Men Than Bullets."

Fig. 7.5. *Frontier Fever: The Scary, Superstitious—and Sometimes Sensible—Medicine of the Pioneers* by Elizabeth Van Steenwyk

An excellent overview of the American Civil War is found in Norman Bolotin and Angela Herb's *For Home and Country: A Civil War Scrapbook* With numerous photographs, quotes, captions, and letters, this book makes for fascinating reading and browsing. This is not the place to look for detailed accounts of Civil War battles, but rather for the details of everyday life, including what soldiers wore, how they amused themselves, and how they dealt with sickness and injury. The chapter "Feast or Famine" is particularly interesting. Tell kids about hardtack, otherwise known as "teeth dullers" and "sheet-iron crackers." Page 36 tells how soldiers would dip the hard flour and water biscuits in coffee or soup to soften them up. Unfortunately, this process also loosened the worms and weevils typically infesting the moldy biscuits. Students might be surprised by the menu items found on page 39. Throughout the book are quotes from soldiers' letters, many of which could be read aloud, and ample photographs for showing to groups of listeners.

At the same time the frontier was settled, other events were happening back east. An engineering marvel is described by Cheryl Harness in *The Amazing Impossible Erie Canal*. After the War of 1812, many Americans wanted to move west, to settle the new land. But they found it tough going getting there. There were no good roads, and there was no good way to ship food and goods from one part of the country to another.

One part of the land that really needed a way to transport goods and people was in New York state. The Hudson River, which ran through New York City, needed to be connected to the Great Lakes. From there all sorts of business could be conducted. But there were 363 miles, going up and down over uneven land, that would have to be connected by a canal.

Could it be done? DeWitt Clinton thought so, and he became the governor of New York. On July 4, 1817, ground was broken for the canal. It took eight long years, but for much of the nineteenth century, the Erie Canal was *the* way to travel.

Today, it is mostly a memory. Trains took over much of its work, then trucks. But while it lasted, it truly was amazing.

Colorful, detailed illustrations highlight this appealing title. Show any of the lovely two-page spreads. The one of the five double-stair-step locks at Lockport may be the most amazing of all.

The Brooklyn Bridge by Elizabeth Mann gives a look at another engineering feat, and will engage even the most reluctant reader. The Brooklyn Bridge story includes all of the ingredients for a good read: vision, drama, death, disaster, disablement, and a strong woman. The pictures illuminate the tale in an exciting and informative fashion. Easy and quick to read, but hard to put down, this is a real winner.

In 1852, John Roebling decided to build a bridge. People in what is now New York City had a hard time getting to and from Manhattan and Brooklyn. Although they were close in distance, there were no bridges, and only a ferry ran between the two. The problem was that a special type of bridge had to be built. Most bridges were built on many supports, with towers sunk in the riverbed to hold them up. Roebling's bridge needed to be a suspension bridge, held aloft by only two supports (show the two-page spread on pages 10 and 11) as it had to allow plenty of room for the boats to go under the bridge.

No one was much interested in such a bridge until the winter of 1867, when the river actually froze over and people who lived in Brooklyn but worked in Manhattan could not get to work. They had to skate across the river! By 1869, Roebling had finished his design—only to die as the result of a freak accident with a ferryboat.

Although he was young and inexperienced, Roebling's son, Washington, took over the job and became chief engineer of the Brooklyn Bridge. The problems he faced were horrifying. When he, too, was injured, his amazing wife Emily assumed much of the actual supervision. It is considered one of the most famous, most beautiful bridges in the world, and it is still standing today.

A common theme in American history is immigration, and many immigrants to America came first to New York City. In any group that you booktalk to, chances are you will have a child who was not born in the United States. To introduce Ellen Levine's book, *If Your Name Was Changed at Ellis Island*, see if a student can tell about his or her immigration experience. Then explain to students what immigration was like in the past.

What if you decided to move to a foreign country far from home? When you got to the check-in place, someone who could not speak English might ask you what your name was. What if the person spelled it wrong? What if they did not even try to spell it but wrote down another name, saying yours was too hard? How would you feel if someone gave you a new name and you were stuck with it? This happened to many immigrants when they came to America through Ellis Island between 1892 and 1922. With colorful illustrations and a question-and-answer format, this book answers questions about what it was like to be an immigrant during the peak years of immigration. A special addition to this booktalk is to describe any immigration stories that you know of personally. Kids love these and might be inspired to ask their relatives for family stories of their own.

Today, Ellis Island is a museum filled with the belongings and memories of the people who arrived there. It is a great place to visit, especially if you know of someone whose name is carved on the circular monument that commemorates immigrants to America.

Another book on a similar topic is Betsy Maestro's *Coming to America: The Story of Immigration*. Wonderfully colorful two-page spreads make this book easy to sell to first through third graders.

All Americans came from someplace else. Ask listeners if they know what country their ancestors came from. Even Native Americans walked into America long ago when what is now Alaska was connected to what is now Russia.

Most people who came to America wanted to come, but some were brought here in chains as slaves who were captured and sold to work for others. People came to America in many different ways, but for almost all of them it was a difficult and frightening experience. More people come to America all the time. Do you know anyone who is new to America and might need to make some friends?

This book is fun to read but tells us a lot about how lucky we are to be here.

After immigrating to America, life was not always easy. *Big Annie of Calumet: A True Story of the Industrial Revolution* by Jerry Stanley, tells a gripping story about an event most people know nothing about. If you have time for a longer booktalk, share this information with your listeners.

In 1913 workers in the copper mines in the Keweenaw Peninsula, located in Michigan's upper peninsula, went on strike. Their town, Calumet, was a company town, where everything was controlled by the C and H Mining Company. Things were not good in the mines. Production was way down. Miners had to dig deeper to find considerably less copper than they had found 30 years before. The straw that broke the camel's back and caused the strike was a new tool called a one-man drill. The two-man drill, which had been in use for 30 years, allowed a worker to watch out for his partner in case of a cave-in or some other danger. Under the new plan, a 150-pound drill was operated by one man. If an accident occurred, the miner was doomed, as the nearest man was 500 feet away. Miners called the new tool "the widow-maker" and feared having to use it. Working conditions had always been appalling—temperatures in the mines ranged from 115 degrees to minus 27 degrees. Workers had no toilets, no water, no food, and no compensation for injuries. They also faced huge rats and breathed poisonous gas.

The C and H Mining Company had been unafraid of a union, for the workers belonged to various ethnic groups who hated each other. But they had not reckoned on the wives of their workers. In February 1913, the wives formed their own union: the Western Federation of Mines Auxiliary Number Five, and with their support, the men went on strike too. The strike was long and bloody, with strikebreakers brought in from New York City. Through it all, the women stood resolute. Their leader was "Big Annie" Clemenc, a Croatian woman more than six feet tall. Only 25 years old, she carried a huge flag in the parades to support the strike and became nationally known.

The most famous incident of the strike was the 1913 Christmas party at the Italian hall. More than 675 people, mostly children, attended the party, financed by donations. In the middle of the excitement, an unknown person yelled "Fire," causing a stampede to the door. Although there was no fire, 74 people, mostly children, were crushed or trampled to death in the mad rush. The perpetrator was never found. Who did it and why? This book provides a interesting viewpoint on a subject not many of us know much about.

Susan Campbell Bartoletti has written another book about the life of miners called *Growing up in Coal Country*. The photograph in the introduction on page 8 will capture your full attention. It shows the grandparents of the author's husband on their wedding day in 1924. He was 20. She was 13 years old. She had her first baby at 14, and they both lived a life of incredibly hard work. They were married for 67 years. He had to retire after 45 years in the mines because of black lung, and she never learned to read, write, or do arithmetic.

Children started working in the mines at a very young age. Pennsylvania did not issue birth certificates, so a father could claim a boy was small for his age. Boys would start out in the beakers, where they would sort out the coal until their fingers became bloody (called "red tips") and hardened as they got accustomed to the work. The boys had to huddle in backless benches which were very uncomfortable. As a boy became older, he could actually work in the mines. A coveted job was that of a mule driver, although the mules could be mean and ornery. You had to watch out for your mule—you never knew when it might take a bite out of you. One boy fell asleep. When he woke up, his left hand was in horrible pain—his mule had bitten off two of his fingers. This, of course, was the boy's fault and caused him to be fired from the mines. In fact, any injury was the fault of the person who got injured, even if the mine caved in. It meant you were no longer employed by the mine.

The book includes great photographs of life in the mines and of the lives of the hardworking, poverty-stricken women and children of the miners aboveground. Read all about it and be glad you did not grow up in coal country in the early 1900s.

In her book *Buffalo Days*, (figure 7.6) Diane Hoyt-Goldsmith tells about Clarence Three Irons Jr., a 10-year-old who lives on a Crow Indian reservation in Montana. The Crow love to remember the days of hunting buffalo because the animals were crucial to their survival. The Crow used every part of the buffalo. They ate the meat and used the hides to make tents, storage containers, and clothing. They made ropes out of buffalo hair. They used buffalo bones to make tools and eating utensils. At that time, vast herds of buffalo roamed over most of the United States, and they were good for the land. They fertilized the land and broke the soil so that seeds could grow in it. But, by 1889, many pioneers had moved into what was formerly buffalo and Indian land. They wanted to build fences, raise livestock, and ride on the railroads which were built over the land. People like Buffalo Bill Cody were paid money to kill buffalo, and by the 1890s, the buffalo was almost extinct. The Crow and many other Native Americans were forced onto reservations.

Today, the Crow celebrate the buffalo, and the buffalo is again being raised so that it can serve the people. On the reservation is a huge open area, surrounded on three sides by water and on the fourth by a high steel fence, where buffalo can roam and graze freely. (Show the two-page spread of this area on pages 12 and 13.) Today, when the Crow round up buffalo, they use cellular phones and all-terrain vehicles!

Every summer the Crow nation holds a celebration of buffalo days. Tepees are put up all over (show the spread on pages 22 and 23), and there is a huge festival, with dancing, parades, good food, and events and activities that keep the Crow traditions alive. This is great fun to read about, and the color photos are excellent to show groups.

Fig. 7.6. *Buffalo Days* **by Diane Hoyt-Goldsmith**

On a different note, a couple of books by Sue Macy tell how women athletes have shown their spirit. *Winning Ways: A Photohistory of American Women in Sports* is a truly astounding, eye-opening book. A few interesting facts:

- The first person to go over Niagara Falls in a barrel was a woman—one who said she was 43, but recent research indicates she was 63!

- In 1928, the pope issued a letter condemning a public exhibition by female gymnasts, suggesting that the athletes should "think first of becoming good mothers of worthy sons."

- In 1967, Boston Marathon officials tried to rip the entry number off the chest of the first woman who dared to enter the men-only race.
- Women's clothing was a primary hindrance to the development of athletic skills and to exercise.
- In 1936 Olympic Committee President Avery Brundage said of women who compete in track events, "Their charms sink to less than zero."
- Writers were obsessed with the idea that women could not be both feminine and athletic. Sexist remarks by male sportswriters were epidemic even in the 1990s.
- As college women's athletics become more popular, more men are coaching women, taking the bulk of the female coaching jobs away from women.

Winning Ways is a good read and will have you sharing with your friends a lot of new facts.

Another book by Macy will appeal to sports fans and history buffs—*A Whole New Ball Game: The Story of the All-American Girls Professional Baseball League*. Remind your listeners of the movie *A League of Their Own* starring Tom Hanks, and tell them that this book gives the true story of America's first female professional baseball players.

SLAVERY AND FREEDOM

The last few years have seen a huge growth spurt in the number of books available on slavery. Many are excellent, and can enlighten and illuminate. Exposing children to these stories can help them to develop compassion and understanding. How would *you* like to be a slave and have no freedom at all to make your own choices? How could any human being justify *owning* another human being? Children are both horrified and fascinated when they find out about slavery in the United States. Kids of all races will want to know more, and these excellent nonfiction books will grab their attention and teach them valuable lessons in history.

Students usually learn the facts about slavery and the Civil War in school, but sometimes it takes a good book to convey what it was really like to live in such conditions. *The Strength of These Arms: Life in the Slave Quarters* by Raymond Bial (figure 7.7) will teach readers something about daily life as a slave. For a heartrending, eye-opening grabber, show children the photograph of the two slave children dressed in rags on page 4. This is what it was like to grow up in slavery. How would it feel to be owned? To live in cold, drafty shacks and sleep on straw, when the people who owned you lived in mansions? And you would know that your work was paying for their luxuries.

Nothing could have been much harder than to be a slave. If the man who was in charge of your work, the overseer, was in a bad mood, you could be whipped for almost no reason at all. Worse even than that, you could be sold—sold away from your mother and your father, your brothers and sisters, even your husband or wife. Life lived as a slave was a life lived with almost no hope. But this excellent book also lets us know how many slaves were able to preserve their old African traditions and to form a loving, supportive community. It is a fascinating and thought-provoking book.

Fig. 7.7. *The Strength of These Arms: Life in the Slave Quarters* **by Raymond Bial**

1853: Daily Life on a Southern Plantation by Paul Erickson features wonderful photographs and art describing what it was like to be a slave or the family of the plantation owner. Many of the photographs were taken on a real plantation in Louisiana.

This book points out that slaves helped make America rich. They worked hard to make their owners wealthy, and many became fine craftspeople who made furniture, built homes, and created works of art. A good male slave cost as much as $2,000 in 1860, which would be about $30,000 today. Skilled slaves, such as carpenters and blacksmiths, were even more expensive. Women and older slaves cost about three-fourths as much as good male slaves, teenagers about half, and children about a fourth. In the best farming areas, where the plantations were, more than half of the population were slaves. But slaves had no rights, and their owners could do whatever they pleased with them.

Slave quarters were usually quite some distance from the main house (show the two-page spread on pages 10 and 11), which did give the slaves some privacy. But most of their shacks had no windows, only dirt floors, and very few comforts of any sort. They had only the clothes given to them by their masters, and children almost never had shoes, no matter how cold the weather got.

Inserting some personal information here will give your booktalk added interest. If you know how cold it can get in Louisiana in the winter, add this. If you have traveled to a relevant location, tell the audience about it. A museum in Richmond displays want ads published as late as the 1890s advertising for ex-slave husbands and wives or children or parents who had been sold away from their families. Obviously, slave families were very close, and many were still trying to find each other more than 25 years after the Civil War ended.

Slaves sometimes did have meetings with slaves from other plantations, and this book describes a Saturday night get-together with dancing, storytelling, and banjo playing. In the plantation described here, the slaves had much better living conditions than in many. Nevertheless, this is a fascinating book with many interesting photos and drawings to examine.

Any discussion of slavery will naturally lead to the topic of how slaves escaped using the Underground Railroad. Virginia Hamilton's excellent book *Many Thousand Gone: African Americans from Slavery to Freedom* tells how the term was coined.

Read aloud or tell in your own words the story of Tice Davids found on pages 53-58. According to Hamilton, after Davids made a narrow escape across the Ohio River, it was his former owner who declared that he must have gone on an "underground road."

This book is perfect for a booktalk because each chapter is a short, fascinating bit of history that reads like a story. Most chapters tell of little-known slaves who escaped or tried to escape in various ways. "All Right, Sir!" (pages 92-95) tells of Henry Brown, a slave who made a special padded box and shipped himself from Richmond, Virginia, to Philadelphia, Pennsylvania. The box was two feet eight inches deep, two feet wide, and three feet long. For a memorable visual presentation, find a box with those approximate dimensions, and let a student try to fit inside. Then ask the student how he or she would like to spend 26 hours in the box. Don't forget to mention that Brown spent quite a few of those hours upside down.

Jim Haskin's *Get on Board: The Story of the Underground Railroad* includes many of the same stories that Virginia Hamilton recounts, and once you get started, it is a hard book to put down. Although much is written about the white people who helped escaping slaves on the Underground Railroad, many African Americans, who were either born free or had escaped, also helped slaves find freedom. Jarmain Wesley Loguen had escaped from Tennessee. He went to Canada first, then settled in Syracuse, New York. He became known as the Underground Railroad King because he is believed to have helped more than 1,500 escaping slaves. He wrote a book about his life in 1859, and in 1860, probably because of the book, his former owner found out where he was. She wrote him a letter:

> I write you these lines to let you know the situation we are in—partly in consequence of your running away and stealing Old Rock, our fine mare. I am cripple, but I am still able to get about. Though we got the mare back, she was never worth much after you took her, and, as I now stand in need of some funds, I am determined to sell you. If you will send me one thousand dollars and pay for the old mare I will give up all claim I have to you. . . . If you do not comply with my request, I will sell you to someone else. You know that we reared you as we reared our own children.

Part of the letter Loguen wrote back to her included this: "You say 'You know we raised you as we did our own children?' 'Woman, did you raise your own children for the market? Did you raise them for the whipping post?'"

This book tells thrilling stories about slave escapes. Part of the reason African Americans were chosen to be slaves was that it was easy to spot them because their skin color was different. As a result of this, any African American traveling through slave-holding areas was in danger. Professional slave-hunters, much like professional bounty hunters in the Old West, scoured the countryside looking for runaway slaves. Some of them were not too careful about in whether the person they caught was the right person or not, and there are several incidents in which free African Americans were captured and became slaves simply because of the color of their skin. Imagine how horrible that would be! But many slaves had white ancestors, as well as black, and they could pass for white. This helped some of them escape to the north.

For more information on the Underground Railroad, try *North Star to Freedom: The Story of the Underground Railroad* by Gena K. Gorrell. This spellbinding and well-illustrated book gives some startling facts about slavery and the Underground

Railroad. Did you know that slave ships carrying slaves from Africa would actually throw all of their slaves into the ocean to drown if they feared they were being pursued? That way no one would be able to prove that the vessel was a slave ship. Just describing how slaves were shackled and confined in horrifying conditions on the ships will command the attention of any group of kids.

Some of the stories of individual escapes clearly demonstrate the intelligence and creativity of the slaves who were held in subhuman conditions. Read the story on pages 53-55 of the two slaves handcuffed and penned with iron collars holding bells over their heads, so that if they tried to escape the bells would ring. How could anyone escape from this kind of a situation? They could and did—read the book to find out how.

Another Raymond Bial work, *The Underground Railroad*, (figure 7.8) provides a wealth of photographs to show. Bial traveled to many historic sites to capture the history of the Underground Railroad on film. On page 4, the last paragraph of his introduction makes a nice read-aloud:

> Many of the photographs in *The Underground Railroad* were made late at night and far from my home. As you page through this book, imagine yourself, as I did, being hunted down as you struggle through a thick and unfamiliar woods or wade through a treacherous swamp. Also imagine yourself being helped by kind people along the way because, despite the cruelty and injustice of slavery, one cannot live without hope and faith in other people. The worst of times always brings out the very best in some people, and such is the story of the Underground Railroad.

You might also want to show the slave announcements on pages 24 and 41 and show some of the photographs as an introduction to the subject of slavery and the Underground Railroad.

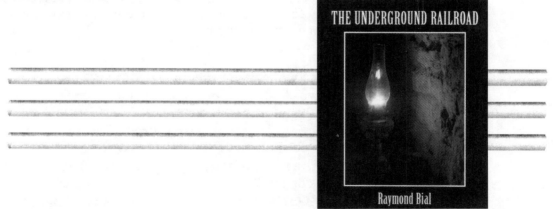

Fig. 7.8. *The Underground Railroad* by Raymond Bial

A Picture Book of Harriet Tubman by David A. Adler makes a great accompaniment to the Bial book on the Underground Railroad. Show younger children the color pictures of Tubman, and describe her story. We do not know exactly when slaves were born, for no one kept records. How would you feel if you didn't know when your birthday was, or even how old you are? Tubman and her family belonged to other people.

Her owners could tell them what to do and could beat them and whip them if they felt like it. Tubman was once whipped over and over again because she ate a cube of sugar.

One of the worst things that could happen to you was to be sold away from your family. Harriet Tubman saw two of her sisters put in chains and sold. She never saw them again. The worst place to be sold was farther south, for it was generally believed that the farther south you were a slave, the harder you had to work and the worse you were treated. Tubman was somewhat lucky in that she grew up pretty far north, in Maryland.

When Tubman was about 14 or 15 years old, her master threw a metal weight at a slave who was running away. It accidentally hit Tubman instead and almost killed her. For the rest of her long life, she had terrible headaches because of that wound.

Tubman desperately wanted to be free, and she knew that she should follow the Drinking Gourd—the North Star—to Canada, where she would be free. She escaped one night with her two brothers, but they decided to turn back. Tubman went on alone, becoming free at last. During the course of 10 years, she returned to the South 19 times to rescue almost 300 slaves.

Like Harriet Tubman, Sojourner Truth was born a slave. Show younger children David A. Adler's *A Picture Book of Sojourner Truth* and ask them to think about what it would be like, and imagine how they would feel. What if your brothers and sisters were sold before you were even born? What if your whole family had to live in a cold, wet one-room basement while your owner lived in a lovely house upstairs? What if you fell in love but the slave you loved was beaten so badly for coming to see you that he never came again? What if your owner made you wash the clothes at night and work in the fields the next day? What if he made you marry someone you did not love just so you would have babies to become more slaves? And what if he promised to give you freedom after nine more years of slavery—and at the end of that time changed his mind? What would you do? Show the children some of the pictures in the book—the one of the family in the cellar is a good one.

Older children will be more interested in Patricia and Fredrick McKissack's *Sojourner Truth: Ain't I a Woman?* which features several excellent photographs of Truth and the people she knew. This text expands one tale of Sojourner Truth's brother and sister being sold away (page 13):

> One morning, Michael and Nancy had awoken to the sound of sleigh bells. The children had run out into the snow to see the big horse that pulled the sleigh. Meanwhile, the driver had gone inside. After a while, he had come out with Master Hardenberg [the slave-owner]. Mau Mau's [Sojourner's mother] worst fears had been realized. Her children had been sold. Michael and Nancy didn't know it yet. Michael saw the man pull Nancy up on the sleigh. How wonderful, the boy had thought. Nancy was getting a ride. But to the boy's horror, he saw his sister shoved into a box and the lid shut and locked.

Michael had run to hide. He cried and begged not to be taken away. But [his parents] had been unable to help them. "My mother mourned for her lost children all the days of her life," [Sojourner] said years later.

Sojourner Truth was eventually set free and spent her life traveling the country, working hard for the rights of all people. One of the many astounding events in her life was that, in adulthood, she did meet her brother Michael, who had been sold the day before she was born.

Another famous slave was Frederick Douglass. You can read about him in William Miller's *Frederick Douglass: The Last Day of Slavery*. Born a slave, Frederick Douglass "never knew his father and saw his mother only a few times. She walked all night through freezing woods, across fields burned white by the moon. She walked all night just to hold him." His grandmother took care of him, but he had to start working long and hard when he was still very young.

Frederick Douglass did something very few slaves ever did. He fought back. He beat up a man who was going to whip him. Read the story to find out what happened.

Show the children any of the pictures in this colorful book. The ones of his mother walking to visit him and the slaves working in the cotton field are very good to use.

One of the most amazing things that ever happened in America was the *Amistad* mutiny and the trial that followed it. The story was made into a popular 1997 movie, and Walter Dean Myers wrote about it in *Amistad: A Long Road to Freedom*.

By 1839, laws had long been passed that said no slaves could be brought to America to be sold. The only slaves that were available were people who were born into slavery. But a person could make a lot of money by disobeying the laws and bringing in more slaves.

In what is now Sierra Leone in Africa, slave traders captured anybody they could find, put them in prison, and waited until conditions were favorable before loading them on stinking, horrible ships and bringing them to America. It was dangerous. British ships patrolled the coast looking for smugglers such as this, but determined slave traders managed to slip through.

Slavery was a very profitable enterprise. You could make so much money at it that you could afford to destroy your ship after four or five trips. Why do you suppose people would destroy a ship? Walter Dean Myers, the author of this riveting book, explains it to us on page 12.

> The reason for this clearly shows the inhumanity of the slave trade. Once taken aboard the ships, the captives would be chained belowdecks and would not be allowed to wash or use any sort of bathroom facilities. When they had to relieve themselves, they had to do it while chained in the cramped quarters. The wooden decks they lay on were soon reeking with waste material, and the captives had to lie in it. If any of them became ill, and many did, they would still have to lie in the filth, often for weeks at a time. Eventually the wood in the decks and body of the ship would be so soaked with the waste material that no crew could stand to be on it. Then the boat would simply be abandoned and another one bought or built.

What happened on the *Amistad* was unique in our history, for the slaves, led by a brilliant leader commonly called Cinque, figured out a way to take over the ship, to escape their chains, and to try to return to Africa. Because none of the Africans knew how to navigate a ship, they kept two of the slave trader seamen alive and told them to take them back to Africa. The seamen played tricks, however, and the ship ended up in New York.

Captured, the Africans soon went on trial. Some Americans wanted to try them for the murder of the crew. Others wanted to sell them. Abolitionists, who hated the very idea of slavery, were determined that the Africans should get what they wanted—the right to live free in their own land.

Show the group the cover of the book, an actual portrait of Cinque, painted from life in 1840.

Children may know the abolitionists who fought for justice and risked their lives to help slaves escape on the Underground Railroad. But they may not realize that others risked their lives to free slaves through more violent methods. Gwen Everett's *John Brown: One Man Against Slavery* gives a very personal view of a controversial historical figure. Using the previously painted works of Jacob Lawrence, a renowned African American artist, the author tells the story of John Brown's raid on Harper's Ferry from the point of view of Brown's daughter, Annie. Everett deals skillfully and straightforwardly with the moral issue of fighting injustice with violence. To introduce the book to students, read aloud from the beginning through page 11 where Annie wonders, "Can one person really make a difference in correcting a national injustice? Is freedom worth dying for?" Tell them to read the book to find out what happens to John Brown's army.

Recommend this book to history teachers and encourage them to read it aloud to their classes. Although it is in picture book format, it is very appropriate for upper elementary or middle school students. In addition to discussing slavery and the Civil War, it could be used as a springboard for talking about African American artists or even the modern-day militia movements.

Another book with paintings by Jacob Lawrence is *Toussaint L'Ouverture: The Fight for Haiti's Freedom* by Walter Dean Myers. The primary reason for this book, surely, is the pictures, which were not originally illustrations. Famed African American artist Jacob Lawrence first exhibited them at the 1940 Chicago Negro Exposition, and they are currently housed at the *Amistad* Research Center in New Orleans.

While most books about slavery focus on the United States, another related struggle was taking place in nearby Haiti. Despite the fact that this is a short book, you can learn a lot from it. Columbus first found "Hispaniola," or "Little Spain," but the people who lived on that island, the Taino and Carib Indians, called it Haiti. The native inhabitants were enslaved by the Spaniards, and thousands died in the subsequent disease epidemics. Captured Africans were then brought to Haiti to be enslaved on the island, which by 1691 was half French (Saint Dominique) and half Spanish (Santo Domingo).

Francois Dominique Toussaint was born a slave in 1743, and was taught to read by his father, who had been educated by the Jesuits. By 1791, Toussaint joined a slave uprising and quickly became its leader. (Before he left, he saved his white masters.) He took the name L'Ouverture, which means "The Opener," after a fierce battle against the French in which he forced an opening in the ranks to gain a victory. By 1800, he and his troops controlled both parts of the island, but they were stymied by Napoleon, who sent ships and troops under the leadership of Charles LeClerc. By 1802, Toussaint agreed to negotiate. The French ambassador not only guaranteed the freedom of the blacks, he also promised to take black officers into the French army. But when Toussaint laid down his arms, he was immediately taken prisoner and sent to die in a dungeon in France in 1803. But Toussaint had ultimately won the big battle, for Haiti signed a declaration of independence on January 1, 1804. Slavery had been defeated in one small corner of the world.

THE CONTINUING STRUGGLE FOR FREEDOM

The Year They Walked: Rosa Parks and the Montgomery Bus Boycott by Beatrice Siegel will interest students if you first provide a little background about the American South in the 1950s. Ask them to imagine a time when African Americans and white people had to drink from different water fountains, use different public restrooms, attend different schools, and ride in separate sections of city buses. Then ask them to imagine what it would be like on their own school buses if white students sat in the front seats and African American students had to sit in the back or stand. This is how it was in Montgomery, Alabama, in 1955. African American passengers paid their bus fare, then had to exit the bus and enter again through a rear door. Bus drivers, who were all white, routinely yelled at and humiliated African American passengers. Seats at the front of the bus in the white section would be sitting empty while African American riders stood, their arms full of packages and children. This was the situation one December day when Rosa Parks, an African American woman on her way home from work, found a place and sat down with her packages on her lap. But the bus filled up, and the driver demanded that Rosa give up her seat for a white passenger. That day, Rosa Parks was tired—physically tired from a long workday, and emotionally tired from years of humiliation. That day she refused to give up her seat, and she was arrested and taken to jail. It was a brave act, and it started a year-long bus boycott that brought the African American community together and started Martin Luther King Jr. on his way to becoming a national leader. This book tells you all about Rosa Parks and how her brave act affected so many people.

Belinda Rochelle's *Witness to Freedom: Young People Who Fought for Civil Rights* provides a fascinating look at how young people made a difference in the Civil Rights Movement. Each of the nine chapters tells the story of one aspect of the struggle and profiles a young person who was involved. Chapter 3, about the Little Rock Nine, makes for a good booktalk, especially if you show the "Keep Our White Schools White" poster found on page 23. After giving some background on segregation and school integration, show the picture of Elizabeth Eckford on page 19 and read her own words on pages 20 and 21. Another interesting chapter, which might appeal to younger children, deals with the Children's Crusade. Thousands of Alabama children (some as young as six years old) marched for freedom and were attacked with billy clubs, fire hoses, and dogs. About 2,000 children were arrested and jailed. Put this into terms your students can understand—tell them that it would be like having every kid in town arrested (or some other comparison that is accurate for your area). The Children's Crusade increased violence in the city, but eventually, stores in Birmingham were desegregated thanks to the young people's courageous witness to freedom.

In *The Story of Ruby Bridges*, Robert Coles tells about a young girl who did one of the hardest things any six-year-old was ever asked to do. Ruby's parents were poor, hardworking people who lived in New Orleans. Her father was a janitor. Her mother scrubbed floors in a bank at night. They went to church every Sunday.

In 1960, a judge ordered school integration. Ruby was sent to first grade in the William Frantz elementary school. She was to be the only African American child in a school that had always been all white. Every single day for two months an angry crowd gathered to scream and yell hateful things at her. Federal marshals had to be brought in to protect her. White people refused to send their children to school, so when Ruby got inside, she and her teacher were the only ones in the room. How would you feel? What would you do? What Ruby did makes for an amazing, wonderful true story.

Almost any of the large and lovely illustrations are great to show, but perhaps the most interesting to a group are the one of Ruby looking at the crowd while the federal marshal protects her and the one of Ruby alone in the classroom with the teacher.

Numerous children's books tell about the most famous figure in the Civil Rights Movement. David A. Adler's *Martin Luther King, Jr.: Free at Last* tells about a great man who fought for civil rights and now has a national holiday named after him. More than 50 years before King was born, his grandfather was a slave. The Civil War freed the slaves, but conditions for them had not improved as much as the ex-slaves and their children had hoped they would. Many states had passed Jim Crow laws. African Americans had to go to separate schools and could not go to many hotels and restaurants. Even in homes for the blind, where children could not see the color of each other's skin, African American and white children were kept apart.

Throughout the country, signs told African Americans people not to sit in certain seats, not to apply for certain jobs, not to buy certain homes. They were often beaten by angry mobs. They were even beaten by police. Can you imagine what that would be like? You would be scared all of the time. You never would know when you might accidentally say something that would get you in big trouble, or be in the wrong place at the wrong time.

King wanted things to change. He wanted African American people to be treated the same as everyone else—to be treated equally. He decided to become a minister like his father, and when he went to college, he read about Gandhi, the great leader of India who led the movement to free his country from British rule by using nonviolent methods. King decided that Gandhi was one of his heroes. His first big chance to make some changes came when he was only 26 years old. He decided to try to help make changes on the buses of Montgomery, Alabama.

Also see Jean Marzollo's *Happy Birthday, Martin Luther King*. This simple but lovely book honors the gains that King worked so hard for all of his life. The two-page spread of the water fountains is good to show to your audience. Another book on King for elementary students is Rosemary L. Bray's *Martin Luther King* (figure 7.9). Colorful, primitive paintings highlight this biography. A good one to show is the picture on page 35 of Dr. King giving his "I Have a Dream" speech.

Fig. 7.9. *Martin Luther King* by Rosemary L. Bray. © 1995 Greenwillow Books.

THE HOLOCAUST AND WORLD WAR II

The Holocaust and World War II are the subjects of thousands of books, and rightly so. Books about both topics are fascinating and appalling; we have trouble even imagining such inhumanity. The Holocaust, one of the most tragic and painful events of the twentieth century, is now part of most school curricula and is a topic of great interest among students. Many excellent books are being written about it, but the most commonly studied is still *Anne Frank: Diary of a Young Girl*. Students who learn about Anne Frank will naturally be interested in learning more about other survivors and victims. Chronicles of individuals who survived the Holocaust are sometimes more accessible than studies of the Holocaust as a whole, for they can personalize the statistics—statistics that are so horrifying as to be almost incomprehensible. This section highlights a few excellent nonfiction books that will expand students' knowledge and touch their hearts.

Susan D. Bachrach of the United States Holocaust Memorial Museum has written an excellent overview of the Holocaust for middle school students. *Tell Them We Remember: The Story of the Holocaust* depicts the horror of the events in words and in pictures. Scattered throughout are stories and photographs of young people who were victims of the Nazis. The well-designed book is divided into short sections, making it easy to read aloud a small amount on a specific topic.

The following books tell about individual children who were victims of the Holocaust. In Germany between World War I and World War II, it was not a good thing to be Jewish or belong to almost any minority group. Sometimes, when we hear the word *Holocaust*, it is hard to imagine it. So many people died. Some say that six million Jewish people died. Most of us have a hard time imagining six million of anything. But one person, a person like you and me, is a lot easier to imagine.

Froim Baum, the subject of David A. Adler's *Child of the Warsaw Ghetto*, came from a poor Polish Jewish family. His father was a tailor whose family lived in back of his shop. They had no running water or indoor toilet. Froim's mother sold candy and cigarettes from the front window.

When Froim was six his father died of diabetes, and things went from bad to worse. His mother first moved the family to a woodshed, and then to an attic. From a very young age, Froim had to work hard to make money to help buy food for his family. Meanwhile, conditions outside his home had become terrible. Adolf Hitler had come to power and anti-Jewish laws were passed in Germany. Then Hitler's army invaded Poland. When Froim was 14, all of the Jews were forced to live in a small area called the ghetto, where there was not enough housing for everyone and very little food. People lived in the streets and starved to death. But Froim was smart, and he figured out ways to get food and to get in and out of the ghetto. And when he was taken to one concentration camp after another, somehow he managed to survive. He is still alive today and now lives in the United States.

The cover of this book is appealing, and the third to the last illustration of Froim escaping from the line of men who were going to be gassed is a good one to show children.

Hilde and Eli: Children of the Holocaust (figure 7.10) also by David A. Adler, tells the story of two children who did not survive the Holocaust. We know their stories because Hilde's brother and Eli's sisters did survive. Ask your listeners to imagine how hard it would be to live in a place where people hated you just because of your religion or heritage. Hilde's father owned a linen store but had to close it shortly before Hitler came to power. He realized that his family must try to escape from Germany, where Jews were forced to wear gold stars and were declared to be no longer German citizens. Hilde and her mother and brother got on the waiting list to get visas to go to America, but her father was too sick to leave. Her brother got out and survived, but everyone else died.

Eli lived in Czechoslovakia. His father was a rabbi, and Eli was a good student. His family, too, wished to come to America, but the Nazis invaded their homeland, and after they took over, Eli was sent to Auschwitz, the most famous concentration camp of them all, where he was gassed in a "shower" and died. He was only 12 years old.

The actual photos of Hilde and Eli on the last page are very moving, and the cover of the book with the illustration of the entrance to Auschwitz in the background is also a good one to show.

Fig. 7.10. *Hilde and Eli: Children of the Holocaust* by David A. Adler

Four Perfect Pebbles: A Holocaust Story by Lila Perl and Marion Blumenthal Lazan (figure 7.11) provides another glimpse of a child who suffered at the hands of the Nazis. Marion Blumenthal was 10 years old and weighed 35 pounds when she was finally liberated from the train that bore her and her family away from Bergen-Belsen, the camp where they had been incarcerated for more than a year. (Ask your audience to think about how much they weigh in comparison to 35 pounds, especially if you are talking to 10-year-olds.) Marion's family was unusual in that, after the war, they were all alive and they were together. Her father, her mother, and her elder brother had somehow survived the war, and the family remained intact throughout the war. This is the story of their desperate attempts to escape the Holocaust.

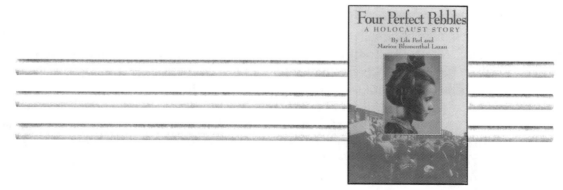

Fig. 7.11. *Four Perfect Pebbles: A Holocaust Story* by Lila Perl and Marion Blumenthal Lazan. © 1996 Greenwillow Books.

Everyone has heard of the concentration camps in Germany, but not many people know the story that Ken Mochizuki tells in *Passage to Freedom: The Sugihara Story* (figure 7.12). In 1940, Hiroki Sugihara was five years old. His father was the Japanese consul to Lithuania. One morning the whole family woke up to see hundreds of people crowded around the fence outside their house.

The people, including many young children, were Jewish refugees from Poland, and they knew they would all be killed or sent to concentration camps unless somehow they could escape. The reason they had come to the Sugihara residence was that Hiroki's father could write visas that would give them permission to go to Japan, to legally leave the country in which they would otherwise be destroyed.

Hiroki's father could legally write a few visas, but not hundreds of them. He asked his government for permission to write as many visas as needed to get these people out of Lithuania. The government said no. He asked again. The government said no. What decision do you think he made? What would you do?

All of the sepia-toned illustrations in the book are attractive to show, but use the third double-page spread of the people standing outside the gate for an effective presentation.

Fig. 7.12. *Passage to Freedom: The Sugihara Story* **by Ken Mochizuki**

Sadako and the Thousand Paper Cranes by Eleanor Coerr tells the story of the other side of World War II. Sadako Sasaki, a Japanese girl who died after the atom bomb exploded in Hiroshima, has been an inspiration for children around the world. This book gives you the chance to combine art, history, and current events in one booktalk.

Sadako believed that if she could fold 1,000 paper cranes, she would be made well again. She folded 644 cranes before her death from leukemia in 1955. People still place paper cranes beneath a statue of Sadako in the Hiroshima Peace Park.

Find some books about origami and learn how to fold a simple paper crane. Tell students about the atom bomb, World War II, and Sadako's story, then let them fold their own paper cranes. This makes an excellent transition to a discussion of how modern kids are working for peace. A perfect tie-in is found in *It's Our World, Too! Stories of Young People Who Are Making a Difference* by Phillip Hoose (discussed in chapter 6) on page 117. The Children's Statue for Peace, a project completely carried out by kids from Arizona, was inspired by Sadako's story.

To introduce Sadako's story to a younger audience, use *Sadako*, also by Eleanor Coerr. Ed Young's beautiful watercolors add to this picture-book retelling of the touching story. A half-hour video titled *Sadako and the Thousand Paper Cranes* is also available from Informed Democracy (1-800-827-0949). The award-winning video is narrated by Liv Ullmann and features guitar music by George Winston.

BIBLIOGRAPHY

Adler, David A. *Child of the Warsaw Ghetto*. Illustrated by Karen Ritz. Holiday House, 1995. 32 p. ISBN 0-8234-1160-5. Grades 3-5.

————. *Hilde and Eli: Children of the Holocaust*. Illustrated by Karen Ritz. Holiday House, 1994. 32 p. ISBN 0-8234-1091-9. Grades 3-5.

————. *Martin Luther King, Jr.: Free at Last*. Illustrated by Robert Casilla. Holiday House, 1986. 48 p. ISBN 0-8234-0618-0; 0-8234-0619-9 (pbk.). Grades 1-3.

————. *A Picture Book of Harriet Tubman*. Illustrated by Samuel Byrd. Holiday House, 1992. 32 p. ISBN 0-8234-0926-0. Grades K-3.

————. *A Picture Book of Sojourner Truth*. Illustrated by Gershom Griffith. Holiday House, 1994. 32 p. ISBN 0-8234-1072-2. Grades K-3.

Bachrach, Susan D. *Tell Them We Remember: The Story of the Holocaust*. Little, Brown, 1994. 109 p. ISBN 0-316-69264-6; 0-316-07484-5 (pbk.). Grades 6-8.

Bartoletti, Susan Campbell. *Growing Up in Coal Country*. Houghton Mifflin, 1996. 127 p. ISBN 0-3957-7847-6. Grades 4-7.

Bial, Raymond. *The Strength of These Arms: Life in the Slave Quarters*. Houghton Mifflin, 1997. 48 p. ISBN 0-3957-7394-6. Grades 4-7.

————. *The Underground Railroad*. Houghton Mifflin, 1995. 48 p. ISBN 0-395-69937-1. Grades 4-7.

Blumberg, Rhoda. *Bloomers!* Bradbury Press, 1993. 32 p. ISBN 0-02-711684-0. Grades 1-4.

————. *The Great American Gold Rush*. Bradbury Press, 1989. 135 p. ISBN 0-02-711681-6. Grades 6-up.

————. *The Incredible Journey of Lewis and Clark*. Lothrop, Lee & Shepard Books, 1987. 144 p. ISBN 0-688-06512-0. Grades 5-8.

Bolotin, Norman, and Angela Herb. *For Home and Country: A Civil War Scrapbook*. Lodestar Books, 1995. 98 p. ISBN 0-525-67495-0. Grades 5-up.

Bray, Rosemary L. *Martin Luther King*. Paintings by Malcah Zeldis. Greenwillow Books, 1995. 48 p. ISBN 0-688-13131-X; 0-688-13132-8 (lib. bdg.). Grades 1-4.

Coerr, Eleanor. *Sadako*. Illustrated by Ed Young. G. P. Putnam's Sons, 1993. 48 p. ISBN 0-399-21771-1. Grades 2-6.

————. *Sadako and the Thousand Paper Cranes*. Paintings by Ronald Himler. G. P. Putnam's Sons, 1977. 64 p. ISBN 0-399-20520-9. Grades 4-6.

Coles, Robert. *The Story of Ruby Bridges*. Illustrated by George Ford. Scholastic, 1995. 32 p. ISBN 0-590-43967-7. Grades 1-3.

Colman, Penny. *Corpses, Coffins, and Crypts: A History of Burial*. Henry Holt, 1997. 212 p. ISBN 0-8050-5066-3. Grades 5-8.

————. *Toilets, Bathtubs, Sinks, and Sewers: A History of the Bathroom*. Atheneum, 1994. 70 p. ISBN 0-689-31894-4. Grades 4-8.

Conrad, Pam. *Prairie Visions: The Life and Times of Solomon Butcher*. HarperCollins, 1991. 85 p. ISBN 0-06-021373-6; 0-06-021375-2 (lib. bdg.). Grades 4-6.

Duncan, Dayton. *People of the West*. Little, Brown, 1996. 120 p. ISBN 0-316-19627-4. Grades 6-up.

Erickson, Paul. *1853: Daily Life on a Southern Plantation*. Lodestar Books/Dutton, 1997. 48 p. ISBN 0-525-675-47-7. Grades 4-7.

Everett, Gwen. *John Brown: One Man Against Slavery*. Paintings by Jacob Lawrence. Rizzoli International Publications, 1993. 32 p. ISBN 0-8478-1702-4. Grades 3-7.

Fisher, Leonard Everett. *The Oregon Trail*. Holiday House, 1990. 64 p. ISBN 0-8234-0833-7. Grades 5-7.

Giblin, James Cross. *From Hand to Mouth, or, How We Invented Knives, Forks, Spoons, and Chopsticks & the Table Manners to Go with Them*. Thomas Y. Crowell, 1987. 86 p. ISBN 0-690-04660-X; 0-690-04662-6 (lib. bdg.). Grades 6-up.

Goldstein, Margaret J. *Eyeglasses*. Carolrhoda Books, 1997. 48 p. ISBN 1-57505-001-3. Grades 4-6.

Gorrell, Gena K. *North Star to Freedom: The Story of the Underground Railroad*. Delacorte Press, 1997. 168 p. ISBN 0-385-32319-0. Grades 4-6.

Granfield, Linda. *Cowboy: An Album*. Ticknor & Fields, 1994. 96 p. ISBN 0-395-68430-7. Grades 5-up.

Hamilton, Virginia. *Many Thousand Gone: African Americans from Slavery to Freedom*. Illustrated by Leo Dillon and Diane Dillon. Alfred A. Knopf, 1993. 151 p. ISBN 0-394-82873-9 (trade); ISBN 0-394-92873-3 (lib. bdg.); ISBN 0-679-87936-6 (pbk.). Grades 4-8.

Harness, Cheryl. *The Amazing Impossible Erie Canal*. Macmillan Books for Young Readers, 1995. 32 p. ISBN 0-02-742641-6. Grades 1-4.

Haskins, Jim. *Get on Board: The Story of the Underground Railroad*. Scholastic, 1993. 154 p. ISBN 0-590-45419-6. Grades 4-6.

Hoyt-Goldsmith, Diane. *Buffalo Days*. Photographs by Lawrence Migdale. Holiday House, 1997. 30 p. ISBN 0-8234-1327-6. Grades 2-5.

Johnson, Sylvia A. *Tomatoes, Potatoes, Corn, and Beans: How the Foods of the Americas Changed Eating Around the World*. Atheneum Books for Young Readers, 1997. 138 p. ISBN 0-689-80141-6. Grades 6-up.

Katz, William Loren. *Black Women of the Old West*. Atheneum Books for Young Readers, 1995. 84 p. ISBN 0-689-31944-4. Grades 5-8.

Ketchum, Liza. *The Gold Rush*. Little, Brown, 1996. 118 p. ISBN 0-316-59133-5. Grades 6-up.

Langley, Andrew, and Philip de Souza. *The Roman News*. Candlewick Press, 1996. 32 p. ISBN 0-7636-0055-5. Grades 4-7.

Lawlor, Laurie. *Where Will This Shoe Take You? A Walk Through the History of Footwear*. Walker, 1996. 132 p. ISBN 0-8027-8434-8. Grades 6-up.

Levine, Ellen. . . . *If Your Name Was Changed at Ellis Island*. Illustrated by Wayne Parmenter. Scholastic, 1993. 80 p. ISBN 0-590-43829-8; 0-590-291009. Grades 2-4.

Macy, Sue. *A Whole New Ball Game: The Story of the All-American Girls Professional Baseball League*. Henry Holt, 1993. 140 p. ISBN 0-8050-19421. Grades 6-up.

————. *Winning Ways: A Photohistory of American Women in Sports*. Henry Holt, 1996. 217 p. ISBN 0-8050-4147-8. Grades 6-8.

Maestro, Betsy. *Coming to America: The Story of Immigration*. Illustrated by Susannah Ryan. Scholastic, 1996. 40 p. ISBN 0-590-44151-5. Grades 1-3.

Mann, Elizabeth. *The Brooklyn Bridge*. Illustrated by Alan Witschonke. Mikaya Press, 1997. 48 p. ISBN 0-9650493-0-2. Grades 4-6.

————. *The Great Pyramid*. Illustrated by Laura Lo Turco. Mikaya Press, 1996. 48 p. ISBN 0-9650493-1-0. Grades 3-6.

————. *The Great Wall*. Illustrated by Alan Witschonke. Mikaya Press, 1997. 48 p. ISBN 0-9650493-2-9. Grades 3-6.

Marzollo, Jean. *Happy Birthday Martin Luther King*. Illustrated by J. Brian Pinkney. Scholastic, 1993. 32 p. ISBN 0-590-44065-9. Grades 1-3.

McKissack, Patricia C., and Fredrick McKissack. *Sojourner Truth: Ain't I a Woman?* Scholastic, 1992. 186 p. ISBN 0-590-44690-8. Grades 5-8.

Miller, Brandon Marie. *Buffalo Gals: Women of the Old West*. Lerner Publications, 1995. 88 p. ISBN 0-8225-1730-2. Grades 5-8.

Miller, William. *Frederick Douglass: The Last Day of Slavery*. Illustrated by Cedric Lucas. Lee & Low Books, 1995. 32 p. ISBN 1-880000-17-2. Grades 1-3.

Mochizuki, Ken. *Passage to Freedom: The Sugihara Story*. Illustrated by Dom Lee. Afterword by Hiroki Sugihara. Lee & Low Books, 1997. 32 p. ISBN 1880000-49-0. Grades 2-5.

Murphy, Claire Rudolf, and Jane G. Haigh. *Gold Rush Women*. Alaska Northwest Books, 1997. 126 p. ISBN 0-88240-484-9. Grades 5-8.

Myers, Walter Dean. *Amistad: A Long Road to Freedom*. Dutton Children's Books, 1998. 100 p. ISBN 0-525-45970-1. Grades 4-7.

————. *Toussaint L'Ouverture: The Fight for Haiti's Freedom*. Paintings by Jacob Lawrence. Simon & Schuster, 1996. 40 p. ISBN 0-689-80126-2 Grades 2-4.

Perl, Lila, and Marion Blumenthal Lazan. *Four Perfect Pebbles: A Holocaust Story*. Greenwillow Books, 1996. 130 p. ISBN 0-688-14294-X. Grades 5-up.

Rau, Margaret. *The Ordeal of Olive Oatman: A True Story of the American West*. Morgan Reynolds, 1997. 110 p. ISBN 1-883846-21-8. Grades 5-8.

Robertshaw, Andrew. *A Soldier's Life: A Visual History of Soldiers Through the Ages*. Lodestar Books/Dutton, 1997. 48 p. ISBN 0-525-67550-7. Grades 4-6.

Rochelle, Belinda. *Witnesses to Freedom: Young People Who Fought for Civil Rights*. Lodestar Books, 1993. 97 p. ISBN 0-525-67377-6. Grades 5-8.

Sandler, Martin W. *Pioneers: A Library of Congress Book*. HarperCollins, 1994. 93 p. ISBN 0-06-023023-1; 0-06-023024-X (lib. bdg.). Grades 3-6.

Schlissel, Lillian. *Black Frontiers: A History of African American Heroes in the Old West*. Simon & Schuster, 1995. 80 p. ISBN 0-689-80285-4. Grades 4-7.

Siegel, Beatrice. *The Year They Walked: Rosa Parks and the Montgomery Bus Boycott*. Simon & Schuster Books for Young Readers, 1992. 103 p. ISBN 0-02-782631-7. Grades 6-8.

Stanley, Jerry. *Big Annie of Calumet: A True Story of the Industrial Revolution*. Crown, 1996. 102 p. ISBN 0-517-70097-2 (trade); 0-517-70098-0 (lib. bdg.). Grades 6-8.

Stefoff, Rebecca. *Finding the Lost Cities*. Oxford University Press, 1997. 192 p. ISBN 0-19-509249-x. Grades 6-up.

Van Steenwyk, Elizabeth. *Frontier Fever: The Silly, Superstitious—and Sometimes Sensible—Medicine of the Pioneers*. Walker, 1995. 144 p. ISBN 0-8027-8401-1; 0-8027-8403-8 (lib. bdg.). Grades 7-up.

Watkins, Richard. *Gladiator*. Houghton Mifflin, 1997. 88 p. ISBN 0-395-82656-X. Grades 4-8.

Weitzman, David. *(The Brown Paper School Presents) My Backyard History Book*. Illustrated by James Robertson. Little, Brown, 1975. 128 p. ISBN 0-316-92901-8; 0-916-92902-6 (pbk.). Grades 4-6.

Author/Illustrator Index

Title Index